ESHIRON
Blue Shadow

BOOK 1
GREYSON GREEN

To my wonderfully, fantastic wife,
without whom this wouldn't have been possible.

CONTENTS

ESHIRON
Blue Shadow

◄PROLOGUE►

A large ship maintains a distant orbit over the planet below, quiet and serene like a slumbering giant. It's the Mayflower, the flagship for the Corporate Coalition's colonization efforts on distant worlds. It's objective-the peaceful planet floating amid the black of space, like a blue marble nestled in a blanket of darkness. It's a world on which rests the hopes of millions confined within the hulking behemoth now lazily orbiting nearby; hopes for a place called Home.

Years of calamities and war have ravaged Earth, creating a struggle for power and dominion. Eager for peace, many pursued ways to live among the stars; away from the struggles and endless warring. At the forefront of these pursuits was the Corporate Coalition, or CC, an organization formed by several corporations and big business owners. They hoped by combining resources, they could find new ways to turn a profit in a failing economy. They believed government regulation stifled progress and they sought to break away; seceding from government rule as their own sovereign entity.

Earth's governmental superpowers united, feeding off the people's indolence to seize total control. This new government took control of the world's industry and economy, automating as much as possible, hoping the people would grow too lazy and complacent to resist their attempts to control every aspect of human life.

A war ensued between this new government, the United World Order, or UWO, and the CC. Tired of the government's iron-fisted ruling, the majority of the people flocked to the corporations of the CC. Still, large numbers stood by the UWO, swayed by their promises of future social and economic equality.

Unbound by restrictions and regulations, the CC advanced their technology at a rampant rate. Oftentimes, they acted without any moral or ethical code to guide them, leading to human experimentation, alteration and genetic enhancements. Armed with these enhancements, the CC staved off UWO military attacks for many years. Unfortunately, the process was both time consuming and expensive, and the CC was suffering significant losses; too large to maintain an adequate military force. Under constant attack, the CC evacuated Earth and fled to their space stations.

Free from the UWO threat for a time, they turned their focus on finding resources to maintain their own space stations and colonies. Cut off from Earth, it was imperative they find habitable worlds and resources to survive. This led to the exploration of other solar systems for a place to call home.

To deal with extraterrestrial environments and wildlife, the CC employed their genetically enhanced, or Genhance, soldiers. Through years of genetic research and development, the CC was able to refine and enhance their soldiers to exceptional levels. The alteration process began after conception in the womb, or created in a lab and implanted in a surrogate mother. The most viable specimens had higher survival rates when carried to term and born naturally. These soldiers were engineered to be more resistant to infection and poisons, tolerant of extreme temperatures and radiation, capable of breathing in low oxygen atmospheres, absorbing moisture through the skin, high immunity to viruses and bacteria, capable of accelerated healing, and designed to be more agile, faster, and stronger than ordinary humans. For those who were not genetically enhanced, cybernetic technology was developed to imbue ordinary people with similar abilities. These soldiers became the ideal shock troops on newly found planets. Armed with these advances, the CC discovered new materials and alternate energy sources, enabling them to explore further from the world they once called home.

To travel deeper into space, they constructed the largest ship ever created, called the Mayflower; named as a homage to early settlers seeking freedom. A completely self-sustained space station capable of interstellar space travel, the Mayflower was so massive it couldn't maintain orbit within close proximity to planets. To compensate, it employed detachable barges that carried all necessary equipment for planetary colonization and resource gathering. The barges maintained orbit in close proximity over target planets and launched dropships to deliver the needed personnel and resources to the surface below.

The Mayflower is capable of producing all its own weapons and vehicles as well as the prefabricated structures used in colonization and military base camps. The largest and most integral of these structures is the base structure or command center. In its deployable mode, it looks like a large metal box with a convex bottom, outfitted with turbojets and thrusters. It's capable of being deployed from orbit without the use of dropships and it can maneuver itself to a safe landing zone. Once landed, the sides fold down, creating a hard, flat surface around the structure. Large doors open, deploying the cranes, bulldozers, and other vehicles used to clear the area for the dropships and additional prefabricated structures. A large contingency of soldiers also deploys from the structure to provide protection until additional defenses are built. Within minutes, a complete base of operations is up and running so other facilities can be dropped in at a later time.

Unfortunately, peace could not be found, even in the stars. Dissensions and contentions led to more bloodshed and the CC eventually abandoned entire colonies or worlds, trying to cut their losses and minimize expenses. Sometimes, whole companies would leave the coalition with their ships, resources, and soldiers and go their separate ways. The main body of the CC fled beyond their explored territories to avoid greater losses. They continued their pursuit of colonizing unknown worlds and amassing more resources by stripping planets of their wealth.

In one such venture, the Mayflower discovered the planet Eshiron. Eshiron and both its moons were Earth-like; habitable and rich in precious resources. They were prime candidates for colonization and resource gathering. Having three such planets in close proximity to each other was a rare treasure and one they couldn't afford to pass up.

The moons, while habitable, were home to many thriving species of extremely hostile animal and plant life. Eshiron itself was peopled with a humanoid race, similar to those on Earth. Their civilizations appeared to be in their infancy, with limited, primitive technology. They wore skins, lived in tents, and were efficient in the use of the bow and arrow, spears, and other simple tools. Believing them capable of little resistance, colonization efforts were put into effect.

It wasn't long before the locals noticed the invasion. Several curious war parties arrived to investigate the large pre-fabricated structures that descended from the heavens amidst fire and thunder. They watched as the large metal doors rolled open and great monsters sallied forth from the hollow depths as if these structures were the very portals of hell emptying the depths below. The large monsters roared and thundered, spewing smoke as they spread across the land, tearing up the earth, plants, and trees in their path. Then the warriors watched as hordes of demons marched from the gates in great numbers, clad in dark, shining blue armor covering them from head to toe. Their eyes were dark and lifeless, their faces void of expression. They did not appear to be heavenly beings sent by the Gods as the natives hoped, but devils sent to ravage the land in smoke and fire. Then, to their dismay, the structure appeared to grow and expand without hands; as if by some unseen power. Within hours, the demon's stronghold was complete and a perimeter established. A tall, black wall stretched around the now barren field surrounding Hell's gate.

Some of the native scouts returned to their tribes with news of the new threat. Others remained to watch and observe the newcomers. Few tribes packed up and moved their people, hoping to outrun the potential onslaught. The others took up arms and journeyed to the landing site in hopes of pushing the demons back through the gates and destroying them before the invaders could spread any further.

As the hours passed, more ships arrived, dropping off additional supplies, shelters, and people. Before long, a temporary settlement sprang up beside the central base of operations. Towers rose up along the wall and soldiers took up position on the battlements. All the while the native warriors moved in around the wall. Without radar and communications being fully operational, these skilled hunters moved in unseen and undetected.

With the sound of the wind, a single spear flew through the air, impaling its intended target, cutting through the body armor and severing the spine of the unsuspecting, blue demon. As if a lethal wind blew over the battlements, several more soldiers dropped to the ground in unison; pierced by spears and arrows. Shattering the silence of the evening, a siren sounded, alerting the camp of danger. Within seconds, the walls were lined with armed soldiers firing into the trees, brush, and empty fields, shooting anything that moved.

And so began the fight for Eshiron; a once peaceful planet floating amid the black of space, like a blue marble nestled in a blanket of darkness. The beginning of a fight for a world whereon lies the hopes of millions tired of traveling among the stars. A fight for a place called Home.

1

Chance scans over the letter in his hands, letting out a slight sigh of frustration. It's more rhetoric from the HR department denying his transfer request to one of the moon colonies. It's coupled with a threatening side note urging him to discontinue his opposing stance concerning many of the company's recent activities and methods or be faced with disciplinary action up to and including termination.

"You get a letter from your mommy?"

The mocking words break the silence created by the humming whir of the ship's thrusters. Another taunting voice joins the first. "Does she send hugs and kisses to her little crybaby, telling you it's okay to come back to the ship if you're too scared? Or did she tell you to suck it up and finally be a man?"

"It's time to cut the belly cord! Oh, I forgot. You probably never had one! It's probably a recall notice telling him his test tube mommy was defective so he'll never grow up to be a real man," retorts the first voice.

The dropship jostles and trembles as it descends through the atmosphere. The two men cease their taunting and tighten their grip on their harnesses. Their uneasiness shows clearly on their faces and they press back into their seats. Chance casts a quick glance at the two as he folds the letter and slips it back into his breast pocket. He recognizes the two taunters from his time on the Mayflower. He remembers once they received their cybernetic alterations, they made a point of going around and aggressively introducing themselves to all the genetically enhanced people in an attempt to prove they were as strong and fast, if not stronger and faster, than those they encountered. It's clear they have no tolerance for anyone they know is a Genhance.

Chance cracks a slight smile as the ship shakes more violently in the turbulence and the two taunters tighten their grip, wincing with greater uneasiness. He can tell they're new recruits on their way to Eshiron Base Camp and they probably have never been outside the Mayflower.

"Approaching the landing zone in thirty seconds. Ensure harnesses are secure and prepare to land," a voice announces over the intercom.

Chance tugs at his harness and rests his head back against the seat, staring at the ceiling. He ponders how much he would rather be landing on one of the moons fighting off ferocious monsters than staring down his scope at people defending their home. His thoughts instantly drift to the letter in his pocket. Blood rushes to his face as the anger wells up inside him. He shakes his head and sighs. "Look at the Mama's boy, pansy scared…" one of the recruits spouts before being interrupted by the ship's jostling. He tightens his grip on the harness once again. "I wish this stupid ship would land already," he groans under his breath, forgetting to finish his previous sentence.

The ship sets down effortlessly beside the main structure on the planet's surface. Instantly, refuelers and unloaders rush in and busily work on getting the ship prepped and ready for another departure. The cargo doors open with a slight whining sound. The harnesses release with a click and all aboard head for the exit. Chance lifts the harness off and slowly steps in line with the others disembarking the ship. When he reaches the exit he feels a hand pressing against his shoulder trying to shove him to the side. In a blinding second, Chance grabs the assailant and pins him against the wall. A second figure approaches from the side and with a quick hit to the side of the neck Chance causes him to drop to the floor. He glares deep into the first man's eyes and recognizes him as one of the taunting recruits. "You should really know who you're messing with before starting something," Chance calmly and coolly explains.

"You can go scr…" The recruit grunts before Chance slams him into the wall again before he can finish his insult.

The recruit grabs Chance's hand and tries prying it from his chest. The mechanics in his arm grind and whir as he strains to even budge it. Panic sweeps across the man's face when Chance pushes in on his chest and he realizes he's powerless to stop him. His partner slowly picks himself up off the floor, looking around in confusion. "You best behave yourselves. I'd hate for anyone to get hurt," Chance smirks as he lets go and steps off the ship.

"You really are a freak!" yells the recruit disdainfully. "We'll meet up again. Just wait!"

"Idiots," whispers Chance. "Not the way I wanted to start my day. HR is going to love me even more now. I'll probably never hear the end of that one."

Shrugging his shoulders, Chance heads to the main building to check in and get the details of his new assignment. He glances around the base camp, familiarizing himself with the layout. He notices the large number of mounted turrets placed along the perimeter wall, as well as the large number of armed soldiers patrolling. Apart from that, the area is unusually quiet. Having grown accustomed to the humming and whirring of space ships, the silence found on terrestrial worlds always left him feeling a little unsettled at first. On the other hand, he always did enjoy the fresh air and the feel of a natural breeze on his face, especially when compared to the stale, recirculated air of the Mayflower. Even in the arboretums with all the plants and trees, the air never seemed this fresh and rejuvenating.

An older, uniformed soldier stops Chance at the checkpoint outside the building's main entrance. "Welcome to Eshiron. Do you have your orders, sir?"

Chance reaches in his pant's pocket and pulls out a folded piece of paper and hands it to the man. He unfolds it and gives it a quick glance. He scrolls through a few screens on his datapad and compares it to the document. "Eshiron?" Chance questions. "Don't planets usually get an acquisition number to identify them, not a name?"

The soldier looks up from his tablet with a crooked smile. "It's the only word we can pick out when these savages are screaming at us before we put them down. It kinda stuck with us," he explains with a chuckle before looking back down at his screen.

He flips through a few more screens then looks back up at Chance with the same crooked smile. "Sorry for the delay, Mr. Haywood. I was told that before sending you to the briefing room, General Manager Gafflin wanted to see you directly. His office is located on the third floor. If you'll proceed straight forward into the building, you'll come upon some elevators to your left. Get off on the third floor and his office will be at the end of the corridor. Have a pleasant day, sir," he smiles as he hands back Chance's orders.

Chance exits the elevator on the third floor and walks down the corridor past several offices and conference rooms. He stops at the door with a General Manager plaque beside it and straightens his shirt. With a sigh, he knocks on the door and waits for a reply. He can hear the buzzing of the security camera focusing in on him from the upper corner of the corridor. Chance looks up hesitantly with a slight smile and then back down at the door in front of him. The door buzzes then opens with a click. Chance steps forward into the spacious office.

Slivers of light break through the blinds covering the only window in the dimly lit room. The walls are covered with accolades and credentials along with some exotic animal trophies, no doubt obtained from other worlds. The smell of pungent cigars hangs in the air. Several monitors sit on the main desk, behind which sits a burly, middle-aged man. He clasps his hands together and leans back in his chair.

"Come in, Mr. Haywood. Take a seat. I hope your trip wasn't too unpleasant. Myself, I've always hated entering the atmosphere in those accursed dropships. Anyhow, I digress. Welcome to Eshiron, the CC's most recent acquisition. As I'm sure you're aware, there's a problem here on Eshiron that's preventing us from meeting our quarterly goals. Initial reports stated the locals here wouldn't pose much of a threat or a hindrance to our operations. Unfortunately, these uncivilized savages have proven to be some of the most resilient, stubborn, uncooperative beings we've come across so far. I mean, they even have some kind of metal capable of piercing our toughest armor. They're using freaking spears here! Can you imagine? We can't even seem to root them out and all attempts to hunt them down end with lots of casualties. They're ghosts," he scoffs in disbelief.

"I find it hard to believe with all those dropships and satellites in orbit that you don't have better eyes on the situation down here. And to be honest, sir, I believe they have every right to defend themselves. We are invading their home, after all. I don't understand why we stay here if they're such a problem.

If you're that worried about the bottom line, why not cut your losses and abandon this world? We have both moons already."

Gafflin leans forward and rests his elbows on the desk, a look of disappointment stricken across his face. He runs his hand over his chin, stroking his tobacco-stained goatee. "I'm aware of the letter you've sent to HR, and I'm well aware of your position on the matter. I can't say I agree with your ideals and frankly, I'm a bit concerned. The fact of the matter is since we are working on three planets at once, our resources are stretched thin. As far as the savages are concerned, it didn't need to be this way. They struck at us first."

"Only because we invaded and started tearing up their world," Chance interrupts.

"Let me finish, son," Gafflin continues. "Certainly we could have come to some peaceful compromise, but they didn't even give us the chance and we've been on the defense ever since. Fortunately for us, it's because of their attack we now know they have a material that can pierce our armor. Do you realize how valuable that is? Surely you as a soldier can appreciate the application of that, especially in protecting our forces. If we can find what it is they are using it will give us an advantage. We have other enemies out here among the stars. We could use the upper hand. I mean, seriously, you've landed on several worlds and led our teams to countless victories. I'm surprised you've suddenly developed a conscience."

"I know how the CC works, sir. Shoot to kill first and don't bother asking questions. I doubt the CC would have given these people the chance at a peaceful relationship. Now the CC is trapped in a corner and trying to clean up the mess they've made. We shouldn't be killing people! I'm used to fighting off plants and animals, so you'll have to excuse my aversion to taking innocent lives!"

Gafflin sighs impatiently, leaves his seat, and paces behind his desk. "You're unique, kid. You're one of a kind, and technically, you shouldn't even exist. You're an anomaly. Whatever freak accident allowed your father and mother to conceive you gave you a unique set of abilities. Genhances aren't even supposed to be able to procreate. Everything comes out deformed and not even remotely human. Heck, they can't even do it in a lab without creating some sort of monstrosity. Yet, here you are; which makes you extremely valuable. You're not like any other; you're better. With those valuable skills and abilities, we need you to lead our teams to success. There was a time when you didn't have a problem with doing that. Think about all the lives you could be saving with a few decisive victories. You've got the leadership skills in ya. You've got the speed and the strength. I mean, it would take nothing short of taking your head off to put you down; seriously! You know, your father was a good leader. He was a good man. Wasn't afraid of anything. Best and strongest Genhance I ever did see. That is until he got tangled up with that cursed woman. She messed everything up. Messed him up big time."

"That's my mother you're talking about, sir," Chance blurts out scornfully.

"And it looks like she did a number on you before she died as well!" Gafflin retorts with obvious disdain. "We need soldiers! Fighters! People willing to do what needs to be done. We've got a job here to do. We don't need some whining little puke who can't pull his head out of the clouds long enough to see what's going on. We don't need anymore weak-minded, coddled fools who can't seem to understand what lies waiting for us on the horizon. They can't see what the future holds; or don't want to see; blinded by their own self-inflicted ignorance. We need people who can see the big picture. Are you going to be weak, like your father? There's a reason you stayed on the Mayflower all those years ago. Now you want to be a mama's boy and sit on some backwoods moon with your self-righteous ideals and shoot at some mindless animals? You used to be a soldier; someone we could rely on. Now you gone soft? What's the deal? Who took care of you when your family betrayed the CC? We did. This is how you want to repay us? By following after them? I just don't get it."

Gafflin pauses for a moment to calm down. Chance remains silent, seething inside. He remembers saying similar things to his parents. He would often argue that they didn't understand what the CC was doing. Their family prospered because of the generosity of the CC. They even trusted his father with command of his own ship. Chance wonders if he was so naïve back then. Or was he being naïve now? He'd hated his parents for going against the CC, mostly because he couldn't understand his parents' point of view at the time. Now that he is older, he can see the CC the same way his parents must have. He remembers his mother, calm as ever, trying to reason with him. He can hear his father's words trying to convince him not to join the Special Forces; that they would exploit him any way they could. Their words fell on deaf ears. He didn't want to believe them. How could the CC be all that bad? After all, they saved mankind from the oppressive UWO and led them to a prosperous future among the stars. His parents always chalked it up to teen angst and rebelliousness, but he really believed the CC was good. It didn't seem right for his parents to abandon the CC, but was the CC justified in what they did? All those innocent lives were gone in an instant. He could envision his parents' faces as their ship exploded in a ball of flames while he stood safe inside the Mayflower as it fired on them. "Was it worth it, Father?" a conflicted Chance thinks to himself.

"We believe," Gafflin continues, "should our forces gain some ground; if we just win a few fights; they'll see that we're strong and that we aren't going away. Perhaps we'll gain enough ground to bring in more dropships without them getting shot down, or our bases from being overrun before they can be established. Maybe then they will be willing to talk to us. Maybe then we can come to some sort of compromise. That's where you come in. We're placing you as Bravo Department Manager. We figure, if anyone can lead our teams to victory, it would be you. You've proved yourself in the past. We're counting on you. Can we still count on you?"

"What of the other available Genhance? Can't you get one of them to lead your troops?" Chance asks.

Gafflin sighs. "We don't have any available Genhance but you. Those we do have are on the moons protecting the colonies and maintaining our footholds there. Their numbers are few and none are as well trained and experienced as you. It doesn't take much to shoot wild animals, as you well know, which is why the CC sent them to the moons and not you. These are not just mindless animals we are dealing with. We're hoping that with your skills and experience that we'll make some headway in dealing with these savages."

Chance looks at the General Manager whose eyes are staring intently at him. After a brief pause, Gafflin continues. "If you don't do this, I can't guarantee what the consequences will be, but for one, the fighting will continue as it is. Who knows how many more of your precious savages will be slaughtered before we see some sort of peaceful solution? And, as you may have realized, we aren't going to leave this world any time soon, bottom line or not. Look at it this way. The Board believes you will be more willing and determined to come to a quick and peaceful solution with these people, whereas, all others are just anxious to get out there and shoot something up. That would only make things worse. Our guys are going to want paybacks for those others that have been killed. The Board hopes you'll succeed where countless others have already failed. So what's it going to be, Mr. Haywood?"

Chance can tell Gafflin is trying to appease his better judgment, but Chance knows, regardless of what he chooses, innocent people are going to die. The problem now was to decide whether to sit back and let it happen, or try to lead the team in the hopes of finding a peaceful resolution. Gafflin may have claimed the Board has high hopes of success with him, but Chance isn't so sure this isn't an attempt to get rid of him. Hoping he'll meet with a quick demise like all the previous department managers. With the letters he has written of his opposing views, things could be more complicated for him if the CC believes he's starting to turn on them. Lately, their methods have become more aggressive toward people who question or cause trouble for the CC. "Well Mr. Gafflin, I didn't think the Board took an interest in the well-being of indigenous life. What's the real reason I was brought in for?" Chance replies with some cynicism.

"If we weren't concerned with the welfare and preservation of the indigenous life here, we would have bombed them into oblivion a long time ago," Gafflin explains, his face turning red with anger.

"I thought the only reason you haven't bombed them into oblivion is that you didn't want to risk losing the only means possible of finding out what this precious metal is and where to get it."

"Do you realize how dire our situation is?" yells Gafflin as he slams his fists on his desk.

"Isn't our situation always dire? Isn't that why we go from

planet to planet? Hoping to gain the edge or advantage over whoever or whatever happens to be our next enemy? Going from place to place hoping that on one of these planets we'll find someplace to call our own? A place to finally call home? We go from place to place, spreading our seeds, hoping at least one will stick and take root. It sounds nice, which is why most people believe it, but I know it will never end. The CC has no intention of ever stopping, not as long as there is the possibility of something to be gained from every habitable world we find. The CC doesn't care about the natives. They never have. They don't figure into the bottom line. I've been around long enough to know that. Who's to say once you find this precious material, you won't just nuke everybody anyway?"

Gafflin's face turns a deeper shade of red. Chance expects smoke to start billowing out of his ears at any moment. He clenches a bunch of papers on his desk, crumpling them in his fists. He inches one hand towards the drawers of the desk. Chance keeps a keen eye on the general manager. He figures Gafflin would know it'd be foolish to draw a weapon since Chance would be on him before he even got a shot off. He wonders if he'll call for security, which would also be futile since it would take a substantial number to subdue him, more than the number on duty that Chance saw on his way up. Before Gafflin has an opportunity to reveal his intentions, Chance continues, "Don't worry, sir. You can count on me. I'll do my best to bring a quick resolution to this conflict. I'd hate to see more lives lost unnecessarily, especially if my skills will help to avoid further conflict."

The words Chance speaks are empty. He says them because he knows it's what Gafflin wants to hear. Engaging him further in this dispute would be senseless since neither side will surrender. If anything, it will put him at greater risk for retaliation. The only reason he risked engaging Gafflin was because he felt like he was being played to begin with. He hoped to drive Gafflin into revealing something that would give Chance a clue as to the Board's true motives. Everything Gafflin told him seemed like more company rhetoric. His skills have only ever been used to kill and destroy. He's not even sure how he's supposed to find a peaceful solution. He usually dealt with hostile plant and animal life, nothing that ever proved to be sentient. Chance has also been bothered by the fact that ever since he's been called to duty on Eshiron, he's never been briefed on what his mission is and what it is exactly they expect him to do. His orders only stated when and where he was to report. They didn't say anything about being a department manager or anything about his team. Usually, he was given the dossier of everyone he was going to be in charge of when he was placed as a department leader. There were too many unanswered questions that left Chance with an uneasy feeling. "Do you mind if I ask what exactly is my mission here?

"Very well. It will be mostly reconnaissance, once the more immediate threats are dealt with. You'll be briefed on specifics along with your team, which you'll be meeting shortly. So far, we've been unable to find any mining operations, and these savages aren't being very forthcoming with the information. We need you to find out where this material they use to pierce our armor is coming from. We need you to get in there and find out how and where they are getting this stuff, along with any other information you can get on them. You'll be given further information as it becomes available. The Corporate Coalition thanks you for your service, young man. You may proceed to the briefing," Gafflin calmly states as he hands Chance a small slip of paper with directions to the briefing.

"And, Mr. Haywood, if you could, please keep these kinds of things to yourself," Gafflin behests, holding up a stack of copies of Chance's letters. "I'd certainly hate it if you ended up like your father."

2

Walking through the halls reminds Chance of the Mayflower's cold, abysmal corridors. The walls themselves seem to drain the flame of life into their cold, steel surface. It was this feeling that led him to seek out the life of a soldier, to seek out the life of excitement and life-threatening thrills. The kinds of thrills that make you feel alive; like the flame hasn't gone out just yet.

This feeling of being drained leads most of the youth to join the CC's armed forces. As soon as they are able, most sign up to go planetside, or jump on different ships, hoping for a chance at some excitement. Many join never considering the danger that comes with this type of work, which leads to the team's breakdown on the battlefield. Chance has seen it many times on other worlds. Young adolescents fresh out of school go through training and join the first crew they find going to one of the planets. Then, when things get tough, they can't handle the stress of combat and panic, ending up as food for the local wildlife. Usually, the ones who pushed through it were those augmented with cybernetics or the Genhances. The cyborgs believe they are invincible with their new found strengths and will step in to rally the teams together, but their training usually amounts to nothing more than knowing how to load and fire a gun. The Genhances are the ones with any real training since they are bred and altered for the purposes of being super soldiers. Their combat training begins at a very early age, and therefore, are the ones really suited for extraterrestrial combat.

The CC counted on this enthusiasm displayed by the youth to bolster their numbers. They were a cheap and quick resource; easy to train and inexpensive to equip. Because so many are so willing to throw themselves into harm's way in the name of adventure and excitement, the CC could fill their ranks with ease. It was also a conventional means to reduce the risk of overpopulation on the Mayflower.

Those opting for cybernetic implants had to be considered adults as well as undergo extensive physical therapy and psychological evaluations to ensure the individuals were able to adjust and adapt to their alterations. These methods were time-consuming and expensive, two things the CC tried to avoid, although they welcomed any who had already undergone the procedures.

The Genhance soldiers, on the other hand, while time-consuming and expensive, are worth the resources. The genetic enhancements occur in a lab, but they have to wait the natural gestation period of the baby, and then wait for the child to grow. The reason they didn't have such large numbers was the parents had to volunteer their children to be part of the armed forces. Procreation between Genhances is taboo, as well as ineffective since most are sterile. Chance was the only known offspring of a Genhance. All other attempts, even in test tubes, failed, creating grossly deformed specimens that didn't survive because of the genetic mutations occurring as a result of the extensive alterations of the parents. This led, however, to what are called Genhance farms. Women are encouraged to offer themselves as surrogates for the Genhance babies. They are kept in facilities where they live and are cared for while pregnant. Once they birth the child, they can re-enter the program as soon as they are physically able, living their lives in the farms, giving birth to several Genhance children. Unfortunately, because of the complexity of the alterations and the extensive amount of gene therapy required to create one soldier, few embryos survive the process, and even fewer babies make it to full term. The farms gave the CC a constant inflow of new Genhance recruits, but not nearly the numbers they would like. The recent lack of resources and a declining number of women willing to participate led to a drastic drop in Genhance numbers, making each one all the more valuable.

Chance, however, grew up not knowing he was any different than the other kids. It never occurred to him when his wounds healed instantly, why all the other kids walked around with scraped knees. Unfortunately, this fact didn't go unnoticed by others. It wasn't long before Chance was ostracized by the other children. As much as his parents tried to keep his gifts a secret, it didn't take long for word to get around there was something peculiar about the Haywood kid. Fearing the eventuality of the CC catching word of her unique son, Chance's mother kept him close by at all times in an attempt to protect him. Even then, Chance was oblivious to his changing circumstances and was completely content with playing on his own.

Chance was ten years old by the time the CC's executives came knocking on their door. They wanted to put Chance in the Genhance program, but his parents refused, hoping for as normal a childhood as possible for their young son. The CC left empty-handed that day, but it wasn't the end of their attempts to bring him into their ranks. In spite of all his parents' warnings, once Chance was old enough, he rebelled against them, and like all youth raised aboard the space vessels, he sought out the life of thrills and excitement.

Glad to finally have him among their numbers, the CC wasted no time enrolling him in their Genhance program. Chance was glad for the change of pace and the opportunity to be among those who were like him in many respects. Unfortunately, as soon as word made its way around he wasn't a true Genhance, he once again experienced the loneliness inherent with being so different from everyone else. To make matters worse, after the first few sessions in the program they discovered his abilities were far superior to the other Genhance's. This led to numerous occasions where several Genhances tried to test Chance's limits, which ended in their defeat and all of them being disciplined. Labeled as a troublemaker, as well as being the son of traitors to the CC, Chance sought any opportunity to overcome the stigma placed upon him, and it was on the battlefield where he proved himself.

Fearless and stalwart, Chance would press forward, even when all others faltered. He stood his ground even when facing overwhelming odds, rallying the surviving troops behind him. Witnesses claimed he was an unstoppable force; a one-man army capable of massive destruction and annihilation. After securing several footholds for the CC, Chance's past seemed to be swept away and he was lauded as the CC's champion. Unfortunately for them, Chance wasn't indoctrinated like the other Genhance soldiers, and his loyalty and trust began to be shaken as he called into question their methods and morals. He saw all those things his parents warned him about were true and sometimes worse.

Now the CC wants to regain his trust by placing him as a department manager. He didn't buy their motives for putting him here and figures their real intentions are to try to get rid of him. That, or cover him in so much innocent blood he'd have no choice but to abandon his morals and throw his lot in with them for good. Either way, Chance determines to do all he can to bring this conflict to a peaceful resolution and hopefully escape from under the CC's grip with his own life, and humanity, intact.

Walking into the conference room felt like being late to his own birthday party. Bravo team was already assembled, sitting in rows on metal chairs. An assistant manager stands at the head of the group giving his presentation. "Normally, your department manager would be briefing you all, but given the urgent circumstances and the fact that your manager has also just arrived and has yet to be briefed, it's fallen upon me to apprise you all of your mission."

Chance walks to the front, scanning the group of faces staring at him. He immediately spots the two delinquent recruits from the dropship. They stop their horseplay long enough to look up and give him the stare down. He recognizes a few of the others from the dropship among the group and a few others he's seen on the Mayflower. It's no surprise to Chance they are all young, freshly trained recruits. There's not a single veteran among them. He can tell by the bewildered, anxious look in everyone's eyes. It's the look of reality sinking in that this job isn't as glamorous as expected and they are really going to have to fight. It's also the sinking fear of death. The fear of inflicting death on another person, as well as the possibility of being the victim. It's a look Chance has seen too often.

The assistant manager nods in acknowledgment as Chance takes his place beside him. "I'll introduce you in a moment," the manager whispers. "Moving on, we've received some crucial intel that requires our immediate action."

The two rowdy recruits snicker and comment that some of the women in the group look like they required some immediate action. "Cut the chatter, you two!" Chance interrupts.

The two roll their eyes and sit back in their seats with their arms crossed. The assistant clears his throat and continues. "As I was saying, there is a situation that requires us to deploy our forces immediately. Scans of the surrounding areas, as well as our orbital images, show a large group of native forces quickly moving this way. Several of our long-range scans are also picking up activity indicating there may be other groups moving in close behind them. We've all heard about the kind of trouble these groups can cause for our teams. Our CEO is sending Bravo Department to head them off and stop them before they reach our base of operations. These hostiles are experts in guerrilla warfare, setting up ambushes and traps and catching our teams off guard before disappearing without a trace. We've been fortunate this time because their groups are so large that they're showing up on all our sensors and radar. Except for the first day on this planet, we've yet to encounter groups this large. This could possibly mean that they've got an ace up their sleeve that we are unaware of, or they've simply grown brazen and feel they have no reason to fear us anymore. Whatever the case may be, we want you to show we're a force to be reckoned with. Use any amount of force necessary to secure our foothold here."

Chance shifts uneasily and clears his throat. The manager casts a glance his way before continuing. "Having said that, we also have standing orders to obtain any and all information we can about these people. We want to know their weaknesses and their strengths. We'd like to know their movements and where they like to hide. If an opportunity arises for you to acquire any intel on these savages, any at all, please take the initiative. We still know very little about the residents of this planet, including the local flora and fauna. Our research teams are being held up by these constant attacks; so, unfortunately, we don't have much in the way of information for you regarding possible environmental threats. Which leads me to this man beside me. This is Bravo Department Manager Chance Haywood, also with the CC Special Services."

"Oh, brother!" sighs one of the unruly recruits.

"Is there a problem, recruit?" asks the assistant impatiently.

"Ya. That guy's a freak even by Genhance standards. One time on the Mayflower, Jacks and I," pointing to his partner in crime, "we went to the weight room facilities while he was in there on the bench press and we turned the magnetic field all the way up. The bench sounded like it was going to collapse under the pressure, but this guy didn't buckle at all. We wondered if he even noticed the change at all. 'Course we got outta there before he saw us, but still, this guy's messed up. I'd say he ain't even human."

The assistant manager crosses his arms and glares at the two young men. "What?" one of them interjects. "It's not like anyone got hurt. 'Sides, that's why they sent us here; our punishment for all the trouble we cause."

The manager turns to Chance, looking for a hint as to how to proceed. Chance stands firm and poised. The assistant shrugs slightly and turns back to the group. "Are there any questions before I turn it over to your department manager? If not, they're all yours," he says, motioning Chance forward while taking a step back.

Chance nods and takes a step forward. He stands silently as he once again scans the faces of his new team. Most look up at him nervously. The two unruly guys sit, shaking their heads in dismay. "My name is Chance Haywood, Special Services Shock

Trooper. My orders were to lead this team to find a peaceful resolution with the native people of this planet. That's what I intend to do. I'm not here to wage war on these people or to go around massacring large groups of them."

"Pfffft! Are you serious, man?" Jacks chuckles antagonistically. "We came to show these animals who's boss."

"Like you did earlier on the dropship? If that's any indication of your skillset, you won't be showing anybody much of anything," Chance retorts.

A few snickers sound throughout the group. Jacks and his buddy lean back in their seats, looking around with embarrassment.

Seeing his hecklers have been silenced, Chance continues. "Anyone here have any actual combat experience?"

A few people sheepishly raise their hands. "Anyone have experience on this planet?"

The few raised hands quickly lower. Chance was afraid this was going to be the case. It fuels the argument the CC is aiming to get rid of him. How is he supposed to achieve the CC's objectives with a handful of soldiers, the majority of which are new recruits seeing battle for the first time? Not only are they fresh out of training, but he has no time to find anything out about them. They are deploying immediately after this briefing if they hope to head their enemies off in time. "Very well. Just follow my lead and let's all try to come out of this with our lives."

The assistant manager steps beside Chance and orders everyone to head to the armory where they will be equipped prior to heading out. As everyone leaves the conference room, the manager grabs Chance's shoulder. "I hope you know what you're doing. They aren't friendly, and as far as we've seen, they don't take prisoners. I don't know what chances you have of pulling off anything peaceful during this mission, but good luck to you. As you can see, you're going to need it."

Chance's helmet visor automatically adjusts to the sunlight as soon as the hangar doors open up. He steps out ahead of his team and walks toward the perimeter wall. The transport vehicles rumble behind him like eager beasts ready to jump into the fray. Two reconnaissance drones buzz past him as they fly out of the hangar ahead of the team. His headset crackles with the lead transport pilot's voice. "Receiving a clear signal from both drones. Ready to roll out on your signal, sir."

Chance waves his finger to signal the transports and hops on one as it drives passed. They proceed beyond the perimeter wall and speed over the terrain toward the tree line in the distance. After the initial attack, the CC sent out the machinery to tear up anything that could be used as cover within range of their turrets. This left a large, barren wasteland around the entire perimeter. Chance imagines how angry the local people would have been to discover such blatant disregard for their world. He remembers instances in Earth's history where much of the same disreputable actions occurred. It was surprising to learn the CC would so willingly engage in these types of actions, but then again, they've never been prudent when taking action to preserve their own interests.

As they close in on the treeline, Chance notices more and more disabled vehicles left abandoned; riddled with rudimentary spears and arrows. He catches sight of a few corpses wearing the CC's identifiable, blue armor. It's interesting to think these people are able to hold off the CC and all their advanced technology for such a long time. The CC spent most of their time on the defensive since landing on the planet. Chance was aware of several other attempts to land in other areas, but they were overrun before being able to set up a defensive perimeter. They even lost several airships trying to provide support, being shot down by the same projectiles capable of piercing their advanced armor. It didn't take the natives long to figure out how to use the weapons they raided from the fallen teams, which gave them an advantage in subsequent ambushes and attacks.

The transports slow down upon reaching the tree line. Chance hops down and walks to the trees and peers down the overgrown pathway leading further into the thick forest. The woods are extremely dense and nature has already overtaken the road carved through them from previous transports. The lead transport reports that the drones show the road is clear of enemies and obstructions. Chance is hesitant about leading his team into such dense foliage. It's no wonder the other teams were so easily defeated when it's nearly impossible to know what's hiding in the brush. He checks his holographic display on his wrist to view the scans sent by the drones. He notices a clearing near their objective destination. He decides to take a position on the edge of the clearing and wait for the Eshironians to arrive. He tells the lead transport to head for the clearing as fast as it can. The rest of the transports should wait a short time and then follow afterward. If anyone ambushes or decides to follow the lead transport, the following transports will hopefully catch the aggressors unaware.

Chance climbs into the lead transport to travel to the designated clearing. While en route, Chance reviews the most recent scans of the enemies' positions. He notices the main group doesn't appear to be too far from the clearing and he hopes they can arrive there to get into position first. At their current rate of speed, they will be cutting it close. A second large group is coming in from another direction but appears to be converging on the main group. There are several smaller outlying bodies along the outer edges of the scans, but none appear to be moving any closer.

The pilot's voice crackles through the headset. "We've lost contact with one of our drones, sir."

"Did it detect anything before losing contact?"

"Negative, sir."

"What was its position?" inquires Chance, worried what the response will be.

"It was the drone patrolling the forest around the clearing. It was a few clicks from the clearing in the direction the enemy forces are coming in from. Our second drone will arrive in two minutes."

"Do current scans show anything? Do we know where they're at? How much longer before we arrive?"

"Negative, sir. We've got nothing. The clearing is still outside our range, plus the density of the woods is making it difficult to get any accurate readings out here. We're still approximately fifteen minutes out."

"Are we able to go any faster?"

"Sorry, sir. The road is overgrown and the rough terrain is making it slow going. We're doing what we can to make up some time. We're trying to get more intel from Home Office, but we haven't got anything back yet."

"Listen up everyone," Chance announces. "We may be showing up late to the party. I want you all to be ready and stay alert. When we get there, get to cover and watch your backs. Transports Two and Three, close the gap, I need you with us now."

"Copy that, sir."

The recruits on the transport with Chance look unsettled. "It helps if you don't think you're already dead," he says calmly to the recruit across from him.

She looks up at him bewildered. "Huh? Oh, right," she stutters.

"Just stay calm and follow your instincts. Envision yourself in control and keeping it together even if it all goes wrong. Stay focused on your orders and trust in your training. And remember, you're not alone. We've all got your back. Follow my orders and you'll do fine."

"Right, thanks," she mutters uneasily.

Chance leans back and looks up at the ceiling. "They're definitely trying to do away with me," he thinks to himself. "A handful of green recruits in some of the thickest, densest vegetation. It's no wonder their teams get decimated. It's near impossible to avoid an ambush or defend when you can't see where the enemy is at."

"Sir, our drone is in position. We're still not picking up anything and still no word from Home Office. We're in range for our scanners, but it's still too thick in here to get anything."

"Very well. Proceed as directed. Continue to scan the area with the drone."

"Sorry, sir!" the pilot interrupts. "Our second drone was just hit. We're still receiving an image, but there's a lot of interference. Its scanners are also offline, so now we're in the dark, and there's still no response from Home Office."

His entire career was spent defending colonies and resource gathering operations from wild animals. Going up against civilized, intelligent opponents, especially ones who are expert hunters, is out of his comfort zone. Chance isn't even sure how to engage these people with hopes of it ending peacefully. He doubts they understand the concept of a white flag and reports have stated they don't take prisoners or leave anyone alive.

"Now you look like the one who's unsure," comes a quiet reply.

Chance looks at the woman in front of him, staring intently into his eyes. She continues to watch him, looking for some assurance things aren't as dire as they seem. He fakes a smile to placate her fears.

It seems like a recon mission would have been more effective to discover the enemies' designs, numbers, and location before constantly throwing troops at them. It doesn't take a genius to discover they're in over their heads, even with the amount of firepower at their disposal. No other teams succeeded before, and these recruits knew it.

"We'll be fine," he tries to reassure her. "You've been trained for times like these. This is what we do. Just remember what I told you. Stay focused, we'll be alright."

"Do you really believe that?"

"I have to, especially if I want to go home in one piece. And I need you to believe it too because I need to be sure someone has my back."

"You can count on me, sir!" she replies with encouragement.

The others in the transport resound with a similar response. The mood aboard the transport has changed from hopeless and desperate to one of confidence and eagerness. Even Chance feels luck may yet be on their side and there still may be light at the end of the tunnel. He hopes these recruits can cling to this glimmer and not buckle if things go sour. The others on board psyche each other up, betting on who will dominate the enemy and send them packing.

Once again, the crackle of the earpiece breaks Chance's train of thought. "Sir, we're coming up on the clearing. Estimated time is thirty seconds."

"Take us to the edge of the clearing and we'll deploy on the outskirts using the trees as cover," Chance orders. "Do we know how long before the other transports arrive?"

"Copy that, sir. The others are approximately sixty seconds behind us."

The transport pulls off the road and plows through the underbrush and lurches to a halt. The transport's camouflage engages and blends it in with the surrounding trees. Inside, the soldiers put on their helmets and ready their weapons. As soon as the door opens, Chance rushes out ahead of his group and takes cover behind the trees. The recruits follow and take up positions beside him. The other transports pull up behind and deploy their soldiers. Atop the middle transport, Jacks hops on the mounted gun turret and shouts. "Woohoo! Bring it on, you savages! I got somethin' for ya!"

Chance whips around. "Cut the noise, you idiot!"

As if in response to the challenge, several arrows fly through the air and strike the recruits rushing off the transport. "We're being attacked! Get to cover, now!" Chance barks.

Two more men drop with arrows piercing their bodies before everyone is able to get behind cover. Jacks whips the turret around towards the direction of the attack and shreds everything in front of him with a constant stream of bullets. Caught up in the moment, the rest of the soldiers fire blindly into the trees. A spear comes from another direction and pins one of the recruits to a tree. "Cease firing! Everyone, watch your backs. They're moving to surround us. Make your shots count. You five, take cover by those trees and make sure no one gets around us. You six get over there and cover our right flank. The rest of you, keep an eye on those trees across the clearing," Chance orders emphatically. "Jacks, keep your cool! The last thing we need is some hothead shooting everything up and getting everyone killed. We've got debris hitting us because of your recklessness. Keep your head on straight and get your act together."

Jacks huffs and rolls his eyes. "I don't need to take orders from you. I've got a way we can end this quick," he mutters under his breath.

He waves for his friend to return to the transport. A mischievous grin breaks across his friend's face, and as soon as Chance's back is turned, he runs to the inside of the transport. Just as he makes it inside, another soldier yells he sees movement in the trees straight in front of them. A few shots ring out through the clearing. A volley of arrows scathes the trees beside the soldiers using them as cover. Chance glances at both flanks in time to see native warriors leaping from the trees and underbrush onto the unsuspecting soldiers. With bladed weapons they dispatch the soldiers in split-second timing.

With blinding speed and lethal precision, Chance raises his rifle and shoots down every attacker rushing in on both flanks before anyone else has time to react. The soldiers closest to the attacks panic and leave their cover to run toward Chance. The Eshironian warriors seize the opportunity and loose several more volleys at them. Several more warriors rush from their cover with spears and blades in hand and charge those soldiers still behind cover. Chance does his best to protect his team, but the attacks are coming from too many directions at once. Their attacks are quick and they're able to retreat behind cover in the blink of an eye. They coordinate their movements to create the illusion of one disappearing behind a tree to reappear instantaneously several trees closer and on the opposite side from the trees they hid behind. Chance feels like he's watching a cartoon where the characters chase each other through doors and come out of completely different doors, alternating the sides they came out of. It's difficult to lock on any one attacker before they get too close, especially while covering his team on different fronts. He yells out orders to keep his team focused on defending their position, but panic is already setting in and they're buckling under the intensity of the attacks. Many fall without even lifting their weapons, too frightened to react. Others go into a frenzy and shoot anything moving. These frenzied outbursts abate the attacks long enough for Chance to regroup his team.

Jacks, feeling invincible behind his gun turret, continues sweeping back and forth along the tree line across the clearing with a steady stream of gunfire. When he finally stops to re-load, Chance tries taking the opportunity to order him where to direct his fire. Before uttering a word, Jacks' partner in crime strolls from the transport armed with shoulder-mounted rockets, a grenade launcher in each hand, and draped with belts of spare explosive ammo. He fires the launchers in random directions, raining debris over everyone. Feeling invulnerable, he presses forward, firing grenades and rockets at every group of trees he comes to; all the while ignoring everything around him. With a newfound boost of courage, the recruits gather their wits and act with equal arrogance; leaving their cover, pushing forward, and firing into every clump of underbrush they cross.

Chance yells at the recruits to get back behind cover while defending his own position, until he notices a group of warriors on the edge of the clearing at the opposite end of the explosions. He raises his rifle and takes aim, but before he pulls the trigger, he notices the warriors seem distracted by something other than the explosions and gunshots. Upon further observation, he sees the warriors are fighting each other. He peeks around his cover in the direction his recruits are pushing and notices there are fewer attacks. In fact, he can see the Esh-ironians running through the trees toward the direction of the warriors fighting each other. Curious, Chance makes his way around the clearing toward the fight, running in the direction opposite his recruits.

Jacks notices his manager's movements out of the corner of his eye and pauses long enough to see what's going on. Seeing where Chance is heading, he spies the warriors in the clearing. He whistles to get the attention of the others and points them in the direction Chance is going. Jacks swivels the gun around and cuts a swath through the trees, mowing down the warriors fighting there.

Chance stops and whips around. He yells at Jacks to hold his fire, but Jacks replies with a raise of the middle finger and another barrage of attacks on the natives now flooding into the clearing.

Chance watches as the natives fall in a deluge of bullets and explosions. For the first time in his career, he feels at a loss. All he can do is stand and watch, his mind racing with a multitude of options, as well as an overpowering curiosity to investigate why the warriors would turn on themselves when it seemed they had the advantage.

As he stands and watches, the pieces of the puzzle fall into place. He remembers the radar scans and satellite images he viewed on the way here. There were two groups converging here. He glances at the warriors in the clearing and notices slight differences in the appearance of the warriors fighting each other, mainly in the colors and designs in the war paint on their faces and bodies. He runs toward his recruits to stop them. "Hold your fire! They're warring tribes! We aren't the enemy! Stop!"

His cries fall on deaf ears. The recruits led by Jacks' explosive companion continue toward the fray, firing at everyone still moving. It isn't long before the recruits find themselves in the middle of the clearing and completely surrounded by the enemy. Volleys of arrows and spears once again slice through the air, penetrating the dark blue armor of the CC soldiers. The clearing soon fills with fighters and fallen warriors from all factions.

Chance uses his radio to tell all his soldiers to fall back to the transports, after which he tries to radio the home office to inform them of his findings. All that comes back in his headset is static. He tries radioing his team again, but no one responds. Chance leaps into action and moves among the warriors in an attempt to reach his team before they're completely wiped out. Unfortunately, in the chaos of all the fighting, gunfire, and explosions, his recruits have scattered.

Like a vision from the Eshironian's worst nightmares, Chance moves like the Blue Demon they think he is, swiftly running through the battlefield as if carried by the wind, though he sheds no blood. With effortless and fluid motions, he disarms anyone trying to stop him all while continually moving across the field to his people. When he reaches his teammates, he disarms the surrounding Eshironians, then tells his teammates to fall back to the transports and get behind cover. He tells them to only fire when absolutely necessary and to defend their position.

He reaches one of the last recruits huddled beside a boulder, with her knees pulled up to her chest and her hands over her ears. Chance slides over the ground to her side and grabs her shoulder. The recruit startles and fumbles for the pistol on the ground between her feet. Chance grabs the gun and lowers it before it's fired. Two more recruits move in next to them just as a group of warriors approaches. Chance has enough time to see the group moving toward them is unaware they are hiding behind the boulder. In fact, several warriors surround a wounded individual escorting him from the battlefield. At the same time, the two joining recruits step out from cover and take aim with their weapons. Chance jumps in between the warriors and his recruits. "Hold your fire! These people aren't our enemy. We're caught between two warring tribes. Lower your weapons."

The Eshironian warriors stop in their tracks, their eyes wide in surprise. They tighten their grip on their spears, but stand in wait. The CC recruits hesitate and slightly lower their guns, keeping them at the ready. Chance turns to the warriors and waves, signaling for them to keep moving on their course. The warriors hesitate at first, then give in to Chance's persistence, continuing their course past the boulder and away from the forefront of the fighting.

In that moment, the world slows to a crawl for Chance and he becomes hyper-aware of everything around him. It's as if the world slowly unfolds before his view. He can sense every bullet and arrow in the air and who their intended target is. He can see everyone's intended motion, every step they're about to take, every swing of their arm, every pull of the trigger. In all the chaos and death, everything feels peaceful; something he has not felt in his life for a long time. Then, as quickly as the silence and peace came, dread clenches his heartstrings when he realizes what is happening. His eyes fix on Jacks' exuberant face, unaware of the arrow flying straight for his heart. Death's stroke causes him to swivel the turret enough to send one fateful bullet straight into his fellow comrade on the other side of the clearing, still firing away with his grenade launchers. With the escape of his last breath, he sends one last explosive streaking through the air. In a sick twist of fate he can't explain, Chance can only watch the horror unfold before his eyes. He remembers the old adage that claims when you die your life flashes before your eyes, but he never heard every fleeting detail of that last moment flashes before your eyes. He doesn't feel much as the explosion swallows him up in flames and debris. All goes black, but Chance can still feel everything spinning. More accurately, he knows he is the one spinning, since he took the brunt of the impact.

His shredded body is blown into the air and tumbles across the ground until he comes to a stop amid a heap of bodies. A high pitched ring sounds in his ears and he tastes blood and dirt in his mouth. He attempts to open his eyes. His helmet no longer covers his face and everything is a blur. He can't feel his left side but the rest of his body hurts. He blinks several times before the haze lifts. The first thing he makes out is a face laying in front of him. He strains his eyes to determine who it is. The eyes stare back at him; a strand of dirty blonde hair lay across the bridge of her nose. It's the woman recruit he spoke to on the transport. Her gaze is lifeless, her face expressionless. Portions of her helmet still hide parts of her face, but he knows it's her. Judging from the damage, he figures she was one of the recruits with him at the time of the explosion. She, however, was not as lucky as him to survive.

He shifts his gaze on his immediate surroundings. He notices movement in front of him, past the body of his fallen comrade. With his right arm, he inches his way in that direction. It's slow going, but he is finally close enough to see who it is. This time, it's not such a familiar face peering at him. He can make out the features of a man, covered in war paint and blood. Numerous, lifeless bodies bury him, and he is fighting to make his way out by pushing the bodies off with what strength he has left. Chance makes his way closer, and with what strength he can muster, tries to help him out. "Hopefully," Chance thinks to himself, "if my life ends here, they can see we aren't all bad."

The Eshironian warrior, exhausted from his struggle, rests on the heap of bodies encumbering the ground around them. He stares at Chance for what seems an eternity, then reaches out and places his hand gently on Chance's head. "Doman gri se chu fo chu kaum grokan. Jurcto jouem Doman[1]," he whispers, his voice weak and fading.

Chance glimpses the crooked smile on the warrior's face before darkness shrouds his vision and his body's strength fails. He slips into unconsciousness with the words of the warrior still echoing in his mind.

---

1   *God smile on you for your brave deeds. Together we go to him.*

« 5 »

*S*hadowy figures sleek from the woods and scurry through the grassy fields surrounding an unsuspecting, native village. Large, black clouds darken the sky and move in over the land, casting a shadow surrounding the collection of small tents. As the shadows draw closer, native warriors line up along the wall surrounding the village with their shields and spears ready to defend their women, children, and homes. The shadow figures lunge at the warriors with ferocious attacks and a battle ensues. The shadow cast by the darkening sky washes over the tents like a wave and they burst into flames, filling the air with smoke and ash. Holes open up in the dark, ominous sky spewing more flame and ash. Shadow figures clad in blue armor drop from the holes above amid thunder and fire, dashing towards the defending warriors as they hit the ground. The native warriors are instantly overwhelmed, allowing the shadows to spread throughout the rest of the camp, hunting down any survivors.

One figure emerges from the other shadow creatures. His body is like the defending warriors' but his head and face are engulfed in darkness, like a ball of black flame resting on his shoulders. His focus centers on a lone, young woman attempting to flee but can't move fast enough. The other shadows surround her, ensuring she can't escape. The dark warrior closes in and reaches for her; the blackness twisting and bending his hand into a menacing claw. His clawed hand closes around her neck and she can feel her breath being pulled from her lungs. Darkness surrounds her and fills her with fear, hopelessness, and despair.

A beam of light breaks through the turbulent clouds and strikes the dark warrior, causing him to fall back and scream in agony as he *vaporizes in the bright light. The beam widens and grows more intense, dispelling the other surrounding, shadow figures.*

With the nearby shadow creatures destroyed, the beam of light shrinks and gathers around a blue shadow figure crouching where the vaporized warrior had stood. The figure slowly stands and the shadow covering him dissipates like a morning mist. He faces the young woman, his eyes glow as brightly as the beam of light had. The armor covering his body resembles the same blue armor as the shadow creatures emerging from the holes in the sky, but his armor is tattered and worn. It's covered in scratches, dents, and several large holes where the figure's pale skin shows through.

Several more shadow figures appear and race over to attack the young woman again. The figure from the light places himself between her and the shadows, effortlessly dispatching them as they get too close. When the attacks cease, the figure steps beside the young woman, peering down at her. His face is youthful and kind, but it's not a face she recognizes. He extends his hand to help her stand. She takes his outstretched hand and as she stands, she reaches up with her free hand and caresses his face. The glow in his eyes fades and he peers deep into her violet eyes. She's drawn into his gaze. Instead of the dread and despair she felt with the dark warrior, she's filled with a sense of hope and a gentle warmth as their eyes are locked onto one another's. His eyes are a color she's not seen before among her people. They are mostly green with hints of brown and amber, like the grassy fields during the warm, dry seasons.

"Katalariana, wake up!"

Katalariana's eyes widen in surprise and the dream slips from her mind. "Come, Kata, the warriors have returned. We must go quickly," her mother's voice urges again.

The tent is still completely dark inside and Katalariana has no idea what time it is. She yawns as she stretches and flings the fur blankets off her. In a half-sleep state, she fumbles around until she feels her healer's satchel. With satchel in hand, she crawls to the entrance of the tent and slowly exits. Her mother impatiently waits outside beside the doorway. "Come, we must hurry," her mother exclaims before rushing off.

Kata rubs her eyes, hoping they'll adjust quickly in the fading moons' light. She can faintly see others rousting from their sleep and emerging from the tents to make their way to greet the returning warriors.

She slings her satchel over her shoulder and heads off to follow her mother, making her way past the growing group of people.

As she increases her pace to try and catch up to her mother, she remembers the strange dream she had and can't help but think a dream that feels so real and intense must be significant. Yet, other than her home village, nothing else in the dream actually exists. She tries remembering the details of the dream, but for some reason, those green eyes are foremost in her thoughts. "How strange. A pale man with green eyes. Of course, such a wonderful creature could only exist in my dreams," she mutters to herself.

Lost in thought, Kata speedily walks down the path out of the village toward the direction the warriors will be returning from. She passes her mother, knowing if she walks at her pace, she'll be tempted to fall asleep again. Not only that, but her mother would want to talk the whole way and it was still too early for that much talking.

As daylight breaks over the horizon, Kata can make out the forms of the returning war party in the distance. She picks up speed to meet up with them. As she approaches them, she puts on a smile and runs to meet up with her father, who should be at the head of the line leading the warriors home. Instead, she's surprised to see another warrior in his place. She hadn't thought about why the warriors would be returning home so soon and risk traveling through the night with their dead and wounded. It makes sense now. Something happened to their beloved leader; her father.

A twinge of pain stings her heart as she considers whether he's wounded or dead. She slows down once she arrives at the head of the returning caravan. Her voice quivers. "Cultac, where is the Eldest?"

The warrior leading the group doesn't stop walking but motions to the group pulling the carts behind him. She passes Cultac to the first cart in line. She races around the warriors guarding the body and stares down at her father covered in furs lying peacefully on the bed of the cart. She pulls back the cover from his face. Keeping pace with the rolling cart, she leans in close to him, hoping to hear him breathe. She can feel her heart in her throat. She knows there's nothing she can do. She already smells death on him. It's a smell she's come to know working as a healer.

Others arrive at the caravan looking for their loved ones, hoping to rejoin with their fathers, husbands, brothers, and sons. The quiet morning is soon interrupted by the wailing of those mothers, wives, daughters, and sisters whose loved ones did not survive. Their cries mimic the sound Kata's heart is making, but she lets no tears fall. She clears her throat and straightens herself up.

She gives her father one last glance. She tries looking past the burned skin and singed hair and the blood and dirt caked on his face. She tries looking past it all and remembers the face of the man who provided for her and her mother and led their tribe through one of the most peaceful times in the tribe's history. "Your strength will be missed, Father," she whispers as she lifts the covers back over his face.

She steps back and watches as the cart continues onward. She hears her mother approaching the caravan. "Kata! Kata?

Where's your father?" she yells not even looking at her daughter but focusing on the cart rolling up beside her.

Her mother throws back the furs and throws herself on the body of her husband with her wailing sobs joining those of the other grief-stricken tribe members. Kata stands aside as the caravan continues to push forward and the cart carrying her parents rolls farther out of sight. A woman falls to her knees beside her, too grief-stricken to walk but determined to stay with the caravan by crawling. She clutches a burned, blood-soaked cloth in her hands, and tears stream down her cheeks. Through the deep sobs, Kata can barely make out what the woman is saying, but it sounds like she's begging some unknown being to tell her where the rest of her life partner's body is at.

Kata looks up and down the caravan and notices there are a larger number of wounded than usual after a battle with a warring tribe. She comes to her senses and remembers her responsibilities as a healer. She tugs at her satchel and approaches the nearest cart of wounded warriors. Some of the wounds are unlike anything she has seen before. Out of curiosity, she moves to the next cart to check the wounds of the other warriors. She's never seen so many holes, burns, and lost limbs before. There are several warriors in the carts who have already succumbed to their injuries and lie dead beside their wounded brothers.

The last cart catches her attention. It's separated from the rest of the caravan and trails way behind the other carts. It's even been left unguarded. Passing the cart puller, who's half asleep and unaware of her presence, she moves to the side of the cart to check the body. She's surprised by the mangled body lying there and initially wonders why he was in line with the wounded. No one could possibly survive those wounds. Apart from that, he doesn't look like one of their warriors. In fact, everything is foreign about him; from his pale skin and short hair to the hard, broken shell covering his body. A stark contrast from the darker skin, long hair, and animal skin clothing common among the tribes. At least among all the nearby tribes she's familiar with.

She's entranced by the stranger's youthful and attractive face, even though it's caked with blood, soot, and dirt. She can't take her eyes away from his calm, peaceful expression, and though she's never seen anyone like him, his appearance is oddly familiar. She turns to ask why this corpse was brought back as the cart hits a bump causing the stranger to groan. Her heart races when she realizes he's still alive. A beam of morning light breaks over the horizon, illuminating his face and glints off the tattered, blue armor covering his body. Her heart pounds harder. "Such creatures do not exist," she mutters incredulously.

With all the blood and dirt on his face, it's hard to know if it's the man from her dreams, but the resemblance is too uncanny. She slowly reaches out and caresses his face, afraid she may still be dreaming. He stirs and she withdraws her hand. Was he reacting to her? He slowly opens his eyes and she stares deep into his bewildered gaze. The color of his eyes is unique, like the color of green grass beginning to dry during the warm seasons.

Kata gasps. How is it possible for the man from her dreams to be in front of her? The only reason she can think is divine providence brought them together. It can't be a coincidence she first sees him in a dream, then he is brought to her in her waking reality. She feels he must be coming to her to be healed, and in turn, he will be there to protect her. Surely this must be

God's will for them. Kata leans in close to his ear and whispers, "Cho chu shere.²"

The stranger closes his eyes and a peaceful calm settles over his face once more. Now having promised to care for him, she wonders how to treat wounds as severe as his. She's never treated someone whose side was ripped open because no one had ever survived such a wound.

A warrior approaches her, gripping his spear tightly with both hands. "Young healer, it would be reason for you not to be near that blue demon. It is extremely dangerous to be so close. I've never seen anything move so quickly before and if it were to wake, we could not protect you in time," he warns.

"Then why was he brought back with you?" Kata asks.

"We are bringing him before the council for them to decide his fate. There are those among our men that claim he helped our Eldest before his death. They say they were found together when your father's body was found. There are others that say because he is a demon, he should be destroyed. Until it is decided, I cannot let you be near him."

Afraid to draw too much attention by refusing to go along, Kata steps away. She heard tales about blue demons from friendly, neighboring tribes, but this was the first contact her tribe had with one. When she thinks about blue demons, the image of the shadow creatures in blue armor from her dream comes to mind; not the youthful man with the gentle eyes strapped to the cart. Surely no demon would have such beautiful and kind eyes. It's not likely anyone will listen to her opinion about him though, especially an opinion based on a dream she had. She takes one last glance at the stranger before returning to the carts to tend to the other wounded.

---

2   *I will take care of you.*

6

Tensions run high around camp. People pace nervously while waiting to hear more about their war party's quick return and the council's sudden gathering. Moments ago, the war party returned with their wounded and dead, but the thing that has everyone uneasy is the man in the blue shell they brought back with them. Word spread like fire through dried brush about the stranger hauled back from the battle, and everyone wanted to see him. Crowds gathered around the body as it was carried to the tents of the healers. Judging by the state of the body, it was impossible to believe he was still living, but, to the amazement of all, he was still breathing and clinging to life.

People questioned who he is, where he came from, and more importantly, why he was brought to their camp. Fears arose and a division formed between the people when word spread he was one of the blue demons they heard about. As much as they wanted to hear from the war party, the elders of the tribe saw it was necessary to call the council together to discuss what should be done with the injured foreigner.

Inside the council tent, the elders take a moment to reflect on the accounts given by the warriors and the council members who witnessed this foreigner on the field of battle. Several of the warriors sit around the elders, waiting to hear the verdict of the one some call a demon, and others call a benevolent force.

"We've heard the rumors spread on the wind across these lands. They spoke of the blue shadows and demons. Many said they would be coming and that they would destroy all things. Now we see that these whispers have spoken truth. The blue demons are now among us. I say we kill him and burn the body. Send him back to the depths before he walks again and kills our women and children. No good will come from keeping him here. It is plain to see he is not like us. Our people fall when their bodies are pierced by arrows and spears or are cut down by the blades of our enemies, but this demon looks like he was eaten by a cleridrac[3] and spit back out and he still breathes. I say let us be rid of him before he shows us what he is truly capable of," sternly argues the young warrior that led the party home.

"What Cultac says carries reason. You are indeed one of our most able warriors, and your words carry much weight here," replies one of the older, gray-haired men. "However, they are not the only words to carry weight here. It is true that we have heard the whispers of dark blue demons coming from the gates that fell from above. This is the first evidence we have seen of these beings, but it would appear there is more to these beings than the whispering winds would ever tell."

Cultac paces defensively behind the elders, casting a disdainful glance at the old man. Another elder speaks up. "We knew nothing of these people, but our warriors say that they were fighting our enemies with fire and thunder. Demons or no, they used great powers to destroy our fiercest enemies. Perhaps they can help us still."

"They killed our warriors too! And they used those same powers to do it!" Cultac rebukes.

---

3   A large, bipedal, bird-like reptile covered in feathers. Also the name of a tribe on Eshiron.

"Many say this man did not. They say he flew through the battlefield on invisible wings and merely took the weapons of those who opposed him. Many witnessed him stand between his people and our Eldest, saying that he saved our Eldest from being slain by their fire, only to then be consumed by it himself. When they found him after the battle's end, he was with our Eldest, lying among our brethren having received the grace of our chiefest."

Cultac grits his teeth after being reminded how the demon was found with the tribe's leader. "Who's to say the Eldest left his blessing upon the demon but was rather defending himself when it attacked him in his weakened and defenseless state?" he slyly refutes.

An old woman stands; her body bent and twisted by many long years. She leans on her staff for a moment to steady herself and then outstretches her arms toward the council. Everyone grows quiet and turns to listen. "The boy speaks with sense and reason. You let demons among us. He lies in wait, regaining his strength while deceiving you all, and when your guard is down, he will summon the others to destroy our tribe and all we hold dear. He drained the life from our beloved leader so that he could survive his wounds, and we blindly allow ourselves to believe that the Eldest has bestowed a blessing upon him. He feigns benevolence, but in his heart festers malevolence and the power to destroy and sow the seeds of chaos on our world. You let him live and he will draw others to him. They will overthrow this council and continue the work of destruction, just as the winds have spoken. I have seen the blue shadow. The winds have shown me how his demons will overwhelm our warriors. I say we destroy him while he is weak or we will end up suffering his wrath as did our beloved Eldest!"

Many among the council nod their heads in agreement.

One of the warriors stands and addresses the council. "Shumakra is certainly wise and her words have foretold much that has led our people to great prosperity and safety in the past, but I do not believe our Eldest, the leader of our people, would have been so easily deceived. I do not believe demons are capable of good, and it would not have served him to protect our Eldest only to be wounded in doing so. He would have gained no advantage in sacrificing himself in the hopes of our people taking him in, especially if his purpose is to destroy all things. He would engulf our world in flames, as the winds have spoken, until he eventually came upon our people and destroyed us then. No, I do not think our Eldest believed him to be evil. In fact, it was his hand upon the stranger, not the other way around. I believe it was his intent to ease the man's passing to join with him in the life after. I believe that in his final moments, he saw the good in the stranger and bestowed his grace upon him, not believing the stranger would survive his wounds. We should not go against the Eldest's final actions. This man should be honored, as our leader honored him with his last breath. We shame our Eldest, both to his name and memory, by doubting his actions.

We should not act in fear and rush to quick judgments. Here is an opportunity to know more about those of whom the wind speaks. If he shows us he is a demon, then we can destroy him just as we destroyed the others of his kind. We know they bleed as we do and they can be killed if necessary, but it would be foolish to let an opportunity pass us that could help our people in times to come. Perhaps we can even learn his powers and use them ourselves, as the winds have made known that other tribes have. Could it not be possible that he is an angel sent to aid our people against our enemies? Just as we have enemies among our own kind, perhaps it is with their kind. An angel comes at the time when demons have appeared."

Others of the council nod their heads in agreement. They all stare into the fire in the middle of the tent and ponder the points brought up. Cultac glares at the warrior who spoke up against Shumakra. He noticed a greater number of the council members were siding with him. "Broltrom speaks foolishly. Like water, always finding the path that is easiest to follow, hoping to flow into calm waters. He would lead us to side with the demons, hoping not to displease them and then in return, not be destroyed as well. While this would seem wisdom, I will not follow those who destroy our world and slaughter our people. Can you so easily forget how quick they were to cut down our brave warriors without hands or blades? Their bodies were pierced as if with arrows and spears, yet only holes were left in the bodies not consumed in the flames. Are you so quick to forget this?" he challenges.

"I do not forget this. I lost a brother on that battlefield by the very powers of which you speak. I must now take his family, so do not think that I have so readily forgotten these things. Not all wars can be won by bloodshed. Bloodshed begets more bloodshed. We cannot allow our people to continue to bleed for the sake of more war. We must be wise about these things. I believe this man can show us a way to bring peace to our people. Were it not so, why did our Eldest not use his blade to kill your demon, when it was well within his grasp? This man can show us things that we do not know," Broltrom pleads.

"There is a reason you were not chosen to lead our people when the great star fell on the Eldest's time. I was chosen! I was chosen because I am a great warrior, and the Eldest knew the seasons were about to change and that our people would need someone that could lead them to victory over our enemies; be they demons or the Toorkrat[4] Tribe. I was chosen because I am the strongest. I was chosen because you are afraid to get blood on your hands. Sometimes, to do what must be done, we must get blood on our hands. I fear no man. I fear no demon, but I will not allow him to live among us to destroy us."

"That will be for the council to decide," interrupts one of the elders.

"You are not the Eldest yet. The time of mourning must pass first," mutters Broltrom in distaste.

"Broltrom speaks with reason. A time of mourning will commence, but now, it is up to this council to decide what must be done with this foreigner. To avoid further argument, this council would ask for all but the elders of the council to wait outside. The words spoken carry much weight and give us much to consider, so we ask for a moment of solace to decide," one of the elders requests.

The warriors slowly exit the tent. The crowd outside waits eagerly for any word about the stranger and is disappointed the elders are still deliberating. Others rush in to embrace the fathers and sons who were with the council before being able to rejoin their families. Shumakra grabs Cultac's arm on his way out. "Do not fear, my boy. I will make sure the counsel sees reason."

Cultac smiles at her and steps outside the tent. She turns and scowls at Broltrom as he passes her. "If the council is blinded by your words, pray that the winds are wrong about the demon."

Broltrom nods with a halfhearted smile pursing his lips. "If I am wrong, it wouldn't have made a difference. The demons would have come for us sooner or later, just as you say the

---

4   *A large bird of prey characterized by spines on its head, massive talons and large wingspan. Also the name of a tribe on Eshiron.*

winds have foretold. We should consider the possibilities if I am right. Imagine what we can gain."

He pats Shumakra on the shoulder and steps out of the tent. His family waits to greet him and runs into his arms. He eagerly embraces his wife and children, glad to be in their company once again. As he holds his wife in his arms, he sees his brother's family standing sullenly to the side, watching expectantly at him. He slowly releases his wife and walks disconsolately toward them. He stands before the widow and her two small children. Tears instantly well in her eyes as she stares into Broltrom's face. Her two children look bewildered, too young to truly understand what has become of their father. Broltrom puts his arms around the distraught woman and slowly leads her and the children to the loving and comforting arms of his family.

This is an all too common scene among the tribe. Old rivalries have led this tribe into wars with neighboring tribes over some of the most fertile hunting grounds in the area. The most aggressive conflicts have been with lifelong rivals, the Toorkrat tribe. Recently, scouts reported a large Toorkrat war party on the move. Fearing an attack to claim their best hunting grounds, their warriors had gone to meet them. Their scouts returned and reported the enemy changed their direction. Fearing they were going to join with other neighboring tribes, they set out to head their enemy off before they could increase their numbers. They traveled three days before finally catching up to the Toorkrats, and it was then that they first saw the blue demons they heard about in rumors.

When the battle ended, the demons were vanquished and the Toorkrats were nearly annihilated. Having taken the brunt of the demon attacks, they were outnumbered and were quickly overwhelmed. The surviving Toorkrats were allowed to return home having suffered a devastating defeat. The wounded were gathered and carried home with as many of their dead as they could find and carry. The bodies of the demons were piled together and then set ablaze. When they found the one demon still breathing and their leader's hand upon his head, it was very unsettling. A heated debate broke out among the warriors as to what should be done with the demon. Some wanted to kill him there and then and throw his body into the flames. Others felt it would be wrong because the Eldest obviously showed him favor, and many witnessed the demon's selfless actions before being engulfed in the explosion that wounded him and ultimately killed their leader. Feeling the urgency to get their wounded home, an agreement was made that he should be taken to the council to interpret the meaning of the Eldest's final actions and decide what to do with the maimed demon.

The journey home was a speedy one. They didn't stop to eat or sleep, but pressed homeward hoping to get their brothers' wounds cared for before anymore died. What drove them harder was a fear more demons would appear to avenge the fallen ones. Also, the smell of blood and death had a tendency to attract large, hungry predators that posed a threat to everyone. Fortunately, they arrived home without further incident. Now it was a matter of waiting for the council's decision, informing the families who lost their loved ones, and getting the wounded to the healers to be treated.

After a short period of deliberation, the council emerges from their tent. The crowd outside the tent becomes quiet and everyone watches as the elders line up in front of them. "The council has gathered, and after much consideration, we have come to an accord," one of the elders speaks out.

Cultac watches intently, hoping to hear the verdict ends in his favor. He spies Shumakra at the end of the line with her head held low, a look of disgust and disappointment stricken across her face. Cultac figures the elders did not see things their way. His blood begins to boil and he clenches his fists. He glares at Broltrom with his family. He now looks forward to the demon's awakening so everyone will see he was right about needing to destroy it when it starts killing them.

"Much has happened," the elder continues, "that the council has needed to discuss. First, we will begin the time of mourning for our Eldest, as well as for those who have gone to the next life with him. At the conclusion of the time of mourning our new Eldest will be appointed. Until then, this council will carry out those duties as is our custom. On the morrow, we will carry out the mourning celebration to celebrate the lives that have enriched our own as they pass from this world to the next to enjoy the company of our ancestors.

Also, the rites of partnership will be given to those young warriors who have returned honorably and are eligible to enter the tribe as men and begin their families."

The spokesman pauses for a moment and looks over at a fellow council member. The other member nods at him as if to encourage him to continue. The elder sighs deeply and clears his throat before he nervously continues to address the crowd anxiously waiting to hear about this stranger. "Regarding this… this foreign warrior that was brought back; it is the wisdom of the council to spare his life, as he spared and attempted to save the lives of our people. It is our belief that the Eldest, with the final embers of his life, sought to honor this man and we feel it is our duty to uphold his judgments. We know nothing of his kind, but it is the wisdom of the council that we welcome him into our tribe, and in exchange, we hope he will join as one with our people and impart his wisdom and strength to the tribe. We know it is a hard thing we ask, but this is the last honor which our Eldest bestowed. To honor our Eldest and to unite this stranger to our tribe, it is the wisdom of the council to invoke the rites of partnership on his behalf; to make him one with our tribe and unify him with one of our daughters. All eligible daughters will be allowed part in this rite, and should he survive his grievous wounds and wake, she will be his according to the rite.

I know many have concerns about the matter, but this is the wisdom of the council based on the words of those who witnessed this man's actions, as well as the actions of our Eldest towards him. Should this man survive and wake from his slumber, he will be watched over by our warriors. Should he prove a threat to our people, he is to be purged from this life and cast into the next for the flames of judgment to take him. We hope this will put your thoughts at peace. May the embrace of our ancestors and the hopes of eternal rest give you comfort in this time of mourning."

Broltrom is glad to hear the council has considered his words and they are giving this stranger a chance. Looking over the crowd that has gathered, he can see many are torn over what was said. Part of them fear the unknown, but others are more curious and anxious for this demon to wake up so they can find out more about him and his kind.

Walking home, Broltrom notices the excitement generated among the young women about the prospect of being the stranger's future partner. Never before had an outsider been allowed to join the tribe, unless it was the occasional exchange with friendly tribes to introduce new blood to reinvigorate the tribe. On the other hand, not all of the parents were so enthusiastic about the idea of offering their daughters, although they understood the reasons behind it. To them, it appears their fair daughters are being offered up as a sacrifice to appease the demons. The daughters, on the other hand, are excited by the fact that it's something different and of such high controversy. They consider the honors and attention they will receive if they are the fortunate woman chosen to be the life partner of someone that could potentially be deity. Many are so excited they already gather outside the healing tents to await the ceremony to begin the rites.

It's the custom of the tribe when an eligible young man has proven himself worthy, either on the battlefield or during a successful hunt, they believe he has gained God's favor and earns his place among the tribe as a man, allowing him to choose a young woman as his partner to begin a family. If an eligible young man is severely wounded and ends up in the care of a healer, he has not yet earned enough of God's favor and isn't considered worthy of choosing his own partner. He can, however, invoke the rites of partnership and submit to God's will for him, conceding his own choice to allow God to choose for him. The eligible young women who wish to be the warrior's partner enter the rite as candidates and are each given a token to determine the order in which they will be allowed to prove their worthiness. They are given half a day and one night to care for and tend the wounds of the young warrior and must stay with him the entire time. Their belief is if the warrior gains favor in the sight of God, he will survive his wounds and recover enough to rejoin the tribe. The woman caring for him at the time of full recovery is considered the choice partner and God will bless their union.

A young man who has been healed may still choose the woman he wants to partner with, but to choose someone other than the one deemed worthy in the rites is considered dishonorable and mocks the rites and traditions of their people. The couple would then be shunned by the rest of the tribe for fear they would bring the displeasure and wrath of God on them.

To have a daughter deemed worthy is considered a great honor for the parents because it reflects on how well they've raised her and speaks highly of her skills in aiding the healers and caring for her intended spouse. While it is an honor to have your child considered a worthy prospect, it is still considered a greater honor for a warrior who returns unharmed, having been protected by God, to choose your daughter among all the available women. While the young women vie for a warrior's affection in the hopes of being chosen, most often the relationships have already been developed over the years of growing up together, and the warriors usually know who they want to choose before they are considered men among the tribe. Because of this, rumors have often circulated that wounded men will feign needing care until the woman of their choosing is the one to care for him, and then they will miraculously be well enough to leave the healer's care.

Tonight, the young women scurry around in an attempt to get themselves ready and over to the healer tents. They are excited for the rites to start so they can begin caring for the wounded warriors and prove their worth. Katalariana is eager to join them, having returned home after hearing the council's announcement about the stranger. She stands outside the door when Broltrom passes with his family. He stops in front of her and bows himself. "My deepest sympathies to you and your mother. Your father truly was a great man and did much to lead our people in prosperity as our Eldest."

"Thank you, Broltrom. Deepest sympathies to you and your family. You and your brother have served our people well. Your brother was a fine warrior and his strength will be missed.

Comfort and peace find you and your family," she replies with genuine tenderness.

"Comfort and peace to you," he responds before stepping back to his family and walking home.

She watches Broltrom and his newly increased family while they walk away. She reminisces about the times when Broltrom and his brother served as the family's protectors and how kind and overprotective they were of her when she was little. It was a shame conflict between them and Cultac managed to end their time with the family. She never discovered the whole truth behind their dismissal, and the brothers were never forthcoming about what happened. She believes it's out of respect for her father they avoided discussing it. She always felt the two brothers were like her own older brothers, and even though they weren't under the family's service, they still always looked out for her.

An older, heavyset woman strolls up to Kata and draws her attention. "Where are you going?" the older woman inquires as she enters the home.

Kata looks at the older woman and forces a smile. "Well, Mother, I was planning on going to the rites of partnership."

"Humph! Oh really?" her mother scoffs. "And why might you be going off to the rites?"

"Well, I was considering participating in them," Kata replies coyly.

Her mother whips her head around and stares wide-eyed at her daughter still standing in the doorway. "I should think not! You know you've already been chosen for Cultac. You won't be participating in any such thing, not if I have anything to say about it."

"The rites say that any eligible young woman may participate. And, well, Cultac hasn't officially chosen me. Therefore, I don't see any reason why I can't participate. It's my choice after all," Kata states in a matter of fact tone.

"Katalariana! You know very well why Cultac hasn't officially chosen you as his wife yet. He's waiting to be given the mantle of the Eldest. You know that this will secure the future of this family when you two are unified. This has been the plan all along. It was your father's desire for you," the older woman explains, becoming emotional as those last words escape her lips.

"I know what Father wanted for me, but don't I have a choice in the matter? Don't you care that I don't choose Cultac, Mother?" pleads the young woman.

She knows the real reason Cultac hasn't officially chosen her is he prefers to spend his time with other girls. If he were under obligation to a woman and was caught with another, he would bring shame and dishonor to himself. He kept his indiscretions a secret, but she heard the other girls talk, and Katalariana saw how they looked at her with eyes that told her she wasn't going to be his first. Of course, no one in her family knew this about Cultac, nor would they believe it if she told them. They are of the mindset there couldn't possibly be a more perfect man for their daughter and scoffed at any insinuation he was anything but an honorable warrior. Katalariana wasn't so easily fooled and she knew it was up to her to change her own fate.

"Of course I care! Why do you think we wanted this for you?" her mother importunes. "No one else could ensure your well being like the one who would become the Eldest. You've seen how well your father has provided for us. We just wanted that for you. So enough of this nonsense. You've already been chosen, so not another word about this. Come, we have our duties to attend to in the healer tents. You should have been there instead of here wasting your time dreaming about such foolish things. You best not let Cultac hear about this."

Her mother busies herself restocking a satchel with healing supplies and asks, "Who were you planning to enter for?"

Katalariana's thoughts immediately go to the events earlier that day when she raced out to the returning war party to tend to the wounded. She can still envision the young man in the tattered blue armor looking at her with those beautifully strange colored eyes. "Tell me, Kata," interrupts her mother, tearing her from her thoughts.

Kata hesitates for another moment. "I was going for the stranger they brought in from the battlefield."

Her mother stares at her in disbelief, almost dropping her bag in shock. Before she can respond, Kata continues. "Before you say anything to me, I want you to know I feel that's my path. Signs were given to me that show I'm worthy to be his. I told him I would care for him," she tries to convince.

"The rites haven't even started yet! How could you possibly believe signs were given to you? They say he is a demon! If anything, I would say it's trickery to cloud your mind and lead you from your true path."

"He's not a demon. He's just a man who has been wounded and needs care. I believe he was sent to me and will wake for me."

"Not another word! I do not want to hear more of this. You are to rid yourself of such thoughts. Come, we have wounded to tend to before the rites begin. Your path is with Cultac and none other. Now let us go and speak no more of such things. Cast such things from your mind or it will lead you to ruin, and I will not have such things for my daughter."

She hands Kata her satchel and walks out the door toward the healer tents. Kata stands holding the satchel, seething for a moment before following her mother to the tents. She knew her mother wasn't going to understand and was hoping to get to the ceremony to participate before her mother found out why she was there. Now that wasn't going to be possible. Even though she would be at the tents during the opening ceremony, it would be to fulfill her responsibilities as a healer and not as a potential partner to the wounded stranger.

To ease the anger she feels welling up inside, she tries convincing herself of all the reasons it was for the best. As much as she didn't want to be Cultac's partner or anyone else's in the tribe, it's reckless to consider a complete stranger as a potential partner. After all, she knows nothing about the man. The rumors of him being a demon don't bother her, as she doesn't believe them anyway. Seeing he was only a man in a blue shell helped confirm her belief. Unfortunately, thinking about it makes her recall the first time she saw him and how attracted to him she was. Remembering the dream she had this morning with him coming to save her doesn't help either. If it wasn't right for them to be together, then why was he well enough to wake up for her as soon as she arrived? Every time these thoughts return, she casts them aside and tries once again to convince herself it's for the best she isn't participating.

7

Arriving at the healer tents, Kata notices all the young women who are waiting for the ceremony to begin. A pang of envy pierces deep into her chest when she spies the large number of women waiting outside the tent of the stranger. Though she can't understand why so many are interested in pairing with the foreigner, it does make her more upset that she isn't one of them.

She finds herself moving from tent to tent as fast as she can, treating the wounded warriors as quickly as possible. Lost in her thoughts and in a hurry to finally see the foreigner again, she often forgets which patient she is working on and offers the incorrect treatments. Even some of the warriors who are well enough to talk have their questions and comments ignored completely while she treats them. Her mother notices how distracted she appears and calls her attention to it. After apologizing, she rushes to finish up and moves to the next wounded person, still lost in her thoughts and ignoring any and all questions and comments.

When she sees her mother is occupied with a severely wounded patient requiring extensive time to treat, Kata decides to sneak off to the stranger's tent. It's a smaller tent off to the side of the larger tents where most of the wounded are kept. Because it's at the end of the row of tents and a little more isolated, it's easy for the other healers to overlook. Once inside the tent, Kata closes the door flap behind her to shut out all the women standing in line, each one trying to catch a glimpse at the stranger inside.

Kata stares at the stranger for a long moment. The warriors who carried him here left him on the ground beside the empty bed, still tied to the stretcher. No one attempted to treat him yet, even with the severity of his wounds. It breaks her heart to think they would treat him in such a manner without knowing anything about him. She knows those responsible are hoping he passes away from his tremendous wounds. Before approaching him, she pushes the door flap aside and asks the guards posted at the door to come inside and help her move him to the bed. The two guards look at each other and scoff at the request. "As a healer, it is my responsibility to see to it that this man's wounds are treated. I intend to fulfill my responsibilities until he no longer needs treatment, or until God takes him home to eternal rest. It is your responsibility to ensure nothing happens to me while I fulfill those responsibilities. What do you suppose will happen to you if I happen to be injured in my attempt to move and treat this man?"

The two guards look at each other again with reluctance in their faces, realizing it would be bad for them if something did happen to her. After helping move the body, they promptly return to their post outside the tent. Kata throws some flaps open on the sides of the tent to let some more light in. She then looks the stranger over to check the wounds. As she cleans his face and head, she notices where his dark hair has been singed and burned away, but there are no wounds. The skin is unscathed even though there is dried blood all over. Once she's checked his head and face and finds nothing that needs to be treated, she feels around the hard, blue shell covering his body. A large hole has been torn through the left side where mangled flesh and broken ribs are exposed. When they moved him to the bed, she noticed crunching sounds anytime the left arm was moved. She knows she is going to have to set the bones in his arm if it's possible. She continues to feel around the armor to ascertain a way to remove it and finds a latch on either arm. After fiddling with the latch, she's able to remove the bracers and gloves. With each piece she removes, it reveals the next latch to remove the next piece. After pulling off the chest plate, she tears off the tattered, blood-soaked cloth covering his torso to reveal his muscled physique. His skin is lighter than what she's used to among her people. There are also several discolored marks on his body as if he had suffered other wounds that healed without leaving heavy scars like the healed wounds of warriors she's cared for in the past.

She removes the boots and shin guards but hesitates when it comes to removing the leggings. Normally a married woman was responsible for handling areas requiring a wounded person to expose themselves, but Kata knows she can't rely on anyone else to help care for the stranger. The last person she wants in here to help her is her mother. For as much attention as this man was getting being brought into their home, they all were reluctant to do anything to put themselves in direct contact with him. That is, except for the line of young women waiting outside for the opportunity to be with him. It's odd that so much attention is given to one individual when the only thing appearing to separate him from them is a slight variation in skin and eye color. There is nothing demonic about his appearance that she can see.

With great hesitation, she finally gets the courage to take the rest of the armor and his leggings off. While the male anatomy was nothing new to her, as it was not unusual for the children to run around nude, it was quite another issue to see a grown man fully exposed. After overcoming the initial awkwardness, Kata is able to clean and dress the wounds on his lower half then cover him in the furs and skins kept in the tent. She can imagine her mother's reaction if it was found out she undressed a grown man and cleaned him without adult supervision. She concocts a response based on the fact she's a healer and no one else bothered.

After cleaning as best she can, she resets the bone in the broken arm and wraps it in a splint to stabilize it. Afterward, she turns her attention to the gaping hole in his side. She has no idea how to even treat such a thing. Never before had anyone been brought to her with such a wound; no one living, anyway. She does her best to clean the wound and extract any dirt, plant material, pieces of the blue armor, or anything that looks like it doesn't belong. Surprisingly, his innards look intact and require little handling. She covers the wound with clean animal skins along with some herbal salves from her satchel. When she finishes, he stirs and once again opens his eyes. She kneels beside him and caresses his face. No words escape his lips but she can see the discomfort and confusion in his eyes as he squints at her. "Whe morshi, cho chu shere,[5]" she calmly whispers.

Once again, Kata feels there must be some divine bond between them because he wakes every time she's around. She's happy to see he's coming around and has the opportunity to talk to him, but a tremendous fear overtakes her. At any moment, the rites of partnership are going to begin and she's not supposed to be a part of it. Woman after woman is going to be given the opportunity Kata feels is rightly hers by divine predetermination. She doesn't want them to get to know him before she has a chance to, and when he is well enough to

---

5   *Don't worry, I will take care of you.*

leave, she will miss out on her opportunity to be with him. Panic begins to set in until she remembers the serum she keeps in her satchel to relieve pain and help people sleep. She grabs her satchel and empties it on the ground.

She rationalizes to herself the serum will keep him comfortably asleep until his wounds are fully healed. She rummages through the different items strewn on the floor and picks up a wooden vial with a stopper. She pulls out the stopper and pours a couple drops in the stranger's mouth. He winces at the bitter taste so she carefully pours some water from a small bowl into his mouth. His body slowly relaxes and he quietly drifts back into a deep sleep. Kata gently caresses his face once more and packs her belongings back into her satchel. She takes one last, longing glance at the sleeping stranger. "I will see you again soon. God willing, we will be together and you'll be the one to save me," she whispers to herself as she slips out of the tent.

She walks back to rejoin her mother, realizing how irrational it is to think those kinds of things about someone she doesn't even know. It doesn't make sense to her why she suddenly has these feelings and why she feels so invested in a stranger. Even walking by all the girls outside the tent, which have multiplied since she first walked passed, fills her with such a feeling of jealousy, and she knows it isn't logical or reasonable. She realizes she doesn't even know his name.

An elder standing in front of all the healing tents calls out to all the young women present, starting the opening ceremonies to the rites of partnership. Kata's heart leaps into her throat and she has to fight back tears. She ducks behind one of the tents to hide and give herself a chance to calm down. "There you are," comes a familiar voice. "Where have you been? What's wrong with you?"

Kata turns to look at her mother walking toward her. "Nothing," she quietly replies.

"The rites are beginning so our part is done again until morning. Let's go home and rest. It's been a difficult day; hopefully the great light will come bearing a better day."

"I'll join you shortly. I just need a moment to myself," Kata explains.

"I'm not leaving you. I don't trust you to refrain from doing something foolish, like entering the rites while I'm not here. Please, let us go home and end this day of sorrow," her mother pleads.

Kata wipes the tears starting to well up in her eyes and slowly walks toward her mother. Coming out from behind the tent, she observes the elders handing out the tokens to the women in the order they will be going for their respective warriors. "I can't believe how many are entering for that demon. I simply do not see the reason behind that at all, but it seems to have attracted a large number of young women. Hopefully, you've come to your senses," complains her mother as she leads Kata away from the tents.

Kata watches the line of young women outside the stranger's tent and the elder as he goes down the line handing out tokens. Her heart aches knowing she won't have a chance when she knows she's the worthy one. She also knows no one will believe her or even allow her a say in the matter. "Are you even listening? What has gotten into you today?" her mother inquires impatiently.

"I just have plenty to think about," Kata meekly responds.

"I feel I know what it is. Has your father's death cast such a cloud over your heart? That would certainly give reason to why you are so distracted today and why you express such an urgency to marry someone to care for our family. Fear not, my sweet daughter, we will be cared for, and after the time of mourning ends, you will have your desires fulfilled. Cultac will choose you as his life partner and take the mantle of Eldest and our lives will be whole once more.

I hear the demon's wounds are too grievous and I doubt he will live much longer. Then he will become no more than an afterthought, erased from our minds and our lives. We will be rid of this nonsense and peace will come again to our tribe. Dispel this cloud and let the great star shine once more in your heart."

Kata tries to fake a smile. She doesn't want to engage her mother any more about Cultac or the stranger. "I will attempt to do so," she concedes.

"Storm winds take me!" exclaims her mother. "I've forgotten my medicine bag in one of the tents and I'm going to need to resupply it for tomorrow."

"I will retrieve it for you, Mother. I shall return with all speed."

Kata has already turned around and runs back to the tents before her mother is even able to respond. She runs down the row of tents, peering into every tent until she finds the bag. With the bag in her possession, she spots the elder who was dispensing the tokens for the wounded stranger's tent. He's completed his task and is preparing to head home. Kata rushes over and walks alongside him.

"Katalariana, my child, I did not expect to see you still here. I am grieved about your father. He was a strong leader and his strength will be missed," the elder expresses, having been caught off guard.

"Thank you, Elder. He will be greatly missed. Before you leave, I would ask a favor of you."

"Yes, what is it?"

"I want to participate in the rites of partnership. I would ask for a token to announce my place."

"You what?" the elder gasps in disbelief. "Why would you do such a thing when you have already been chosen by another?"

"I have not been chosen yet, though he has expressed his intentions to do so at some later time. However, the choice is still mine to make, and I want to participate in this," Kata corrects.

"Does your mother know of this? I tell you, I do not feel comfortable about this. I do not believe it would be in your best interest."

"Please, Elder! The choice is mine and the rite claims every eligible young woman may enter. Am I not considered eligible? Would you go against our traditions and deny me the right to enter?" Kata pleads in desperation.

The elder looks around uneasily. With a heavy sigh, he opens his bag containing the tokens. "Which warrior is it you are willing to join yourself with? And I assume you understand the rules pertaining to your part in the rite."

"Yes, I do understand. I choose the foreigner to unify with."

"What!" the elder yells out, unable to contain his shock.

"Please, keep your voice quiet," Kata urges.

"What do you mean the foreigner? You must be playing a game with me. I did not agree with this in the beginning, and I cannot go along with this now. I would be skinned alive if I allowed the Eldest's child to join with the demon. I cannot do this!"

"I have my reasons for believing this is meant to be and that this is my path. This is still my choice, and if it is meant to be, then God will allow it. If he demands it be otherwise, then we will not be unified. After all, I am the last one to receive a token in a long line of women; he may not survive long enough for me to have my chance, or he may wake and be healed for another. Regardless of the outcome, the choice is still mine and mine alone."

The elder ponders for a moment while Kata waits impatiently as they walk closer to where her mother is waiting. "Elder, please!" Kata begs again.

"I do not agree, but it is your choice. God spare me if this goes awry."

He pulls a token from one of the pouches and slips it into Kata's hands. "Thank you, Elder. You have my confidence, I only ask for yours in return."

"I want nothing more to do with this. Please watch out for yourself."

The elder pats her hand and departs. Kata clenches the token in her hand and continues on her way. She looks up and sees her mother is only a few paces away walking to meet up with her. Kata hastens her steps to her mother's side. "What did the elder want, Kata?" her mother asks.

"He expressed his sadness at Father's passing from this life and that his strength will be missed."

"Is that all?" her mother pries.

"Yes, Mother. That is all he wanted to say to me. Here is your satchel."

Kata hands the satchel to her mother, who stares at her intently, gauging whether that is the whole truth or not. Kata looks into her mother's eyes to assure her there was nothing more to their conversation. "Let us go home then," her mother finally surrenders.

Kata lays in her bed after returning home and stares up at the ceiling of the tent. Every time she attempts to close her eyes, she can only see the stranger's eyes staring back at her. She rubs the token between her fingers, envisioning the day when it will be her turn in the rite. It's a long shot the stranger will survive his wounds, or even last the night, but in her heart, she feels there is more to this man than anyone realizes. She's anxious to find out what it is, but for now, she's content with being the one to care for him. While eager for the morning, she knows she can't fall asleep yet.

She listens intently for her mother's breathing. Her mother lies at the opposite end of the tent in her bed, separated only by a hanging fur. Kata spent the waning hours of the evening consoling her mother over the loss of their patriarch. Her mother was able to show a strong face during the day by keeping herself busy with the tribe's wounded, but once evening fell and their responsibilities were complete, there was nothing left to distract her from her grief. She even went to bed still crying. It was only moments ago Kata heard the last of the sniffling, and now she was listening for the loud breathing noises she makes when she sleeps. After a moment of listening, she can hear the heavy breathing.

Kata quietly slips out of her bed and grabs her pouch with the sedative in it. She creeps to the entrance of the tent and peeks out. It's a clear night and the two moons illuminate the camp. She looks down at her mother, who appears to be sleeping quite peaceably now. She quietly steps outside and makes her way toward the healer tents, sneaking past the guards by hiding behind the residential tents along the way. Staying in the shadows, she finally reaches the healer tents. There are still two guards huddled on the ground outside the stranger's tent so she slips through the shadows to the back. Carefully lifting the bottom edge of the tent wall, Kata peers under and spies the bed with the stranger still upon it in the dim light of a dying fire. Close by the bed is the form of a young woman huddled on the ground asleep, swaddled under heavy animal furs with only strands of her bright red hair flowing out from underneath.

Kata slides under the tent wall and crawls to the stranger's side. She gently caresses his face and he stirs and groans. Kata startles, surprised the sedative has already worn off, but also worried his groans will either wake the girl or draw the attention of the guards. She calmly whispers into his ear in an attempt to quiet him, but it has no effect. He mutters something she can't make out. She'd love for nothing more than to hear what he has to say, but panic is setting in and every second she lingers puts her at greater risk of being caught. She digs in her satchel and pulls out the vial. In a hurry, she carelessly pours the liquid in his mouth, more than she would normally give to put someone to sleep for the better part of a day. The bitterness causes him to choke and cough, at which point she doesn't know whether to hide, flee, or try and help him. She instinctively grabs a bowl with water from close by and brings it to his lips. He stops coughing and gulps down the water; his body relaxes and he settles back into sleep. Kata wants to stay longer, but her nerves have her on edge. The young woman stirs and Kata dashes to the side where she came in from and slides under. She looks around to make sure she can get away unnoticed. Sticking to the shadows, she once again makes her way home.

Her mother lays exactly how she left her, still breathing as heavily and loudly as when she snuck out. Kata crawls back into her bed and lays staring up at the ceiling. In the quiet of the night, she can hear her heart beating like a drum in her ears. Never before had she felt so exhilarated and alive. It's the first time in her young life she remembers having something to look forward to every day. With every passing moment, she feels the attachment with this stranger growing ever stronger. Her only fear is the length of time she'll be able to maintain these nightly excursions without getting caught. She was able to accomplish her plan without getting caught, even with the close calls, and she considers herself fortunate for that.

A loud horn sounds in the early hours of the morning commencing the time of mourning and calling all to gather at the council tent. Kata was already up and gathering supplies to put in her healer's satchel. She hurries and leaves the tent as her mother stirs from her sleep. Kata makes her way to the gathering place, observing all the people as they stumble from their tents while trying to wake up. The morning air is crisp and cool, so it doesn't take long for people to snap out of their lethargy. The early hour and the grayness still hanging in the breaking dawn add to the somber mood of the tribe as they gather together.

The council lines up outside their tent while the people gather around them. The people gather close together, hoping to generate enough body heat to take the edge off the morning air. Kata is feeling impatient and anxious to go about her duties and find out whether the stranger lasted through the night. She grieves her father's passing, but their relationship was not a close one. Being the Eldest of the tribe meant he was gone on long hunts and countless war parties defending their hunting grounds and tribal territories. She grew up spending most of her time with her mother learning the ways of the healer. While she loves her mother dearly, even their relationship was not a close one either, as her mother preferred spending her time gossiping with the other women of status in the tribe. She preferred Kata run off and play with the other children than spend her time following her around the healer tents. While respected by the people because of her family's position in the tribe, Kata never had many close friends and felt more comfortable associating with the older members of the tribe. Usually, she was with the other healers or Broltrom and his brother. When the other healers saw Kata showed great natural skill as a healer, they were more than willing to take her under their wing to train her. This never stopped Kata's mother from boasting Kata had gotten all her skills and know-how from her and taking the credit for Kata's success. This led Kata to forge out on her own and stop following her mother around from tent to tent and began treating patients on her own, gaining renown as a skilled healer among the tribe. This renown coupled with her parent's positions in the tribe drew several suitors vying for her affections. They were met with disappointment as she wanted nothing to do with someone who was only in it for the prestige. Her lack of effort in finding a life partner led her parents to arrange one for her with the strongest and most able, young warrior of the tribe. The one who her father chose to succeed him as Eldest when the time came. This young warrior had been pining for Kata since childhood.

Now the time was near for the succession of the Eldest to take place. At the end of the time of mourning, Cultac would be taking his place as Eldest, however, in order to legitimately be considered for the position, he needed to be considered a man in the tribe. To be considered a man required he take a life partner to begin his family. Her saving grace now is she is in mourning over the death of her father. Therefore, she is unable to be partnered until the end of the time of mourning. Time is still on her side, though she knows it's not going to last long. She hopes the stranger will be well enough in time and then she will be considered his worthy companion. She will then be outside of Cultac's reach and unable to be used as some status symbol or conquest trophy. A lot is riding on this stranger. Her dream takes on more and more significance the more she considers her future. She can see Cultac as the dark warrior with the ball of flaming shadow for a head, and it will be this stranger as the blue shadow that saves her from him.

Being in the large group waiting for the council made her uncomfortable and more eager to be done with the meeting and carry on with her day. She looks around at all the faces, and while they are all familiar to her, none are the friendly faces she could use right now. Then, like a light illuminating the darkness, a familiar voice floats through the morning air like a warm breeze. "Little Riana, you're up early. Are you well?"

Kata turns with a big smile on her face. "Trom Trom!"

She steps beside Broltrom and puts an arm around him while laying her head on his chest. "This is a bit unusual. Are you sure you are well this morning?" a concerned Broltrom asks.

"I am well. I just needed to see a friendly face right now."

"Where's your mother then?"

"She was just waking when I left this morning," Kata curtly replies.

"Well, this is unusual. Since when do you ever get up before your mother? I don't recall a time when you ever got up this early, even when it was for something important like this," mocks Broltrom with a large smile on his face.

Kata smiles back, knowing all too well it was the truth. "I'm sorry I didn't stay around yesterday when we spoke. I needed to take my family home and move in my brother's family as well," Broltrom apologizes in a somber tone.

"I understand. There is no need to apologize. It is a hard

time for us all. Doltrom's strength will be missed. How is his family?" Kata inquires sympathetically.

"They are having a difficult time. They are behind us with my family. My brother was with your father in the end. He was escorting your father to safety after he was wounded. They were helped by the stranger that is now in our healer tents. The stranger stopped his own kind from attacking them before they were all consumed together in the flames and thunder. I witnessed the events from afar, and that is how I found the stranger with the bodies of my brother and your father. I know hearing these things must be difficult, and I apologize. How is your mother?"

"She wears a brave face, but I know it is difficult for her also. She stays busy in the healer tents to pass the time and to keep my father from her mind. She is also eager for me to begin my life as a woman," she expresses woefully.

"Katalariana!"

Her name rings out over the crowd of people, this time sending shivers running down her spine. A large figure pushes through the groups of people, making his way toward Kata and Broltrom. Broltrom feigns a smile and gives Kata a squeeze. "I will speak with you another time. Be well, little Riana"

Broltrom retreats to be with his family as Cultac struts up beside Kata. He watches Broltrom with a disdainful glare and then returns his attention to Kata. "I was hoping to see you today, though I did not expect to find you with such poor company. I do not understand why you continue to associate with him or his family. They disgrace this tribe and contradict everything your father has done for us. Oh, and I'm sorry about your father. His strength will be missed," Cultac rambles scornfully then dismissively.

"Broltrom and his brother are good people. They have done much for this tribe as well, and they would gladly give their lives for our people," Kata chastens.

"Then he should have given it alongside his brother. That is beside the point. I wanted to show you my recent trophy from this last battle. It's a headpiece from one of those demons. I took it myself. Caught the demon unaware and took it clean off his body. I personally made sure that none were still standing at the end of the battle. It was glorious to be sure, to send them back to the fiery depth from which they sprang. I've never seen anything like the headpiece. It's hard as stone and as cold as frozen water and a dark blue like the sky when the great star descends at the end of the day."

Kata's mother interrupts him as she walks by on her way to the front of the crowd. "Now this is what I like to see. Cultac, hopefully you can help her see reason."

She smiles at them and pats Cultac on the shoulder before making her way through the groups of people to where all the spouses of the council members congregate. The elder in charge of the ceremony has already begun to address the crowd regarding the time of mourning and the activities transpiring throughout the day and the days to come. Cultac looks at Kata in confusion, still wondering what her mother was talking about. Kata sighs and looks up at the sky. How she longs to be away from the crowd, from the hustle and bustle and all the talking. "Katalariana?" Cultac looks at her inquisitively.

"It isn't anything. We had a difference of opinions and she must be hoping you'll help me see reason," Kata halfheartedly explains.

"Do you think that after this ceremony, we can meet up and spend some time together? The council has been saying that we will need to go on another hunt because our rations are running low, so I won't be able to spend time with you for several more days."

Kata scrunches her face as she pretends to remember all the things she has to do today. "Today won't be good. I have to go to the healer tents and perform my responsibilities, and there are a lot of wounded. I don't believe I will have the time before you leave again."

"Even this afternoon when the rite participants arrive to take your place? And what about this evening's mourning festivities? You aren't planning to go even though your father was the Eldest?"

Kata runs her hands through her tangled mess of dark hair. "I'm usually exhausted after I finish at the healer tents. I didn't even consider going to the mourning festival tonight, and you know I don't like being in large groups of people."

"I don't understand what your issue is with large groups. You're around people every day. You're going to have to get over it when you become my life partner. You should at least come join the celebration for a little bit tonight. The tribe celebrates the life of the departed ones and sends off their spirits to a better life. I think that you have much to celebrate in regards to the life your father lived since he has done so much for us. It would be a disgrace to him if you didn't at least come for a little while. So I will see you there after you are done at the healer tents."

Cultac tries to look into Kata's eyes for an affirmation she will be there tonight, but she refuses to look up at him. Instead, she stands with her arms crossed staring at the ground, moving some pebbles around with her toes. "One more thing," he adds. "Have you heard anything about the demon? Do you know if the hellspawn was sent back to the depths from which he came? If not, I ask that you stay away from him. The council may not see him for what he is, but I will not be fooled, and I will not allow others that I hold close to fall prey to that foul creature. I know you have responsibilities at the healer tents, but please take care, and use reason when working there. If he wakes while I am still here, be sure to find me quickly, and I will come to take care of him before he's allowed to destroy all we hold dear. I will take his head for a trophy to go with the head plate I got from the other demon. Do not risk your own life, Katalariana, and do not put yourself in a situation that will put you at risk with coming into contact with him. Do you understand?"

Kata finally looks up at him and stares defiantly into his stern eyes. She wants to defend the stranger, but she knows it will be futile and lead to more issues between her and Cultac. That's the last thing she wants in front of all these people. She looks back down at the ground and continues to play with the pebbles. "I do what I must as my duties require, but rest assured, I do not place myself at risk. Since I have not yet been there this morning, I know no more than you do about his current condition."

The elder announces the end of the meeting and summons all the warriors to gather around him. As the people disperse, Cultac looks behind him toward the gathering group of warriors. A few of his friends motion for him to join them. He motions in acknowledgment and looks back at Kata. "I'll see you this afternoon," he asserts before running off to join his friends.

Kata is glad the meeting is over and rushes to the tents. She ignores everyone and doesn't stop to talk to anyone greeting her when she passes. Her chest feels as if it's about to burst with anxiety. She wants to run to the stranger's tent before helping anyone else, but she feels it would draw too much attention to her and others may question her reasons. Not that she cares what others say about her, but it's the few individuals she would rather not find out, like her mother and Cultac. She knows she needs to work quickly and efficiently and there will be plenty of time to spend with the stranger.

When Cultac joins the group of warriors, he looks back to watch Kata, but she has already gone from his view. Seeing she is out of sight, he turns his focus to some of the young women lingering nearby. He tries to make eye contact with them, but the meeting starts and the girls leave the area.

The elders announce the need for another hunting trip. This last war trip took all available warriors, leaving enough to protect the tribe's residents, but not enough to continue hunting and bringing in a steady source of food. They need a large group of warriors to go to the hunting grounds and gather enough food for the tribe, as well as enough for the festivities that will transpire for the rites of partnership and the time of mourning.

While the request for the hunt is not out of the ordinary, the situation in the tribe has changed. The council addresses the concerns many in the tribe have that the warriors will be leaving while a demon still sleeps in their home. The council asks for volunteers to stay to protect the village instead of going on the hunt. Cultac steps forward from the rest of the group. "I say that the one who wanted to keep the demon among us should be the one to stay. Broltrom should take the responsibility," he yells out spitefully.

The group turns and looks at Broltrom for a reply. "It would be an honor for me to stay and defend our tribe to put their fears at ease. However, my family has grown, now that I have my brother's family to care for, and so my need to go on this hunt is great. With all respect, I cannot stay. Since you deem him such a threat, Cultac, and since you claim to be the strongest of us, why do you not stay?"

"My place is at the head of this hunt. My responsibility falls on providing for the whole tribe, and not my family alone. I must also go on this hunt."

The group bustles with whispers. A member of the council steps forward to hush the crowd. He looks at Cultac and then at Broltrom. "This is not what was asked of you. We asked for those who would be willing to stay and watch over those left behind. These harsh words and tones are like embers that will continue to grow until they are all-consuming. You would do well to put aside your differences and embrace each other as brothers. That will keep our people strong. Such behaviors as those displayed here a moment ago are not becoming of great leaders, but of weak minds. Now, as was asked, are there those who will volunteer for the honor to serve our people? If not, this council will decide."

The elder steps back in line with the rest of the council members. There is some talk among the group, and one by one, some of the older warriors step forward to volunteer and fill the needed spots. Once the spots are filled, the council informs them all they have two days to rest and prepare before dismissing them all. As the warriors separate to begin their day, Broltrom approaches Cultac to apologize. "Brother, forgive my actions. I spoke shrewdly and it was inappropriate. As brothers should be, let us brothers be."

He extends his arm in fellowship to which Cultac returns it with a cold stare. "It would be reason for you to learn your place. As my brother, it is not. The Eldest should have shamed you and your brother years ago. Though I respect the decisions made by the Eldest, believe me when I tell you, I will not be so lenient when I am Eldest. I will not tolerate your insolence, nor will I listen to and be swayed by your poison as the council has. You will find it reason to stay away from me as well as from Katalariana and her family."

Cultac turns away and walks off with his group of friends. Broltrom can hear them laughing and mocking him, making comments like, "My brother he is not, but my sister he is," and, "there are already so many women in that tent, I'm certain they're waiting for a real man to join them."

Broltrom clenches his still outstretched hand, trying to hold back the rage building up inside. He reflects on the words of the elder and tries to let the anguish go. He wishes his brother was still around to back him up, which causes the anguish to turn into deep sorrow and grief. He swallows the lump building in his throat and tells himself Cultac isn't worth wasting his time over and he has more important people to worry about. He knows his family needs him and relies on him, and doing anything to jeopardize his family's position within the tribe, especially when Cultac becomes Eldest, isn't worth the effort. Deep down he knows he is the better man and no one can question his morals or values, and to him, that's worth everything.

9

Every morning, the healers go to the tents of the wounded and relieve the young women who stayed the night. They then proceed to administer whatever healing care the warrior needs for the day. At midday, the young woman whose turn it is for the rites comes and takes over the responsibilities. They stay the rest of the day and all through the night until the healers return in the morning. The process continues until the warrior is well enough to return to the tribe, or the injuries take the life of the warrior. If the warrior is not well enough by the time all the participating young women have had their turn, they go around again in the same order as before for as long as it takes. Those men who have a partner already, are cared for by their partner during the later hours until they are well enough to go home.

Kata is the first to arrive after the morning meeting to relieve some of the young women. The young women try talking to her and ask about what was said during the morning gathering. Too distracted to say much, especially since she didn't listen to anything said by the council; she mutters something random about the festivities in the evening, then makes herself busy. She bustles about until the other healers show up. When they arrive, she finishes with the patient she is working on and slips away to the foreigner's tent.

The young woman she relieves is extremely disappointed he is nowhere near being able to leave the tent on his own. Kata's heart takes courage and she hopes the young women begin to drop out, disqualifying them from further participation in the rite. She steps inside the tent where the stranger lays peacefully sleeping. She kneels beside him and caresses his face, which is becoming a habit when she greets him. He doesn't look quite as pale as he had the previous day, and several of the scratches and bruises on his body have already disappeared. She thinks it's curious, as it should have taken several more days before that occurred, and even then, there would be some sign the wound had been there. She checks the splint on his arm to ensure it's still tight, and then removes the covering on his side to clean the wound and redress it. She prepares herself for the gruesome sight but ends up being surprised. It appears as if his ribs are already healed together, and new tissue is already growing around the open wound. She redresses the wound and decides to check his arm again out of curiosity. It seems the bones have healed in his arm as well. She leaves the splint on for good measure and checks the rest of his wounds; which all appear to be healed. She's amazed at these discoveries and feels it must be God preparing him to be healed by the time it's her turn. She can barely contain her excitement at the prospect and it solidifies her commitment to the choices she's made going against everyone else's plans for her. She feels he must be someone important and carries a great destiny within her tribe.

She sits on the ground beside the bed and talks to him, telling him all her cares and concerns, and about life in the tribe. When it's almost time for the other young women to show up, she once again pours several drops of sedative in his mouth; since the large amount appears to be keeping him asleep for now. She tenderly caresses his face to say goodbye then leaves the tent. She goes to the other tents to make sure everyone else has been taken care of before the relief comes.

While she walks to the other tents, she's reminded by the noises coming from the other side of the camp of the celebration being held this afternoon. People have already started the festivities. She feels a deep dread and a complete lack of enthusiasm about going. It would be disrespectful not to at least make an appearance, especially since she and her mother would be the honored attendees, being the family of the departed Eldest.

Kata walks slowly home thinking about the stranger and his miraculous recovery. She plans to repeat last night's venture to the healer tent to give him the sedative. Then she realizes the festivities usually carry on through the night and there will still be plenty of people out. Sneaking around unseen may not be so easy, unless she pretends to be out for the celebration, even though the celebration is not allowed near the healer tents.

As she gets closer to home, she can smell the fires and the food roasting over the open flames. She can hear the music and the singing all around her and see the people dancing along the pathways. Near the council's tent, there are a few large piles of timbers built up for the funeral pyres for later in the evening. Other bonfires have been built up around the camp where the people are gathering to celebrate among their families and friends. The tribe is already in full swing for the celebration. Kata feels she should be more involved in the activities, but she can't help but feel she wants it all to be over and the new day to arrive. The quicker the days pass, the more the stranger will be healed, and the sooner her turn will be to take part in the rite of partnership. A smile crosses her face as she imagines her mother's and Cultac's faces when they find out what she has done. She imagines the rage they will have toward her, but it will be too late for them to do anything about it. It is her choice anyway, she thinks to herself.

Walking up to her tent, she spies her mother exiting. "Be sure to come to the fire ceremony. It will be starting shortly. It will be the last time to see your father in this life before sending him to the next. For once, please be there on time," she pleads as she rushes off to join her gossip companions.

Kata steps inside the tent and immediately feels the difference in temperature. The skins making up the tent walls insulate the tent well from the external heat. She enjoys the cool air inside and slumps into her bed and flings her bag on the floor next to her. She slowly drifts into sleep until she hears the horn call announcing the start of the funeral rites. Not wanting to disappoint her mother on this significant day for their family, she darts from the tent and runs as fast as she can to the pyre. She sees her mother standing with the council in front of the gathering crowd. Kata pushes her way through and rushes next to her mother. Her mother gives her a stern look of disappointment and pulls her in closer. "I asked you to be here on time. And couldn't you have cleaned up some before you came?"

Kata sighs in annoyance and runs her fingers through her hair to try and tame it. One of the council members begins the ceremony by motioning for the piles of wood to be lit. A torch is set to the dry wood that ignites into large red flames. A nearby group plays their instruments composed of an assortment of drums and flutes. Others within the group sing to the music in a soft, serene tone. All in attendance bow their heads in silence; many are brought to tears as they reminisce about their departed loved ones. A procession of warriors walks through the gathering carrying the bodies of the deceased to the pyres. The first body brought in is the Eldest's. Kata feels more emotions than she thought she would at the sight of his carefully wrapped body being carried toward the fire. The elder leading the procession motions for Kata and her mother to approach the body to pay their respects before the body is placed in the fire for his spirit to be carried on the smoke to the next life. Kata's mother becomes extremely emotional and sobs over her companion's body. Kata feels a pang of guilt for not wanting to attend. Perhaps it was an attempt to protect herself from feeling the grief. If she avoided it, she wouldn't have to face the reality that her father is really gone, all while trying to justify the emotional distance using their lack of a close relationship. At the time, it felt as if he was gone on another hunting trip as he often was, but to see his body one final time forced her to accept the reality. She remembers seeing his body when the war party returned. At the time, he looked peaceful and at rest, like he was sleeping. Yet reality never set in that her father was dead and she hadn't accepted the fact he was gone from this life. Maybe, even, being a healer from a young age and being so familiar with death stripped her of those initial feelings of grief. In any case, she can't help but feel the grief now, especially as the warriors take her father's body to the flames.

One by one, the other bodies are brought to the flames where the family is given a chance to say their goodbyes, and then the body is hefted into the flames. Kata stands by, watching body after body be thrown into the flames. She's mesmerized by the flames and drifts into numbness, her thoughts and emotions become blank and empty again. She feels a hand gently squeeze her shoulder. Looking up, she sees a sullen face looking down at her. She recognizes Broltrom's sharp features and it brings a smile to her face. She embraces him and the rest of his family as they walk past to the body of his brother. Doltrom's wife breaks down into hysterical weeping as she clings to the lifeless body. Kata closes her eyes and turns away to block the sadness from welling up again. Doltrom had always been there for her, even more so it seemed, than her father. It was usually Doltrom who gave her the scoldings every time she misbehaved or had a rebellious streak running through her. Even when he was being stern with her, she could always feel the compassion and love he had for her and her well being. He was an integral part of her life along with his brother. He was truly going to be missed.

Once the last body is cast into the flames, the tribal musicians play another slow, quiet song. Shumakra chants the song of departure, sending the spirits to the next life with the assurance they will not be forgotten and their families will be taken care of. Once she finishes the chant, the music's pace picks up and gets louder. Another elder steps forward to address the tribe. "Now let us celebrate their lives and live our lives to honor them. Let our lives be a reflection of the strength they have imparted to each of us. Their strength will be missed but lives on through us."

The tribe continues with its celebration, dancing and singing to the music, as well as feasting and drinking. Kata's mother leaves Kata to go join with the elders and their wives in their celebration. Kata makes her way back home, hoping to avoid running into Cultac. When she nears her tent she hears loud, boisterous chatter and laughter coming from nearby tents. She recognizes one of the voices as Cultac's. She picks up her pace to get to her tent, but she's not fast enough to escape being seen. She can hear Cultac calling after her before she reaches her tent. "Katalariana, we were just coming to get you. Come join us at my family's fire."

Kata stops walking and slowly turns to face Cultac and his group of friends. It's apparent in his speech and movements he and his friends have started celebrating early and are heavily inebriated. She doesn't like being around him or his friends when they're drunk because of how loud and aggressive they are. Cultac stumbles over to her and clumsily puts his arm around her, pulling her toward the group. "I don't feel like celebrating tonight, Cultac. I really prefer to just go home and rest. These last days have been difficult and I would like to rest. Thank you for the invitation, however."

Cultac laughs and pulls her tighter into him. "Sure, sure! Always needing to rest. Tonight is supposed to be celebrating and being with friends. We should be together during this time."

Kata pushes the clay jug away that Cultac keeps pushing into her face. She tries to squirm her way out of his embrace, which causes him to pull her in tighter. "Please, I just want some time to myself and just rest tonight. I don't feel like celebrating," she pleads in frustration.

"I saw you with Broltrom again today. You can embrace him, but you push away from me? We are together; we are supposed to be partners. It's time you start acting like you're mine. Tonight is a celebration and we are going to celebrate together."

Cultac's eyes fill with fury and he tries forcing Kata to drink while all his friends watch and laugh. Kata tries fighting him off and pushes the drink away from her face. Cultac becomes more aggressive as he forcefully pushes the drink into her face while pulling her into the middle of his group of friends. Kata tries fighting her way free, but she knows she's outmatched in strength. She would scream, but every time she opens her mouth Cultac tries pouring in the vile drink. She manages to knock the jug from his hands and it shatters on the ground. Cultac becomes more determined and tries kissing her. She can feel the others in the group groping her as she struggles to free herself. Growing more frustrated by her constant struggle, Cultac tries leading her between some of the nearby tents. "It's time I show you your place," Cultac breathes into her ear.

"Cultac, stop!" Kata begs, trying to pull herself away from the group.

Her cries embolden Cultac further and he tries rushing the group to the space between the tents, all while pulling at Kata's skirt to loosen the straps. She feels the fingers of despair closing in around her until she hears her mother's voice calling for her. The group goes quiet and they all turn their attention toward the voice. Cultac releases his grip on Kata and she side-steps from the group as her mother rounds the tents into view. "Kata, are you…? Oh! I didn't realize you were with Cultac, I thought you might be home, so never mind."

"No, Mother. Cultac was just bringing me home. I was feeling tired and they were dropping me off. What is it you need?" Kata explains as she casts a disgusted look at Cultac.

"Never mind, my daughter. Someone from the healer tents came saying someone needed a healer's care. I will find someone else to go."

Kata stops her mother before she leaves and tells her she will attend to it. She dashes from the group and steps into her tent to grab her bag and heads straight to the healer tents. Cultac and his friends are still near the tent talking and drinking among themselves when she leaves. Cultac watches her intently until she is out of sight, then rallies his group and leads them elsewhere.

Kata rushes through the tents in a hurry to get away. She can still feel all the hands groping her and it sends a shiver over her body. She feels so filthy and violated and it's near impossible to get the images of the event out of her mind. Her legs feel weak and she struggles to stay on her feet, but she doesn't want to slow down in case Cultac is following. Her heart pounds intensely as if trying to jump from her chest and tears flow uncontrollably from her eyes. She arrives at the healer tents and leans up against the outside of one of them. She props herself up and takes a moment to catch her breath. Her chest is tight and her lungs burn as if she'd been holding her breath the entire time. She takes several deep breaths and tries wiping the fountain of tears pouring from her eyes. She stares up at the sky and tries calming herself down. More and more, the dream she had seems real. It was like the shadows came and were surrounding her, only they came in the form of Cultac and his band. She's filled with a sense of gratitude and continually thanks God her mother showed up in time as the ray of light this time.

After calming down enough to focus, she makes her way to the tent to address the issue her mother sent her for. She takes her time at the healer tents, hoping Cultac and his friends will have moved on and forgotten her in their inebriated state. She also decides to put a plan into effect, hopefully allowing her to give the sedative to the stranger before she leaves. After finishing her mother's task, she goes from tent to tent to see if the girls need a short break before she leaves. She hopes they will take her up on the offer to allow even more time to pass.

By the time she reaches the stranger's tent, the darkness of night begins to fall. She politely asks the young woman if she would like to be relieved for a moment, since Kata happens to be there for an emergency. The young woman is grateful for the opportunity, claiming time is passing too slowly and she's extremely bored. Some fresh air and a chance to stretch her legs is a welcome offer. Kata says she is glad to help and excuses her.

A small fire burns inside, casting just enough light for Kata to see. She gently kneels beside the stranger and caresses his face. She is happy to see him once more and finds herself wishing he was awake. She remembers what happened with Cultac earlier and convinces herself this stranger wouldn't have let it happen, but instead, would have come to her aid and taken her from the group. Tears roll down her cheeks as she tries to block the emotions and the images from her mind. If only the stranger had been the ray of light showing up and crushing Cultac and whisking her off to safety. Her heart yearns for the stranger's companionship and friendship. She's not sure why the feelings exist because she doesn't even know him, but looking at his calm and serene face in the dim firelight, it's hard to imagine he would be anything different than what she imagines him to be. She feels it's God impressing these things on her heart to prepare her for when he wakes, as well as to give her a ray of hope. She can sense the dark cloud hanging over her future if she doesn't end up with the stranger and is forced to be with Cultac, like the overcast shadow in her dream. She tries not to allow her thoughts to go there, but there is an ever looming fear of the worst.

Kata administers the sedative and kisses the stranger on the forehead. She feels a bit embarrassed for having done it when she realizes what she did, but the impulse felt almost natural in the moment. She's opened her heart more than she ever has in her life, and the emotions are driving her mad. It's not something she's used to, and she's not quite sure how to handle them, especially since he can't reciprocate those feelings yet. For now, all she can do is wait. Wait to see what the future holds for her and this man who's become such a focal point in their tribe and in her life.

The young woman returns and Kata quietly slips from the tent after casting one last glance at the stranger. She avoids the groups of people still celebrating outside as she makes her way home. She keeps an eye out for Cultac and his group, and fortunately, she avoids further confrontations with them.

As she lies in bed staring up at the ceiling, she hopes tomorrow will be a better day. Drifting off to sleep, she feels there is certainly a brighter hope for the future as long as all goes according to her plan. A hope brighter than there ever had been up to this point in her life.

◄10►

For the next three days, Kata wakes up early every morning to go to the healer tents and begins her duties. She rushes to finish taking care of the tribal warriors so she can spend the rest of her time tending to the stranger. Before the rite participant shows up, she pours the sedative in his mouth to help him sleep longer. Every night, when everyone is sleeping, she sneaks out to his tent and repeats the administration of the sedative and returns to her own tent unnoticed.

The majority of the warriors have left on the hunt and will be gone for many days. Kata is relieved not to have to worry about Cultac during this time, and considers herself fortunate she had no further run-ins with him. She figures he was regretting what he did and stayed away, or he drank so much it took time for him to recover enough to lead the hunt. Either way, Kata was glad for the reprieve.

On the fourth day, Kata gets up early and begins her day as she's done for the last three. By now, some of the less severe cases have left the tents, so the workload has been reduced considerably. Kata goes about working happily, knowing she will get to spend even more time with the foreigner once she's completed all her tasks. His condition has drastically improved over the last few days and she knows it won't be long before he is healthy enough to leave the tent. Furthermore, word of his severe condition on the first night spread and caused a majority of the young women to forfeit their place as possible life partners. In a few more days it will be her turn to stay the night with him.

She speeds through her work and races to the stranger's tent. She flings the door flap aside and steps inside. She stops dead in her tracks and watches another woman bent over the stranger. Hearing Kata rush in, she turns to look at who it is. "Ah, Kata! What are you doing here?"

"Mother?" Kata exclaims in surprise and confusion. "I was just coming to see if you needed any help."

Her mother smiles at her and waves her hand to gesture there was no need. "I figured I should come and look at this demon while he's still sleeping. I didn't think anyone had been taking care of him since they were all too afraid he would wake up to tear them apart. Apparently, whoever is caring for him during the nights must have knowledge about bandaging wounds like us healers. It's more than I feel he deserves. Though I do have to say, he's not near being in the condition everyone who first saw him said he was in. The hole in his side is certainly a serious wound, but not nearly the mangled mess I was told it was. This makes me think that there isn't a reason why he should be sleeping so much. The other thing is that he's awfully pale looking for a blue demon. They say he came covered with a hard, blue shell. I wonder what became of his shell. I certainly hope that none of those young women undressed him. It certainly is not their place to have to be exposed to such indecency until they have their life partner."

Kata looks longingly at her patient while her mother rambles on and tends to the stranger's wounds. Kata sighs as she considers what she'll have to do to administer the sedative without her mother noticing. He hasn't woken up again since she started giving him the sedative, but she didn't want it wearing off again anytime soon. "Do you need me to help you here, or take over for you?" Kata interrupts her mother's ramblings.

Her mother looks up at her again. "Oh no, there isn't much to do here. If everyone else has been taken care of, we can be done early. I do like days like this, where everything goes quick and smooth. No sense spending more time here than necessary. It isn't like we are participating in the rites and have to stay with these men all the time. Especially this one. I wouldn't even consider him as part of our tribe."

She grumbles under her breath he shouldn't have even been brought back and obviously someone wasn't using their head. She continues mumbling and Kata has a hard time hearing her. "Well, I will not linger any longer if you do not need me," Kata interrupts again.

"Very well, I am done here anyway. By the way, I will not be home to eat tonight; I was invited to another's home for a meal. I will see you afterward."

Kata hesitantly makes her way to the doorway, gazing at the stranger's calm and relaxed visage. She can barely pull herself away when she hasn't been able to spend her time with him today. Kata's mother notices her awkwardness and watches as her daughter leaves. She stands and goes to the doorway and steps outside. She watches as her daughter rushes away from the tents. "Tell me. Who has been caring for the demon during the day?" she asks the guards.

The guards look across at each other, unsure why she would ask. "Your daughter has, Grand Healer," they respond.

She catches Kata looking back at the tent before walking out of sight. "Is there a problem, Grand Healer?" one of the guards asks, noticing some concern on her part.

"No. All is well."

She replies all is well, but in her mind, she recognizes several clues that insinuate not all is well. She thought it was odd Kata was waking up early these last several days when it was always a struggle to get her out of bed. She has also been keeping to herself during the latter part of the day after her responsibilities at the tents are done. It also explains why Kata has become so careless in her work and isn't in the other tents much. Her thoughts go back to the first night the demon was brought to the tribe and how Kata expressed her desire to enter the rites for partnership with him. She figured that night was the end of it all, but she should have known her daughter wouldn't drop it so easily.

Realizing there is possibly more going on than she cares to believe, she turns to the guards at the doorway. "From now on, let no one else enter this tent, including my daughter. I will take care of this demon while he remains here. I don't want anyone else to put themselves at risk."

Kata finally slows down once she's out of sight from her mother. She's concerned about how she is going to give the stranger the sedative without her mother growing suspicious of her. She doesn't like deceiving her mother, but she knows her mother will not approve or permit her to have any interaction with the stranger. She plans on waiting for her mother to leave the tents for the day and then going back to the stranger under the pretense of picking something up her mother had forgotten.

She walks around the camp until she catches a glimpse of her mother going home, then races back to the healer tents to carry out her plan. When she reaches the stranger's tent, the guards in front stop her. Bewildered, she claims she's there to pick up something her mother left behind.

The guards insist she cannot enter and it was her mother who forbade her from entering.

Panic swells in Kata's chest. Was her mother aware of her actions? She hopes it's only as a precaution to protect the younger healers from being exposed, or needlessly being in contact with the one they claim is a demon. Regardless of the reason, the panic does not subside.

She excuses herself from the guard's presence, claiming her mother will have to collect the item herself in the morning. She backs away from the tent and makes her way along the other tents as if she were going to check on someone else. Instead, she dashes between the tents and makes her way around to the back of the tent. She tries to move quietly, but she does not have the cover of darkness to aid her from being spotted. Fortunately, no one is behind the healer tents.

She gently lifts the tent side and slides underneath. She can hear the guards asking each other if they heard something as she's halfway underneath the tent. Kata scurries back out right as the guards look inside. She sits on the ground outside, listening for the guards. She tells herself to move slower so the tent doesn't move so much or make a lot of noise crawling on the ground.

Waiting a moment after she hears the guards return to their post and claim it was the wind or some scurrying animal, she tries crawling under again. Going as slow and carefully as she can, she crawls to the stranger's side and draws her vial out.

She's dismayed at having to hurry and not getting to spend her time with him. She's so panicked and stressed, she forgoes caressing his face so she can hurry up and administer the medicine.

Immediately after dripping the fluid in his mouth, she hears the guards talking outside. Their relief has shown up to allow them time to eat and take a break. Knowing they check on the stranger before switching, Kata scrambles to the tent wall, her heart racing the entire time. A lump wells up in her throat as she fights back the tears. The guards take their time to chat with each other, giving Kata the time she needs to get out unseen.

She slinks from tent to tent until she knows she's in the clear and then breaks down in tears. She tries to keep moving but she can't seem to stop the tears. She's so disappointed she didn't get to spend her time with him, and the stress created by having to sneak around is getting to be too much for her to take. Her disappointment turns to anger. Her mind floods with thoughts that fuel her anger. Why should she have to sneak around? Why can't she choose what she wants for her life without the interference of her family and tribe members? Her anger turns toward her mother and Cultac, for all they continue to do to force her into a position she doesn't want to be in. She's angry with herself for not having the strength to make a stand. As she mulls over and over these questions and thoughts in her mind, one question rings out. Why go through all this for someone she doesn't know?

The question causes her to stop and she falls to her knees. The tears well up again. Once again, she can't explain to herself why she feels so attached to this man. It seems silly to place so much time and effort for a future that wasn't guaranteed. Doubt fills her thoughts and she wonders if it's really divine influence bringing her so close to him, or is it desperation to get away from the life everyone wants for her? With every doubtful thought and question, her heart sinks deeper into despair. Then she remembers how happy she has been and how bright the future seems when she's with the stranger. She tells herself to trust in those feelings. She picks herself up off the ground and brushes the dirt and the tears away. Just a little longer and the stranger's wounds will be completely healed and it will be her turn in the partnership rites. With a somewhat renewed conviction, she makes her way home.

For the next few days, Kata's mother says nothing to her daughter about the demon, but she keeps continual watch over her. Her behaviors have started returning to how they used to be, but there is still something different about her, like she is still being evasive. Even meal times were extremely quiet and they seldom ever spoke to each other. Kata stopped waking up so early to go to the healer tents, but she still didn't see her working there as much as she used to. According to the guards, they never saw Kata approach the demon's tent after she restricted access to it.

The other unusual thing her mother noticed was she spent a lot more time going off on her own, taking long walks in the nearby woods or spending a lot of time near the bathing area at the river. It was like she was living in her own world. She considers the thought that perhaps she overreacted and misjudged her daughter, and perhaps the awkwardness was derived from her daughter mourning her father.

One morning, as she treats the demon and thinks about her daughter's odd behavior, a flash of light catches her eye. She looks around the tent and notices the wind blowing the edge of the tent wall, causing it to lift enough for light to shine under it. She walks to the tent wall and notices the ground is disturbed and looks as if someone has worn a path under the tent wall, or even tried to dig a shallow indentation large enough for someone to pass underneath. She looks back at the demon and then back at the disturbed earth. Once again, the pieces come together in her mind. She's not sure what her daughter is doing, but she's determined to find out.

That night, when all is quiet and still, Kata's mother lies in her bed. She fights the sleep trying to subdue her. She spent the day trying to follow her daughter around, but once again, she spent most of her time wandering the woods and sitting at the river's edge. She hopes to stay awake to keep an eye on her activities, but sleep is forcibly encroaching. As she is succumbing to slumber, she hears her daughter moving about the tent. Pretending to sleep, she allows her daughter to slip out of the tent into the night. Once she knows her daughter is away from the tent, she herself slips out into the night. The dual moons light the night sky with a brilliant blue glow. She spies her daughter's form moving among the shadows of the tents. Seeing she is heading toward the healer tents, Kata's mother quietly makes her way there, keeping out of her daughter's view. She watches her daughter scurry across the open area in front of the tents, staying in the shadows and avoiding being found by the guards. She sneaks behind the tents out of her mother's view. Her mother waits hiding in the shadows until she sees her daughter returning after a few moments. Kata's mother notices her daughter clutching her bag in her hands as she slinks through the shadows. She hurries home, hoping to stay ahead of her daughter. She arrives home first but hides behind another tent along the path her daughter is traveling. When she hears her daughter's footsteps close by, she reveals herself by standing in her path. "Mother!" her daughter whispers in surprise.

They stare at each other for a long time, Kata's eyes wide with terror, and her mother's eyes slanted in disappointment. Kata is speechless, wanting to ask what her mother is doing, yet knowing full well she would have to answer the same. Her mother's voice is quiet yet stern and cuts through the quiet night like a blade. "Awfully late to be out by yourself, isn't it?"

Kata swallows hard, still unsure of what exactly to say. Her mother reaches over and snatches the bag from her hands. She rummages through the bag and pulls out the wooden vial. She knows instantly what it is, what it does, and what it is Kata has been doing. She wants to unleash her rage against her daughter, but to do so would wake those in the tents around them. Waking everyone around them would reveal what her daughter has done, placing their family in a shameful position. "Do you realize what it is you have done? Do you know what will happen to our family if the elders are made aware of your actions? We would be shamed or worse; cast from the tribe for interfering with sacred rites. How could you do this? It is forbidden and you gave no thought to the consequences? You are no longer permitted near the healer tents. You are no longer allowed to assist those who are wounded until that demon is removed from this place!"

Her mother spits the word "demon" from her mouth with such hatred and disdain. Kata looks at the ground, once again feeling the dark clouds moving in over her future. "You speak reason, Mother. I am sorry for my actions, but I felt I had no choice."

"No choice?" her mother echoes in disbelief.

"I tried to speak to you of my choices and my feelings. I tried telling you what my heart wanted and what I felt God had led me to, but you wouldn't hear!" Kata explains in defense.

"I do not accept that God would want a demon as your companion. You were chosen by Cultac, and you will be his life partner. I will keep these things from the council, but you will no longer go near that monster. Is that understood? If I find out you have disobeyed once more, you will face a swift retribution. Enough about this demon, you are not to be with him! I will not allow you to destroy our family!"

"You care nothing about this family or what I want! You only care about your position in the tribe. You're afraid that if I marry someone other than the Eldest, you will lose your place and will be considered the same as any other member of the tribe; no longer welcome among the circles of the council," her daughter retorts.

Kata forces her way passed her mother, tears flooding her eyes. Her mother grabs her arm and squeezes tightly. "You will not shame me and you will do as you were always meant to do. You are forbidden from going near that tent."

"You can't stop me!" Kata spits in defiance, producing the token for the rite of partnership and holding it in front of her mother's face.

"What is this that you have done?" her mother exasperates.

She takes the token from her daughter and stares at it with wide, incredulous eyes. Her shock melts into fury. She tosses the token to the dirt and steps toward her daughter with a stern finger pointed in her face. "This means nothing!" she spits venomously. "You are forbidden and I will see to it that you go nowhere near him."

Kata goes to where the token is on the ground and picks it up and runs into the tent. Her mother stays outside, letting the night air cool her anger. She no longer trusts her daughter to obey and decides she will have to keep a closer eye on her actions. She will not let her daughter destroy the best future possible for their family, even if it means following her everywhere until she is rid of the demon as a potential partner. Now that she has stopped Kata, hopefully he will awake and be well enough to be claimed by another. If things with her daughter continue to escalate, she may be forced to take matters into her own hands, dealing with the demon on her own terms and rid the tribe of him. But for now, she is willing to abide by the council's decision to let him live and allow things to transpire of their own accord.

By morning, clouds have moved in and unleash torrents of rain. It reflects Kata's dark and sullen mood. She stands in the tent's doorway with the flap open watching the raindrops falling. Her mother set out earlier to the healer tents and informed the guards someone was sneaking in from the back and showed them the worn out indentation on the ground. After informing the other healers she and Kata wouldn't be there to help, she hurried home to stay with Kata. Every time Kata attempted to leave, her mother prepared to go right along with her. It didn't matter much since she really had nothing to do today anyway, and she knows it isn't going to be possible to see the stranger. No doubt they placed more guards or placed one in the back and one in the front to keep her out. Her greatest fear is of him waking before it's her turn in the rite. She expects the elder to come to her anytime and notify her it's her turn. She hopes the stranger stays sleeping until then, though the chances are slim. Her other concern is of her mother doing something to get rid of the stranger or wake him up as soon as possible. His wounds are nearly healed completely, so there is no reason for him to stay in the healer tent once he awakes.

Kata spends a lot of her time praying she gets her chance, but more and more, she feels all her deception and dishonesty may have disqualified her. She regrets not having made her stand earlier when confronted by her mother. She clutches the token in her hand, hoping for a ray of sunshine amid the dark clouds. She wonders if telling her mother was the best idea. Perhaps she let her anger get the better of her and rushed into a rash decision to spite her. Her mother would have been furious regardless, but Kata wonders if she would risk her position within the council to stop her daughter from participating in the rite. Perhaps she is so against Kata partnering with the demon the risk is worth it. Deep down she feels it really doesn't matter now. There is no way of stopping nature's course and the demon will soon wake.

Time passes by slowly, making for a long day, but when night finally comes, Kata can't sleep. She lays in her bed tossing and turning, too anxious and worried to sleep. She still listens to her mother's breathing, wondering if it's worth the risk to try and venture out.

She rolls over and peers down to the end of the tent where her mother sleeps and sees her sitting up in bed. In the faint light of the burning embers she catches the glint off of her mother's eyes. She appears to be wide awake; making sure her daughter makes no effort to leave during the night. Kata rolls onto her back and stares at the ceiling. Tears once again roll down her face. The rain starts again, and Kata allows herself to be lulled to sleep by the pitter patter of the rain on the tent. She prays the morning will bring brighter skies and the rain will have washed away the sorrow of today.

In the morning there is an unusual buzz of energy going through the camp. Kata wakes up with a start and looks around the tent. Her mother is no longer in her bed and there is a lot of noise outside. She goes to the doorway and peers out. The first rays of morning light are breaking over the horizon. Kata rubs the sleep from her eyes and looks around. People rush past her tent heading in the direction of the healer tents. Her heart beats hard in her chest. She races in the same direction as everyone else. The closer she gets, the faster her heart beats and the faster she runs. A large crowd gathers around the healer tents; a council member stands outside trying to calm the crowd and keep them back. Several of the warriors are armed with their blades and spears, standing around the council member. Kata reaches the crowd and tries pushing through everyone toward the front. The people are so crammed together it's difficult to make any progress. The elder continues to shout at the people to calm down and to be patient.

Kata's heart continues to race and she chokes back the tears trying to force their way out. It wasn't supposed to happen this way; he was supposed to be hers. She tries looking over everyone to see what is going on in front of the group. She can barely see the doorway to the stranger's tent, but she sees it open and the tops of people's heads coming out. She recognizes one of the heads as her mother's, judging by the hair. The other person appears to be the young woman who stayed the night. Kata can't see her face, but recognizes the hair. There was only one person in the tribe with red hair, and that's Reshiara.

Kata only knows of Reshiara because of her situation, but never actually had any associations with her. Both of her parents died when she was very young and she had no other family in the tribe. Tribe members helped to take care of her, but she lived on her own most of her life. Because of all the unfortunate circumstances surrounding this young girl's life, there was inherently a negative stigma placed on her. She never had friends that Kata knew of, and she entered every rite of partnership she could with the hopes of finally having her own family.

Reshiara and Kata's mother walk over to the elder, who listens to them intently. Kata doesn't see the stranger anywhere and fears the worst. Had her mother, in her anger over her daughter's actions, gone and poisoned the stranger, killing him in the night? Had the young woman caught her in the act? Or did something else happen, and because her mother was in charge of the healers, she came to the stranger's aid and failed? Kata's mind races with all sorts of possibilities, each one casting more fear in her mind.

The elder looks up over the crowd and raises his arms to silence them as he prepares to address them. Quiet falls over everyone in the crowd as they eagerly await the news regarding the foreigner. "As many of you have no doubt heard," the elder's voice echoes over the silent crowd. "The demon has awoken! According to our Great Healer, he appears to be healed and able to leave the care and shelter of the healer tents. By rite of partnership, this daughter of our tribe has been found worthy to be his companion for life. After his ordeal, he is still weary and plagued with confusion. After he is clothed and fed, he will be released from the healer's care into the care of our fair daughter, Reshiara. We, the council, are aware of the concerns many of you have over the safety of this tribe now that he is awake. We assure you he will be guarded by our strong warriors and they will be with him wherever he goes. We know nothing of this man yet, what his intentions are, or what he is capable of. Until we do, we ask that you treat him as a welcomed member of our tribe, and pray that he sees fit to treat us in kind. Let us do all we can to make him feel welcome. One more point we wish to bring before the tribe is that because we know nothing about this man or how he came to be healed so quickly from such grievous wounds, we ask of one of the healer's to stay with him until we are sure he no longer needs a healer's care."

The crowd remains silent as they look from one person to the next. Katalariana's mother steps forward as a voice rings out over the crowd. "I will take the responsibility! I am willing to watch over this man."

The elder bobs his head side to side trying to catch a glimpse of the person yelling from the crowd. The crowd parts and Kata makes her way to the front. "Very good, Katalariana. You will be an excellent choice," the elder confirms.

Kata's mother approaches the elder and tries to inform him she should be the one to take the responsibility. "The council has accepted Katalariana's offer. We would not impose this upon you as you are still needed here at the tents. Your daughter is more than capable of caring for any issue this man may have. This is the choice of the council."

Kata's mother glares at her with disapproval, but she knows it is already too late for her daughter to be in a relationship with the demon. Reshiara has already been given to the demon as a partner, and as far as she is concerned, it is an ideal match. Once Cultac comes home, Kata will have no other choice but to join with him.

◄ 11 ►

A cool draft blows in from the night air through the gap under the tent wall, sending a chill rippling through Chance's body. He slowly opens his eyes and blinks several times to clear the haze from his vision. The smell of a smoldering fire enters his nostrils and he wonders if he's still lying on the battlefield. He tries to move but his body feels extremely stiff and sore.

Images flash through his mind of the last things he saw before blacking out. He remembers being hit by the explosive and then the numbness he felt throughout his body. His body definitely wasn't numb anymore.

His vision finally clears and he sees he is no longer in the field or even out in the open. His memory is still a little hazy as he tries remembering the events following the explosion. A woman's face also flashes through his mind. A woman with a youthful and attractive face, dark hair and purple eyes. Certainly not one of his teammates.

As he tries to remember anything else, his head throbs and the room feels like it's spinning. He closes his eyes and takes several deep breaths. Nauseousness tightens his stomach, but he can't tell if it's from the room spinning or because of how hungry he is.

Once the room stops spinning, he tries to move again and sit up. All his joints ache and his muscles feel tight. He works on moving his head to glance around the room. He obviously wasn't picked up by a CC medical team and being held in the cold, steel confines of a CC infirmary. He is in some kind of tent with a framework of wood poles holding up the walls and a long pole holding up the center of the ceiling. At the foot of his bed is the doorway covered by a flap of the same material as the rest of the walls. On the opposite side of the tent from the bed are the smoldering embers of a fire and the huddled shape of a sleeping person beside it. The faint glow of the embers reflects off of red strands of hair and he can vaguely make out a face. It looks like the face of another young woman he doesn't recognize.

He props himself up on his arms and all his joints crack and pop. He slowly sits himself up, wincing in pain as he does. Upon sitting up, he discovers he is without any clothing. He looks around for possible clothing but finds nothing but the skins he is laying on and the one covering him up as a blanket.

Covering himself the best he can, he continues to work his muscles and joints. He pulls his legs to his chest and rotates his shoulders and head, getting all the popping and cracking done with.

While rubbing the knots out of his leg muscles, he hears stirring on the far side of the tent. He looks over and sees the young woman sitting up and watching him. Both sit in silence, trying to size each other up. She says something under her breath that he can't make out. He remains motionless and silent, so as not to scare her. After a silent moment, she says something even louder, but it's a language Chance doesn't know.

In quick response, two men with spears charge into the room from the doorway. They utter more gibberish and point their spears at him. Chance raises his hands in the air to show he has no ill intentions. They tell the young woman something, but she remains motionless, staring at him. They yell at her again before she makes her way to the door and flees outside. The two men stand menacingly over him, still pointing their spears at him for a long time.

The young woman finally returns with several others. The inside of the small tent becomes crowded, but Chance doesn't move or say a word. He keeps his hands up to show he means no harm, while the rapidly growing crowd gawks over him. The two men with spears are having a hard time covering him and keeping the people back.

A woman's harsh voice causes all but the two spearmen, one older gentleman, and the young girl with the red hair, to leave the tent. Once everyone else has vacated the tent, the woman yelling at them enters. She talks to the older man and then crouches beside Chance. She grabs his face in one hand and moves it from side to side and then stares into his eyes.

She yells at the small group behind her and the young woman rushes to the fire pit, throwing on more wood to stoke it up and create more light. The woman looks back at Chance and continues her examination.

The older man speaks to the woman and then exits the tent. Chance can hear a lot of commotion outside that instantly subsides once the older man addresses them. Chance gets the idea he's become a matter of great interest among these people. He's never felt more like a zoo exhibit in his life. He becomes a little concerned when he thinks about what they may have done to him while he was unconscious, especially if just his waking up has caused this much ruckus.

As the woman examines Chance, he watches the people in the tent with him. He hoped to talk to these people, but he didn't expect it to be under such circumstances. The young woman with the red hair squats down beside the fire, wrapped in several skins, watching the older woman doing the examination. Whenever Chance looks into her eyes, she beams with excitement. She appears to be quite young; if he were to guess, he'd say she was in her late teens or early twenties. She has long, fire red hair that glows in the light of the flames.

The two men guarding him both have long dark hair and chiseled features that accentuate their stern expressions. They appear to have a muscular physique under the animal skins draped over their upper bodies. They stand approximately six feet tall, close to Chance's own height of six feet and two inches. From his earlier encounter with their warriors, that seems to be the average among them; tall and muscular.

The older woman doing the examination is a shorter, heavy set woman with dark, curly hair peppered with gray. Several necklaces and bracelets made of bone and colorful stones hang around her neck and arms. Unlike the others, she wears no skin or fur coverings to protect her from the cool night air other than a skin wrapped around her waist. She's methodical in her approach to the examination, suggesting she is most likely the primary medical practitioner.

After being poked and prodded extensively for what feels like a long time, the older woman finally stands, whispers to the young girl, and then they leave the tent. The two guards remain inside, although they have since raised their spears and now stand watch over Chance. Chance can hear people speaking outside the tent; he assumes it's regarding him. He sits on the bed with only an animal skin covering him, waiting for whatever happens next. He hopes whatever it is has to do with food and clothing.

As he sits and waits, listening to the strange words coming from outside, a voice breaks his concentration. He doesn't understand the words, but the voice resonates with familiarity. He perks up and tries to listen some more, but all he hears is the older man's voice along with the older woman's. Chance feels the urge to go see who it is, so with the strength he can muster, he stands on his feet. He feels awkward and unbalanced and his legs are like gelatin. After gaining his footing, he secures the skins around him and starts for the door. The two men guarding him step in to intercept him.

Chance raises his hands to show once again he has no ill intentions, and then points toward the door. He points at his eyes and then points to the door again, trying to tell them he only wants to look. The guards look at each other, unsure of what this stranger is doing.

Chance continues to the door with his hands raised and steps outside. A gasp sounds over the group still gathered around the healer tents. The two guards step up behind him and several other men waiting nearby rush to meet him with their spears at the ready. Chance keeps his hands raised and steps away from the doorway, careful not to walk into the spears or make any sudden or aggressive moves.

He scans over the crowd, hoping to find the one with the familiar voice. In the front of the group, he spots a slender young woman with dark, wavy hair and deep purple eyes. Her eyes seem to glisten with oncoming tears, but she has a large smile on her face. He recognizes her from the images in his mind, but he has no idea who she is or why she is so familiar. Regardless, he's comforted by the fact there is a familiar face among the crowd of gawking faces. Her smile drops from her face into disappointment when the red haired girl walks toward him.

The red haired girl's amber eyes gleam with excitement as she approaches Chance. She slowly reaches out her hand and places it on his arm and then slowly runs her hand down into his own hand, slipping her fingers between his and tightening her grip. She looks up at him longingly, which confuses Chance even more as he tries to figure what is going on. The confusion and anxiety take their toll and everything feels like it's spinning again. He falls to one knee and hunches over the ground as a wave of nausea washes over him. The majority of the people in attendance view it as an act of submission, bowing himself before the mercy of the tribe, but Kata can see the distress in his expression and rushes to his aid. Reshiara still clings to him when Kata approaches and kneels in front of him. She bends down and looks him in the eyes, which happen to be shut tight. He breathes in deeply, hoping the nausea will pass, but it isn't until he feels the gentle hand on his shoulder that fills his body with a calm energy. He opens one eye to look at her and then he whispers, "Water."

Everyone looks around at each other with unsettling confusion. Chance looks up long enough to see their confusion. "I need water, please!" he mutters again, this time moving his hand to his mouth to simulate drinking.

Kata turns to the tribe and tells them to bring some water and then turns her attention to the councilman. "This man is not ready to be released from the healer tents. He is still too weak, and I think he should stay for more time."

Reshiara clings more tightly to Chance and looks desperately at Kata. "But he was declared well enough to leave the tent. He can't go back, he's already mine. I will care for him, he just needs to rest at home," she pleads.

Kata's mother steps toward them with a scowl on her face. She glares defiantly at her daughter who still kneels by the demon's side. "Do you challenge my abilities as the Great Healer? Did he not leave the tent on his own strength?"

"Clearly this man is not well!" Kata interrupts.

"I see nothing wrong with him. Clearly he humbles himself before the tribe. Fear has seized this demon because he knows his end lies within our hands and that he is alone. It's fear, nothing more. Do you not feel capable of caring for him as you volunteered to do, and so you need others to help care for him here? Or do you have another reason for keeping him here longer?" her mother questions cynically.

Reshiara glances at Kata distrustfully and pulls in closer to Chance. Kata withdraws her hand from his shoulder while bashfully glancing at the others witnessing the debate. "No, I have no other reason than this man's welfare in mind. I do not doubt my abilities and feel I am more than capable to accompany him and attend to his needs when necessary. I desire no disrespect to anyone; I was only concerned he was not well enough, as he appeared distressed."

Someone brings some water which is poured into a dish and given to Chance. Kata is grateful for the distraction and Chance is glad to finally have something to help calm his stomach. The dizziness has subsided, but the weakness and nausea still overwhelm him. He sips the water and empties it, handing it over for a refill. It has been a long time since he remembers having such fresh and clean water to drink. He's used to the stale tasting water aboard the Mayflower. The fresh water is reinvigorating as it goes down his throat, and he continues to drain the dish each time it's passed to him.

Feeling a little better, Chance lifts his head and looks at Kata. Her smiling face looks back at him, and in habit, she reaches her hand out to caress his face. Realizing she's in the presence of the tribe and with Reshiara watching her closely, she stops her hand and instead feels his forehead and wipes the beads of sweat off. She swallows the lump forming in her throat, trying to force its way out again. It's hard for her to accept she's lost her chance with him. She tells herself it isn't over and some way, they will end up together even though their chances are slim. All she can think about is how unfair it is. Her mother kept her from entering the rites, and then kept her from going to him on a daily basis. She was denied the opportunity and now he belongs to someone else.

Before she can move her hand from his forehead, he reaches up and places his hand on top of hers. Her skin feels soft and cool against his face. She's surprised by this act, along with several of the nearby tribe members. Several of the warriors close in with their spears but Reshiara steps in to intercept them. Kata jerks her hand away and moves back, though she wants the moment to go on forever. The warmth of his hand on hers filled her with a sense of protection and compassion, almost as if he knew her anguish and sought to ward it off. It feels like they are linked with each other. It's the sudden flood of emotion that surprised her and caused her to pull away. Though it pained her to do it, she was glad she pulled away, as it may have given her secret away about her feelings for him.

Chance holds his hands in the air to show he still means no harm and the warriors withdraw their spears. It was that her hand felt so familiar to him. It's perplexing how familiar this young woman is to him even though he can't recall ever having seen her before. The only contact he had with these people was in the fight that got him blown up by his own people, and he certainly doesn't recall her there. When he looks into her eyes, however, they do remind him of the warrior he helped in the battle. And while the eyes may have been similar, the face of the warrior was much older and more masculine, so it's unreasonable he would be confusing the two. While his memories before he blacked out on the battlefield are still vague, the image of her face is still clear in his mind and it's unmistakable when he sees her in person. It's her face he envisioned when he awoke.

Thinking about it makes his head throb even more, so he turns his attention to those around him. At any other time, he could have made quick work of these warriors and made his escape unscathed, but weakened by his injuries he isn't so sure he can get away so easily. Not only that, but he's naked and unarmed. He has no provisions or means of even finding his bearings. As he considers the next course of action, he remembers the words of the assistant manager during the briefing. He said they were to take every opportunity to learn what they can about these people, and this is a perfect opportunity to do just that. Especially if he hopes for a peaceful relationship between the CC and these people. Once he's well enough and has learned enough about the people, then he will consider going back to the CC, assuming these people plan on keeping him alive long enough.

With some renewed strength and a determination not to engage in any hostile actions, Chance stands again. He slowly approaches the elder, whom he assumes is the leader, and bows before him. Unsure of these people's customs, it's the best way Chance knows of to show his respect. Hopefully it isn't a gesture they view as a challenge or aggressive in nature and the warriors won't jump him to protect their leader.

After bowing, Chance stands upright and introduces himself to those present. "I am Special Services Shock Trooper Chance Haywood, Department Manager of Bravo Team. I mean you no ill will and stand ready to serve your people."

A silence settles over the tribe. Not a noise is heard, not even in the wind. Everyone looks at one another hoping at least one person understood the noises coming from the demon's mouth. Chance notices the confusion in the elder's expression as he stares into his face. A calm whisper stirs through the crowd. Even Kata and Reshiara look at each other in wonder. Chance points to his chest several times while facing the group. " Chance Haywood. My name is Chance Haywood."

"He-wold?" stammers the elder.

Chance nods his head. "Haywood. Yes. My name. My name is Haywood."

Grasping what the stranger is trying to say, the elder repeats the name again and nods his head. He directs his attention at the rest of the tribe and recites the name over and over with the rest of the people. "Hewold. Hewold."

After they repeat it several times, Chance points his hand at the elder. "Your name?" he asks.

The elder stops repeating the name and looks questioningly at the stranger. Chance points again to urge a response. "Your name?"

"Nem? U nem?" the elder mutters unassuredly.

Chance points to himself again. "My name…Haywood. Your name?" he points again at the elder.

"Nem Hewold?" he repeats, then, realizing what Chance is asking, he excitedly responds. "Nem, Umochak!"

"Humochak." Chance repeats with a smile.

He approaches slowly and extends his hand toward the elder. The warriors are on edge and tightly grip their spears and stand ready to attack. The entire tribe holds their breath with anticipation as they watch the events unfold. The elder looks doubtfully at the extended hand. Chance offers it again, urging the man to take his hand. Hesitantly, the elder extends his hand and takes Chance's. Chance firmly grips the man's hand and shakes it with the biggest smile he can muster on his face. "Hello, Humochak. I'm Haywood. I'm honored to make your acquaintance."

A little afraid at first, the elder's demeanor shifts and he hardily returns the hand shake. "Hewold!"

Assured of no ill will, the elder waves for others to come forward and meet Hewold. The warriors back up a step but remain on high alert. Several from the crowd approach and readily take his hand while spouting out their names. Chance tries to repeat the names and acknowledge everyone that approaches, but he soon becomes overwhelmed by the numbers gathering around him. Several others stand on the outskirts of the group, despising the fact the demon has been allowed to stay among the tribe. Many of them leave the area to go about their daily routines while others stay behind hoping to see the demon turn into something more malevolent and fearsome and tear the demon supporters apart before the warriors are able to put a stop to him.

Kata hangs back from the rest of the group so as not to get trampled. She also wants to be able to have her one on one time with him without feeling rushed by several others trying to get acquainted with him. Reshiara, on the other hand, pushes her way back to Hewold's side after being pushed aside by the masses rushing in to meet him. It's her first claim to any kind of family in years so she feels the need to make her presence known and take her place by his side, especially since she knows there were several girls trying for partnership with him in the rites. Though he may not know the customs of the people, the women know them and as is their tradition, the rites only claim a woman is worthy, not that they are guaranteed to be partners. The man still has a choice in the matter and Reshiara doesn't want to give any other the chance to inform him of that. The council has claimed her as his partner only because they have made exceptions to appease him if he was a monster bent on destroying the tribe, but that won't keep some from trying to stake their claim on him and push Reshiara out. She already has the fact she's an outcast working against her and she fears they will use that to take him away or convince him to choose them instead.

Chance does his best to keep up with everyone introducing themselves to him, but the language is foreign to him so he has no idea whether people are telling him their names or are trying to speak to him. He smiles and nods his head, shaking as many of the hands as are thrust towards him. In his weakened state, the activity is too overwhelming and he can feel his stamina fading fast. His head continues to throb more and more, and the dizziness is returning, but he does his best to stand his ground so he doesn't offend anyone. For all he knows, to faint or collapse while shaking someone's hand could be a bad omen dooming the person for life.

Looking around, he spies the blazing red hair standing out among the dark skin and dark hair of everyone else. By the expression on her face, Chance can see the girl is distressed as she tries in vain to make her way toward him. He's not sure who she is exactly, but it pains him to see someone in such desperation and he feels the need to help her. She may be his guide, or more likely, his nurse, but either way, she was near tears trying to reach him. By helping her, it may also give him some reprieve from all the introductions and allow his body time to calm down and recuperate. He stops shaking hands and raises them into the air in an attempt to calm the people crowding around him. The commotion dies to a quiet calm once more as they try to figure out what's about to happen next. The warrior guards are on edge again, gripping the spears firmly in their hands and ready themselves for quick action. Those observing with hopes of seeing the power of the demon, wait with baited breath when it appears he is about to cast some evil magic over everyone. Once the crowd has grown quiet, he points at Reshiara and extends his hand for her to grab hold of it. The surrounding people give way to let her through until she is able to reach his extended hand. She's overcome with relief to be back by his side, and even happier it was by his own actions. To those observing, especially those of the council, it solidifies Reshiara as the chosen one to be his life partner; to all those observing except for one lone person. Kata witnessed the events unfold, from Reshiara's desperate and vain attempts to fight through the crowd, to the stranger pulling her to his side.

The ever-present lump is working its way back into her throat. It's almost too much to bear, and fortunately everyone is so distracted by Hewold they don't see the tears welling in her eyes. She remembers envisioning her fantasy of the stranger coming to her aid, taking her from the troubles and woes around her once he was awake. Like the dream where he rescued her from the shadows.

Now she witnesses the very act portrayed before her eyes with the man she has been pining for and a hapless girl considered a pariah among the tribe. Her heart shatters when she sees him pull her from the mass of bustling bodies into a protective embrace. She wants nothing more than to run away and hide her face, but responsibility compels her to remain. She wishes she tried pushing her way through. It should have been her he noticed and pulled from the crowd.

Her regret festers even more when hearing the last words she ever wanted to hear. "They make a perfect couple, don't they?" her mother inquires as she steps beside her. "The perfect choice, I would say."

Kata doesn't bother to look away from the scene in front to acknowledge her mother's presence. Her mother looks at

Kata conceitedly. "See reason, my daughter. Put on a face that is becoming of the Eldest's daughter. We can't allow new members of our tribe to see our weakness, now can we? You didn't really expect to be with something like that, did you? Not when you have someone like Cultac waiting for you. If it was meant to be as you said, then would he be standing with that girl by his side? As you can see, he never paid you any attention and left you standing here alone with your broken heart. You should have followed my counsel from the start. If he was truly meant for you, and he truly wanted you, he could have chosen you, and all here would have witnessed his choice. Who could dispute that?" she goes on adding insult to injury, knowing the demon has no knowledge of their customs or the rites he was involved in.

As Kata listens to the words that sting like daggers in her heart, and watches the red-headed girl beside the stranger, she remembers the first night she snuck into the tent and the red hair visible under the heap of furs. Only one girl in their tribe had such red hair. In order for Reshiara to be with the stranger for a second night, all others seeking partnership had to have had their turn. Kata realizes she was skipped. Last night should have been her turn. Driving the daggers even deeper, she now knows her mother was behind the oversight of the elder responsible for notifying her. A mix of anger and sadness swirl inside her as she realizes her mother's cruel betrayal. It's impossible to hold back the tears.

"That should be me up there right now. That should be me in his arms. It was you who denied me that. You denied me my happiness; the happiness that I had chosen for myself."

"You will thank me when he turns out to be a monster. You will be glad it is that sorry girl and not you in those arms when he finally decides to show what he truly is."

"So convinced are you that he is a demon? I do not think a demon would be so concerned for the welfare of someone he does not even know. So concerned he would stop everyone to help her. You will be sorry you thought of him so, when he shows you the demon does not exist and he is a friend to the people. But more so, you will be sorry for betraying your only daughter."

With those last words, Kata turns and looks at her mother defiantly, the anger and frustration still evident through her red, teary eyes. Her mother remains as stern and smug as she always has been, but with nothing more to say. She knows it would be futile to engage her daughter anymore. She figures her daughter will see reason soon enough, especially when the demon spends all his time and attention on the orphan girl. Then her daughter will have no choice but to let him go and move on with her life.

Seeing the crowd has calmed down a bit, the elder in charge tries to regain the attention of the remaining people. As he addresses them, Chance listens closely but still has no idea what is being said. He sees the man is pointing at him while he talks, so he knows it must be about him. Chance looks around at the guards, but none appear to be making any aggressive gestures, so he figures he isn't receiving the death sentence. The red haired girl beside him clings to his arm, holding him close to her. It's a bit odd for a nurse to be so attached to their patients, but then again, he is on an extraterrestrial world. Perhaps she's afraid of being separated from him in the crowd again and doesn't want to lose him. The thought crosses his mind that perhaps she's supposed to be more to him than he is aware of. It seems absurd at first, but a growing fear wells up inside making him a bit uncomfortable. Could it be they gave him to her? Several possibilities cross his mind as to why they would do such a thing, none of which makes him feel any better about the situation. Was he standing in some strange, alien, marriage ceremony that he has willingly played part? She did seem awfully pleased to see him awake, and she hasn't left his side since he awoke. In fact, she had been clinging to his side the majority of the time. In his state of distress and confusion, he hadn't paid any mind to what she was doing, it seemed natural for a nurse to be close by and watch over their patient.

Reshiara senses the tension building in her companion and she looks up at him to assure him everything is fine. She gives him a smile to which he responds with an unnerved, crooked smile. She reaches up and strokes his face to ease the tension, but doing so causes him to become more anxious. Afraid she's done something wrong, she lays her head on his shoulder and pulls his arm closer to her chest. Sensing her disheartened demeanor, Chance feels bad for allowing his thoughts to get the better of him, especially when he has no idea what is transpiring. For all he knows, she's overly friendly and trying to help him feel welcome. At least that is what he is hoping is the case. He pats her hands with his free hand and gives her a more sincere smile to assure her he is well. With that, she moves under his arm, wrapping her arms around him and pulling herself closer to his body. Chance swallows hard. It's harder and harder to convince himself she isn't anything more than a friendly nurse, but he doesn't want to offend his hosts. Playing along until he figures out what's going on seems the best course for now.

To distract his thoughts, he scans the crowd around him for the girl with the familiar face and purple eyes. He finally finds her with the older woman standing just beyond the group of people. It's clear she is unhappy with her arms crossed and biting her lip. Her eyes seem puffy and red as if she has been crying. When their eyes meet, she looks away, and the sadness she had been holding back shows again on her face. She kicks at the ground and looks around to avoid making eye contact with him again. He continues to watch her, wondering what it is that has made her so upset. Not even awake an hour and he already feels entangled in a heaping mess he doesn't know how he got into or even how to get out of. It makes him long for the days he spent hunting down dangerous predators preying on the colonies. At least then, he knew his position and what he was involved in. It was kill or be killed and end up in the stomach of some voracious, alien beast. Of course things couldn't be so simple now. He offends without knowing he's offending and involved in a relationship that may or may not be a real relationship without even knowing how he got into it to begin with. On top of that, he's standing in the middle of a group of people with a woman he doesn't know clinging to him, in the nude with only a blanket to cover himself.

Reshiara tugs at Chance's arm and steps out from under it. The crowd parts and a woman approaches him with a small bundle of skins. She places the bundle in his arms and steps away into the crowd. Chance lifts the top skin and watches it unfold as he holds it in the air. The skin is a dark gray color and feels smooth like snake skin, but heavier and more durable like leather. The skin unfolds into one broad piece with smaller straps hanging from opposite corners. Hoping this is a sling for throwing rocks and not what he's been given to wear, he looks at what else he was handed. He picks up the next skin which looks like a small vest, and underneath is a smaller package, wrapped in a softer, white colored skin. Inside the smaller package is what appears to be dried strips of meat. Reshiara puts her hand under his and pushes it up to urge him to eat it. Chance smiles and, with some hesitation, grabs a piece and bites a chunk off. The texture is similar to the beef jerky he's tried before. Meat was a rarity because livestock didn't fare well enough in space to be useful. The CC had a few colonies which specialized in raising beef and poultry, but when the people rebelled and were breaking away, those colonies were lost along with the meat they produced. Chance has eaten the flesh of a few different species on different planets, but none ever tasted as good as the meat raised from Earth animals. The meat he was eating at the moment was better than a lot of those others he's tried and it comes as a welcome offering since he's sure the last time he's eaten was while he was aboard the Mayflower. The body's healing process is also quite taxing, and without a source of constant nutrition, it has been especially so for Chance. He'd like to tear into the meat with gusto, but he feels it would be quite rude to do so in front of everyone still watching. He wraps the meat back up and thanks them for the food and clothing. He's met with the same blank stares he's been receiving all morning.

Hoping for some time away from all the excitement and attention, Chance turns to the elder and asks if it would be possible to wash before he dresses himself. He pretends to scrub his body to help them understand. He's met again with the same blank, questioning stares. He bends down and grabs some mud and rubs it on his arm and then points and asks for the water they brought for him to drink. The person appears puzzled but hands over the water. Chance pours a small amount on his arm to wash the mud off and then points all over his body and pretends to wash himself again. Reshiara talks to the elder who then nods his head. He points to the nearby guards and then back at Chance. He speaks at Chance, but he still doesn't understand what is being said. He figures, based on his own blank expression, the elder can see he doesn't understand and uses his own gestures to try to explain. Chance watches intently to figure out what he's saying. He points again to the warriors with spears and then back to Chance. He walks in place and points toward the horizon. He places both his hands together and walks in place. He speeds up his walk and separates his hands, points at Chance, then covers his face with his own arm, then points once more to the warriors. He points emphatically at Chance then signals for one of the warriors to step up. He takes the warrior's spear and thrusts it toward Chance.

Chance gets the idea he will be accompanied by these warriors and if he attempts to hide, he will be killed. He nods his head to acknowledge he understands.

The elder turns to the crowd and speaks to them again. "Now we must decide where to keep this man, now that he is well enough to leave the healer's tents. While he goes to the waters, we must prepare a place for him until he is able to complete his own home. Our warriors will continue to keep watch over him, so there is no need to fear. Is there one here who is willing to keep him until then?"

Kata's mother stares sharply at her daughter to make sure she doesn't volunteer their home. Kata glances at her mother, but forgoes any attempt to volunteer. Reshiara cries out to the elder before anyone else has a chance. "What of my home? I am alone and have plenty of room, and besides, I am his chosen life partner. I will keep him in my home."

The elder lowers his head and thinks for a moment. "No, it cannot be so. The rites have not been completed for your union, and we will not risk the virtue of our daughter until they have been completed and you are truly given to each other as life partners. It cannot be as you desire at this time. Is there another willing to volunteer?"

"Respected one, I have an idea. Let the young woman stay elsewhere; as I am sure most will be more comfortable with that arrangement than keeping the demon in their home while the men are still away. Then you can keep the demon in her home without fearing any inappropriate acts before due time," Kata's mother suggests. "I would honorably accept this young one for the time requested."

Kata whips her head around and glares in disbelief at her mother's offer. A devious smile breaks across her mother's face when she realizes her daughter is watching. Not only does she have to watch the man she was pining for with another girl, but now she will have to share a home with the same girl.

"Very well, Wise Healer. Your offer is accepted. The young one will stay with you while she awaits the day her rites should be completed and they be joined. Young one, go make all things ready in your home and prepare to reside in the Eldest's home. Katalariana, accompany the guards and this man to the waters to wash himself. You men watch over her with your lives and do not allow him to escape. Should he attempt to leave, you are to ensure he does not return to his people. After all, we still know nothing of his people or his ways. Katalariana, are you sure you still want this responsibility?" the elder asks concernedly.

"I am sure. I do not fear this man," she claims with confidence.

She approaches Chance and points toward the direction of the waters. When Chance fails to walk with her, she mimics the washing gestures he made previously and points again toward the waters. Chance nods and starts in the direction she is pointing. Reshiara grasps his hand tightly, not wanting to let him go. "Reshiara," she says, still holding his hand and placing her other hand on her chest.

She pats her chest a few times and says her name again. Chance repeats the name, to which she nods her head. She points to him saying his name and points to herself again, saying her name as she does. She puts his hand to her chest and repeats both their names together. Chance understands it's her name she is repeating, but he's hoping the gestures she is making don't mean what he thinks they mean. He's hoping he's her pet star man; and while not ideal, it's easier to accept than being paired with someone he's never met before. He nods to indicate he understands, but she refuses to let his hand go. She holds it to her face and closes her eyes, as if enjoying the warmth of his hand on her skin.

Kata, who's becoming impatient, turns to her. "I promise I will return him unharmed and that nothing unfortunate befalls him. The sooner you let him go, the sooner we can return."

With reluctance, Reshiara lets him go, but not before kissing his cheek. Chance is shocked at the sudden gesture, but gives her a smile and waves at her as she backs away. He turns and continues toward the waters with Kata and the guards. He sighs with relief and is glad to be getting away from all the attention.

ᐊ12ᐅ

The guards walk close behind Chance, but the young woman with the purple eyes walks several paces ahead of him. Her demeanor is considerably different now than when he first saw her. He clears his throat to try to get her attention, but she ignores him and walks faster. Chance grabs at the blanket wrapped around him to keep it from falling off as he tries to keep up, all while juggling the clothing and food he was given. He tries rushing to be by her side with the hopes of being able to talk to her. "Excuse me. Excuse me, miss," he calls out, hoping she'll finally acknowledge him.

She slows down a bit and looks over at him. As soon as their eyes meet she looks away. Chance can see there is something bothering her and hopes it isn't that they're taking him out to the woods to dispose of him permanently. He's not too worried because he knows his own strengths and abilities, and most likely they're unaware of what he is capable of. Regardless, the last thing he wants is to engage in any type of conflict, let alone offend any one of them. "So, what's your name?" he finally asks.

Kata looks at him for a brief moment before continuing to stare down the trail. "Your name?" Chance repeats.

She wants to ask him why he's so concerned with her when he already has someone, but she knows he won't understand. She'd like to unleash her anger and sorrow at him, but she knows it's useless. Instead, she remains poised and her sight fixed straight ahead. "Po chu morshi[6]?" she berates.

She feels a warm hand on her shoulder that instantly floods her body with a warm sensation. Her emotions well up into her throat again. She realizes it's all she wants, for him to be near, to be able to feel his warmth and his affection. "Excuse me. Is something wrong? Did I do something?" Chance quietly asks.

Kata shrugs his hand off and swallows the lump in her throat she's fought off all morning. She tries to remain poised and cold because her heart aches and she blames it on his ignorance. Yet, she also wants to melt into his embrace and allow all the sorrows and cares to fall away. She feels so frustrated and it's getting harder to contain her emotions; but if she were to soften her heart to him, it would leave her vulnerable to be hurt even more. It's already difficult letting him go to be joined with someone else. At the same time, she doesn't want to lose his friendship, or even the possibility of them being together. "Katalariana," she finally blurts out.

"Katalariana," whispers Chance. "Chance Haywood. A pleasure to meet you, Katalariana."

Kata looks down at his extended hand and slips her hand into his. Her hand feels small and slender compared to his large, strong hand. He shakes it slightly then lets her hand slip back out. Her demeanor changes a little, but she's still a bit stand-offish toward him and walks without engaging him any more. Chance looks back and sees the guards don't appear too happy about how friendly he is with her, so he backs away.

As they walk, Chance takes the opportunity to check his surroundings to see how these people live, hoping to gain beneficial intel for the CC that leads to an end to their fighting.

---

6   *Why do you worry?*

The tents all seem to be similar in construction. They appear to have the wood frame on the inside to support the structure covered in animal skins. The simple wood frame allows for different sizes to accommodate the family size or the need for separate rooms. They all have the same pointed roofs created by the pole supports in the middle. There is little grass in the immediate area from people walking everywhere. The common paths the people walk on are made evident by the packed dirt from frequent travel. Surprisingly, the dirt is soft and comfortable under Chance's bare feet, even though it is still muddy in most places from the recent rains. There are still many puddles, several of which have small children playing in them.

As they walk through the grounds, the people are busy at work. Plumes of smoke exit the flaps of several tents from the fires inside, as well as several smaller fires being started outside. Several people seem to be cooking, making the morning meal or preparing food for later in the day. Other people are using branches to sweep the dirt outside their tents, or bringing blankets and rugs outside and hanging them up on wooden frames and beating the dirt off of them. Others are walking back from the direction Chance and his group are heading, carrying large pitchers of water. Surrounding the residential area of the camp is a wall made of sturdy, wooden poles with stretched skins between them. Chance is curious how skins form an effective wall, so when they venture close by, he touches them to see what they are like. The skins are thick and a dark gray, mottled color, and when dried, they feel as hard as stone. Even tapping on it sounds like tapping on rock. With animals sporting skins like these, it's no wonder they developed weapons capable of piercing the armor of the CC's soldiers.

Chance notices the guards eyeing him suspiciously and Katalariana giving him a strange look. He realizes it must seem odd for someone to be feeling their wall, and the guards are probably thinking he's gauging their walls for weaknesses. He smiles sheepishly at them and rejoins them to continue walking to the water.

Outside the walls are several large gardens with people working and harvesting the produce. Children carry full baskets of produce home for today's meals. Beyond the gardens are more open fields and what appear to be groups of large birds roaming around. From this distance, Chance can't tell exactly how large they are and what exactly they look like, but they do appear to be of considerable size. Considering their proximity to the camp, they must not be hostile, and possibly even domesticated by the tribe.

Beyond the open fields and gardens lies the forest. Upon entering the woods, Chance notices right away they aren't as thick as the ones he traversed through the day he was almost killed. There is even a pathway cleared through the woods to where the waters are. The trees are cut back far enough away from the path to avoid ambushes by enemy tribes or unfriendly animals. The pathway leads from the edge of the woods into an open field surrounding a large, serene lake. Chance makes his way toward the water's edge, but Kata grabs his arm to stop him, nearly causing him to lose his blanket. "Whe, whe joue et chuay! Um rukshar!⁷"

Chance stops and looks at Kata in confusion. There is water here, and as far as he can see, it looks clean, but she is adamant they don't stop. She pulls on him to keep walking along the path. She looks disappointedly at the guards for not

---

7   *No, don't go that way! It's dangerous!*

trying to stop him from approaching the water's edge and they respond with a smirk.

Figuring he wouldn't understand the explanation they would give him, Chance continues to follow Kata further along the trail. They follow the path beyond the clearing into the woods again. After walking a short distance, Chance can hear the sound of running water, and before long, he can see through the trees where a river runs parallel to the pathway. There are a few people along the running water filling up their water containers to take back home. After a short ways further, there is a rocky outcropping the water flows over and down into a pool. They follow the declining path to the edge of the pool. The guards sit on a couple of stumps along the side of the pathway while Kata and Chance walk closer to the pool of water. She points to the water and signals for him to go on ahead, and then points to a tree along the ridge where she will be waiting. Chance nods and thanks her before going down to the water.

He places his belongings on a nearby stone and wades into the water. The water is cold and sends a shiver through his body. He waits for the water to calm down and stares at his reflection in the water. He rubs his hand over the several weeks' worth of facial hair covering his face. He wishes he had a razor to get rid of it since it was getting awfully itchy, but he doubts they would trust him with sharp objects yet. His hair was also getting longer than he preferred it, except on the side where it was singed off in the explosion; which fortunately is growing back. He kept it short while he was on the Mayflower, but often let it grow out while he was planetside during missions.

He also takes the chance to look over the new scars on his body. The first one he notices is the tender, red blotch covering a large part of his left side. Several smaller scars mark his arms and legs, but all his wounds appear to be healed. He'd like to see what his armor looks like after the explosion ripped through it and left his body in such a condition. The materials used in creating the armor are found on another planet and have proven to be stronger than any of the Earth metals. Up until landing on Eshiron, they found nothing on any other planet able to penetrate the armor created from the bluish material, except the weapons made using the same blue metals. Shrapnel from the explosive must have contained pieces of this material, weakening his armor's integrity and opening it to further damage from the explosion. He wonders what became of his armor since it wasn't in the tent with him when he woke up. Wondering about the armor's location makes him wonder if any of his other squad mates survived and were brought here to be taken care of. These were questions he was going to have to try and ask the young woman escorting him.

While Chance wades in the water looking at his scars, Kata sits on the ridge overlooking the pool, pulling at blades of grass to pass the time. Her curiosity gets the better of her and she can't help but turn around to get a quick peek. She looks out of the corner of her eye first to make sure he isn't watching. When she sees his back is turned to her, she fully turns around. She's apprehensive at first, but then becomes enthralled staring at Chance's physique and watching him as he bathes himself. She fantasizes what it would be like to be with him had she not been denied her place in the rites. To live in the same tent together and start a family of their own. He would no doubt become a great hunter and provider for the family while her pale skinned children with dark hair and purple or brown green eyes run through the camp playing games with the other children. It was not something she could ever see with Cultac, nor was it something she ever cared to entertain.

Consumed in her fantasy, she didn't notice Chance turned around and is now watching her stare at him. Realizing she's been caught staring at a naked man bathing, she tries acting innocent. She knows he wouldn't understand any explanation she could try to give, so she smiles nonchalantly and nods, turning back around and continues pulling at the grass. Facing away from him, she sighs in disbelief. How could she have been so careless? She feels the blood rushing to her face in embarrassment. All she can hope is he believes it's what her people do when others are bathing. They watch each other to make sure they are well. Kata feels pleased with her rationalization, and hopes if she has to explain, he will believe her story and won't be upset. Although, he didn't seem too upset to have caught her watching him in the first place. In fact, he returned her smile.

Kata can hear Chance getting out of the water, but she is hesitant to turn around again. She waits a moment before turning around to make sure he is well and wasn't falling into the water or passed out on the shoreline. She looks again to find him sitting on a flat boulder with the blanket over his lap. He has the vest on, but holds the other piece of clothing in the air with a look of doubt and confusion on his face.

Chance isn't sure how to put on the bottom piece. He isn't too keen on having so much of his body exposed, especially among a group of people he's just met. Most of the men he saw this morning were covered in several layers of skins. How is it then, that he is given a large, leather slingshot to cover his entire bottom half? He was never one to wear tight underwear, let alone thongs, so wrapping himself up in a leather strap isn't his ideal choice of clothing. As soon as he is able, he figures he will try to get a hold of some fabric materials and make himself a pair of shorts. That, or hope they kept the clothing they found him in, though he doubts they would be in good condition after what he went through. He had never sewed a piece of clothing in his life, but he was willing to try over having to wear what was given to him.

He fidgets around with the straps, trying to figure how they go on, when he notices Katalariana walking toward him from the ridge. He feels a bit embarrassed, although there probably isn't much she hasn't seen of his already. She has a sympathetic smile as she approaches him and signals for him to stand up. She reaches over and grabs the bottom from his hands and steps behind him. She tugs at the blanket for him to take it off. Chance sighs as he reluctantly unwraps the blanket and places it on the boulder. Kata reaches around him and places the loin cloth around his waist and wraps the straps around a couple times before tying it off. She places her hand between his legs and grabs another strap hanging from the bottom edge and pulls toward his back and ties it off on the straps around his waist. Chance can't help but feel more and more awkward with every passing moment. It's not every day there is a young woman he barely knows reaching between his legs and dressing him.

After tying the bottom strap, she reaches out as if asking for something more. Chance looks at her hand and then back at her. He shakes his head and shows her his empty hands. She looks around the area for something, but Chance knows the only other item with the clothing was the dried meat. He picks that up off the boulder and shows it to her. She waves her hand and acts as if she is wrapping something invisible around her waist and tugs at her own skirt. Chance halfheartedly looks around then shakes his head and waves his hands to tell her there was nothing else. She lets out a sigh of slight frustration and throws her hands up. Chance isn't thrilled about having a leather strap riding up his backside, but another skin, even if it was a skirt, would have been nice to cover up even more. He imagines he looks like a male stripper in his leather vest, leather thong and wet, unkempt hair.

Kata can tell Chance is uncomfortable in the clothing, but can't help laughing at his awkwardness. It's quite comical to see the tall, pale skinned, muscularly toned man wearing a small skin vest and groin cover. She knows it isn't polite to laugh at the expense of another, but it's a welcome distraction from the stress and sorrow she's been feeling the last several days.

Chance knows how awkward he must appear to her and laughs along with her. He realizes there may not be too many differences between their peoples keeping them from under-standing one another even with the language barrier. "Cho sushu[8]," Kata laughs.

"Cho sushu?" Chance repeats.

Kata looks disappointedly at Chance as she ponders how best to explain what she is saying. She points to herself and repeats the word cho[9]. She points at him and says the word chu[10]. She repeats this a couple times until Chance nods to show he understands. He points at himself and tells her I. He points to her and says you. They both repeat each other's words together before she tries to explain the next word. She pauses for a moment to think about how best to explain sushu. She pretends to laugh and then points to Chance and puts on a scowling face. She pretends to laugh again, then stops and covers her mouth while shaking her head. She bows a couple times while repeating the word sushu. She looks up at him in the hopes he understands what she is saying.

---

8   *I'm sorry or I apologize.*

9   *I*

10 *You*

Chance thinks about it for a second before realizing what she is saying. "Oh, I'm sorry!" he exclaims.

Kata's face lights up with excitement when she sees he understands. She's even more excited when she sees his attempt to speak to her in her own language. "Cho sushu cho…uh…" he stutters and pauses again.

He shakes his head and uses his hands like mouths talking. Kata watches him, intrigued by his efforts to speak to her, although she isn't sure what it is he wants to say. He looks puzzled as he considers how to get her to know what he wants to say. He wants to say he's sorry he can't speak her language, but she's more humored by his attempts than actually understanding what he's saying. He figures he might as well start off simple before trying to speak full and complete sentences on his first day of learning. His face beams as he comes up with an idea. He shakes his head repeatedly while saying no. He then nods his head and repeats the word yes. Kata catches on and follows his actions. She shakes her head while saying whe[11] and nodding her head while repeating nue[12]. Chance repeats the words until he is sure he's saying them correctly.

He sits down on the boulder to rest and grabs the package of dried meat. He takes a piece and then offers some to Kata, who sits beside him on another rock. She declines the offer and urges him to eat it instead. While he eats it, Kata looks around and notices a plant nearby. She runs over and pulls some of the fruit from it and returns to Chance's side. She breaks the fruit open and hands him a piece. He takes it and watches her take a bite first to make sure he knows how it's meant to be eaten. He sinks his teeth into the juicy flesh of the fruit and scrapes it from the rind like she did. The fruit

---

11 *No*

12 *Yes*

is very acidic on the tongue, yet it has a pleasant taste to it; nothing like he's ever tasted before. Kata holds up the fruit and waves her other hand over his body then squeezes the muscles in his arm. She makes a stern face and puffs herself up to make herself look bigger and tougher. Chance assumes the fruit toughens the body and makes it stronger; something he feels he can use right now.

While Chance eats a breakfast of dried meat and alien fruit, Kata sits quietly and observes him. He can tell she really wants to talk to him, but the hassle of playing charades prevents her. The guards check on them and return to their seats on the stumps, leaving them alone once more. Again, Chance can see the wheels turning in Katalariana's mind and finally she breaks her silence. "You Chanz Hewood. No Hewood?"

Chance thinks for a moment what she is asking, apart from being pleased to hear her using the English he has already taught her. Then he remembers the group calling him Haywood, but when he introduced himself to her, he used his first and last name. Now she's confused by the different names. "Yes. My name is Chance Haywood. Chance. Haywood."

Kata is still confused by the different names and why he would tell her something different than the rest of the group. She's been wondering about it since the time he first introduced himself to her, but she hadn't quite figured how to ask him about it. To try and explain it, Chance draws in the dirt at their feet. He draws a stick man and a stick woman. He draws several smaller stick figures beside them to represent children. He circles the family and writes Haywood above it and says it out loud to her as he does it. He circles it several times while repeating the name. Then he points to each individual as he lists their names. "Dad, Mom, Brother, Chance, Sister. Dad

Haywood, Mom Haywood, Brother Haywood, Chance Haywood, Sister Haywood," he explains.

To emphasize the point, he draws another family and circles it, separating it from the other family. He draws a line above them then points to each individual and repeats the names, substituting Katalariana's name for his own. He points to the Haywood family while saying the name, then points at Kata and urges her to say a name. She smiles at the simplistic drawings, something she usually sees the children doing when they play in the dirt, but the symbols aren't familiar to her. Her people have no system of writing other than the symbols the men paint on themselves during hunts and battles. Those symbols don't look like any of the ones drawn in front of her. Other than the painted symbols the men use, everything else is passed along orally from generation to generation, which in turn, creates numerous variations of history and languages. Even those of neighboring tribes may not understand each other perfectly, and have their own sets of beliefs and traditions; which is also the cause for a lot of conflict between tribes.

While not accustomed to interpreting drawings, Kata believes she understands what Chance is drawing; at least she understands they're people, though she is not sure what he is asking her. Puzzled, she points to the group of people she was included in and then points back toward the tribe. She points at the Haywood name, then at Chance, and then again toward the tribe in an attempt to clarify if Chance was indicating the name of his tribe and was wanting the name of her tribe.

Chance shakes his head and scratches it in frustration. He points at the drawing at the two larger figures in the family, then points to himself and then to Kata as he tells her a man and a woman join together, to which he clasps his hands together, then points to Kata and simulates a large stomach while telling her they have children and create a family. Judging by the bashful look appearing on her face, he realizes it may have looked like he asked her to have children with him. Stuttering with embarrassment, he tries to apologize and tell her he didn't mean they were going to have children.

Kata watches the flustered Chance in amusement as he tries to explain himself. While difficult and confusing at times, she still enjoys the time getting to know him, but she didn't quite know how to respond when he pointed at them both and then insinuating she would have a pregnant stomach. While she was eager to be with him before, now it was really happening and it's all a bit shocking as reality sets in. She was sure he didn't mean to imply they would have a child together, but the idea stirs emotions she's been harboring for days. The thought of him implying being with her would be her deepest desires coming to fruition. She considers carrying on the conversation making him believe that's what she understood and insist he take her as his partner, but deep down she worries it could scare him away. It wouldn't be fair to Reshiara either, but it should be her with him and not Reshiara to begin with. It's tempting to inform him of the rites and that he still has a choice who he wants as his life partner, but what are the odds he is going to understand her well enough? If he did understand, who's to say he would choose her once he got to know others of the tribe?

Kata realizes her thoughts are taking her to a place she doesn't want to go and bringing up emotions that are affecting her demeanor, which appears Chance is picking up on. He has stopped trying to explain his point and appears unsettled by the sudden change. She tries to fake a smile to put him at ease and focuses on his drawings again. Looking at the drawings and remembering what Chance described with her being pregnant, she understands the drawings depict families and not tribes.

She taps on Chance's knee excitedly and points to the families and spurts out an excited, "Yes!"

The excitement fades when she realizes she isn't sure if Haywood is the word for family in his language, or the name of his family. "What?" Chance asks desperately. "What happened?"

Kata points to the first family and repeats Haywood; then points to her family and repeats the name again. She rapidly scratches out a drawing of another family and asks, "Haywood?"

Before Chance responds, she holds up her hand to signal him to wait. She points to his family and says the name and then points to her family and uses her own name, points to her drawn family and uses Broltrom's name. Chance nods his head in affirmation. He points to his stick figure and recites his name once more. He points to her figure and waits for her response. She looks at him disappointedly and shakes her head. "Katalariana," she mutters, seemingly regretful she had no other name to give him, as their families didn't have separate names.

Seeing she has no other name like his people do, he points toward the tribe wanting to know its name. Kata perks up a bit and with a smile she responds with, "Cleridrac."

She in turn asks the name of his tribe. Chance thinks for a moment how best to answer the question, since he has a number of options to choose from: Earth, the CC, Mayflower, Special Services, or simply stick with his family name. For ease of conversation, he chooses to go with the CC. She then inquires how large the CC is by using hand gestures. Chance stretches his arms out as wide as he can to Kata's dismay. He wonders if it's because they fear or hate his kind so much. He's surprised she doesn't ask where he's from, which makes him wonder if she believes he's from this world, just from another area.

They sit and try communicating for a while longer, but the two guards are eager to get back to the camp and urge them to follow. When Chance and Kata reach the trail, the two guards can't contain their laughter when they see Chance wearing only half his clothing. A quick look from Kata and they compose themselves more seriously until their backs are turned again and continue smirking. Chance tosses the blanket over his shoulder hoping it hangs down far enough to cover everything until he can acquire more suitable attire back at the camp.

They slowly make their way back toward camp, though, unlike the trip to the waters, Kata is a lot more talkative. She and Chance still try to communicate as best they can with each other. She asks Chance about his family and where they are, trying to use what words she remembers and trying to refer back to the drawings left in the dirt along the shore. Chance explains he has no family, that he is the only one left. Kata feels awful for having asked and tries explaining she recently lost her father in the fight where he was wounded. She remembers it was said Chance was found with her father when he died, so she tries telling him as best as she can. Chance listens and watches her intently while trying to remember who she may be talking about. A burst of images runs through his head as he remembers the older warrior he helped before blacking out. Chance nods his head to acknowledge he remembers the person she is talking about, and apologizes for not being able to save him.

They continue talking to each other until they reach the body of water they kept Chance from approaching. Chance notices some breaks in the water's glassy surface and ripples spreading to the shore. Chance is mesmerized as he tries to catch a glimpse of what swims beneath the surface. He approaches the shoreline again, but Kata and the guards try to halt him from getting any closer. He shrugs them off and creeps closer, not taking his eyes off the surface of the water. There is some splashing coming from the center of the lake, but he can't make out what is creating the disturbance. He crouches in the tall grass and keeps watch. Kata and the men stay on the road and don't dare follow him so close to the water. They continue to call him back with hushed voices, but Chance ignores them.

The water grows calm once more to Chance's dismay. He watches a moment longer, and before he is about to return to the road, a large creature breaks from the water and snatches a flying creature from the air before plummeting back into the depths. Chance stares in amazement, even long after the creature has submerged. The large ripples crash onto the shore. It was a large animal to be sure, and it's no wonder the others are so afraid to approach the water's edge. Even animals flying overhead are not spared the creature's appetite. With the brief glimpse he got, it appeared serpentine with large fins at its side. Its head was massive, with a large mouth full of long dagger-like teeth. The head also appeared to be covered in spines and fins. Chance imagines it was similar to sea monsters from ancient Earth mythology.

After watching the water for a moment longer, and without further appearances by the beast, Chance slowly backs away from the water. When he is able to turn around after being a safe distance from the water, his traveling companions are not standing where he left them. He glances up and down the dirt pathway for any sign of them. He spots movement among the trees at the end of the clearing where the path enters into the woods. Kata stands behind a tree waving for him to hurry over to them. He smirks and jogs to where she and the two guards are waiting. They're still apprehensive about leaving the tree's protection, but he can see the scowls on their faces for his carelessness in endangering their lives. Upon reaching the group, Kata punches him in the chest and chastises him with words he still doesn't understand, though it doesn't take an understanding of the language to know more or less what she is saying. The two escorts simply shake their heads while she continues her rant. Chance stares innocently at her, sorry he allowed his curiosity to get the better of him, although now he's more aware of the dangers residing so close to camp and why they're so afraid to go near the water. It doesn't take long to figure he wasn't the first to get too close to the shoreline. Yet, more than likely, he's a lot more fortunate than the previous people.

Chance and Kata don't talk much the rest of the way back to the camp. Chance's disregard of their warnings dampened the mood, though Kata at least continues by his side while they walk. Chance can tell she is still a little upset and he doesn't want to bother her further with his queries. He felt it wise to let her cool down before approaching her again.

As they cross the open fields near the gardens, he notices the large, bird-like creatures are a lot closer and there are people with them. His guess they are domesticated proves correct. Surprisingly, they tower over the people who are tending them. The tops of their backs are as high as a man and they have long, extended necks with large, angular heads; like those of reptiles. From this distance, he can see light, golden feathers forming a crest on the top of their head. Shorter tufts of feathers run down the spine of the long neck and body to the end of the tail. Several large plumes fan out at the base and tip of the tail. The wings look more like small arms covered in smaller, golden feathers. The legs are thick and powerful and end in large talons. Their skin is dark and scaly in stark contrast to the golden tufts running down their backs. Chance imagines they look like a cross between Earth's ostrich and a dinosaur. He wonders what other creatures inhabit the camp and what they are used for.

Kata notices Chance's attention being drawn to the animals in the field and stops him. "Cleridrac!" she exclaims, pointing to the creatures in the field.

Chance looks puzzled, believing the tribe's name was Cleridrac, yet now she points to the creatures and gives them the same name. He wonders if he's been misunderstanding the whole time. He points toward the tribal camp and questioningly repeats the name. He then points to the animals and again repeats the name. Kata smiles seeing his confusion and nods her head, confusing him further. He supposes their tribe must be named after the creature and they are an integral part of their tribe.

Kata mimics the creatures movements and acts as if attacking Chance. The guards chuckle at her gestures and roll their eyes. Kata ignores them and continues the charade. Chance watches her inquisitively as she prances around like the cleridrac and then stands tall and firm. She pounds her chest and stomps her foot, posing herself like the guards holding the spears. "Chuem shum li cleridrac.[13]"

"Chuem? Chuem shumli?" Chance repeats seeking clarification.

He believes he understands her gestures, but he is still eager to learn the language. Kata smiles with pride, happy to be his teacher and explain, even though the guards would rather

---

13 *We are like the Cleridrac.*

move on. Kata points at all of them together and repeats the word chuem. Chance nods. "We, or us. Chuem means we. And shumli?"

"Shum li cleridrac," she clarifies.

Kata pauses as she contemplates how to explain what shum means. She looks at the guards, who appear less and less amused to be stuck watching the two as they attempt to communicate with one another. She realizes how similar the two are and rapidly points at them. "Chue shum chue!"

Chance raises an eyebrow. "Chue[14]?"

Kata points to each person repeating the corresponding words. "Cho, chu, chue, chuem."

"Him, or them! Okay, I get it!" Chance responds. "He shum him?"

Chance observes the guards and ponders over the statement. "He is like him! Shum means like. We are like the cleridrac. I understand. You're all like a bunch of dinosaur birds. Hence the name. I get it!"

Chance nods to Kata's delight. She's happy to be making headway and hopes it won't be long before they can have a real conversation they both understand. She's also glad he's willing to learn and speak with her as well as teach her his language. It certainly doesn't come off as a behavior a demon would display. If he really was as monstrous as her people made him out to be, he certainly could have acted out and destroyed them long before now. Other than his rapid recovery, everything about him indicates he is as fallible and mortal as the people from her tribe.

The guards urge them to continue moving toward the camp. Kata once again engages in sharing with Chance; both

---

14 *He, she, or they*

learning and teaching each other their own language. Passing the gardens near the camp, a pit develops in Kata's stomach. She fears Reshiara will be waiting near the entrance for her betrothed to return. Chance senses her distraction and asks her what's wrong. She shakes her head and feigns a smile and urges him to continue exchanging words. She isn't ready to let him go yet, though she could still technically stay with him as a healer, she won't have his sole attention. She wants to lead him elsewhere, but she knows the guards won't allow it. Odds are the elders would send out a hunting party to track him down if they did manage to sneak away, and he would probably be too clueless to know what was going on and get them caught. She hopes Reshiara isn't waiting at the entrance to take him away.

When the entrance is within sight, several children playing nearby spot the group approaching. One of the boys runs into the camp, hollering as if sounding an alarm. The other children, mostly boys, grab sticks from nearby and line up along the pathway. As Chance and his group walk by, the children grip their sticks tightly and point them towards him like spears. They glare at him while he passes; some even snarling and lunging as if attempting to attack him with their pretend spears. Chance merely smiles at them and nods his head. He's rather amused at their actions, but it's clear not everyone is as content to have him among them as the people he met this morning. All he can do is show he's not their enemy and stick close to those who are friendly until he learns their ways and language. Then, he can hopefully put their minds at ease.

When he passes the child sentinels, he hears them snickering behind him. He turns to see what's so humorous and finds them pointing at him and laughing. He realizes the blanket isn't covering him as well as he thought, exposing his backside to the amusement of all those behind him. He does his best to hide his exposed areas, having completely forgotten his missing apparel during the walk. He's glad to be reminded before going the rest of the day walking through the camp half dressed.

Kata allows herself to laugh as well. Relieved to find Reshiara is not waiting for them near the entrance, she lets herself believe things are starting to go her way. She gets to continue spending time with the foreigner, getting to know him without having to share or compete for attention. She'll have to let him go eventually, but for now, it fulfills the desire to be with him.

She slips her hand into his and gives it a slight tug to keep him moving away from the entrance before a crowd gathers. It won't be long before people gather again since the boy from the entrance ran off alerting the camp that Blue Demon had returned.

The guards stop her before she gets too far with him. She turns to face them, squeezing Chance's hand even tighter, not wanting to let him go and fearing now they are back at camp they will take him away. "Where are you going, Katalariana? His tent is in that direction," they point down another pathway.

Kata clears her throat and glances down the different pathways. "I was going to show him other areas before returning him. I promise we will stay within the walls. Don't worry, I'll be fine if you don't want to follow. There are always warriors nearby no matter where we go if I need help," she rationalizes. "We won't take long before I bring him home, I promise."

The guards look at each other and mumble something between themselves. They look back at Kata and after a brief moment, wave her on. One of them calls out, "Don't make us regret this. Remember, you promise not to take long."

Before he can finish his sentence, Kata drags Chance down the pathway towards the healer tents. If she goes toward her home, they're more likely to run into Reshiara or Kata's mother and she wants to avoid them. When they reach the healer tents, Kata stops and explains to Chance she works in these tents. She shows him her satchel carrying all her healing herbs and salves. She shows him the tent where he was kept and tries explaining she was the one who cared for him. Thinking he understands, Chance realizes this must be why he recognizes her face and touch. He stands still and watches her point out on his body where all his wounds were. When she touches his side, she pauses and slowly runs her hand along the discolored area on his skin. He watches Kata's face as she slides her hand along his side. Judging by the look on her face, he must have been in bad shape. She must be wondering how he survived. He also sees something more in her expression and how she touches him. Something running deeper than mere professional concern. He wonders why, if she is so invested in his care and nursed him back to health, why was another woman in the tent when he woke up? "Resherra shum Katalariana?[15]" Chance asks, pointing to the tents.

She pulls her hand away and looks up at him with wide, worried eyes. She glances around her and becomes visibly uneasy. "Reshiara?"

That was the last thing she expected to hear from him. What's she supposed to tell him? Sooner or later, he's going to find out his tie to that girl, but this is her time with him. What can she say so as not to lose him? Should she try to explain the rites to him and tell him he has a choice?

"Nue Reshiara. Reshiara shum Katalariana?" Chance repeats.

"Whe! Reshiara whe shum cho![16]"

Kata's uneasiness shifts to disdain. Chance is almost sorry

---

15 *Is Reshiara like Katalariana?*

16 *No! Reshiara is not like me!*

he asked and her response makes things even more confusing. So much for the clingy nurse theory. Now his concern shifts to whether his other theory is true.

Kata knows why he's asking but she doesn't want to give the answer. Hearing him repeat that girl's name again causes her blood to boil and she doesn't want to waste the time she has with him talking about her. She can't even bring herself to expend the energy to try and explain it to where he can under-stand. Unable to hide her disdain for Reshiara and hoping to avoid explaining, she looks into his eyes and smiles, grabs his hands and tries leading him from the healer tents to continue the tour.

Chance hopes the answer comes before he ends up having to spend the night with a stranger again. Seeing Katalariana's change in demeanor at the mere mention of Reshiara, he de-cides not to pursue the issue for now. He wishes he knew more of their language and it fuels his desire to learn it quickly.

They race towards the far side of camp, passing several rows of tents to a small, secluded hutch. An old woman dressed in a medley of skins, feathers, bone, and other small carvings and trinkets, sits in front, surrounded by several young adolescents. They all look up at Kata and Chance as they approach. The old woman's eyes narrow in disgust when she spots Chance. Kata, oblivious to the old woman's demeanor, runs to her, eager to show off the awakened stranger. "Shumakra, I bring the out-sider to meet you," she exclaims with glee.

"Demon!" she hisses. "You dare bring that monster to my home."

Kata looks at her in surprise. She figured of all people, the Wind Talker would be most curious about the stranger. The winds brought many rumors to the old woman's ears of these foreigners. None of which were favorable, but Kata hoped that seeing one in person would prove otherwise. Rumors stated they were demons covered in a near impenetrable blue shell, and everywhere they tread, they were followed by thunder and fire, death and destruction. Clearly, none of these was true about Chance, but on the contrary, he appears to be like any other man.

Chance stops behind Kata and watches as the old woman slowly stands, points a crooked finger at him and utters the most wretched sounding words at him. She doesn't look away from him or blink, but keeps her gaze locked on him. He doesn't need an interpreter to know whatever she's saying isn't very nice. She almost spits the words at him, like darts tipped with a venom concocted of hatred and disdain. A quick look at Kata and he can see she's as shocked as he is at the woman's behavior. The woman continues to rant as she slowly backs towards the entrance of her hutch until she disappears inside. He can still hear the old woman muttering from inside.

Kata takes the opportunity to leave. She looks into Chance's eyes and he can see the worry and concern in her countenance. She tugs at him to follow, but before they take two steps, Shumakra re-emerges from her hutch holding a clenched fist to her lips. She slowly uncurls her bony fingers and blows some kind of powder towards Chance. The dust is caught in the wind and slowly floats away from them. Shumakra utters a few more words and spits on the ground. Kata tugs on Chance again and pulls him away towards another group of tents near the center of the camp. As they hurry away, the old woman continues to call after them, but her voice isn't so spiteful and it appears she's speaking to Kata. Kata ignores her words and hurries Chance along the path.

Kata slows once they are far enough away from the secluded hutch. She looks at Chance apologetically and then back down the pathway.

"Katalariana?" Chance utters cautiously.

Kata sighs with uneasiness and continues looking down the path. She was aware of others in the tribe who were against Chance being among their people, but she had never before been confronted with such hatred, and it breaks her heart. As much as she tries to forget what was said, the old woman's words still echo in her mind. She repeated over and over that he is a demon and nothing good would come from his presence here. In fact, Shumakra viewed his presence here as the end of their tribe. She muttered curse after curse upon him, even calling upon the winds to carry his evil away using the dust and ashes of their fallen warriors. She warned Kata to remove herself from the blue shadow's side before he claims her soul or taints her with his evil, cutting her off from joining her ancestors in the afterlife. The last thing she yelled at Kata was the winds had shown her this blue shadow demon appearing and coming for her.

"Katalariana," Chance repeats. "What's ruke sherluke?"

Kata sighs again and hangs her head disparagingly. She walks a few paces before turning to face him. "Ruc Zherulk?[17]"

She hoped he hadn't picked up on those words, though it was understandable he would, since it's been repeated several times by multiple people. The more time she spends with him, the more it's apparent he's a very intelligent and observant person, surprising her on several occasions by his aptitude for picking up on the language. Still, she finds it hard to find a way to explain what Ruc Zherulk means and she isn't sure

---

17 *Blue Devil/Demon*

she wants him to know. How would he react to the name her people gave him?

She looks around her and spies a small bowl of drying, blue flowers sitting in the sun beside one of the tents. She takes a pinch of the petals and rubs them between her fingers. She shows Chance her fingers which are now coated in a blue dust. "Ruc," she replies.

"Blue? Ruc is blue," Chance nods.

Kata grabs his hand and tries walking again. "Katalariana, what's Zherulk? Blue what?" he presses.

She shakes her head, refusing to divulge the meaning. Chance sees a tear run down her cheek. He wonders what has her so upset that she refuses to tell him and brings her to tears. He only met her today, but already she's awfully concerned for him. He guesses the words don't mean blue flower, or something just as harmless. The old woman did seem pretty spiteful towards him, which makes him more interested in the words' meanings.

He reaches over and wipes the tear away. She grabs hold of his hand and presses her face against it. A warm sensation runs through her entire body. This is something she's longed for all her life, and she doesn't want to ruin the moment by dwelling on Shumakra's hateful words.

Chance urges her again, to which she lets his hand go. "Chanz, cho whe nano dajir chu. Losheer chu whe feza. Losheer![18]" she pleads with him.

Chance shakes his head. "Cho whe? You no? You no what? I still don't understand enough. Please, I want to know. Nue cho I don't know! Tell me. What is it?" Chance urges emphatically, frustrated by the language barrier.

---

18 *Chance, I don't want to tell you. Please don't ask. Please!*

"Chanz," she hesitates, looking into his eyes with desperation.

She doesn't see the demon or shadow the others see. She dreads what he will do when he knows, but he's persistent and she can see the frustration in his face. It pains her, but she also doesn't want to cause more frustration. She doesn't believe he'll suddenly become the killer they think he is at the mere mention of being called a demon, but she worries about his feelings towards her. She hopes he'll know she doesn't think the same as the others in her tribe.

She crouches to the ground and draws a straight line in the dirt and then pats the ground and points back to the line. Chance crouches beside her and nods. "The ground, okay."

Using stick figures like those used earlier in the day, she draws one figure floating above the line and points up into the sky. Chance nods again. She then draws another figure below the line and embellishes the drawing with squiggly fire lines surrounding him. She rests one finger on the figure below the line and reluctantly whispers one word before the tears fall again. "Zherulk."

It makes sense now as Chance reflects on people's attitudes toward him since waking up. He can understand being cautious with a stranger, especially when every contact with his people ended in bloodshed. It's even more understandable knowing they viewed him and his people as devils and demons.

"Chanz, chu Ruc Zherulk," Kata sobs as she wipes the drawing away.

"Blue Devil," Chance repeats. "Katalariana, it's okay. I'm not a devil. Cho whe zherulk."

He places a gentle hand on her shoulder to calm and reassure her. Kata is relieved to hear him say so, and it confirms what she's believed all along. She looks up to meet his smiling face and is relieved he isn't upset with her. She attempts to lean forward to embrace him, but another's voice calling out to her stops her. In a blink of an eye, several warriors surround them, all with their spears pointed in Chance's face.

❧13❧

Chance is beginning to feel accustomed to having spears pointed at him, only now it makes more sense why everyone is so jumpy. He holds his hands up in front of him while staying crouched to avoid appearing aggressive. Two more warriors grab Katalariana and drag her away from Chance's side. She screams at them and when they finally release their grip, she addresses the old man leading the group of warriors. Chance recognizes him as Umochak from this morning. With him is the older woman who gave him the physical when he woke up. Behind her are the two warriors who escorted him all morning. They look at the ground as if downtrodden and ashamed. Umochak and the woman try to calm the girl, who's inconsolable at the moment. Chance tries listening to the conversation and can pick out some of the words he's already learned. It's obvious the conversation is about Blue Devil. Katalariana is on the defense, insisting he is not a devil. She's speaking rapidly and he can't pick out more than that. He clears his throat and calls out to the older couple arguing with Katalariana. "Whe cho Ruc Zherulk.[19]"

The group goes silent and all eyes fall on the stranger. No one expected him to know their language after one morning. "Whe cho Ruc Zherulk," he repeats with even more confidence.

---

19 I'm not Blue Demon

With tears still streaming down Katalariana's face, she manages a smile. The others in the group are still in shock, with the exception of the older woman. She stands with her hands on her hips, glaring at Chance with eyes that could cut through stone. She slowly steps toward him, not taking her eyes off for even a second. Umochak protests but she silences him with a quick gesture of her hand. The warriors step aside to let her through and she stops in front of Chance, still holding his gaze. She leans forward until her face is a few inches from his. He sees the same disdain and contempt in her face that was in the elderly woman's face only moments ago. She looks deep into his eyes for what feels like an eternity. Chance imagines she's trying to glimpse into his soul to see what he really is. He can see her eyes shift as she searches and her frustration builds when she doesn't find what she's looking for. Finally, she lets out the slightest sigh. "Ruc Zherulk. Chu whe engan cho. Chu whe joue chuay om froinya,[20]" she whispers sternly before standing and walking away.

Chance wonders if every older woman he'll meet is going to treat him with such hatred. So far, he's been a hit with the young women, but every older woman treats him like a villain. It's a contrast that has him confused. How can people from the same village have such a divided opinion of him without getting to know him?

The older woman passes Katalariana and waves her hand. The warriors standing nearby grab Kata by the arms and attempt to lead her away. Kata struggles to free herself from their grip, but realizing the futility in trying, she calls out to Chance. "You, I, uz. Uz," she repeats.

Chance watches her until she's led away down the path be-

---

20 *Blue Demon. You don't fool me. Stay away from my daughter.*

hind more tents. Once she's out of sight, he turns his attention to the men still pointing their spears in his face. Umochak steps toward them and motions for them to raise their weapons and for Chance to stand up. Chance can tell he's unsure what to do next. There's a hint of curiosity, no doubt spurred on by Chance's use of their language, but there is also a sternness in his presence indicating his disapproval finding him unguarded. After a brief pause, he motions for Chance to follow him. "Hewold, jurcto jouem[21]," he sympathetically mutters.

The words ring in Chance's ears and he sees flashing images of the fight where he was wounded. He remembers the face of the old warrior on the ground in front of him reaching over and placing his hand on Chance's head. The words he spoke echo in Chance's mind. "Doman gri se chu fo chu kaum grokan. Jurcto jouem Doman.[22]"

They are the last words he remembers hearing before blacking out, yet they are as vivid in his mind as the moment they were spoken. He figures it's best to ask Katalariana the meaning, assuming he ever sees her again.

Chance and Umochak walk in silence toward the center of the camp. An entourage of warriors follows behind them. Chance thinks he hears Katalariana's voice in the distance getting closer, still angry and yelling. He feels bad she's in that position because of him. What concerns him even more are the words she yelled before she was taken away. It was clearly something meant for him to know since it was in his language, but he's unclear at the meaning. Was it her way of saying they were supposed to be together?

As Chance considers the meaning and is lost in his thoughts, a young woman rounds the corner and stops in front of him.

---

21 *Together we go, or we go together.*
22 *God smile on you for your brave deeds. Together we go to him.*

Chance recognizes the blazing red hair from this morning. An ecstatic smile crosses the woman's face when she realizes it's Chance she almost ran into. With a glee she can't contain, she hops to Chance's side and slips her hand into his, seemingly unswayed by the fact he is being escorted by several warriors. "Hewold, jurcto jouem," she exclaims with an enthusiasm Chance has only seen in Katalariana.

Eager to lead Chance away, Reshiara pulls him in the direction she came from. Hesitant to follow, he looks at Umochak to know whether to follow her or not. Umochak calls Reshiara's name and signals for her to come closer. As he whispers in her ear, her enthusiasm slips away. Her grip on Chance's hand tightens more and more as Umochak explains the situation. Once he's finished speaking, she looks into Chance's eyes with her own pleading eyes. It's as if she's searching for something; perhaps the same thing the older woman was looking for earlier. After a moment, she turns and pleads with Umochak. Chance can only pick out a few words he's learned, but it sounds the same as what Katalariana had been pleading with him. He hears over and over the same phrase; that he isn't the Blue Devil. After pleading with him, Umochak slowly nods. Her enthusiasm returns and she throws her arms around Chance, squeezing as tight as she can. Then, with the same enthusiasm, she grabs his hand and tugs, urging him to follow. Umochak signals for two warriors to follow.

Chance sighs, wondering how often he's going to have to go through the same thing. He feels he went through this with Katalariana, and now it appears he will be doing the same thing with Reshiara. He wonders if he's their new pet and they're taking turns walking him around the camp. He hopes at least this trip doesn't end up with several spears pointing in his face.

Before going too far, Umochak once again stops them.

Reshiara acts a little impatient but is inclined to stop. Umochak pulls one of the escorts to him and whispers in his ear. Chance notices their gaze pointing toward his exposed posterior. Remembering his lack of clothing, he once again feels the blood rushing to his face. With all that's happened, he forgot about it. He hopes it isn't one of the reasons for being jumped by the warriors while he was with Katalariana. It's not as though he intended on walking around half naked.

Reshiara's face turns red and she turns away when she realizes what they are talking about. Chance does his best once again to adjust the furs draped over his shoulders to cover himself. The warrior nods after Umochak finishes speaking with him and takes his place behind Chance as an escort. He pats Chance on the shoulder and points for him to go on. Reshiara takes the lead and guides Chance through rows of tents. A short distance down the path they are on, a large tent stands encircled about by the rest of the tents. In front, Chance sees Katalariana and the older woman still talking. They stop when they spot the group approaching. Katalariana doesn't wait for them to get closer before disappearing inside the tent. Chance feels disappointed he won't get to talk to her again to apologize. He never intended for anyone to get into trouble because of him. After all, he was there to learn their ways.

Reshiara stops outside the tent and faces Chance. She points to herself and then points to the tent. She waits for him to acknowledge he understands, and although he does, he's still thinking about Katalariana. He looks at the older woman outside, still standing with her hands on her hips and the same hateful look in her eyes. It's like she's waiting for him to step out of line so she can let him have it. He recognizes the angry, mom look and it clicks in his mind why she was so quick to haul Katalariana away from the blue devil. If there's one thing he's come to know in his career is never cross a mother and her young unless you're expecting a good fight. He certainly didn't come looking for that.

"Cho sushu,[23]" he calls out. "Katalariana, I'm sorry. Cho sushu"

Reshiara faces Chance with a surprised expression. A tinge of jealousy pierces her when she hears him call Kata's name in their native tongue. He hasn't said anything to her since this morning. She turns and looks back at the tent as the woman goes inside without a word.

"Hewold, chu lom hulne im chu lom wundcham?[24]" Reshiara questions.

Disappointed Katalariana doesn't respond, and not winning any points with the older woman, Chance looks up into the sky and sighs. He feels Reshiara's hand caress his face and then pull downward until their eyes meet one another. "Hewold, chu lom hulne im chu lom wundcham?" she repeats.

Chance simply shakes his head. "No, I don't understand. Whe. Cho whe whatever. I don't understand. Sorry. Cho sushu," his voice trails, frustrated by the way things are playing out.

Reshiara looks up at him, biting her lip, trying to make eye contact. She tenderly brushes a few strands of hair off his forehead and gazes expectantly at him. "Hewold," she whispers, trying to keep his attention and cast away the frustration. "Hewold lom hulne."

She repeats the words while gesturing something coming from her mouth. She then points to her ear and traces a path in the air to the top of her head while repeating the word "wundcham."

---

23   *I'm sorry.*
24   *You can speak and understand?*

Chance watches her and nods. "Hulne is to speak and wundcham is to hear and understand. I get it. Cho wundcham."

The brightness in Reshiara's expression returns and she claps with joy. Chance finds he also feels better. He still has someone with the patience and eagerness to teach him the language, though Reshiara is a bit more clingy and more outwardly affectionate, which is a bit awkward for him. The only other person in his life who showed him affection was his mother when he was a child. Life as a Genhance soldier never left him with the time for anything more than training or missions on other worlds. While not opposed to Reshiara's affection, it's something he's not used to.

Reshiara, in her excitement, points to everything she can see and tells Chance the word for it in their language. She skips along the path, never letting his hand go, reciting the words and having Chance repeat the translations. Chance was able to remember things easily with his eidetic memory, but it took Reshiara more time to learn and remember the words. It's her insatiable desire to learn his language that keeps her eager to learn, despite the difficulty pronouncing the words. She's also happy to have someone pay attention to her and spend time with her. That's something she has longed for most of her life.

Along the path, one of the escorting warriors stops the two and enters a nearby tent. After a brief moment, he returns bearing a piece of clothing made from similar material as the clothing Chance is already wearing. He tosses it to Chance, who gladly wraps it around his waist and ties it off. It looks like a miniskirt extending to his mid thigh. He's glad to at least have something to cover himself with, even if it is a skirt. Since all the other men are wearing similar clothing, he feels confident they didn't give him something inappropriate to wear for their amusement. He'd feel more comfortable in pants, but the skirt works for now.

Properly clothed, Chance follows the others down the pathway to a small tent on the outskirts of the village. Reshiara lets Chance go and races to the tent and opens the door flap, motioning for him to go inside. As Chance approaches, Reshiara points and says, "Eshiron.[25]"

Chance pauses, recognizing the word used by the CC to name this planet. Chance repeats the word inquisitively, awaiting Reshiara's explanation of what it means. He knows it's not the word for tent, because she already taught him that on the way here, and he doesn't recall hearing it at another time. She looks at him slightly puzzled and motions again for him to enter the tent. Chance crouches and enters the tent with Reshiara following close behind. The two escorting warriors take up position outside the door.

The sunlight shines through the doorway and lights up the small interior. There is a smoldering fire in a pit on one side and several heavy furs making up a bed on the other. Bundles of dried flowers hang from the top of the tent. There are a few clay pots, bowls, jugs, and some baskets stacked on one end, but little else in the way of possessions. It's not very spacious with barely enough room for both of them to be standing inside.

Reshiara points at the bed and ushers Chance over to sit on it. Chance sits on the bed while Reshiara gleefully watches him. "Tro eshiron? What is eshiron?" Chance asks again.

Reshiara waves her hands pointing all around the tent and then points towards him. Chance thinks about it for a second and realizes she's telling him it belongs to him. "Home? This

---

25 *Home.*

is my home? Om eshiron?" he asks, hoping he understood correctly.

Reshiara smiles wide and nods, barely containing her enthusiasm. "Nue, chu eshiron.[26] You hom," she repeats, attempting to copy the word in Chance's language, waving her hands around again as if showcasing a new prize he had won.

Chance finds it ironic the CC happened to name this planet using a word they heard the natives use when attacking, only for the word to mean home. It was exactly what most of the people on the Mayflower were hoping to find for some time now; a place to call home. Chance is reminded of his objective to learn what he can so the CC can expand its foothold on the planet. The hopes of thousands of people rests on his shoulders and his ability to find a resolution to the conflict so the people can finally settle. Chance wonders if it will ever be possible with the CC's aggressive methods for dealing with inconveniences. Regardless, it's a fitting name, whether they realized it or not.

She mumbles something and leaves the tent in a hurry. Chance runs his hands over the thick furs. For being on the ground, the bed actually feels quite comfortable. A small breeze blows through the open doorway and causes the embers in the fire pit to glow. The dried plants hanging from the ceiling rustle in the breeze and send out a pleasant aroma. Chance takes the moment of quiet to ponder on the day's events. He closes his eyes and takes a deep breath. The aroma of the plants fills his nostrils and is quite relaxing. He feels isolated from everything around him, and there's a quiet he still isn't used to. On the ships, even in the most isolated areas, it's possible to hear the rumbling of the generators, the whirring of turbines, or even

---

26 *Yes, your home.*

the fans in the ventilation. There was always noise, as subtle as it might be, it was always there. Here, on the planet, there is a different quiet. It's the sound of a gentle breeze, the rustle of grass and leaves, the hiss of burning embers. It's natural and calming, and everything Chance loves about being planetside. Even on the most hostile planets, Chance would always find moments to be still and listen to the sounds of nature, away from the humming, whirring, and whining of machines. It was always reinvigorating and something Chance had a hard time letting go, even though it took some time to get used to at first. Duty as a Genhance in the Special Services kept him on the move, going from one place to the next, from one battle to another. It's nice to be free from that pressure, even if it is for a little while.

Reshiara reappears through the doorway carrying a shallow bowl filled with food. She sits beside him on the bed and hands him the bowl, motioning him to eat. The bowl is filled with dried meat and an array of assorted fruits and vegetables, the likes of which he has never seen before. Chance takes the bowl and nods in gratitude. He takes some of the fruit and offers the bowl back to Reshiara. She declines and watches for him to eat. Chance slowly bites into the fruit, which is harder than what he ate earlier, and also has an acidic taste, like the core of a pineapple. While Chance eats, Reshiara goes to the fire, throws some wood onto it and stokes it up. She grabs the largest dish from her stack and sets it on the fire. She goes to the baskets and pulls a large, oblong egg from one of them. With a wooden utensil, she breaks it open and pours it out onto the dish in the fire. She stirs it and makes what looks to Chance like scrambled eggs, which she serves to him in a separate dish.

Reshiara sits next to him again and urges him to try the egg. With his fingers, he scoops some up and puts it into his mouth.

It has a bold, earthy flavor and could use some salt and pepper, but overall, Chance feels they are satisfying. With the amount of time he's been unconscious and with all the recovering his body has gone through, it's a welcome meal.

Reshiara is enthralled with watching him eat. Feeling a little self-conscious, he offers her the food again. She declines but Chance insists. She bashfully accepts and shares the plate with Chance, happy not to be eating alone. As they eat, Reshiara points to everything and continues to teach Chance the language. They spend the evening eating and exchanging words in each other's language.

When darkness falls, Reshiara gathers the dirty dishes and sets them outside. She crawls back to Chance's side with a forlorn look. She peers deeply into Chance's eyes and again brushes hair aside on his forehead and caresses his face. She leans in and kisses his cheek and wraps her arms around him. She squeezes as tightly as she can. Chance, with his arms pinned to his side, tries reaching over and pats her on the back. "Thank you for the food. Cho loshome chu fo sustev,[27]" Chance whispers.

"You welcome. Whe morshi,[28]" she whispers back. "Bemelen wus.[29] Good rest."

She slowly backs away toward the doorway. With a smile and a wave of the hand, she steps from the tent into the night, closing the door flap behind her. The glowing embers of the fire cast a dim light throughout the tent. Chance shakes off the top fur making up the bed before settling down for the night. He reflects on the events of the day and looks forward to the morning. He hopes it will be slightly less stressful and put him

---

27 I thank you for food.
28 Welcome (No worry).
29 Good rest (Good night).

in contact with more people who are friendly towards him and don't treat him like a devil. He knows he's going to have to gain their trust somehow, and hopefully tomorrow will shed some light on how to do it. Letting sleep overtake him as he nestles into the furs, his last thoughts are of the young woman with the dark hair and purple eyes and how he hopes to see her again. "Good night, Katalariana," he whispers.

⫷14⫸

Kata sits huddled on her bed, seething over what happened in the afternoon. Just when she felt like things were going her way, they were ambushed by the elder and his warriors. She tried explaining nothing happened, but they wouldn't listen. Why would they, with her mother poisoning their minds against her new friend, Chance? She tried telling Chance they were meant to be together before being dragged away, but she doubts he understood what she meant. If only she had more time to explain things. More time to teach him the language. The hunters would be home soon and the rites of partnership would be enacted thereafter. She would lose him to Reshiara and she would be left alone, or worse, forced to be with Cultac.

To the public eye, she and Cultac seem like they would make the perfect partnership, but on the inside, they were very different people with very different views. Even as children, she never cared much for Cultac. He had always been a bully to all the kids. Being the son of an elder on the council, he always felt entitled and behaved as such, even picking on Kata from time to time. When he would get caught by their parents, he pretended to be helping her after she got hurt or convinced them he defended her from the kids who were bullying her, even when no other kids were around. Her parents found it endearing, that even at such a young age, he was their daughter's protector. It didn't take long for them to decide Cultac was the best match for her.

As for Cultac, being the son of an elder, or even the prospect of taking his father's place on the council couldn't satisfy his hunger for power. He wouldn't settle for anything less than becoming the Eldest. Kata was his way in, which was something he recognized even at a young age. Because of that, no other boys were allowed to be friends with her, or they risked facing Cultac's wrath. As he got older, he proved himself in combat and during the hunts as one of the best, though Kata learned it was at the expense of others. Being a healer, she cared for those who were wounded during the expeditions and a few were forthcoming about Cultac's treachery. Those few expounded on how they came to receive their injuries. When Cultac felt his position within the tribe was threatened because someone else proved to be better, that person usually ended up injured, attacked by an unknown assailant or unknown beast. Fearing Cultac would finish the job if they divulged how they were injured kept most people quiet, and if others knew, they weren't about to challenge Cultac and end up injured as well. Knowing no one dared challenge him, Cultac often claimed the largest kills, or the most kills, even when they belonged to someone else.

Kata always suspected he was also behind the events leading to Broltrom and Doltrom being expelled from her father's service. But once again, no one dared question Cultac, whose voice was loudest in accusing the brother's and turning her father against them. Broltrom was in line to be the next Eldest until Kata's father's favor was turned toward Cultac. Now, Cultac's arrogance knows no bounds and he goes about unchecked. With the Eldest's mantle passing on to him soon, there will be no one to stop him. No one, perhaps, except Chance.

Kata wonders if Chance's presence within their tribe isn't by coincidence, but by divine intervention. Could Blue Demon really be Blue Angel, sent to correct the injustices wrought within their tribe? Or the angel from her dream, come to save her from the choking grip of those trying to control her life. In her opinion, Cultac is the true demon that she and her tribe needs to be rescued from.

However, Cultac is not the only obstacle. She remembers the words her mother spoke to her after having been dragged away from Chance and brought back to the tent. Her mother was more determined than ever to see that she and Chance didn't end up together. When everyone went to the entrance to see Kata and the others returned safely and found they ran off, her mother was the first to incite fear and rally the warriors together to find the blue demon who swayed her daughter into following him. It was also her mother who confronted the warriors that allowed Kata and Chance to run about unattended. Fearing they and their families would be shamed and cast from their homes, they were quick to comply and cooperate, though how they will be punished has yet to be seen.

When they finally caught up to Chance and Kata, her mother was there accusing him of some devious plot, even though nothing happened. Kata argued nothing happened and that it was her idea to lead him around to show him the layout of their camp. Once again, her mother was quick to insist her daughter was under the demon's influence and had her daughter taken away. Kata fought the whole way, accusing her mother of being unfair and a liar. Her mother remained silent until they arrived at home and the warriors left. She had gripped Kata's arm, pulling her close until they were face to face and eye to eye. "I will not tolerate any more of your insolence. I warned you to keep away from him. You thought that with your little trick this morning that you could outwit me, but you are wrong. It was his filth that took our beloved

Eldest, my partner and your father, from us. I will not allow him to take you from me as well. He has no place here. I told you to stay away from him, and you will abide by my reason as your mother and as your superior. Attempt anything further, and you will come to regret it."

"You wouldn't dare oppose the council. I have been appointed as his healer to escort him as needed. You wouldn't risk losing your place by questioning the wisdom and reason of the council," Kata spitefully rebuked.

"Disobey the council? No, I would not disobey the council, but that will not stop me from protecting what is mine. Even if it means destroying the demon. A poison in his food or drink and the job is done. Do you question my resolve? Do you question my ability to fulfill my words?" her mother threatened.

"If he is the demon you claim him to be, what makes you so sure poison will even affect him?"

"The question you should be asking is what will happen to him if he's not a demon, as you claim?" her mother retorted with a wicked smile.

Kata can still see the look on her mother's face as she reflects on the conversation. She remembers it was shortly after their exchange that Chance and the others showed up. All she could do was to get out of sight. Her mother was the one variable she always underestimated, and now it seems she has the upper hand. She feared what would happen if Chance lingered any longer while her mother was there outside the tent. It broke her heart to hear him call out to her, apologizing for something he didn't do. It wasn't his fault. It was never his fault. It was all her mother's doing. Her mother was the cause of her sadness and the despair she felt circling about her.

Kata sits huddled in her tent, alone on her bed, more resolved than ever to not let her mother keep the upper hand. She has to find a way to get out from under her mother's controlling grip. Kata decides she will see Chance again. She can't let her mother win. Perhaps she can go to the council first and explain her mother's plan.

As Kata contemplates her next move, Reshiara arrives at the tent. Kata is reminded her mother is not the only one she has to overcome if she's to be with Chance. Her mother greets Reshiara and offers her some food, which she politely declines stating she and Hewold ate together. Knowing Kata is listening, her mother presses Reshiara for more details on how her day was with him. Reshiara, glad for the attention, expresses with great enthusiasm how her evening went and how she can't wait for the union ceremony to take place. Kata sinks her face into her arms, not wanting to hear the girl gush about her time with Chance.

After a brief conversation with Kata's mother, Reshiara excuses herself and enters the room where Kata sits on her bed. She stands beside Kata's bed and looks down at her. Unnerved by the awkward silence, Kata slowly raises her head and looks up at the red-headed girl. She sees the disappointment in her face. "Welcome, Reshiara," she meekly utters, mentally preparing herself for the verbal barrage she's about to receive.

"What happened, Katalariana? You told me you would keep him safe and bring him back to me. What were you doing? What were your intentions? Why didn't you bring him back?" Reshiara questions with a tone in her voice carrying more pain in it than anger.

"I'm sorry," Kata responds, knowing those simple words alone won't abate Reshiara's discontent.

"Sorry? Sorry? Do you realize they weren't going to let me be with him? They were going to take him away from me because of what you had done. Why would you risk disobeying the council? Was it your intent to have him destroyed like so many others here want? I know he's not a demon and that he's not evil and I hoped you did too. So why risk him being killed when you knew he couldn't be without our men to watch him? Please tell me why."

Kata knows she can't give her the real answer, not if she ever wants to see Chance again. She has to choose her words carefully, because giving the slightest hint of her true feelings for him, Reshiara will see to it that Kata never has any contact with him again. She'd probably even go to the council to ensure Kata couldn't see him again. She also knows her mother is listening to every word being said. Kata can see her sitting in the other room with a sly smirk on her face. There's no doubt in Kata's mind her mother would go out of her way to help Reshiara if it meant keeping Chance from her daughter. Kata knows she has to be careful indeed. "I...I only wanted to show him his new home and where everything is."

"Do you not think it my place to show him? And that doesn't explain why you would go alone with him."

"You have reason, Reshiara. It should have been your place to show him. I was overzealous. I also knew we were within our walls and if anything were to happen, our men were always close by. I am sorry. I did not intend for there to be trouble, and I certainly did not mean for him to be taken away. It...it was foolishness. It won't happen again."

Kata hopes she appeased her rival and this conversation will end. Reshiara looks at Kata with disapproving eyes and shakes her head with a sigh. "He is all I have now, Kata. You were only supposed to keep him well."

"What did he respond?" Reshiara asks.

"He said he is not a blue demon."

With that, Kata lays down with her back to Reshiara and pulls the furs over her. Reshiara can see Kata is done talking and decides to let the subject rest for now. She stares at the ceiling, eager for the new day to come. Kata lays motionless, glad to be done with the conversation. Tomorrow she will rise early. Tomorrow she will go to Chance and tell him everything. Her mother and Reshiara are not going to keep her from her destiny.

⥺15⥷

Chance wakes with a chill. The fire has long died out and the cool, morning air seeps into the tent. He sits up and rubs the sleep from his eyes, remembering where he is at. His body is still a little stiff, but not nearly as bad as the previous morning. As he works out the stiffness in his muscles, he hears movement and voices coming from outside his tent. The door flap is thrown back and Chance is greeted with a familiar, smiling face. Even in the dim, morning light, he can make out the features of his early morning guest. Kata stretches out her hand and signals for him to come along.

The brisk morning air outside the tent helps drive the drowsiness away. Katalariana is eager to get moving, but the two guards are slow to respond. One sits crouched on the ground under a heap of skin blankets while the other stands watch on the opposite side of the doorway with his spear in hand. Chance can see the fatigue of being on watch all night taking its toll on him. The other crouched on the ground appears to have gotten some sleep and is slowly rousing. He grumbles in a tired voice, irritated about being woken up so early. The sun is barely over the horizon and there doesn't appear to be anyone else awake. Katalariana replies curtly to the grumbling watchman, grabs Chance by the arm and walks away. Chance is hesitant to follow after how things ended the previous day but gives in to Katalariana's persistence. The two guards begrudgingly take up position behind Chance and keep pace.

They huff and puff and grumble some more, but Katalariana ignores them and increases her pace. She leads Chance around the outer edge of the camp toward the entrance they went through to the bathing area. Chance wonders why they don't cut through the middle of camp, but it's apparent Katalariana has her reasons. One of the escorts, still annoyed about being awake so early, barks out something to Katalariana. She stops, walks back to him, whispers sternly to him, then returns to Chance and continues leading the way. Chance isn't sure what's happening, but the two escorts seem less than pleased about the position they're in.

They walk in silence for a while before Chance speaks up. "Katalariana," he starts.

"Kata," she interrupts. "My nem Kata."

She looks at Chance and smiles. Chance smiles back and nods. Before he can speak up again, Kata points in the direction they are heading and makes the gestures of bathing, answering what she believes is his question. As fast as she is walking, it's as if she's trying to stay ahead or get away from someone. She's in a lot better mood than the last time he saw her, and he wonders what's changed. "Kata," Chance repeats. "Cho hulne chu.[30] I want to talk to you."

Kata slows down and looks again at Chance with a smile. It seems as though there is a weight lifted from her shoulders allowing her to exude sheer happiness. Even the grumbling escorts behind them can't damper her spirits. She acts fearless and resolved. Chance can see something has definitely changed in her. Even as they pass the entrance, she merely waves at the sleepy guards posted there, as if nothing that happened yesterday has any bearing on her this morning. Before he asks

---

30   I speak to you.

what's changed, there's something that's been nagging at him for a while, something he felt he should ask only Kata.

"Kata," Chance starts again. "Cho hulne chu. Doman gri se chu fo chu kaum grokan. Jurcto jouem Doman.[31]"

Kata stops dead in her tracks. She turns and faces Chance again. This time, instead of a smile, she has a look of intrigue and curiosity. "Chanz, Reshiara hulne chu?[32]"

"Whe," Chance responds. "Chue shum chue.[33]"

Chance points to one of the guards to show Kata that the person who told him was like the guards. He points to the spots where his wounds were and mimics an explosion. He points to one of the guards again and puts his hand on Kata's head, repeating the phrase he was told. Kata remembers being told Chance was found with her father. His hand was on Chance's head when he was found, but Chance was the only one alive in the pile of bodies. Tears well up in Kata's eyes and she drops to her knees. Even her father, in his last moments could see Chance was not a demon, and in fact told him with his last breath they were going together to meet their god. If the others knew this, perhaps they would see even the Eldest favored this man. Perhaps, even then, her mother could not deny nor forsake this man's presence in their lives. There were few honors the Eldest can bestow on someone, but to be asked to accompany him anywhere was considered one of the greatest, even in death.

Chance is hesitant to kneel beside her, since last time he did, he ended up with several spears in his face. He crouches down and puts a hand on her shoulder. He looks up at the two guards for any objections. They both seem uninterested and

---

31 *God smile on you for your brave deeds. Together we go to him.*
32 *Did Reshiara tell you this?*
33 *No. Someone like him.*

are propped against their spears. Chance leans in a little closer to Kata. "Kata?"

"Om Domoinya[34], Chanz," Kata explains through teary eyes.

She tries to remember the words Chance taught her by the water. Instead, she scribbles a group of stick figures in the dirt. She points to one and repeats her name. She points to the largest figure. "Om Domoinya."

"Your father? That was your father?" Chance questions woefully.

She then draws a large circle around the group and waves her hand pointing to the entire camp. She points again to her father and then to the camp again. "He was the leader as well? I knew he was important, I just didn't realize how important. Cho sushu[35], Kata," Chance mutters. "Domoinya is father. What is Doman[36]?"

"Doman?" Kata asks.

She points to the sky and repeats the word. She draws a similar drawing on the ground as when she explained what a devil is, but this time she draws a figure floating in the sky surrounded by smaller floating figures. She points to the larger figure and tells Chance it is Doman and the smaller ones are called Aerulk[37]. Remembering all the times people said "jurcto jouem", Chance realizes it means "going together." Kata's father told him they would be going to meet God together. Though they were the final words he remembers, it doesn't explain what the first part means.

Before Chance asks, he hops up into a defensive stance

---

34 *My Father.*
35 *I'm sorry.*
36 *God, or The Divine*
37 *Angel*

as a large, reptilian creature bears down on them, screeching, hissing and snapping in Chance's face. Chance restrains himself from killing the monster when he notices a rider sitting atop. The rider looks down at Chance with scorn and distaste. He continues to ride his mount in a tight circle around Chance and Kata, never taking his eyes off of Chance. Noticing the escorting guards have kept their distance and are making no efforts to intercede, Chance relaxes his defensive stance a little, realizing this must be a tribe member. The man appears to be young, but carries himself with a sense of pride and authority. He wears several thick skins and furs to protect him from the morning chill, but even with all the skins, Chance can tell he is large in stature and as fit and toned as all the other men he's seen in the camp. His long, dark hair blows across his face with the morning breeze, but Chance can still see disgust in his expression. Chance also notices what looks like dried blood or mud covering the right side of his face. These designs continue down his neck under the furs he's wearing and down along his right arm, which arm he's using to keep a spear pointed at Chance.

The creature itself is as tall as Chance. It looks like a large, bipedal lizard covered in down feathers. It snaps at Chance with a mouth filled with rows of small, razor-like teeth. Chance recognizes the animal as the cleridrac, though it's his first time being so close to one. Several more cleridrac riders approach and circle the group as well.

Kata jumps up after realizing what is happening. "Cultac! What are you doing? You're all back?"

Cultac stops his cleridrac and slides off next to Kata. "Kata, what are you doing? Why are you with this monster? And why are you leaving the village so early? How is it this demon is allowed to wander freely?"

The two escorting warriors step forward to interject, but they are met with Cultac's cold, disapproving glare, and they shrink back. Kata stands between Chance and Cultac and tries moving Cultac's spear to the side away from Chance. "Cultac, he's not a demon. I was given the duty as his healer to watch over him," Kata explains.

"Who dares place you as his healer? This will not stand. No one disrespects the departed Eldest's daughter and future Eldest's partner by placing her in the company of demons and within harm's reach. He may wear the skin of a man, but he is not like us. He is not one of us nor will he ever be. I will see to it once I am Eldest. The council does not see reason now, but they will in time. I should destroy him now, right where he stands!" Cultac threatens, raising his spear towards Chance.

"It was my choice. I chose to be his healer. He is not a demon. It was also my father's..."

"Enough!" Cultac cuts Kata off before she can say another word. "This cannot be! I will not tolerate more of your insolence or your betrayals. You will not be permitted to help him any longer. I command it! Now see to the wounded."

Kata stands firm between Cultac and Chance. She stares defiantly into Cultac's face. She hates him. She wants nothing more to do with him. Such arrogance to assume she would be his partner. Not if she gets her way. Not if it truly is the Divine's will she and Chance remain together.

"Now!" Cultac yells. "Are you not a healer? Then fulfill your duties for those who truly are in need of your skill and who truly are brothers to you. Do not defy me any more."

His last words tempt Kata into standing her ground, but she fears how the situation will escalate if she makes that choice. She doesn't know what Chance is capable of since he was a warrior for his people, and she fears he will attack Cultac in an attempt to help her. Doing so could get Chance killed or exiled and Kata would lose him forever. She also hesitates because she planned on explaining to Chance the rites of partnership with the hopes he would choose her. If she leaves now, she misses her chance before Reshiara finds him again and keeps him in the dark regarding the rites. In the end, Kata knows there isn't anything she can do without jeopardizing Chance's safety and the possibility of them being together.

Knowing she has a responsibility to tend to the wounded brought in from the hunt, she decides to dismiss herself without further argument. She turns one last time and peers deeply into Chance's eyes. She swallows back the emotions building up in her throat. She managed to escape her mother and Reshiara to be confronted with yet another obstacle she didn't count on; the return of Cultac.

"Chanz, I you Hewold. No you Reshiara," Kata whispers in a quick attempt to explain her plans before leaving to tend to the wounded.

Cultac eyes her suspiciously as she walks away toward the approaching caravan of hunters and their spoils. With Kata gone from the group, Cultac drops his spear and draws his knife. He leaps at Chance and holds the blade to his throat; their faces inches from each other. Chance sees the fury in Cultac's eyes as they stare each other down. Chance remains calm, even though every muscle in his body twitches, yearning to take action and defend himself by putting this fool face-down in the dirt. He constrains himself, eager to prove he isn't a malicious demon, but a loyal ally and friend. Chance's calm demeanor enrages Cultac more.

"I'm not afraid of you, Demon," Cultac spits. "I will destroy you and take your head as my prize. I will display it for all to see and they will know that I do not fear your kind. I will be known as Demon's Death. I will hunt your kind and drive them back to the depths of this world. All will fear me and submit to me. First, I will rid this world of you. I will not allow you to corrupt my people or my home."

"Leave him be, Cultac!" interrupts another voice. "You cannot. He is our guest and you risk displeasing him. To do so would defy the wishes of our wise council."

Cultac steps back and turns toward the voice. When he sees it's Broltrom speaking, he can barely contain his fury and storms toward him. "I do not take counsel from you!" he bellows.

"He speaks reason, Cultac. This man is our guest, and for now, he will be welcome here," interrupts an older man as he rides up beside Broltrom. "You will put away your weapons and treat him with due respect. That is the word of the council."

Cultac stops his advance. His knuckles whiten as he grips his blade even tighter while trying to suppress his anger. "As the council decides. Forgive me, Elder Tumok. I meant no offense. It appeared as though he was attempting to harm one of our own. I acted rashly," Cultac apologizes, still fuming on the inside.

"As you can see, all is well," the councilman points out.

Cultac bows his head and then slowly walks back to Chance. He picks up his spear from the ground and mounts his cleridrac. He gives Chance one last, disdainful look and spits on the ground in front of him before riding away. Chance watches as he rides off and gives Cultac a big smile and a wave goodbye. Cultac kicks his cleridrac to pick up the pace and races off in a huff.

Chance has no idea what the problem was or what was even being said, but he's glad it's over. One thing was for sure, he determines he will no longer crouch beside Kata any more.

Both times he crouched down beside her, it ended with someone hateful towards him appearing and making sure he was aware of what they thought of him. This time was the most extreme, but Chance was able to pick out enough of what was said to know it was once again about him being a devil. This time, however, Chance was surprised to see others who are more accepting of his presence here.

Broltrom approaches and pats Chance on the shoulder. He's clearly impressed to be standing in Chance's presence. He pats himself on the chest and introduces himself as Broltrom. Chance nods and introduces himself. "Cho Chance Haywood. Bemelen wumcham chu.[38] It's good to know you."

Broltrom raises an eyebrow and studies Chance for a moment. A large grin breaks across his face. He pats Chance heavily on the back and laughs, happy to see Chance already knows some of the language. "Bemelen wumcham chu, Chazhewold. Chuem gardhrallim.[39]"

"Garjralleem?" Chance questions.

"Gardhrallim!" Broltrom repeats.

He pauses and thinks for a moment. Chance has gotten used to the waiting game as people try to figure out how best to explain what they are saying. As he watches his new charades partner, Chance notices there is something different about Broltrom than the other people he's seen in this tribe. There is a positive light about him that's more inviting than the seething disdain and hatred expressed by many others. He wonders if it's because of his lighter colored hair, or if there really is something lighter in his demeanor. Unlike the dark brown or black hair prominent in the tribe, Broltrom has more of a dark, sandy colored hair peppered with white and gray.

38 *I'm Chance Haywood. Good to know you.*
39 *We are brothers/brethren.*

Although he appears somewhere between his late thirties to early forties, there is a youthful energy about him as well. He stands just short of Chance's height, and like the rest of the men in the tribe, he has a toned physique, though he is slightly broader in the shoulders. As Chance observes him, there is something familiar about his face, like he's seen him before. He racks his brain to remember, and it finally comes to him. He saw someone bearing a resemblance to Broltrom among the group of warriors escorting Kata's father on the battlefield. A pit forms in his stomach as he ponders on what happened to that man. He attempted to protect them, but fate had something different in store for them.

Broltrom doesn't take long before he figures a way to explain the word Chance asked about. He places his hand near Chance's heart and his other hand near his own heart. He beats on both their chests as he repeats the word. When he sees Chance still doesn't understand, he thinks for another moment before clasping his hands together. "Chazhewold im Broltrom chuem gardhrallim.[40]"

"Friends?" Chance asks. "We are friends?"

"Frenz?" Broltrom repeats. "Chazhewold im Broltrom frez!"

With a big smile, Broltrom puts his arm around Chance and pulls him in close and walks him toward the caravan, excitedly repeating the word "frez." Chance attempts to correct his pronunciation with little success. Having the correct pronunciation doesn't seem as important to Broltrom as just being able to speak to him. Chance is also glad to have one more person to add to his small circle of friends.

---

40 *Chance Haywood and Broltrom are brothers.*

◀16▶

Walking with the caravan, Chance sees the camp has come alive with activity. With the return of the hunting party, everyone is rousting from their slumber and running to briefly greet their loved ones before unloading the dead game and returning to their tents to clean and prepare it. Several of the returning men are riding cleridracs, while others walk beside them carrying their bundles of spears, bows, and quivers of arrows. There are also harnessed cleridrac dragging sleds filled with dead game or bundles of furs and supplies behind them. Some of the cleridrac have the burdens placed directly on their backs while their owners lead from the front. At the end of the caravan are a few sleds carrying the wounded hunters.

Chance and Broltrom walk beside one of the sleds being dragged by a cleridrac. Chance's escorts continue to follow behind until Broltrom realizes they are there. With a questioning glance, he turns and speaks to them. After a brief conversation, they leave Chance in Broltrom's care and they go to join their families. Chance can tell Broltrom is a little upset after the conversation, but when he notices Chance staring at him, his large smile returns. He pats Chance on the back and points ahead, signaling for him not to worry and to keep up with the caravan.

Chance looks over the cargo on the sled they are following. There are stacks of furs as well as bundles wrapped in skins stacked neatly on a sled built from wooden poles lashed together by vines. Laying neatly across the bundles are an array of small, dead animals, ranging from large rodent-type animals and reptilian creatures to some larger bird-like ones. On the front of the sled, Chance notices what appears to be some type of water container made from dried animal skins. Chance peers inside to discover the container is filled with bloody water and several fish-like creatures. Upon closer inspection, the fish-like creatures look like miniature versions of the large, dragon-like monster haunting the body of water on the way to the bathing area. Chance thinks it's odd they keep them in water since it's added weight and the creatures are already dead. Broltrom leans over to Chance to see what has caught his attention. "Rashudrac,[41]" he tells Chance.

"Rashudrac," he repeats. "Rashudrac get big?"

Chance holds his hands up to show the size of the smaller ones and then stretches his arms out as wide as he can. He then points back in the direction of the body of water while repeating the name. Broltrom nods uneasily. He holds out his hands out wide as well. "Gebeeg!" he says enthusiastically. "Rashudrac gebeeeeg!"

They both chuckle, but Chance can tell from Broltrom's demeanor they don't take the large rashudrac lightly. As they continue to walk, Broltrom explains the nature of the rashudrac. Through acting and hand gestures, Broltrom tells how the juvenile rashudrac have the capability of walking on land. Once they reach a certain size, they leave their home and cross over land, using their fins to walk until they find bodies of water to call their own. Chance gathers they are a nuisance because they can infect any body of water, no matter where it's at. Broltrom also expresses how dangerous they can be. He shows Chance

41 A type of carnivorous, freshwater fish capable of traversing across dry ground.

one of the small ones and the rows of sharp teeth as well as the spines in their fins. He worries they won't have any safe water sources nearby. Chance asks why they don't kill the big one. Broltrom shakes his head. He holds up one finger and points to the rashudrac bodies, then he counts out several warriors and makes the gesture of them being eaten. He shakes his head again, and Chance nods in acknowledgment.

Broltrom calls out to the cleridrac driver and they separate from the main group of the caravan. They walk a little way before stopping near a group of tents. Several children and two women emerge from one of the tents. All the children gather around Broltrom, each one vying for his attention. He does his best to acknowledge each child before leaning over and kissing one of the women. He signals for the other woman to approach and they give each other a hug. He then turns and waves for Chance to come meet his family. "Chazhewold, chue om amogar.[42]"

They all stop and stare at Chance. Chance sheepishly waves at them, still unsure of the proper protocol for introducing himself. Broltrom pushes the children toward Chance, but they are all bashful and try hiding behind each other. Chance crouches down and extends his hand towards them. One of the small children slowly approaches and grabs a hold of Chance's fingers. Chance shakes the child's hand, making the child laugh. The other children approach and extend their hands to be shaken. After shaking each child's hand, he steps over to the women. Broltrom grabs the woman he kissed by the shoulders and tells Chance her name is Imelka. She hesitantly steps towards Chance and extends her hand. "Bemelen wumcham chu,[43] Hewold," she greets.

---

42 *They are my family.*
43 *Good to know you.*

"Hewold?" Broltrom interrupts. "Whe chue Hewold. Chazhewold![44]"

The two argue back and forth over who's correct about Chance's name. After some explanation from his wife, he finally looks at Chance for clarification. "Chu Hewold?[45]"

"Nue, cho Haywood,[46]" Chance explains, realizing Broltrom's wife must have gotten his name on the morning he woke up. "Cho Chance Haywood."

Broltrom looks at his wife with vindication. "Chazhewold! Chue Chazhewold.[47]"

Imelka shakes her head and rolls her eyes at her husband's stubbornness. She takes Chance's hand and gives him a smile. "Bemelen wumcham chu, Hewold," she repeats, half whispering his name.

Chance shakes Imelka's hand and greets her in return. He then turns his attention to the other woman. The mood becomes rather sullen. She is withdrawn and depressed and barely makes eye contact with anyone. Broltrom clears his throat and waves for her to come closer. Some of the children gather around her and cling to her legs when she approaches. Chance extends his hand and greets her, waiting to hear her name. She slowly takes his hand and mumbles her name under her breath. Chance asks her to repeat it. Frustrated, she turns and runs back into the tent. Chance is left standing with his hand extended. Imelka smiles at Chance and excuses herself before going after her into the tent. Bewildered by what happened, Chance looks to Broltrom for an explanation. Chance can see the hurt and disappointment in his eyes. "Yulnay," Broltrom

---

44 *Hewold? He's not Hewold. Chazhewold!*
45 *Are you Hewold?*
46 *Yes, I'm Haywood.*
47 *He's Chazhewold.*

mutters. "Chue copegka lo om gardhrall, Doltrom.[48]"

Broltrom tries explaining to Chance that Imelka and him are partners, while Yulnay and Doltrom were partners. He explains Doltrom is dead, and judging by everyone's sadness, Chance knows it was recently. Broltrom hesitates before recounting how Doltrom died at the time Chance was wounded, confirming Chance's suspicions the man he saw on the battlefield was his brother escorting their chief. Broltrom explains as best he can that he now has responsibility for Doltrom's family.

It is then Chance realizes the word he thought meant friend, was in fact, the word for brother. Broltrom claimed Chance as his brother. That realization hits Chance like a ton of bricks. He figured everyone saw him as nothing more than an evil devil. He was thinking the only reason most people were nice to him at first was because they feared him. To be considered a brother to someone he just met was a bit shocking, but also gives insight into Broltrom's character.

It also gives insight into Yulnay's behavior, and why it was so hard for her to interact with someone she perhaps felt was responsible for her husband's death. However, Broltrom seems eager to prove Chance isn't to be feared.

After explaining their family situation, Broltrom rallies his family to the sled to unload everything and pile it beside their tent. Yulnay and Imelka return to help with the work. Once they have unloaded everything, Broltrom hands the cleridrac driver some of their provisions as trade for his services before leaving. Meanwhile, the family cleans and prepares the animals for cooking and drying.

Yulnay and the children stay out in front of the tent, skinning and cleaning the smaller animals, while Broltrom and his

---

48 *She's the partner of my brother, Doltrom.*

wife take Chance to the back of the tent to a large, flat rock. With a speed Chance has seldom seen anyone move before, Broltrom and his wife work in tandem; cleaning, skinning, and butchering the small rashudrac. With efficiency and skill, Broltrom swiftly skins the animal, tosses the skin aside and separates the various parts of the animal, throwing the bones back into the tub of bloody water. His wife takes the skin and stretches it over a wooden frame. Chance watches in awe at the skill and speed at which they work, and before long, they have the container emptied of rashudrac, their skins stretched, the meat hung for drying or wrapped in large plant leaves.

Without stopping for a break, Broltrom moves to the tub of bones and separates them by shape and size. He motions for Chance to come closer. He pulls his knife from his belt and grabs a large, broad rib from the tub. With his knife, he whittles down one of the edges until it resembles a curved blade. He places it on the flat rock, takes a smaller stone and taps the rib to flatten it out. He then hands it to Chance while he works on the other bones.

Chance runs his fingers over the bone blade. It's slightly gray in color with a glossy film over it. The whittled edge feels soft and flimsy, like a stiff, fibrous gelatin, while the rest of the bone is still slightly rigid. Not something that would be effective as a blade. Chance bends it a little between his fingers to see the bone is soft enough to be malleable, which he has never seen with bones. As he handles the bone, it gets darker in color and more rigid as it dries.

He looks down at Broltrom's pile and sees they are all changing in color. Broltrom has created an array of blades, arrowheads, and spear tips out of the different shapes and sizes of bone, and he lays them neatly across the stone table. He rushes to get as many pieces cut from the bones as he can.

Imelka has since built a fire and sets the racks of meat close by to be dried. She then picks up the carved bone pieces, as well as Chance's blade, and places them in the fire. Chance finds it curious they would put them in the fire and wonders if it's a way of tempering the bone, which is also something he's never heard of.

From time to time, the children come around and hand Imelka the work they have finished. Imelka takes the meat and hangs it with the rest and works on tanning the hides. The family has rack after rack of drying meat set around the fire. It looks like a bomb made entirely of meat exploded and covered the area in chunks of flesh.

Chance sits back and watches, feeling like he gets in the way anytime he tries to help. He listens to Broltrom and his wife playfully banter back and forth between each other as they continue to work. It reminds Chance of his own mother and father. It seems so long ago that he was with them, but he can still remember his father trying to help his mother with the chores, while his mother constantly chided him for not doing it correctly, or at least not in the way she wanted it done. He remembers his father smiling back at her, many times messing up on purpose just to hear her correct him.

Chance can't recall there ever being a time when they didn't get along. They always seemed so in love with each other. His mother was always by his father's side, especially when he was being accused of betraying the CC. His father never denied doing so, and often spoke out against the CC's methods.

Chance never knew what caused his father to go from being one of the most skilled and decorated Genhance soldiers to leaving the CC. He does remember his parents trying to convince him not to join and stay away from the CC. They tried to convince him to join them on their ship the day they left the Corporate Coalition. He refused, claiming his parents didn't know what they were talking about. They said they were going to leave and start somewhere fresh. They would finally have a place to call home that wasn't floating in space. The only life he had known was aboard the Mayflower and briefly on his father's ship. A place to call home other than in space didn't mean anything to him at the time.

His parents claimed the CC was going to allow them to leave, as long as they promised never to come back or engage them in conflict. He didn't go see them before departure. Instead, he decided to go to the observation deck and watch their ship leave. He had been convinced they were traitors and was better off without them. Being young and gullible, he believed those words before fully comprehending the consequences of his choice.

The CC let them leave along with everyone else wanting to part ways with the CC. Several families boarded that day, hoping to finally settle down in a place they could call home.

Chance watched as their ship floated away into the emptiness of space. Before they engaged their main thrusters to take them to their new home, the Mayflower opened fire on them, destroying the vessel and everyone aboard. The CC wasn't about to risk possible threats getting away to cause problems for them in the future. They lied to his parents so they would leave peacefully and never suspect the CC's true intentions.

Chance's sorrow at the loss of his family eventually turned to anger; anger at his parents for the choice they made. It was their fault for leaving, after all. Or so he thought. His anger served him well in the armed forces. He quickly rose in rank and skill until he was accepted into the Special Services. With each mission, his anger ate away at him until he no longer cared about anything. It wasn't long before he felt nothing at all. He became nothing more than a killing machine; a tool to be used by the CC to further advance their agenda.

It all changed when he was given a mission to root out a group of deserters on one of the CC's planet acquisitions. He found their camp deep in an exotic and hostile jungle. Several families deserted the CC hoping to make a start on their own. Once again, the CC feared rebellion, and therefore, their bottom line. They didn't dare risk it, and as was their custom, they were going to ensure dissenters were never able to rise in rebellion.

Chance remembers walking into the camp with his rifle at the ready. He pointed the barrel at the first sign of movement. There, in his sights, was a mother walking with her child in hand. She looked at Chance in surprise and jumped in front to shield her child. He hesitated with his finger on the trigger, and before he could pull it, shots rang out around him, decimating the entire camp. His team rushed in, sweeping the area and finishing off any survivors. The job was completed with Chance never firing a shot. He, instead, continued to stare at the bodies of the woman and child through the scope of his rifle; not having moved a muscle during the skirmish.

It was the first time Chance felt something more than indifference in all the years he worked in the Special Services. It was guilt and shame. Everyone in the camp was unarmed and most were women and children. They posed no threat. He never had reason to question the CC's methods as long as he was killing hostile creatures, but staring at an innocent person at the other end of his barrel gave him a glimpse of what the CC had become. It opened the door to all those questions he had always turned a blind eye to. It was the first time he ever asked himself if this was something he should be doing. His team laid waste to their camp while he fought a different fight inside his own mind. It was then that he realized the CC couldn't be trusted. While at one time they stood for progress and freedom, they now were ruthless murderers and tyrants interested in their own profit and power. They had become what they originally fought against. He could see what his parents tried to tell him, and he was sorry he ever doubted them.

❮17❯

Kata passes the incoming caravan of hunters to the end where the wounded are being carried. She seethes over her plans being spoiled. She was so close to telling Chance he didn't have to partner with Reshiara and could choose another. With all her heart, she believes he would choose to be with her. There's a connection between them that she can't deny. He's always so genuine and caring towards her. If she was able to tell him the truth about his situation, it would have been a short wait before her time of mourning was finished and they could be together. If he chose her and she accepted, there would be nothing anyone could do to stop it. Not her mother, not Reshiara, and certainly not Cultac. If only her mother hadn't meddled, she would have been his and she could have avoided this whole mess.

Now the hunters are back, it won't be long before the council ends the rites of partnership, and Kata knows she has to act fast. She has to find a way to tell Chance before she loses him to that girl.

"You're here early. That's so unlike you to be the first to attend the wounded," her mother's voice startles her. "I know you were up early. I wonder what you were up to."

Kata gives her mother a quick glance before focusing back on her patient. She can tell by her mother's sly, cynical tone that she is up to something. She ignores her attempts to engage in conversation and tends to the wounded man in front of her.

"Remain silent if you wish. I passed Cultac on my way here. He told me he saw you with the demon. I believe I told you to stay away from him. You leave me no choice, Katalariana," her mother chides.

Fear creates a pit in Kata's stomach. She tries to remain focused on her task, but all she can think about is how much she wants to turn and scream at her mother. She tries swallowing the lump building in her throat. She turns and leaves her mother behind to go to the end of the caravan and start working from there. She expected her mother to follow, but she didn't. Instead, her mother turned her attention to the wounded and left Kata alone.

Kata lets out a sigh and tries not to let her mother's words get to her. Nothing was going to stop her from being with Chance, especially since they were meant to be together. She tells herself it's necessary to go through these difficult times to better enjoy the times she does get to be with him, and in the end, when they are together, all this hassle will have been worth it and made them stronger for it.

A smile breaks across her sullen face until she arrives at her next patient. He's been battered and beaten severely and bloody bandages cover several open wounds. It looks like a large animal mauled him. Judging from the amount of trauma, he's lucky to be alive. His breaths are shallow and wheezy and he doesn't appear to be conscious.

Kata pulls bandages away to more closely examine his wounds. Upon close examination of his chest, she finds what looks like a knife wound among all the bite marks and scratches. It appears deep, like a stab wound rather than a cut. As she examines the wound, the man startles and grabs Kata's arm. He squeezes hard and looks at her with eyes filled with terror.

"Cultac," he stutters. "Cultac left me to die."

He struggles for breath as he tries to explain his plight but the pain becomes too unbearable and he passes out again. Troubled by his words, Kata turns to the cleridrac driver and asks if he knows what happened. He glances around, afraid of who might hear him. He motions for Kata to come closer and whispers to her about what he saw happen.

He tells her he isn't sure how he was attacked, but he is sure the wounded man was in Cultac's hunting party, exploring a large wooded area for larger game. He explains Cultac claimed to know nothing about how the man ended up alone and victim to a gruthraller[49] attack.

The driver looks around again and leans in closer to Kata. "Cultac claims not to know anything, but I believe he does. I've told no one of this, but I am sure I saw him running away from the attack when we heard the screams. We ran toward the screams as soon as we heard them, and saw the gruthraller attacking this man as he tried to defend himself. The gruthraller was too large to be able to fight alone. We fought it as best we could, and some others were wounded in the attack. When we finally brought the beast down, Cultac jumped in at the end with his spear, declaring his was the killing blow and claiming the beast for his own."

The driver shakes his head in disbelief before continuing. "No one dared defy him, and we were all too exhausted after the fight to care. We let him claim it while we tended to the wounded. He didn't seem concerned with the wounded, and when we asked where he had gone, and where the others in his party were, he claimed not to know and it wasn't his concern. When we found the rest of his party, they claimed Cultac and this man left the group to chase after game they spotted run-

---

49 *A large, aggressive, gorilla-like creature with four arms.*

ning through the trees. I asked this man about what happened, but all he could say was Cultac left him to die. It seems reason to me they ran into the gruthraller while chasing the other animals. I believe Cultac wounded this man and left him for the gruthraller so he could run away. I should not say this, for it is not wise to speak ill of the future Eldest, but I believe he is a coward. A coward, but a dangerous coward. Be careful when speaking of these things, young healer, and do not mention me. I have no desire to be a player in Cultac's foul schemes. I have a family that depends on me."

The driver respectfully bows his head to Kata before urging his cleridrac to speed up to stay with the caravan. Kata lets the caravan go on ahead as she stands in the road, pondering the information.

She had heard similar stories regarding Cultac's misdeeds, but the closer Cultac came to becoming the Eldest, the more vicious and heartless his actions have become.

As Kata watches the caravan of wounded get farther away from her, she thinks about the wounded man. She isn't familiar with who he is, but she knows Cultac's hunting party usually consists of those he considers friends. Most seem as self-centered and cruel as Cultac, but it doesn't sit well with Kata that he would so readily turn on his friends to save his own life.

It solidifies that Cultac is not the one she wants to spend the rest of her life with; as if she needed another reason. If only she could get her mother to see him for what he really is. The problem is no one on the council will challenge Cultac and hold him accountable for his actions. No one will believe the stories even if someone is brave enough to come forward. The council seems more willing to accept Cultac's word over everyone else.

Perhaps this is her opportunity to rid herself of Cultac by bringing the council's attention to his actions. How could they dispute the wound in the man's side as well as the witnesses who say he was hunting with Cultac?

Kata marches toward the council's tents. Along the way, she goes over in her mind how she's going to plead her case and convince them to look at Cultac's actions more closely. If she can convince them he shouldn't be the Eldest, then she won't be expected to be his partner.

Caught up in her machinations, she doesn't notice Cultac with another woman in his arms hiding between two tents. When she passes him on the road, he dismisses the woman and steps out to the road. "Kata, aren't you supposed to be tending the wounded?" he hollers, snapping her from her thoughts.

Kata startles and looks at him bewildered. "Cultac?" she mutters in surprise.

"What are you doing? I thought I sent you to tend to the wounded."

Kata stumbles over her words as she tries gathering her thoughts. Cultac looks at her impatiently, waiting for her response. Without thinking, Kata opens her mouth and the words that escape her lips fill her with sudden dread. "What happened to your friend during the hunt?"

Cultac looks at her incredulously. "What?"

Kata clears her throat and poises herself as if she meant to start this conversation. "There is a man who was part of your party that was wounded. I want to know what happened to him."

Cultac rolls his eyes and shakes his head impatiently. "The careless idiot ran into a gruthraller and was nearly torn to pieces. What does it matter?"

Kata wrings her fingers nervously. "I'm talking about the knife wound in his chest."

Cultac's body tenses and he glares at Kata with an icy cold stare that sends a shiver through her body. "What do you mean? The man was fool enough to take on a gruthraller on his own; he got what he deserved. I had to bring it down just to save him. He's lucky I came along when I did."

"What I mean, Cultac, is that there is a knife wound in his chest that didn't come from the gruthraller attack, and I believe you know something about it," Kata challenges.

Cultac steps up to Kata, gritting his teeth and puffing out his chest. "It would be reason for you to watch the words you speak to me. I do not like what you are accusing me of. I told you what happened, and that is the end. That is all you need to know, so go back to your duties."

Kata stares defiantly into Cultac's eyes. "It seems like reason to me that the council should hear that one of our own was fed to a gruthraller so the other could run away like a coward. The council will hear of this and justice will be done."

Cultac grabs Kata by the arms and lifts her up close to his face. "You will do no such thing. It would be reason for you to know your place and keep your mouth shut. Do not defy me, Katalariana. I will be the Eldest and you will be beside me. I will not have you turn against your chosen one."

Cultac lowers Kata but still keeps a firm grip on her arms. "I did stab him, but he was the weaker warrior. I needed him to distract the gruthraller so I could kill it. If I hadn't done it, he would have led the animal to the rest of the warriors, and they would have all been killed. No one will dispute it. Likewise, I won't allow you to destroy the peace of our people with your vile accusations against me, your Eldest. How often are our people asked to sacrifice themselves for their Eldest? How is this any different?"

"You are not the Eldest!" Kata refutes with utter disgust and disdain.

Cultac shakes Kata and brings her closer to his face again. "Careful, Katalariana. I don't want to have to tell the council that you have been corrupted by that demon; but I will, and the both of you will be destroyed. I will send you with that demon back to the abyss where it belongs. Speak anymore of this to anyone, and I will tell the council how you revile against me, your chosen partner and future Eldest. Forget these things and go back to the healer tents and attend to your duties; where you belong!"

Cultac lets Kata go and heads down the road. Kata remains still, tears pouring down her face. Cultac's fingerprints are embedded in her arms and red welts begin forming. She crumbles to her knees and sobs into her hands. Now more than ever, she wishes Chance was beside her to console her.

She doesn't know how or when, but she knows Cultac will get what he deserves. She hopes she's there to see it when he does.

18

Chance watches as Imelka pulls the assorted bone fragments from the fire and places them into a large jug of water using a pair of twigs. Broltrom sits next to him, telling story after story, most of which Chance doesn't understand but listens to all the same. He tells his stories while he whittles on a piece of wood.

When all the pieces have been pulled from the fire and cooled off in the water, Imelka separates the pieces by type. When she comes to the knife, she hands it to Chance. He takes the blade and immediately examines it. It feels as hard as steel, and the thin edge is as sharp as a razor. Rubbing his fingers over the dark, glossy surface, he realizes this is the material the CC has been after. This bone has been tempered to be hard enough to pierce even their strongest, most advanced armor.

Chance chuckles with excitement, having finally discovered the source of this mysterious material. He laughs at the thought of the CC trying to piece all the bones together to make ships, or armor, or whatever else they planned for this stuff. Unless they could find a way to duplicate it, tempered bone wasn't going to be as useful for their purposes as they had planned.

Broltrom reaches over, asking Chance for the blade. Chance hands it to him and watches as Broltrom fits it into the piece of wood he was whittling on. He walks over to the stretched skins near the fire and cuts a thin strip off. He wraps it tightly around the wooden handle of the blade and then holds it close to the fire for a moment.

He hands the finished blade to Chance and then disappears into his tent. He returns with a sheath attached to a long strap. He hands it to Chance and mimics putting a belt on. Chance ties the sheathe on around his waist and slides the knife in. It fits securely into the weathered skin sheath.

Chance thanks Broltrom and Imelka for their generosity and continues to examine the knife. Broltrom pats Chance on the shoulder then helps his wife sort the rest of the pieces.

As he examines his new blade, Chance hears a familiar voice speaking to the children in front of the tent. Chance sheathes the blade as the children run over with Reshiara in tow; happy as ever to see him.

Broltrom and Imelka look up, confused about why she would be there. She points to Chance and explains her reason for showing up. Broltrom permits her to proceed and she struts over to Chance and takes his hands. Chance notices the questioning look in her eyes as if to ask where he's been all morning.

Before she asks, a loud horn bellows through the camp. Broltrom looks at his wife, who nods, and he hops up and pats Chance on the shoulder. "Chazhewold, jouem,[50]" he says as he points in the direction of the horn.

"Hewold!" Reshiara and Imelka both correct Broltrom in unison.

Broltrom looks at both women and shrugs his shoulders. Chance grins and looks apologetically at Broltrom, who shrugs again and leans in close. "Jouem, Chazhewold," he whispers mischievously, leading Chance toward the sound of the horn.

---

50 *We go or let's go.*

Chance chuckles as he follows Broltrom from the fireside. Reshiara keeps hold of his hand and follows close by. Chance looks down at her, curious as to why she remains so close, almost as if she's afraid to let him go. She meets his gaze with an endearing smile.

Chance remembers what Kata said earlier before departing and wonders if there is a rivalry between the two for his attention. He hasn't spent much time without one or the other since he woke up. It would also explain why Kata was in such a hurry this morning. She was trying to make sure they were gone before Reshiara showed up. It also explains why Kata tried telling him he should be with her and not Reshiara.

He wonders why they are vying so much for his affection. He knows Kata is his nurse, but he also sees there is something more by the way she looks at him. Every time he looks into her eyes, he can see she longs to be with him. He finds, though, he is also drawn to her. She constantly invades his thoughts. It doesn't help that he also woke up with the image of her face in his mind and has felt a connection to her since the first time he saw her. The problem is, everytime they are together they get interrupted and their time is cut short, especially when they really start connecting. It's like everyone is working against them, unlike the times he's with Reshiara.

When he looks at Reshiara, he can also see the longing in her eyes, but he gets the feeling she just doesn't want to be alone. That's why she's so desperate to hold on to him every time they are together. She's enjoyable to be around, but he doesn't feel the same connection as he does with Kata, and he almost feels bad about it.

He counts himself fortunate it's only the two competing for him though. He doesn't know what drew these two girls to him, but oddly enough, he's glad he isn't having to deal with several people vying to spend time with him, especially since he isn't from this planet. He also counts himself lucky the majority of his time is spent with people wanting to be around him on a constant basis and not having to constantly defend himself from people berating him for being a devil.

It isn't long before Chance and the others walk into a crowd gathering around a large tent. In front of the crowd is a row of older men standing side by side. Chance recognizes Umochak, as well as the man that showed up earlier today with Broltrom.

One of the oldest looking men steps forward onto a large, flat rock and raises his arms to try and calm the gathering crowd. Once silence settles over the group, he addresses everyone in a loud, booming voice.

"To honor our skilled hunters and give thanks for a fruitful hunt, we will have our celebration at sundown. It is customary to hold it the following night, but the council has judged it necessary to complete the rites of partnership on that night for all those who are ready and have had to wait for the hunters to return. Remember, the ceremony will be fulfilled for all those who are not in mourning."

The crowd breaks into loud cheering. Reshiara squeals with excitement and jumps with glee while squeezing Chance's arm. Chance looks around, hoping to get an idea of what everyone is so excited about. As he looks around, he spots Kata among the boisterous crowd. She appears to be the only one not excited about the announcement. In fact, her eyes appear red and puffy. He tries to make his way towards her but is halted by Reshiara's tight grip on his arm.

Reshiara notices his perplexion but is unable to see what he is staring at through the crowd. She tugs on his arm to get his attention. Chance looks at her briefly and looks back at Kata who has disappeared into the crowd. Chance is disappointed he isn't able to speak to her again. She looks like she could use a friend.

Reshiara doesn't need to see who it is to figure out who has Chance's attention. She's seen that look on his face before. She loosens her grip on Chance's arm, about to surrender him to her competition, but thinks better of it. He's hers as determined by rites, and she isn't going to give him up so easily. After all, he will be the only family she has and can't let Kata-lariana interfere. "Hewold!" she hollers in an attempt to draw his attention.

Chance looks back at her, realizing he missed his opportunity to talk to Kata again. As he's about to respond, Broltrom comes up beside him and pushes him towards the front of the crowd.

"Elders! Elders!" Broltrom hollers over the noise of the crowd, trying to get the council's attention. "I come on behalf of the outsider, Chazhewold. I ask the council to reconsider keeping guards with him at all times. It seems reason to me that if he were as dangerous as some had thought, he would already have displayed his intentions. I understand the reason for it while we were away hunting, but we are returned and there are plenty of warriors now if the need arises. We have welcomed him as one of us, it is reason to see that we should treat him as one of us. He has already shown an eagerness to learn our ways and our words. If it is the wisdom of the council, allow him to walk freely among us, and I will take full accountability for his actions."

The elders cast glances at one another before they all nod at the elder standing on the rock. The elder on the rock turns and faces Broltrom and Chance. Cultac has been standing close by, listening to Broltrom's request and steps from the crowd toward the council. The lead council member takes notice and asks Cultac if he has any objections. Cultac looks over at Chance with a smirk on his face. "I have no objections. Let him see we have lowered our guard, and when he does strike, I will be the first to destroy him and send him back to the fires of the underworld, and with him, Broltrom as well," Cultac boasts with confidence, casting a sly glance at Broltrom.

"Then it is the wisdom of the council that he should be free to roam within our walls. It is also our wisdom that should he go outside our walls, he be accompanied. Though we have accepted him, he may not have accepted us, and we cannot risk him returning to his people and leading them back here."

Broltrom thanks the council and looks back at Chance with a smile and claps him on the shoulder. Chance pats him back on the shoulder and shrugs, not having any idea what was discussed. Broltrom pats Chance's chest and steps back with his arms out wide and points all around. He shakes his head and poses as a pouting guard, and tells Chance there won't be any guards. Believing he understands, Chance nods and smiles. Finally, they are putting a little more trust in him; all thanks to his new friend, Broltrom.

◄19►

The sun is setting and music fills the air. The scent of roasting meat permeated throughout the camp the entire day, and now the festivities are beginning. Chance is excited to see more of the tribe's activities, and most of all, eat the food he's been smelling all day.

He spent the rest of the day with Broltrom and his family, helping prepare their food for storage as well as practicing the language with Reshiara; who hasn't left his side for even a moment. Now they all walk together to where the crowd gathered earlier to participate in the celebration.

People gather from all around the camp, each family preparing something to share with the tribe for the feast. The food is gathered on a platform made from wooden planks and flat stones encircling a large bonfire.

The platform also encloses several dancers between the food and the fire. The dancers prance and sing around the fire as everyone else gathers around the food, eating at their leisure. Several small groups of people sit scattered around the circle playing the music for the celebration. The instruments consist of a variety of drums, flutes, and horns; all made from wood, animal skins, and bone.

Several smaller fires burn in pits scattered around the larger, central bonfire. Smaller groups of people gather to socialize around the smaller fires, extending the festivities beyond the central gathering place.

"I know," Kata interrupts. "All I want is for him to be happy and well also. I thought if he was familiar with our home, he would be more comfortable and happy here."

Kata feels everything she wants to say would give her away. She really hopes Reshiara ends the conversation and leaves her to her thoughts. The last thing Kata wants to hear is Chance is all Reshiara has. It's all she feels she has right now as well. She wants to tell Reshiara that Chance should know what he's involved in and he should get to choose his partner, rather than have the choice made for him because he doesn't understand their ways. Kata also thinks about telling her it was her mother inciting panic and fear that nearly got Chance taken away, but she knows Reshiara would see it as her way of avoiding responsibility. On top of that, she would have her mother in the room joining with Reshiara and she barely has the energy to continue. For now, she holds her tongue.

Reshiara sits down on the bed across from Kata. She stokes the fire placed between them before laying down and making herself comfortable on the furs of her bed. She looks up at the ceiling of the tent, contemplating the conversation. She looks back at Kata, who still sits huddled on her bed. "Why did he apologize to you? Why did he call out to you when you went inside? Why is he so concerned for you?"

"Reshiara," Kata replies impatiently. "I don't know. It would be reason to think he feels responsible for me being taken away. He understands that he's seen as a demon among us."

"You told him!"

"He asked me to. He heard others calling him Blue Demon and he begged me to tell him the meaning. After that is when the others came and took me away. He would have discovered the meaning soon enough."

The council and their families sit together around the bonfire with an empty space left for the Eldest. Those of high status and position within the tribe gather on either side of the council, followed by their family and friends. Rarely do the council and their family members leave the bonfire to socialize with the other parties, but stay among themselves, whilst the rest of the population mingles and scatters throughout the camp, usually carrying on the festivities well into the early hours of the morning.

Chance's eyes widen at the amount of food gathered and placed around the fire. Though he has just arrived, it appears as though many of the people have already been celebrating, lounging in small groups with their bellies full, or staggering around the fire, already inebriated and trying to dance to the music.

Broltrom grabs Chance's shoulder and directs him to the food, pointing out several of his favorite dishes. He hands Chance a small, clay dish, and fills it with food from the tables. Reshiara grabs a plate and hurries to keep up, grabbing what she can without letting Chance get too far from her.

Chance's eyes widen at the amount Broltrom continues to stack on his small plate. When the plate is heaped to overflowing, he pats Chance on the shoulder and leaves him to rejoin his family. Reshiara laughs as Chance juggles his plate and all the food that keeps rolling off. She points to a spot where they can go sit and eat before Chance loses everything. As they make their way to the spot, Chance hears someone call his name. He turns to see the head councilor calling for him to sit beside the council members.

Reshiara's smile drops from her face. She's never been allowed to sit with the council at a celebration and her discomfort shows. Chance notices her hesitation and smiles at her to ease her anxiety and nods his head in the direction of the council. "Jouem, Resha,[51]" he implores encouragingly.

Reshiara's heart takes courage and her confidence returns, not so much for being asked to join him to sit with the council, but because of the name he called her. Never in her life has she been so close to someone as to be given a nickname, or referred to by an endearing name. Hearing the name and seeing his smile causes all her fears to melt away. She links her arm into Chance's and they sit together with the council. The rest of the council members nod to acknowledge his presence before returning their attention to the dancers and the food in front of them.

Chance wastes no time digging into his food. Given everything was cooked over a fire, there is still a variety of flavors. All the different herbs, fruits, and vegetables combined with the varying meats make some unique and flavorful dishes. Chance expected to find dried or fire roasted meat and perhaps some plant roots or raw vegetables straight off the plant. Instead, it's as if every dish is as unique as the family that prepared it.

Chance eats with gusto, eating everything on his plate and grabbing more from the table in front of him. He feels like it's been a long time since he's had a sufficient amount to eat. Since waking up, he's only eaten some dry meat, some fruit, and a scrambled egg. He can feel his body absorbing the much needed nutrition and it's extremely rejuvenating. He can sense the effects spreading throughout his entire body and it feels as if a heavy, draining fog is being lifted off his body. Feeling the renewing energy surging through his body, he eats with even greater relish.

While shoveling the food into his mouth, he notices Resha

---

51 *Let's go.*

and several council members watching him; awestruck by how much food he is able to eat in such a short amount of time. He smiles bashfully, "Cho loshome chu fo sustev.[52] Thank you for the food."

They all chuckle and motion for him to continue eating. Resha shakes her head and laughs at him. She pokes at his belly and then mimics a fat person, puffing out her cheeks and pretending to scoop food into her mouth by the handful. While she mocks Chance, her demeanor changes and she immediately looks down and picks at the food on her plate.

Chance looks around to see what has caused her sudden withdrawal and he spies Kata taking her place in an empty seat between the council members.. She's in a sullen mood, trying to disappear into the group of council members and their families, until she sees Chance watching her. When they make eye contact, her spirit is lifted and she can't help but smile; that is, until she feels a hand weighing down on her shoulder. She turns and looks up to see her mother standing over her; a look of displeasure and malcontent stricken across her face. Kata shrinks under her mother's stare and firm hand, and once again, tries blending in with the people around her.

Her mother goes to the food table and grabs a small bowl. She pours something from a nearby jug into the bowl and then disappears into the crowd. A short minute later, she reappears beside Chance.

He looks up at her as she stands beside him. She tries smiling at him, but Chance can see through the facade. He's not sure what her game is, but he smiles and nods back at her. She mumbles something and slowly hands him the bowl with the liquid inside. Chance graciously accepts it and thanks her

---

52 *I thank you for food.*

as he peers into the dark blue liquid swirling around. She bows her head and takes a step back before looking over toward her daughter.

Kata watches with sheer dread. She knows exactly what her mother is up to. She wants to yell at Chance not to drink it, but she knows he won't understand her, and no one else will believe her mother is trying to poison him. She won't be able to run to him in time to take it from him either. Her mother would stop her before she reached him anyway. Even if she was able to reach him after he drank it, without knowing what poison she used, it would be impossible to give him the right antidote in time. All she can do is watch. Watch and pray.

Chance raises the bowl to Kata's mother and then brings it to his lips. The smell of sweet fruit emanates from the bowl. It tastes even sweeter as he gulps it down; sweet and refreshing. He empties the bowl and raises it to Kata's mother once again, nodding his head to show his appreciation.

Kata watches with bated breath. Her mother stands by as well, waiting for the effects of the poison to manifest. Chance goes back to eating until he realizes Kata's mother is still standing there; watching and waiting. He looks at her with a questioning stare. She stares back at him, her friendly facade giving way to uneasiness. Instead of confidence, she now displays nervousness. It's then Chance realizes there must have been something in the drink she gave him. He thought it was odd for her to be so generous towards him when she's been nothing but spiteful towards him since the day he woke up. He looks over at Kata, who's more and more relieved as time passes with no symptoms.

After a minute of the three of them looking back and forth at each other, Kata's mother hurries into the crowd with a huff. Chance shrugs his shoulders, smiles and winks at Kata, then goes back to eating. Once again, his enhanced genetics saved his life, and though he managed to live through this attempt on his life, he wonders what sort of ramifications this will have. They already believe he's a demon. Will surviving being poisoned confirm their suspicions? He worries it will lead to greater hostility towards him.

He finishes the food in front of him and watches the dancers prancing around the fire, hoping to take his mind off this latest attempt on his life. Worrying about it won't change anything now anyway. Perhaps they'll be too scared to attempt killing him again for fear of a demon's retaliation and he won't have to worry about it. Afterall, he hasn't been held up at spearpoint yet as a result of surviving.

Mesmerized by the flames and music, his mind wanders. Resha notices Chance entranced by the dancing and decides to enter the ring, hoping to attract his attention and entertain him with her dancing.

Chance is surprised to see Resha get up and leave his side. She looks back at him with a large smile as she passes the ring of food and joins the other dancers. He smiles back at her, interested to see her dance.

When she rounds to the other side of the bonfire, hidden by the pyre and towering flames, someone pulls on the back of his vest, pulling him over backwards. He jerks around to see who the assailant is and finds Kata trying to drag him away into the crowd. Feeling bad about leaving Resha's dance, he hesitates to follow, but wanting to talk to Kata all day, he gives in to her persistent tugging. She waves her hand urging him to hurry, leading him from the fireside and disappearing into the masses.

Once they break through the crowds, she leads him past the tents; running as fast as she can towards the edge of camp.

She doesn't stop for anything or anyone; making sure to stay away from other large groups celebrating throughout the camp. Chance calls out for her to stop and explain where they are going, but she doesn't relent in her pace or in her course.

Chance notices she is avoiding the campfires and people by staying in the shadows. He feels nervous about leaving the party and Resha behind. He imagines how she will react when she finds him again. It also seems others take issue whenever he and Kata are alone, and he fears what will happen if they are caught again. He guesses that's why Kata is determined to keep away from others.

Guided by moonlight, they stop near the wall at the edge of camp. Even in the moonlight, Chance can see Kata vividly, even her nervous expression. She paces in a small circle trying to catch her breath; glancing in every direction to see if they were followed. When she is sure there is no one following, she throws her arms around Chance and tries burying her face in his chest.

Chance slowly puts his arms around her and rubs her back. He feels her body jolting, as she sobs uncontrollably. He slowly pulls her away and lifts her chin up towards him. Tears stream down her cheeks. Not wanting him to see her like this, she tries burying her face in his chest again.

Chance holds her steady and doesn't let her hide her face. "Kata, losheer chu hulne cho.[53] Please, speak to me," Chance pleads.

Kata shakes her head and sobs. She starts falling to her knees, but Chance doesn't let her. He pulls her into him and lets her cry a little more on his chest. He casts a quick glance around; paranoid someone is going to suddenly jump out from

---

53 *Please speak to me.*

behind the wall and stick a spear in his face or have a cleridrac snapping at him.

Kata lets him cradle her in his arms. It fills her with a warmth that comes from inside and not from the heat of his body. It gives her a comfort she has longed for and knows she could never find among the people of her tribe. Everyone she is close to is too cold and callous to ever generate this kind of feeling. Everyone she knows except Broltrom; though he was too honorable ever to be found embracing the Eldest's daughter, especially when he had a family of his own.

Somehow, she knew she could find it with Chance. He was turning out to be everything she dreamed he would be. Everything she dreamed of except he was to be given to another woman. Another woman that perhaps longed to be with him as much as she herself did. It didn't feel right that the decision should be taken from him.

"Chanz?" she finally breaks the silence. "Chanz, you famly Kata?"

Her voice is timid and almost desperate as she chokes back the tears and the lump in her throat. She looks deep and longingly into Chance's eyes, which shimmer in the moonlight. Chance takes a step back as he ponders what Kata is asking. He remembers what she said earlier in the day before they parted.

He gazes back into her eyes, looking for some hint as to what she is asking and why she would be asking it. It makes him even more nervous being alone with her, away from all the other people. He thinks back on their first conversation and how he implied he got her pregnant and had a family. Did she misunderstand what he was saying and now thinks it's what he expects from her? He just met her. It was too soon to be considering having a family. He admits he finds himself drawn to her and thinks of her quite often, but two days is far too little to get to know someone and decide to start a family. On the other hand, this may also be a way for the tribe to finally accept him as one of them. Still, a family is something he never thought he would have for himself, especially as a Genhance soldier. War and fighting was all he ever knew.

Kata can see the fear in Chance's eyes and his hesitation to answer her question. She wants to break down in tears again, but she knows that will make it harder for them to communicate and there isn't much time.

"Chanz, you famly Reshiara?" she queries with extreme hesitation, hoping for some kind of answer.

Chance nods, even more confused. Now he's wondering if she wants to know which family he wants to be a part of. He doesn't know how to answer and he doesn't want to offend. After all, it was only her, Resha, and Broltrom that treated him like one of their family and not some evil monster. He wonders why she would take him to the edge of the camp at night, away from everyone else, just to ask which family he wants to be a part of?

"Kata, cho whe wundcham.[54] I don't understand."

Kata huffs in frustration. She moves her hair out of her face and paces in a small circle, pondering on what exactly to say. Should she tell him he has a choice whether to take Reshiara as his partner tomorrow or not? Judging by his expression when she asked if he wanted to be with her as a family, he wasn't receptive to the idea. Rather, he seemed frightened by it. How does she tell him what she wants him to know in the time she has? No doubt Reshiara has noticed them missing and is out looking for them. It wouldn't surprise her if the whole tribe is out hunting for him. She doesn't have time to think

---

54 *I don't understand.*

about it but now is all the time she has, and quite possibly, will have before losing him to that girl.

Kata steps in close to Chance and softly wraps her arms around him. She gently rests her head on his chest and squeezes him as tightly as she can. She feels engulfed in his embrace and it fills her with warmth once again. Chance holds her tight and rests his cheek on top of her head. Kata's heart races, beating as hard as she's ever felt it beat before. Her mouth feels dry and a lump builds up in her throat. A fluttering sensation fills her stomach. She feels excited and scared all at once.

She leans her head back and looks into his shimmering eyes. She slowly stands on her toes and with one hand, pulls his face closer to hers until their lips meet. The warmth she once felt now feels like a raging fire instantly spreading through her body. She feels his fingers caress her cheek and slowly move to the back of her neck, while his other hand is on her back, holding her close to him.

For a brief moment, the world stands still and all her sorrows melt away. Finally, she has the love of her life in her arms, returning the affection she has so much desired. For once, she feels like there is no one else, and for once, she feels like he is hers. Deep down though, she knows he isn't. As badly as she wants it, no one else will allow it. Not her mother, not Cultac, and certainly not Reshiara. Tomorrow, he will be Reshiara's, and only Reshiara's.

Kata hates the thought, but is powerless in the end to change it. Her only consolation is this one moment; when he was hers, and only hers, first. No one has the power to take this from her.

As their lips part, it feels like time resumes it's hasty course. Kata feels weak in the knees, and her hands tremble. She wants to stay. She wants this moment to go on, but it makes it harder to give him up. She caresses Chance's face, as she has many times before, and then slips into the dark without another word.

Chance watches her slink away through the shadows back toward the main celebration; too stunned to give chase. His heart pumps faster and he can feel the adrenaline coursing through his body. The kiss was unexpected but not unwanted. Even more unexpected was her sudden departure. Chance replays the kiss over and over in his mind. He wonders if he's supposed to go after her; if that is what she's wanting him to do. He feels so lost and confused and it's hard to think straight. She talked of being a family. If he gives chase, does that mean it's a done deal? Or was this simply a kiss? If he doesn't follow after her, does that mean he loses her?

Unsure of this tribe's courtship rituals, but not wanting to lose her, Chance heads in the direction Kata left. He speeds up, hoping to catch her before she reaches the bonfire.

Her face constantly flashes in his mind and he can still feel her lips against his. He wishes she spoke to him more before running off. He wonders why she was in such a hurry to leave, but more than anything, he wants to continue holding her in his arms.

He feels his stomach tingling and twisting in knots and his knees feel weak and trembling. A cold sweat spreads over his body. He's not sure if it's the poison or something more making him feel this way. This has never happened before. He's not in pain, but it feels more like an intense anxiety, one he can't shake. It's like the feeling he gets before going into battle, only without the fear. It's a feeling he's never felt before and it intensifies every time he thinks of their lips pressed together and their hands caressing each other. It's a feeling he doesn't want to go away and his heart pains him whenever he thinks about not finding her.

He wonders if this is what it's like to have deep feelings for someone. He thought it was too soon to feel this way about someone he just met, but somehow, kissing her changed everything he thought before. It's as if kissing her dismantled all of the CC's brainwashing to suppress emotions and forced his true feelings for her to the surface.

As he races through some tents, he catches a glimpse of fiery-red hair in the light of the nearby fires. He comes to a halt and watches Resha going from group to group looking for him. He's instantly filled with guilt. He watches her for another moment before leaving the shadows to join her. He wants to chase after Kata, but he can't leave Resha frantically searching for him. If she panics, she'll notify the tribe she can't find him and he'll have all their warriors coming after him.

At first, she smiles when she sees him and runs to meet him. She slows down and stops before reaching him. The smile fades and Chance can see the hurt and anger in her eyes. She looks around and notices several people from the nearby groups watching her. She takes Chance by the hand and leads him away from them, back into the shadows.

Once they are out of sight, she lets his hand go and steps away. She turns and looks at him with pain and disappointment on her face. He sees the anguish in her eyes and it pierces him to the core.

"Katalariana?" her voice sounds strained and higher pitched than usual.

Tears well up in her eyes. She stares at him, waiting for an answer. Chance looks at the ground, his mind still muddled from earlier.

"Cho sushu, Resha,[55]" Chance finally manages to mutter, looking up from the ground into her eyes.

He knows a simple sorry isn't enough to make up for hurting her feelings, but he doesn't know what else to say. Realizing that, Reshiara sighs and holds out her hand. Chance takes her hand and they trudge back to the bonfire.

They don't speak another word to each other the rest of the night. After watching the dancers and listening to the music a while longer, they go back to their tents. Chance drops Resha off at her tent, parting ways with a simple, "Good night."

Chance walks in the dark back to his tent. He never saw Kata again at the bonfire, not that he dared look too extensively for fear of Resha's scorn. He felt bad enough without adding further injury. Though he didn't see her again, she was never far from his thoughts. He did feel bad about leaving Resha and running off, but he couldn't help but run the thought of their kiss over and over in his mind. It was his first kiss after all.

He had crushes on girls when he was young, but as a Genhance, or rather, as a child of a Genhance, he wasn't able to pursue a relationship with them. Then, after joining the CC's armed forces, he learned not to feel anything for anybody. It made the job easier when you didn't have to worry about what you were aiming at or when watching your teammates get torn to shreds by the local wildlife. And so, there never was time for girlfriends, or crushes, or any close relationships.

It wasn't until recently that he felt anything again, and then, it was because he grew tired of doing the same thing day in and day out. He was tired of being a robot whose only purpose was to kill and destroy. It was an empty life and he wanted more. It wasn't until tonight he realized what it was he was missing.

---

55 *I'm sorry.*

He can see now how his father was able to give up his career to have a family. For the first time in Chance's life, he seriously considers what it would be like to have a family. As he lay in his bed, staring up at the ceiling of the tent, he thinks about his family and how he wishes they were still around. This is unexplored territory, and he wishes he had his parents to council him. It was all new to him. It's thrilling and fills him with excitement and he's sure his mother would be thrilled for him as well. He finds himself eager for morning to arrive so he can find Kata and be with her again. She is all he can think about until sleep finally overcomes him.

While Chance is thrilled at his future prospects, Kata sits alone on her bed dreading hers. She raced home as fast as she could, worried Chance would try and follow her. If he had managed to catch up to her, it would have made it harder to let him go. It was hard enough to leave after their kiss.

Thinking about the kiss causes her feelings to stir again. She feels the rush of adrenaline going through her body and she can't help but smile as she fantasizes being with him again. She wonders why she was so quick to leave him when she finally had the chance to plead her case, especially when it was clear he also has feelings for her.

While disputing with herself over whether she made the right choice to leave Chance or not, Reshiara enters the room. She stands menacingly over Kata, glaring at her with intense fury. Kata looks up at her and then turns away when she realizes who it is. "I don't want to talk now, Reshiara," Kata states in a tone reflecting her lack of interest in the girl.

"You don't need to talk, Katalariana. You need to listen. I know you were with Hewold. I know it was you that took him from the celebration. You told me you only wanted for him to be happy and well, that you were only acting as a healer, but now I see that is a lie. You are trying to take him from me."

"No," Kata tries interrupting.

"Don't speak! I will not let you destroy him. He is all the family I have in this world. You have family. You have someone to be your partner. I do not. I have been alone most of my life. I will not let you get between me and my chance at a family. If I discover you with him again, I will go to the council and tell them you are with another chosen man. Then your family and your home will be taken from you and you will be dishonored. Not even the daughter of our former Eldest or the chosen of the future Eldest can escape punishment."

"They will destroy him as well. You would risk losing him?" Kata tries calling her bluff.

"I will explain he does not know our ways and that it was you who led him astray. They will see reason in this. I will make them see reason. I will see that you are the only one that suffers."

With her final threat, Reshiara goes to her bed and hides completely under the covers, with strands of her long, red hair flowing from underneath. Kata rolls over and stares at the wall until sleep overtakes her. She falls asleep with the consolation she was with him first, before Reshiara was even in the picture, and for one passionate moment, though brief, she was his and he was hers.

◄20►

Chance wakes with a start. A loud horn blows several times in quick succession. He sits up and listens. He can't hear anything indicating there is an emergency, but the horn was different and more urgent sounding than at other times. He throws back the door flap and steps outside. A chill hits his exposed skin sending shivers over his body, chasing away any sleepiness he still had.

The sun is still low on the horizon and shines in Chance's eyes as he tries scanning the nearby group of tents for activity. Men emerge from their tents, weapons in hand, and run in the direction of the elder's tents. Chance grabs his knife from inside the tent and runs to join them. He knows the signs of an impending battle all too well.

Chance arrives before many of the other men as they gather in front of the elders. The effects of last night's festivities still linger with many of them as they stumble, half asleep and half drunk, into the growing crowd. Those sober enough to recognize Chance are shocked to find him among their ranks. Many greet him with awkward stares and uneasy smiles. As he watches the growing army, he feels a hand grip his shoulder along with a familiar greeting. "Chazhewold! Bemelen bruk.[56]"

"Good morning! Bemelen bruk, Broltrom," Chance greets in return, facing his new friend. "What's going on? Tro?[57]"

56 *Good morning.*
57 *What [is happening]?*

Broltrom points toward a pillar of thick, black smoke rising in the distance. Chance feels a little silly for not noticing it
earlier. Usually he was more observant, especially when danger
was imminent. Chance tries asking if Broltrom knows what it
is, to which he shakes his head.

The elders approach from their tent and address the
gathered warriors. "As many have seen, fires burn close to our
home. Some claim to have heard thunder shortly before the
smoke appeared. The skies are clear and we fear the thunder
comes from something else. There are those who fear the blue
demons approach."

"Do you not see?" interrupts Cultac as he emerges at
the front of the group. "It is reason to believe they come for
the blue demon we keep among us. It was not reason that he
should have lived, and now he brings death upon us!"

The crowd turns to face Chance, many tightly gripping
their weapons. Chance preemptively raises his hands in front
of him and waits for the spears to be pointed in his face at any
moment. He didn't have to understand all of what was said to
see what's in everyone's eyes.

Broltrom jumps between Chance and the frightened
warriors. "I do not see the reason in this. Chazhewold knows
nothing of the fires and joins with us to add his strength. It is
reason to believe if the demons are coming, he would not be
here as one of us, but finding a way to join his kind."

"The demons are cunning. He would have us go to our
deaths while he remains and attacks when our warriors are few
and all that is left are our women and children. He will bring
the fires here!" Cultac incites.

"Do not let fear taint your reason," Broltrom pleads.

Broltrom grabs Chance's hand and runs his blade across

it. He holds it up for all to see as blood runs from the cut. "Do you not see that he bleeds as we do? Let us take him to the flames to prove his intent. If he does not join his strength with ours, I will spill his blood again. I hope the council will see reason in this."

The elders deliberate among themselves, but before Cultac can protest further, Shumakra emerges behind him and pulls him aside. "Future Eldest, I advise you to bide your time. Let the demon join you, and when he shows his true form, strike him down along with those closest to him. The council will have no power to question you afterward, and we will finally be rid of the demon. If you act now, you risk angering those tainted by the demon's influence. You must first release them from his control before you can control them," she slyly whispers.

"I see the reason in your words, wise Shumakra. I will do as you say and rid our people of those with weak minds and easily swayed by this demon's power. I will make our people strong once more," Cultac concedes.

Shumakra interrupts the elders and advises them to heed Broltrom's words. Cultac nods submissively and the council agrees to allow Chance to accompany the party. They assign the most able and sober warriors to join Cultac and Broltrom and bid them a safe journey.

Normally, Chance wouldn't allow just anyone to cut him with a blade, but he trusts Broltrom. Although, now that he's being led by Broltrom and several other armed warriors toward the edge of camp, he wonders. He could understand enough of the conversation to know it was about the devils and that's what they think the smoke is from. Is he being led to his execution before the other devils arrive?

Broltrom sees the concern in Chance's eyes and pats him on the shoulder to console him. "Whe chu morshi, Chazhewold. Jurcto jouem shum gardhrallim.[58]"

"We go as brothers. Jurcto jouem shum gardhrallim. Thank you. Cho loshome chu. And I'm not worried. Cho whe morshi,[59]" Chance assures him, while deep down knowing not everyone in the party feels the same.

"Cho sushu fo chu yumin,[60]" Broltrom apologizes as he grabs Chance's hand to check the wound he made.

Chance fails to pull his hand away before Broltrom sees the wound has healed. Broltrom pulls his hand closer to inspect it, bewildered that all that remains of the cut is some drying blood. He looks questioningly at first, then his expression changes into one of amazement. He pulls Chance close so they walk shoulder to shoulder. He pats Chance on the chest and whispers in his ear. "Whe chu morshi, Chazhewold. Cho whe dajir,[61]" Broltrom reassures with a smile.

Broltrom may have promised to keep his rapid healing a secret, but Chance worries others will find out. It'll be hard to explain his ability without coming off as a supernatural being. He's grateful Broltrom is so accepting of it, but he's only one in a minority of people that tolerates him and is so understanding.

They travel for nearly two hours toward the pillar of smoke. Some of the warriors riding cleridracs ran ahead when the trip began to scout the area. They've returned claiming there are no living demons, but there are signs of them nearby. They increase their speed and enter some thick woods before arriving

---

58 *Don't (you) worry. We go together as brothers.*
59 *We go together as brothers. I thank you. I'm not worried.*
60 *I'm sorry for your hand.*
61 *Don't you worry. I won't tell.*

at some wreckage deep within. Cultac and the other warriors urge Chance to approach first while they remain close behind.

Chance examines the wreckage and sees the CC's logo emblazoned on the crumpled armor plating of the fallen reconnaissance airship. Broken arrow shafts protrude from the hull. Thick, black smoke billows from one of the engines. The cockpit is smashed open and the charred remains of one of the pilots hangs out. The other seat is empty, but the safety harness has been cut loose. In the loose dirt immediately around the crash site there are traces of boot prints leaving the area.

Several of the warriors slowly approach the wreckage with their weapons at the ready. They've never seen anything like it. Cultac steps up behind Chance, keeping a close eye on him and asks if it's a gate to bring more demons.

Chance casts a sly glance at him. "It's...a bird."

He puts his hands together and mimics wings flapping. Cultac scoffs and the other warriors laugh, incredulous that something so big and heavy could actually fly. The warriors investigate the ship to figure out what it is, but Cultac keeps a close watch on Chance, following his movements and spots the tracks as well. He turns to the others and quietly signals for them to search the area. Within seconds, the warriors dash into the woods in search of the survivor. Cultac examines the prints and follows them into the woods, leaving Chance by himself.

Chance creeps in the direction the prints are heading but stops a short ways from the downed aircraft. He crouches down and listens. He can hear the faint sounds of the warriors searching the nearby area. He closes his eyes and focuses even more. He picks up the sound of rustling leaves and something rubbing against the bark of a nearby tree. He sneaks to the base of the tree and looks up. He can see the tattered uniform of a CC pilot among the branches above. "Come down here," Chance orders. "I'm not here to hurt you."

He hears a nervous chuckle as the pilot makes his way down. "Ah, you're one of us! Thank goodness. I thought I was dead for sure," the pilot exclaims in relief.

As soon as he sets foot on the ground, he looks Chance up and down, barely containing a laugh. "What's with the get up? Someone steal your uniform when you weren't looking? How'd you get out here so far?" he questions mockingly.

Upon closer examination, he recognizes Chance. "It's you! But... Wait... You...you were supposed to have died. I watched the vids. We all saw you get blown to pieces. No it can't be. You must be one of them. But how? I thought..." the pilot's voice trails as he tries to wrap his mind around Chance's sudden appearance.

"What are you talking about? What vids? How did you get videos? And one of who? What are you saying? You aren't making sense. And try to keep your voice down. There are still people out here hunting for you," Chance warns, curious about the pilot's ramblings.

"The vids? They had a drone watching your fight. That was an impressive amount of destruction you guys caused, until you blew yourselves to pieces. But watching you in particular was something special. I never seen anyone move like you do. Too bad you didn't bother wiping out all those savages. You might not have gotten yourself killed so quick."

"A drone? All our drones were taken out before we arrived. We lost contact with Home Office early on and were unaware of other drones in the area."

"Lost contact?" the pilot smirks and shakes his head. "You had no idea, did you, man? You were a liability, man! You all were. Surely you noticed all the dropouts and rejects in your team. They were just taking out the garbage, as it were. And you especially. I only heard rumors, course, but word spread you were going soft; losing your killer instinct. You were starting to stir the pot, and you of all people know they don't take kindly to that. They figured if anyone survived, they earned the right to rejoin our ranks."

Chance clenches his fists. His blood starts to boil again. It was as he suspected. They didn't count on him surviving. "They caught everything on camera," the pilot continues. "They wanted to see what you would do. Sorry to say that you disappointed them. They really hoped you would shine, even against the odds, but you turned on your own and wasted time taking weapons away instead of winning the fight. I do have to say though, I'm impressed you survived. I just can't get out of my mind watching your body flying through the air like some ragdoll. It was like watching some air gymnastics. It was wicked, man!"

"My objective was to find a way to end the fighting peacefully. We were fighting two different tribes. We weren't even their intended targets. We got caught in the middle of a tribal war. If we could have shown them we were friendlies, it may have been our ticket in," Chance tries to explain.

"Man, it doesn't take a genius to see that was the perfect opportunity to wipe them out. Keep a few alive in the end as prisoners to get the information we need. I heard you were smarter and more experienced than that. We don't have time to play nice with these people, man," the pilot mocks.

"How do you know all this? What are you doing out here anyway?" Chance asks, tired of being mocked over his tactical prowess, or lack of it in the last battle.

"You really were out of the loop, weren't you? We're a pretty tight group back at base. We all know what's going on. Things are getting pretty serious, man. Our resources are spread thin trying to cover three planets, and our forces have dwindled with all the losses on this planet. It's been difficult getting a good foothold here, and what's more, this place has the metal the CC needs to ensure our claim here."

"What do you mean? The CC has footholds on several planets. What's one planet? If they're losing so much, why not pull out? If they're spread so thin, why are they so willing to throw away the lives of their soldiers? I don't understand why this stuff is so important; why it's worth all the effort. Are they so obsessed with becoming the most powerful force in the universe that they're willing to risk it all?" Chance asks impatiently.

"Wow. You really don't have any idea, do you? Where have you been, man? I figured everyone knew by now. The UWO, man! The UWO are coming. We've lost contact from several of our outlying colonies. We received reports that UWO was on their way before losing contact with them. They're coming for us, and we need to be prepared. Who knows how long before they show up here. They're obviously strong enough to wipe out several of our colonized worlds, and reports continue to come in that they're still on their way.

In case you didn't notice, the Mayflower ain't doing too good. It's practically on it's last leg, man. Our resources are practically depleted, and we don't have the manpower to keep throwing at the enemy. We can't afford the losses. They got rid of you and the others because they couldn't risk you reaching out to the enemy. They didn't want any weak links in our defense. Besides, they couldn't allow a group of savages that large to get so close to our base. We could have ended up losing far more than you guys.

As you can see, we can't keep running. There is nowhere for us to go now. We're going to have to make our last stand here, unless we can get that metal stuff, beat the UWO with it, and take their resources. Until then, we need a place to call home, and this is as close as we are going to get, man. You were meant to be the ace up our sleeve until you started going sideways. The admins were really hoping they could count on you. I'm surprised you didn't know any of this. Now more than ever, we need that metal to give us the edge."

"That stuff isn't going to be very useful to the CC," Chance divulges.

"What are you talking about, man?"

"It isn't going to be as helpful as they're hoping. It's not what they think."

"What are you talking about? Have you seen what that stuff can do? In the right hands, we'll be unstoppable. Could you imagine our troops armed with that stuff? What are you talking about; it isn't useful?"

"It isn't metal. It isn't something you can just dig up and forge into weapons and armor. It's bone!" Chance tries explaining.

"What? You've got to be joking, right? You're messing with me, man. You seen my ship? You telling me that some bones did that? I don't think so, man," the pilot shakes his head incredulously.

"That's what I'm saying. It bones from a fish..."

"Fish bones! Now I know you're messing with me, man," the pilot interrupts.

"I've seen it made," Chance draws his knife. "It's bone that's been tempered. That's why I'm telling you, the CC won't be able to use it like they hope."

"Aw, man! This isn't good at all. We need to notify the CC as soon as we can. I assume you can get us out of here safely?"

"I'm not leaving. I'm still..."

"What do you mean you're not leaving? What's your deal, man? We don't have time for this. Let's go," the pilot urges in a frustrated tone.

"I told you my mission was to get intel on these people; to find out all I can about them to end the fight with them permanently. If what you say is true, we'll need their help," Chance rationalizes.

"Intel? Don't you think you got enough intel? You told me plenty. And look at ya, man! You seem to have taken the job a little too seriously. I doubt they intended for you to become one of them."

"They didn't intend a whole lot of anything for me, it seems," Chance interrupts.

"Listen. Your personal issues aside, we still need to let them know the metal stuff isn't going to work. They can still move forward with their other plans. It's vital to all our survival. It's more important than you getting all chummy with these savages, man."

"What other plans? What are they planning to do?" Chance asks quietly.

The pilot sighs in frustration. "Come on, man! We don't have time for this!"

"What plans?" Chance sternly asks again.

"What do you mean what plan? The plan with all you guys."

Chance looks at him in confusion. "What guys? My team was wiped out, you said."

"No, not them. You know. You guys. The other ones of you, man."

"Genhance? I wasn't aware that the CC had any other Genhance in service on Eshiron. What are they doing with them?" Chance presses further.

The pilot looks dumbfounded with Chance's lack of

knowledge and shakes his head. "I heard they were part of a classified program but I thought at least you would have known about them. I guess not. Knowing what you're capable of and seeing how much damage your team caused in your last fight, the CC assembled a kill team with four of you to go around and wipe out potential threats. They're going to start off by clearing out the closest threats and spread outward, clearing more territory for more dropships to move in and set up more base camps. Hopefully, we'll be able to set up several defensive outposts before the UWO arrives. By then, the kill team will be battle-hardened killing machines capable of carrying out offensives against the UWO forces. My mission was to scout out the area for the largest concentrations of enemy encampments so they would know where to hit hardest. Unfortunately, I got shot down by a bunch of them hiding in some trees a few miles from here. We tried flying back until we lost our engine and crashed here, man. So as you can see, since I lost my co-pilot, it's imperative I make it back. So if we're done here, let's get going, man."

"I can't leave. Not yet. I suggest you stick around as well. They'll hunt and kill us if we leave," Chance tries persuading, hoping he can get back to warn the Cleridracs of the kill team.

"I don't believe this, man. I'm not staying. Haven't you heard a word I've said, man? Don't you care, man?" the pilot asks, growing more irritated by the second. "We've got more than our lives at stake here. Everyone back home on the Mayflower is counting on this information as well. They expect us to complete our mission."

Chance contemplates his next move. With everything he's heard, it's hard not to want to go back just to spite the CC and let them have a piece of his mind. On the other hand, when the pilot mentioned going back home, his mind went to the camp with Resha, Broltrom, and Kata. He no longer feels the CC is his home. It didn't feel like home for years. Despite the animosity some of the people have toward him, there are those among the Cleridrac that feel like family; like when he had family.

"They will kill you if they find you. You're better off coming back with me. Maybe then we can figure out a way for you to get back," Chance proposes.

"Unbelievable! I don't get you, man. I told you, I can't stay. The kill team is on the move. They need the intel I have. You need to decide whose side you're on, man. Where do your loyalties lie? Just be warned, no mercy will be shown to you if you stay. They'll cut you down like the rest of the filth you're playing dress up with. They're ignorant cavemen with no redeeming qualities. We've evolved past this. You just think about that when you're playing house with them and we come busting down your door."

The pilot looks at Chance in disgust, shakes his head, and scampers off into the underbrush. Chance stays crouched against the tree for a moment, thinking about everything he's discovered. The CC's actions solidified Chance's sentiments toward them. How could they be so reckless? It made more sense to enlist the help of locals to carry out an effective campaign against the UWO; but once again, they didn't want to invest the time and effort to do things the right way from the beginning. Their refusal to see the bigger picture was going to be their ruin, and Chance is worried no one is going to be spared the consequences, no matter the side they are on now.

Chance goes back to the wreckage with the hopes of finding some useful supplies to take back to camp. Unfortunately, the fire and subsequent explosions caused during the crash destroyed most everything.

While searching the wreckage, Chance hears screaming coming from deeper in the woods. It isn't long before the warriors emerge from the woods dragging the pilot with them. Cultac walks close behind them, seeming proud of himself as they walk directly toward Chance. The warriors dragging the pilot drop him a few paces from Chance and step aside. The man was shot in the back with an arrow and they also cut his legs to ensure he can't run away.

The pilot lifts himself on his elbows and sees Chance in front of him. He pleads with tears streaming down his face. "Please help me!" he sobs. "Help me, man. Please! Don't let them kill me. I'm sorry, man. I'm sorry. You gotta help me, man."

Cultac steps over the pilot and lifts him onto his knees by his hair. The pilot wails while trying to pry Cultac's fingers loose. Cultac looks spitefully at Chance, waiting to see what he might do. Tired of the screams and the struggle, Cultac draws his knife and runs it across the man's neck, replacing the screams with gurgling. Never taking his eyes off of Chance's, he continues working his blade into the man's neck, taking his head completely off. He lets the body fall forward and tosses the head at Chance's feet. With the blood on his hand, he draws a symbol on his chest, then, with arms outstretched, he spins for all to see. "Zherulk Dozhkar![62]" he yells, casting a sly glance toward Chance.

Chance feels a familiar hand on his shoulder. "Jouem, Chazhewold,[63]" Broltrom insists.

Having just arrived after hearing the screams, he doesn't want to linger and directs Chance toward home. He has no interest in celebrating merciless bloodshed. Cultac continues to

---

62 *Demon Killer or Demon Slayer*
63 *Let's go.*

boast as the other warriors gather around him. "Their attempt to infect our land has failed. I have stopped their invasion. I am Demon Killer!"

Seeing Chance and Broltrom are leaving, he halts his boasting and signals for the others to follow. He doesn't want to let the demon out of his sight and miss any opportunity to destroy him

Afflicted by the gruesome scene, Chance walks slowly through the woods. He had long been desensitized to seeing his people be violently killed during his years in the CC special services, but this was the first time he voluntarily allowed it to happen. He knew by helping the pilot, he would be giving the warriors a reason to strike against him. Deeper than that, though, it felt like he was making the choice between the CC and Eshiron. It would have been an easy feat to kill the warriors, save the pilot, and return to the CC; but what would he be returning to? The CC had already written him off once. How long before they would have done it again? Perhaps it's for the best that he jumped ship. One thing is for sure; he isn't going back. He can't bring himself to go back.

Trudging through the woods, he stops when he hears movement nearby. He checks on the warriors walking nearby, but no one else seems to have heard the sounds. A low rumbling noise grows steadily louder as a large overcast shadow envelops him from behind. Chance slowly looks upward and his eyes meet two shimmering, red eyes glaring back at him from a towering, dark silhouette. The rumbling sound turns into a growl and Chance rolls out of the way right as four large fists smash the ground, sending dirt and debris in all directions.

"Gruthraller!" yells one of the nearby warriors, alerting everyone of the danger.

Broltrom turns around as the other warriors run past him away from the danger. He sees Chance on the ground in front of the gruthraller. "Liet,[64] Chaz! Liet!" Broltrom screams, signaling for him to run away with the others.

Chance hops to his feet to run but gets slammed in the chest, sending him hurling through the air, crashing into a tree and falling hard to the ground. His lungs burn as he gasps for air. He's sure some of his ribs are broken and the taste of blood fills his mouth. He looks up and sees Cultac nearby paralyzed with fear. Cultac looks from the gruthraller down to Chance and then back at the gruthraller. Coming to his senses for a brief moment when he notices Chance wounded on the ground, he knows it's his opportunity to finally be rid of the demon. He takes a quick step toward Chance with his spear in hand, but changes his mind when the monster bears down on their position. He, instead, turns and runs, leaving Chance as bait to allow them all to escape.

As Cultac sprints away from the area, he catches the eye of the gruthraller and it gives chase. Panicked, Cultac yells for the others to save him. No one heeds his calls, knowing it would mean death to face such a large, rampaging beast.

The gruthraller runs past Chance, tearing it's way through the foliage in a frenzy as it closes the distance to Cultac. Recovering just enough, Chance gets up and races toward the monster. The gruthraller stands over ten feet tall and is several hundred pounds of pure muscle covered in black fur. To Chance, it looks like an overgrown gorilla with four arms, glowing red eyes, and a taste for blood.

He catches up to the beast and uses his blade to slice into the back of its leg, hoping to cut the ligaments and slow it

---

64 *Run!*

down. In one swift motion, he swings around the side and runs the blade across the beast's neck as it stumbles forward.

Cultac pauses long enough to see Chance has stopped the gruthraller from pursuing him, but continues fleeing with the other warriors. Chance holds his ground and watches as the gruthraller picks itself up off the ground and thrashes about, flinging rocks and large branches in random directions. After its brief tantrum, it focuses on Chance and slams on the ground with concussive force, letting out a deafening roar. It slowly circles, using its arms to help it walk. Chance's blade was sharp enough to disable one of the legs, but not enough to cause more than a superficial wound on its neck. It's going to take more than his knife to get through the thick musculature of this animal. It's easy to see why the others ran even when equipped with spears and arrows.

The beast rushes Chance, and in turn, Chance charges the beast, gripping his knife tight, positioned to strike deep. Before they meet, the beast raises it's fists to attack and Chance leaps into the air, plunging his blade into the gruthraller's exposed throat. The force of Chance's strike causes the gruthraller to spin and fall onto its side, sparing Chance from being crushed under its weight.

Mortally wounded but still not ready to give up the fight, the beast grabs Chance with two of it's clawed hands and squeezes. Chance can feel the burning in his chest as the beast's claws pierce his skin and the air is squeezed from his lungs. The gruthraller tries getting up using it's other two arms while struggling for breath. With his free hand, Chance grabs his blade still embedded in the beast's neck and jerks it out. Before the gruthraller rips him in half, he drives the knife through the beast's eye. It's head whips back as it's body falls into a limp heap. It groans as the last breaths of air escape it's lungs, then all is quiet and still.

Chance picks himself up off the ground and sits atop the fallen beast and reclaims his knife. He takes a moment to catch his breath and let his body heal. He takes a deep breath and looks up at the sky through the treetops. He hears footsteps approaching slowly from the woods.

"Chazhewold?" a familiar voice breaks the silence.

Broltrom sits down next to Chance, looking over his handiwork. He pats Chance on the back and laughs. "Chu heb silme we Doman, Ruc Aerulk.[65]"

Chance smiles back. It's the first time he's been called Blue Angel, or that he came from God, but it explains why Broltrom is so friendly when others are not.

Broltrom dips his fingers in the gruthraller's blood and paints a symbol on Chance's shoulder. Chance looks at him to ask the purpose of it, but Broltrom smiles and signals for him to lead the way back to camp.

When they exit the woods, they are met by the other warriors of their party. They're surprised to see Chance still in one piece. Broltrom sees their shock and steps up beside Chance. He pats Chance's chest and points to the blood symbol. "Gruthraller Dozhkar![66]" he proudly announces.

Chance recognizes the term is similar to one used by Cultac when he killed the pilot. It appears the symbols represent their kills and then they take the title of whatever trophy they've claimed.

Being known as Gruthraller Killer instead of Blue Devil would be a welcome change, especially if it helps change the peoples opinion of him.

---

65 *You must come from God, Blue Angel.*
66 *Gruthraller Killer or Gruthraller Slayer*

The other warriors cheer, acknowledging Chance's victory, all except Cultac. Cultac grits his teeth in disgust and leaves the party, making his way back to camp. He failed in his plans to turn the others against the demon, and not only that, but the demon managed to save them from a large threat, earning him even more renown. It'll be harder to discredit the demon and get rid of him if the people start to respect and trust him.

Broltrom informs the cleridrac riders of the gruthraller's location and they run back to retrieve the animal to bring home. With the riders taking care of the animal, Broltrom hurries the rest to get back to camp. Chance is curious why Broltrom is in such a hurry to get back, but he'll be glad to get home and rest.

As they march home, the others start to include him in their conversations. Most of the conversations currently consist of retelling their side of the gruthraller attack and poking fun at those who were quickest to run away. The more immersed in their language listening to their stories, the more he picks up and understands. Chance feels like he's finally making headway into ending the conflict between these people and the misconceived, Blue Demons.

❖21❖

When the group reaches the camp, they are met by a throng of people who cheer them on and usher them through the camp. Chance is last in the line and watches as large groups of people flock around the men, eager for news on the demon threat. They celebrate after hearing the threat was resolved and the lone demon was eliminated. Chance knows the danger is still yet to come, but he lets them have their moment to celebrate.

Resha pushes her way through and joins Chance, leaping into his chest and wrapping her arms tightly around him. Unlike last night, her face is once again beaming with excitement and happy to have him back in one piece. After squeezing him tight, she steps back and looks at him from head to toe. His appearance is disheveled and he's covered in blood and dirt. All the other men returned looking in as good a condition as when they left. She becomes visibly upset but tries hiding her disappointment with a forced smile. Resha looks at Chance's shoulder and at the large symbol painted with blood marking his kill. "Hewold, chu dozhka li gruthraller?[67]" she asks, bewildered he could possibly have been the only one responsible for killing the gruthraller.

Resha checks over Chance's body, looking for any wounds, surprised there aren't any. She becomes more upset, feeling like

---

67 *You killed the gruthraller?*

Chance was the object of a cruel joke. She grabs a nearby warrior and asks him what happened. As he explains, the cleridrac riders return, dragging the massive gruthraller on a makeshift wooden frame behind them. The cleridrac squawk and shift uneasily under the tremendous weight.

The large group of celebrating people surround the massive beast and are astonished to see such a large specimen. Broltrom pushes his way through the crowd to stand next to the body and points to Chance, yelling for all to hear who Gruthraller Dozhkar was and how he saved the rest of the war party from decimation. The people flock around Chance, all cheering in unison, praising him as a great warrior and hunter. Even Resha, though still disappointed he risked his life in such a reckless, yet selfless act, joins in celebrating his accomplishment. With a smile, she slips her hand into his hand and ushers him toward the council tents while the crowd continues in their raucous celebration.

They arrive near the council tents where the bonfire has been reset and in full roaring splendor. The round table is set with assorted foods once again piled high. Around the exterior of the table, several young men already sit, feasting on the bounty before them, engaged in conversation and storytelling. Resha leaves Chance at an empty spot at the table and races off, giving him one last, big smile as she slowly slides her hand from his.

The other men fall silent and watch as Chance takes his seat. He feels slightly out of place, wishing he was more presentable before joining the party. He wonders if this was a feast for the warriors who just returned, but looking around at the faces watching him, there are none he recognizes. For a brief moment, they all stare at each other in awkward silence. One of the elders sitting nearby invites Chance to partake of the food. Chance nods and thanks him, grabbing from the food closest to him. Conversations soon begin again and more people arrive until the festivities are as they were the night before.

Chance tries to engage in conversation with the others, but they seem more awkward and uncomfortable about it than he is. He's seen Broltrom a few times, but he's more interested in telling others the story about the Gruthraller Dozhkar than actually talking to him. More than anything though, he wishes Kata were here. He's noticed the empty space at the table where she and her mother sat the night before. Although a lot happened during the day, she was never far from his thoughts. He thinks of the night before and their kiss. The same feelings from the night before wells up inside and his heart races again. He needs to see her again. It's to the point where he can't contain the thought of it anymore. He needs to take action before he ends up losing her for good.

The closer it gets to sundown, the more the area looks like it did the night before. Large numbers of people have arrived and gathered around the bonfire into their familial groups to celebrate. The bonfire's flames burn high and the musicians have started playing music while dancers take up position around the fire. With the party in full swing and thinking no one would miss him, Chance steals away from the activity and makes his way to Kata's tent.

He avoids groups of people as much as possible and tries to act natural; as natural as a pale skinned man classified as a demon, from space, living among an indigenous tribe, wearing nothing but a leather vest and skirt, and covered in blood and mud, can. Most people are too consumed in their conversations and dancing to notice him walking around camp.

When he arrives at the large, Eldest's tent, he quietly calls out Kata's name. Chance waits by the door and nervously glances around for passersby. When he doesn't hear anything, he calls again a little louder. The door flap swings aside and Kata emerges, surprised to see Chance at her door. "Chanz? Tro chu gulbha pri?[68]"

He steps up to her, looking deep into her violet eyes and caresses her bare arms. "Kata! Kata, cho alret hulne chu. Cho alret vipav chu.[69] I need to speak to you. I need to see you."

"No, Chanz! You, no," she pulls away, shaking her head. "You, them. Chu alret joue.[70]"

She tells Chance to leave, pointing to the celebration raging on nearby. She steps further away from him, not wanting to look him in the eye. As much as him being here fulfills her every desire, she knows it's too late for them. She hoped leaving him last night would have let him know that. It breaks her heart to see him calling on her and having to send him back to that girl who took him from her.

"Cho whe wundcham. I don't understand, Kata. Last night...li pruk...[71]" Chance stutters, trying to remember the right words for what he wants to say.

"Cho sushu, Chanz,[72]" Kata interrupts, realizing how hard this must be for him.

She looks away, fighting back the tears that always seem to be on the verge of flowing. Not wanting to drag this goodbye on any longer, she steps toward her door. "Cho sushu. I soary."

"Kata, losheer. Please, talk to me. Chu hulne cho. I want to understand. Cho nano wundcham.[73]"

Chance grabs her hand as she steps closer toward the door

---

68 *What are you doing here?*
69 *I need to speak to you. I need to see you.*
70 *You need to go.*
71 *I don't understand...the night...*
72 *I'm sorry.*
73 *Please, talk to me. I want to understand.*

and gently pulls her toward him. He lifts her chin to look her in the eye and sees the tears welling up. "Cho sushu, Kata. I'm sorry," he whispers as he wraps her in his embrace.

It breaks his heart to see her cry, and though he doesn't understand what's going on, he doesn't have it in him to walk away and leave her like this. As he holds her, a warmth spreads through his body and he feels weightless. Even in a strange place, with people he doesn't know, he feels like he's home when he's with her. Holding her now makes everything else melt away and he wonders if she feels the same.

Kata gives in to his embrace and lays her head on his chest. She smiles thinking of him pulling her into his arms. The tears she fought so hard to keep inside now roll freely down her cheeks. She feels protected and safe in his arms, just as she expected she would. As good as it feels, she reminds herself of the dangers inherent with being seen embracing someone already given to another, and slowly pulls herself away from him. Wiping away the tears, she looks up at him and smiles, letting him know she is alright. Looking into his face, she notices the dirt and blood marring his face and body. Her training as a healer kicks in and she looks his body over for injuries.

"Chanz, tro guldra chu?[74]" she asks while trying to wipe his face clean.

"What happened? Oh, I killed a gruthraller. Cho dozhka um gruthraller,[75]" he says with a smile.

Kata chuckles incredulously, waiting for him to tell her what really happened. When she sees he's being truthful, she inspects him more thoroughly for any wounds. Chance laughs as she lifts his arms and has him turning around while she looks him over. She runs over to some pitchers nearby and fills

---

74 *What happened to you?*
75 *I killed a gruthraller.*

a bowl with water. Grabbing a cloth, she returns to Chance and cleans the mud and blood off to get a better assessment of any injuries. He reassures her he is alright and waves for her to stop worrying. She stops searching and their eyes lock onto each other's gaze. She reaches up and moves a strand of hair from his forehead and caresses his face. He leans his head into her hand. Everything in them yearns to be closer to one another. Chance steps closer and leans in to kiss her.

"Ruc Zherulk!"

Chance whips his head around to see Cultac approaching. He clears his throat and slowly turns to face Cultac. Kata steps back and to the side of Chance. Seeing Katalariana with the demon, Cultac's brow furrows and he speeds toward the pair. Kata steps in front of Chance to intercept him. "Cultac, what's wrong?" she asks, knowing the answer but hoping to distract him.

"Katalariana, go inside. I will rid us of this demon!"

"No, you can't kill him. He has done nothing wrong," she pleads, trying to hold Cultac back.

"You know our laws. He belongs to another and I find him here with you. He must be punished. I cannot allow this filth to spread his taint through our home by forcing himself onto our women, especially the Eldest's chosen partner," Cultac threatens, trying to push past the young woman.

Chance readies himself, wondering whether to step in and help Kata, prepare to defend himself, or avoid the conflict and the ensuing consequences by running. Not wanting to abandon Kata to Cultac's tantrum, he stands his ground, ready to jump in if things get physical between Kata and Cultac.

"Cultac, stop! You are not the Eldest, and I am not your

chosen partner. This man has done nothing to me, and is innocent of any wrongdoing," Kata yells.

She pushes Cultac back with as much strength as she can muster. Cultac scowls at Kata, angry at her words, but he doesn't want to turn his attention away from the object of his true contempt. He stops trying to push Kata aside and paces back and forth like an angry gruthraller in front of her, as if blocked by some invisible wall keeping him from tearing his target apart. "Then why is he here and not at the rite of union?"

Kata looks back at Chance and then at the furious warrior in front of her. "He," she pauses, looking for a reasonable excuse. "He came to me as his healer. He did fight a gruthraller and I was tending to his wounds."

Placated for the moment, Cultac stops pacing. He struts over to Chance, puffing his chest out and stands face to face with him. "Cho Ruc Zherulk Dozhkar,[76]" he declares as a warning he has no problem killing demons by referring to himself as Blue Demon Killer.

Chance smiles facetiously. He holds his hand up with his thumb and forefinger extended with a small gap between them. "Zherulk chue miza.[77] They're small," he taunts, and then extends his arms out wide. "Gruthraller chue mozha. They're very big. Cho Gruthraller Dozhkar.[78] I'm Gruthraller Killer."

Cultac bares his clenched teeth and balls up his fists. "Cultac," Kata interrupts. "He needs to get back."

"Then I will see to it he gets there," Cultac grumbles.

He backs away from Chance and signals for him to leave. Chance smirks and walks toward the bonfire. "Good night, Katalariana," he says fondly.

---

76 *I am Blue Demon Killer.*
77 *Demon's are small.*
78 *Gruthraller are big. I'm Gruthraller Killer.*

"Goot ebeneen, Chanz," she responds in a forlorn tone.

She watches Chance walk away, escorted by a bitter Cultac. Every part of her screams to chase after him and beg him to take her away from here; somewhere far where her mother, Cultac, and Reshiara can't stop them. She slowly enters her tent once Chance is out of sight and falls to her knees on her bed, sobbing uncontrollably. How could life be so cruel as to keep her from the one thing she longs for? She finds the token for the partnership rites among her bedding and picks it up. She rubs the surface with her fingers, wishing the outcome was different and that she wasn't denied her place. She flings it across the tent with a scream of frustration and collapses on her bed. She pulls the furs over her and tries to sleep, not wanting to think about her situation or what's about to happen tonight.

Chance returns to the table as the last gleams of sunlight fade behind the distant peaks on the horizon. Cultac takes his place by the elders near the table, keeping an eye on Chance. As Chance expected, no one, other than Cultac, seemed to notice he left. He sits and partially listens to one of the leaders who has since stood and addresses the group. He can understand portions of what's said, but he's too distracted to follow everything, and his mind soon wanders.

He thinks about Kata, wishing she was here, or that he was still there with her. He's disappointed his time with her was once again interrupted. Now that he has a babysitter, he won't be able to sneak away to see her again so easily. Being watched reminds him of Resha and he wonders where she has been this whole time. It's not like her to leave him alone so long. At least he would have someone to talk to.

After trying to listen to the speaker again, he remembers being in mission briefings that seemed to go on and on; much the same way this speech is going. His missions were always about protecting the colonies or clearing out animal dens. It never made sense why the mission briefings were so long. He laughs to himself thinking about how the assistant managers and department managers liked hearing their own voices. It somehow made them feel more important to stand in front of a captive audience and go on and on about nothing useful or relevant, as if he had any interest in the CC's bottom line and profit margins. All he needed to know was where his target was and how long he had to find and destroy it. Nothing else mattered to him. Not that he had much in his life that mattered. No family or friends anyway.

Being here with the Cleridrac people makes him feel there is something more than the mission, though he's using the mission to justify staying. Here, among these people, there's the possibility of belonging and being a part of something that matters; assuming he can convince them he's not a devil. Perhaps he will even be able to pursue a relationship with Kata.

Chance is startled when the man who was speaking is standing behind him, as if waiting for him. Chance sheepishly turns from the table to face the elder. The elder places a hand on his head and recites something, but he does it so rapidly Chance has a hard time picking out the individual words. When he finishes reciting, he moves over to the young man beside him and repeats the same thing, going down the line until he has laid his hand and recited over every young man's head. Chance watches, wondering if this is some ceremony inducting him into their tribe because he killed a beast and protected their warriors, proving his worth.

The crowd parts and several women walking in a single file line enter and surround the stone table. They all wear similar short, light colored, skin tunics and their hair is adorned with beads and feathers.

Chance watches eagerly, expecting this to be the entertainment. The young women step toward the men and Chance recognizes the fiery, red hair, now braided and adorned with colorful beads and feathers.

Resha's face beams as she takes Chance's hands and pulls him to stand beside her. Surprised and confused, Chance tries to feign a smile and follows the young woman. They line up behind the other pairs of young men and women, all waiting to stand before another of the elders. As each pair stands in front of the elder, he places a colorful ribbon adorned with feathers over their joined hands, and loosely wraps them together. Once they've received their ribbon, they race off through the throngs of people toward the tents near the center of the camp.

Chance swallows hard, wondering if this is part of the celebration he missed last night. Resha feels something is wrong and strokes his face. He looks at her and feigns another smile. "Bemelen pruk,[79] Resha. Good evening," he greets, making an effort not to hurt her feelings for a second night in a row.

Resha bows her head to acknowledge the greeting, a precocious smile parts her lips. "Goot ebeneen, Hewold. Bemelen pruk."

They stand in front of the elder and he loosely wraps the ribbon around their hands and gives them a squeeze. Chance can feel Resha tighten her grip, and she has a glint of excitement in her eyes. When the elder lets their hands go, Resha races off, dragging Chance behind her.

They race through the crowd of people and away from the festivities. Chance feels his adrenaline start to pump. He feels excited to be a part of something, even though he's not sure what they are doing. He has no idea why everyone is running

---

79 *Good evening.*

away, or why they're following suit, but he's eager to find out, while at the same time, hoping it isn't what it appears to be.

As they race between the tents, he catches glimpses of the others running away. One by one, the pairs duck inside different tents along the same path he and Resha are running along.

Slowly, he puts the pieces together. What was excitement now turns into dread. He no longer follows with as much enthusiasm, though it doesn't stop Resha from continuing to pull him along.

As they run along the path, Chance recognizes Kata's tent. "Jouem,[80] Hewold!" Resha yells as loud as she can when they pass.

Chance's heart drops, realizing Kata must be inside and well aware of the events transpiring, but Resha doesn't let him stop. She pulls even harder on his hand as she tries picking up the pace toward their destination. She looks back, and for the first time, her smile is no longer that of the innocent girl he had gotten to know these last few days. On the contrary, her smile now reflects bitterness and disdain. Chance gets the sense her words were out of spite and retaliation. Was this what Kata was trying to ask him last night?

His fears are being realized. How was he to know he was betrothed to someone this whole time? His mouth goes dry and his palms start to sweat. He feels a pit in his stomach and the blood rushing from his face. He doesn't know what to do. He feels weak in the knees and he wants to stop, but Resha doesn't let up. She keeps moving along as fast as she can until they arrive at the tent he has been staying in.

He swallows hard as Resha leads him inside. She ushers him toward the side of the tent with the bed on the floor. She

---

80 *Let's go.*

remains at the door to ensure it is closed and tied shut. She turns around, breathing hard from the long run, but still with a smile of satisfaction on her face. She takes a deep breath and sighs; taking a step toward Chance.

He looks at her, wide-eyed, trying to swallow, all while trying to think of a way to get out of this. Resha giggles with overwhelming joy. She's obviously beside herself with excitement. She's waited for this day for a long time, and now she finally has him all to herself. She stares at him, not even aware of his apprehension, and slides the tunic strap off her shoulder, letting the dress fall to the ground in a heap, exposing herself entirely to Chance.

Chance's throat tightens and he tries averting his eyes. He looks at the ceiling and sighs, trying to collect his thoughts and pull himself together. He feels Resha's hands slide over his chest and push his vest off. He remains motionless as she leans in to kiss him. She stops, sensing his uneasiness. He looks her straight in the eye and clears his throat. "Cho sushu, Reshiara. Cho whe lom.[81] I'm sorry. I can't. I can't do this," he whispers.

Her face turns red, and she tries covering herself, fumbling for the clothing at her feet and slipping it over her body. She crosses her arms in front of her as if the dress wasn't covering her sufficiently. Tears fill her eyes and panic tightens her chest. She looks around the tent frantically, as if there was something else in there to blame for his rejection. "Cho sushu," Chance repeats as he steps toward the door.

Reshiara throws herself in front of him to keep him from leaving. "Whe, whe, whe! Chu whe lom![82]" she yells, pushing him back inside the tent.

---

81 I'm sorry, Reshiara. I can't.
82 No, no no! You can't.

The tears run uncontrollably down her face. Chance feels extremely sorry for her. He has no intentions of hurting her; but how was he to know this was their plan? Staying seems like it will make it harder for her.

"Cho sushu, Resha. Losheer chu joua cho.[83] Please, let me go," Chance pleads once more.

"Whe, whe, whe. Whe! Losheer whe joue![84]" she begs, not wanting him to go.

She looks mournfully into his eyes. Chance can see the hurt, but more than that, she is afraid to let him leave. His heart aches to see her this way and he understands the humiliation she must be feeling. She's been nothing but kind and helpful to him since the day he woke up, but that doesn't mean he's ready to take their relationship to this level, especially since he never felt romantic towards her. She's attractive, gentle-natured, and would make a good wife for somebody; at least by his standards. Though, he never considered she would be his. He was just getting used to the idea of being in a relationship and that's only because Kata kissed him. Before then, he hadn't seriously considered the option.

He wonders what the motivation is for pairing them together. Whatever the reason, he isn't comfortable with the idea, though he feels terrible leaving her like this.

He watches her in silence for what feels like hours while she stands sobbing in the doorway. When he tries leaving again, she looks up at him. The deep sadness is gone from her eyes and is replaced with fierce anger.

She charges toward him with gritted teeth, pointing her finger at him. "Katalariana! Katalariana chue gulbha! Chu chue

---

83 *I'm sorry, Resha. Please let me go.*
84 *No,no,no. No! Please don't go.*

yusell, nue? Po chu whe yusell cho im po chu whe donjru cho, ul whe?[85]"

Unable to fully understand, Chance still has an idea why she is mad. "No, it's not because of Katalariana. Whe, Katalariana whe gulbha. Yusell? I don't even know what yusell is, but I can tell you this has nothing to do with her."

Hearing his answer, her anger subsides, though she doesn't fully believe it and the tears stream down her face again. She falls into his chest and sobs. Chance holds her and rubs her back. After a moment, Chance slowly sits her on the bed and caresses her face. She looks longingly at him, wishing the night turned out better. Chance gives her one last smile before heading for the door.

"No, Hewold. Losheer. Plez, Hewold. You, me," she woefully pleads, outstretching her hands toward him.

Chance sighs and looks up at the ceiling again. He feels the touch of her soft fingers sliding into his hand and then a slight pull towards her. She pulls him down beside her on the bed. She places her hand on his cheek and looks meekly into his eyes. "Plez, Hewold. No lev me. Cho chu yusell.[86]"

"Yusell?" Chance repeats.

"Yusell? Cho im chu,[87]" she responds, placing her hand on her heart, and then placing it on his heart.

"Love?" Chance mutters.

Blood rushes to his face again and his heart races. He wonders if it's possible for someone to fall in love after a few days, but then he remembers the feelings he has for Katalariana. He cares for Reshiara, but he wouldn't go so far as to say he loves

---

85 *Katalariana did this! You love her, don't you? That's why you don't love me and why you won't take me, isn't it?*
86 *I love you.*
87 *Love? Me and you.*

her, at least not the way she wants. It also makes it harder for him to walk away knowing how strongly she feels about him, but he doesn't want to lead her on.

He shakes his head and removes her hand. "Cho sushu, Reshiara. Cho joua.[88] I'm going. I'm very sorry."

Reshiara throws herself at him, screaming for him to stay. She appears more afraid than sad about him leaving. She behaves as if it were a matter of life and death. Chance doesn't have the heart to tell her no again, especially when she's so afraid. He grunts in frustration and rubs his hands through his hair and over his face. "What do I do?" he whispers as if seeking advice from an unseen entity.

He paces around the tent before finally crouching beside the fire. He places more wood on it to keep out the night's chill. He looks over at Resha, who sits quietly on the bed, watching his every move. The tears are no longer streaming down her face but her eyes are puffy and red. After staring at the fire for a few minutes, he sits beside her on the bed and puts his arm around her. He pulls her into him and kisses her on the top of the head before resting his cheek there.

He holds her well into the night until she falls asleep. When he knows she's asleep, he gingerly lays her back onto the bedding and stands to leave. Resha wakes from her sleep and sits back up. She grips his arm and the tears well up in her eyes again. "Hewold, losheer.[89] Plez," she pleads once again.

She pats the bed beside her and pulls on his arm. Unable to bring himself to break her heart and not wanting to see her cry anymore, he reluctantly slides in beside her. She pulls the top cover over them and rests her head on his chest. She reaches

---

88 *I'm sorry, Reshiara. I'm going.*
89 *Please.*

her arm across him and squeezes tight, pulling her body as close as she can to his.

Chance stares at the ceiling of the tent until the fire dies out, leaving the ember's faint glow to illuminate the room. Hours pass before he is finally able to fall asleep, his mind having mulled over everything that's transpired in his short time on Eshiron. If these last few weeks are an indication of how life on this planet is going to be, and if the pilot's information was true, then Chance was preparing himself for some troubling times ahead. His only ray of hope and light amid the turmoil is the thought of Kata and their first kiss. Hopefully it won't be the last blissful moment he has.

«22»

Chance stirs, wondering when it was he finally fell asleep. He looks to his side and sees Reshiara still asleep, curled up beside him. He sits up as best he can without waking her. The faint glow of the breaking sun sneaks in around the flap of the doorway. He crawls over Resha and makes his way to the door, grabbing his vest off the floor and slipping it on, making sure not to wake her.

He opens the flap and steps outside. Several men posted outside the door greet him. The moment they see him, they break out into loud cheers and hollers. Chance winces at the sounds and hurriedly tries shutting the door flap; knowing it does nothing to block out sounds. He feigns a smile and holds his hands up for them to desist their ruckus. The foremost person in the group is his new friend, Broltrom, who steps forward and heartily pats Chance on the shoulder.

Within seconds, Reshiara exits the tent, holding a fur blanket close around her. The cheering and hollering erupts again. Broltrom steps over and gives her a hug. She puts on a large smile and returns the greeting. She casts a questioning glance at Chance, wondering if he's told them anything, but judging on everyone's excitement, they are unaware of last night's events, or the lack thereof.

Chance wonders how long they've been waiting outside, and figures they were posted as witnesses to the occasion. It's understandable why Resha was so insistent he stayed, but what would the consequences have been if they caught him leaving? They must be severe to instill such fear in her.

Unable to escape undetected, Chance surrenders himself to whatever his friends have in store for him. He intended to sneak away and find Kata, hoping to finally have an uninterrupted moment with her and explain what happened to him. It's not an option now. He's surrounded by several people who seem eager to take him elsewhere.

He follows close behind the group as they lead him to another part of the camp. Reshiara clings to his side, as determined as always not to let him out of her sight. They come to an empty lot near the last row of tents. There is a small square sectioned off with several small rocks at each corner.

Broltrom steps beside Chance and anxiously slaps his shoulder, then points at the empty, sectioned piece of ground. Some others step up and hand him several, large furs and other smaller bundles. They set down larger bundles in a neat pile on the sectioned piece of ground. With a huge smile, Broltrom pats Chance on the chest and continues pointing at the square. He's been given this plot of land as his own, along with some gifts to help him get started on his new home.

He looks around at other marked off, empty plots nearby. Some of the plots already have young men working at putting a wood frame together. Chance recognizes them from the table last night.

He's been made a member of the Cleridrac people and given a plot to build a home for him and his bride. Resha's spirits seem lifted and she's a bit happier than last night. She clings to his arm, opposite of Broltrom, and jumps with joy at the prospect of a new home.

After leaving the gifts, everyone leaves, including Broltrom. Chance figures they must have been outside their tent all night and were eager to go home. Resha says little before she kisses his cheek and heads back to the tent, leaving Chance to sort through the piles of gifts to see what supplies he's been given.

Never having built a tent, he's not sure where to start. The size of the square looks like it would house a tent twice as large as the one he's been staying in, and unfortunately, there is nothing here large enough to make a complete tent. Sorting through the available materials, he finds several tools, one of which looks like it could be used as an ax to cut the poles for his frame.

With nothing else to do and not wanting to fall short in his new responsibilities as a landowner and new member of the tribe, he takes the ax, some dried meat, and makes his way towards the woods near the water source. Along the way, he spots a large group of men gathered together, cheering and chanting. As Chance draws closer to have a look, he notices the men are forming a large ring; watching whatever is happening in the middle. Chance approaches the circle and makes his way through to the inside. Small stones are placed side by side, making a ring the men are gathered around. Inside the ring, two men are fighting each other.

Chance recognizes the one everyone calls Cultac, or as he calls himself, Zherulk Dozhkar.[90] The other man is unfamiliar and also appears to be on the losing end of the fight. He stumbles around while the other haughtily prances around him. After prancing around and taunting the man, Cultac unleashes a quick barrage of punches that sends the loser reeling backwards over the stone ring and landing on his back.

---

90 *Demon Killer*

The crowd parts and lets the man fall, then stoop over him and laugh as he lay beaten and near unconscious. A few of the men help him to his feet and steady him while they wait for the next challenger to enter the ring.

The winning fighter struts around the ring with his arms outstretched, challenging anyone to face him. Chance watches from the sidelines, unamused at the man's arrogance.

He shakes his head and attempts to leave but feels several hands on his back shoving him into the ring. He stumbles over the stone boundary into the ring. He looks back and several faces watch him with sly grins. Chance tries retreating back into the crowd, but they push back, keeping him from escaping the ring.

"Ah! Zherulk[91]," the winner addresses Chance with delightful anticipation.

Chance faces him and watches as he paces back and forth, taunting Chance to fight him. Chance shakes his head. He's not eager to fight anyone, and he's certainly not going to let someone beat on him just to hide the fact he's different. It would take one quick jab to end the fight, but in the end, what would it accomplish besides strengthening the argument he's a devil? That's the last thing he wants, especially since he's recently been accepted as one of their own.

While the two face each other, the crowd chants Cultac's name. Several people break off from the crowd, running into the camp screaming the devil and Cultac are fighting. The chanting boosts Cultac's ego, causing him to strut around the ring, basking in his own resplendence.

Chance shakes his head. "I'm not going to fight you. Cho whe dozh.[92]"

---

91 Demon
92 I won't fight or I'm not fighting.

Chance turns and tries leaving again. Cultac laughs and scoffs at Chance trying to run away. "Look at the demon, how he tries to scurry away like a tuprit.[93] Without their blue shell to protect themselves they are weak and powerless. He would shame himself and his family before facing me in the circle. I cannot blame him. He is not strong like the Cleridrac. He will never be one of us. No matter what he tries, he will always be weak. The demons are no match for my strength. Look at the coward. Look how fear grips him. I should be merciful and end his misery," Cultac boasts; inciting the crowd to join in the mockery and keep Chance trapped within the ring.

By now, others have started gathering to see Cultac fight the demon. People push their way in to see what's happening; anxious to see Cultac take the demon down. Others are excited to see what the demon is capable of and want to see what he will do to Cultac.

Among those arriving to see what the fuss is about are Broltrom and Kata. Upon seeing Kata in the crowd, Chance is eager to speak with her and feels the frustration of constantly being pushed back into the ring. He doesn't feel up to playing into the antagonism. His whole life, he's had to defend himself from the insecurities of others thinking they needed to prove something by beating him in a fight. Fed up with being mistreated, Chance forces his way through the crowd, crossing the stone border surrounding the ring. The crowd gasps in disbelief that someone would willingly leave the circle after entering it.

"Witness the shame and disgrace he brings to himself and his family!" cries Cultac. "He has no honor. See how he flees the circle and refuses to defend what honor he may have had."

---

93 *Small, rodent-type animal that lives in burrows underground.*

Broltrom forces his way through and jumps into the ring. A silence falls on the crowd. Chance continues pushing his way towards Kata, eager to get away from all the people, and ignores what is happening in the ring behind him.

"Chazhewold knows nothing of our ways. He cannot be held to the same standards, seeing as he has only recently joined our people," Broltrom pleads on Chance's behalf.

"If he wishes to remain as one of us, is it not reason that he should be held to the same standards? What fault is it of mine that he chooses to dishonor himself? He chose to enter the circle and face me, but then he could not hide his fears and cowardice. He is weak and will always be a weak demon. He will never be Cleridrac. He hasn't the strength or the honor," Cultac reiterates.

Hearing his name and recognizing the voice, Chance turns to watch Broltrom in the ring. By now, the crowd has closed around him; everyone impatiently waiting to watch the match between Broltrom and Cultac. Now Chance feels torn between watching Broltrom or taking advantage of the distraction to get away with Kata. He's sure Kata has seen him by now and he hopes she doesn't leave before he can talk to her. At the same time, he's sure Broltrom has entered the ring because of him, and it would be a shame to walk out on a friend.

"If that is the way you choose to follow, then I will take his place. I will fight you in his stead," Broltrom interjects.

A wicked smile crosses Cultac's face. He looks like a voracious predator finally finding its prey after an extremely long hunt. "I accept this challenge," Cultac readily replies. "I have longed for this opportunity. To destroy a shameful traitor instead of a cowardly demon is a welcome trade."

"I admit, I have also desired this opportunity to repay you for the shame that was wrongfully placed upon me and my brother when you tainted the Eldest against us," Broltrom responds indignantly.

Cultac laughs aloud. "A shame he is not here. Now you will never regain your honor, for when I am Eldest, I will ensure you will receive the justice you deserve and the shame you should have received all those years ago. It would be reason for you to bear in mind the nature of those you associate with, especially when they are our enemies."

Cultac laughs again; seeing the anger in Broltrom's face. "It was you who betrayed the Eldest's trust. I know you were colluding with our enemies to destroy the Eldest, and when we confronted you, you accused us of your crimes. In time, our people will know you for what you really are," Broltrom warns.

Cultac glares at his rival. "And what am I?"

"You are the true demon that hides among us!" Broltrom boldly answers.

Cultac lunges at Broltrom, who sidesteps, narrowly missing a punch to the face. Broltrom retaliates and catches Cultac with several punches to the face and body. Cultac stumbles backward before regaining his footing. Growling with anger, he rushes Broltrom again and is struck several more times. Broltrom unleashes several more jabs to Cultac's torso, knocking the wind out of his opponent. "I'm going to put you in your place. You don't deserve to be Eldest," Broltrom threatens.

Cultac grunts in pain as he falls to his knees. He wipes blood from his mouth with the back of his hand and looks at Broltrom with a devious smile. Broltrom rushes in, taking advantage of his faltered victim. Cultac throws a fistful of dirt into the air to distract his charging opponent. Broltrom tries ducking out of the way, but Cultac leaps up and shoves Broltrom into the crowd. He lands against one of the spectators, but manages to stay inside the ring. Regaining his balance, he steps forward to rejoin the fight but feels a piercing pain in his side. He looks down at the blood trickling down from a stab wound in his side. He glances briefly and notices one of Cultac's friends concealing a small knife in his hands.

Before he can react, Cultac is on him, unleashing a barrage of punches of his own. Broltrom reels over backward and is shoved back in by the people on the sidelines. He stumbles and falls to one knee. As he tries to stand back up, Cultac leaps over and stomps on Broltrom's leg. His knee snaps inward and he screams out in agony. He rolls on the ground holding his broken leg while Cultac stands back and admires his handiwork.

Broltrom clenches his teeth and tries coping with the pain long enough to crawl to the edge of the ring. He knows Cultac isn't finished with him. Not until he's dead, or close to it. Cultac doesn't wait for him to reach the edge, but walks over and kicks him over and over again.

Broltrom does his best to defend himself, but the pain is too great. With a kick to the face, Cultac knocks Broltrom unconscious. His limp body rests on the ground and Cultac throws in a few more kicks. He reaches down and rolls Broltrom over on his back and sits on his chest.

"Am I the demon?" Cultac spits. "Am I really the demon? What will you say about me now? Remember that it was me that put you down when you go to meet your brother!"

He punches Broltrom in the face a few more times before lifting his head up by the hair. He pulls his fist back and readies to deliver the final blow.

Someone grabs his readied fist and yanks him off Broltrom; throwing him onto his back in the dirt. When he looks up to see who dared to interfere with his fight, he sees Chance standing over him.

"Cultac, that's enough! This has gone too far!" screams a woman's voice.

Cultac looks over and spots Kata crouched on the ground beside Broltrom's battered body. Cultac jumps up and charges toward them. Chance places himself between them, stopping Cultac's advance. "Katalariana? You know it is forbidden for a woman to enter the circle! You defy our traditions and defile our sacred circle!" Cultac exclaims, infuriated about his fight being spoiled.

"Are you mad? You would have killed him! Where is your reason?" Kata retorts.

"You question me? Know your place, woman!" Cultac seethes.

He attempts to make his way to her again, but Chance blocks his approach and pushes him away from Kata and Broltrom. "Your fight is with me, Cultac. Cho dozh chu,[94]" Chance challenges.

He remains between Cultac and Broltrom until Kata and a few others are able to carry Broltrom from the circle. Cultac paces back and forth on the far side of the ring, scowling as he watches them carry his foe away; like a predator cheated out of its prey.

Once they have left, Chance steps forward to face his adversary. Cultac laughs, thinking to make a mockery of the outsider again until he notices Chance's demeanor is completely changed. He can see the fury in his eyes as he closes the distance between them. He tries laughing off the fear overtaking him. "You will meet the same fate, Blue Demon! I will finish you, and no one will stop me this time," Cultac boasts, trying to build up his own courage.

---

94 *I'll fight you.*

Chance stops a few paces from Cultac and takes a defensive stance. He motions for his opponent to engage him. Cultac spits on the ground in front of him and sneers. "If it's your desire to die this day, I will gladly deliver it to you."

Cultac rushes toward him, swinging and kicking, but Chance evades every hit. He spins and ducks, dodging everything Cultac throws at him; not letting him make contact. Cultac grows more frustrated with every missed punch and kick. He grunts through gritted teeth and charges his opponent. Chance rolls out of the way at the last moment and Cultac crashes into the people lining the circle. His friends ensure he keeps his balance and doesn't step outside the ring to lose the fight.

Chance is surprised how quick and agile the Eshironians are. Their speed and strength rival some of the weaker Genhances he's known. It's no wonder they've been able to keep the CC at bay and decimate every attack force the CC has sent out. As quick as Cultac is though, Chance knows he can still easily outmaneuver him. He also notices Cultac is losing stamina; slowing down considerably in his wild attacks and stumbling as he chases Chance around the ring.

Tired of being made the fool, Cultac draws his knife from his belt and readies to face the demon again. An unnerving quiet falls over the spectating crowd. One of the spectators comes forward, stepping up to the stone ring. "Cultac, you know weapons are forbidden in the ring!"

Cultac slowly turns his head with an expression of pure hatred, and with one glance, the man slinks back into the audience. He returns his focus back to Chance, who smiles back at him, waiting for the fight to continue. Infuriated, Cultac screams and lunges at Chance, trying to plunge the knife deep into his chest.

Chance sidesteps, and like before, avoids every one of Cultac's attacks. Swing after swing, Chance twists and bends, staying away from the razor edge of the knife. He would love to turn the knife back onto his opponent and drive the blade deep into his skull, but he's also relishing the humiliation he's meting out to someone who was so sure of his own strength and abilities. Putting him down with his own knife might be a fitting end to one who gave no consideration to the life of another, but he worries about the repercussions his actions will have on the tribe. He hopes by showing mercy and only humiliating Cultac, it will convince people he isn't an unscrupulous monster.

Cultac hunches over, trying to catch his breath. He hefts the knife in his hand, pondering where the best place to embed it in his opponent. If he could, he'd take the demon's head off without a second thought, but the demon is too agile. He paces around the demon, watching and waiting for the right moment to strike.

Chance remains in one spot, letting Cultac circle him. He's ready for this fight to be over. It seems crossing the stone boundary counts as an automatic loss, and perhaps one of the more humbling ways to lose the fight. He'd like to knock Cultac out of the ring, but Cultac's friends are likely to keep him from falling outside the line.

With Chance's back to him, Cultac keeps low to the ground and runs up behind him with his knife at the ready. In a blink, Chance has Cultac on the ground, holding Cultac's knife to his throat. Confused about how he ended up on the ground with Chance on top and a knife at his throat, Cultac panics. He struggles to push the knife away, but he's powerless to move Chance's hand.

Seeing the fear of death in his eyes, Chance relents and stands up. He throws Cultac's knife into the ground beside his head and grabs Cultac's ankle. He drags him to the edge of the ring while Cultac claws at the ground trying to escape. Standing at the edge of the ring, the crowd parts, clearing the area immediately surrounding the stones. Even Cultac's friends are obliged to stand back. Chance turns and smiles at Cultac, and with a quick jerk on his leg, he sends Cultac sliding over the stone boundary.

Cultac, while glad to still be alive, pounds on the ground with his fists, enraged by the demon. His friends crowd around him and try to help him up, but Cultac pushes them away. He stands up and marches toward Chance, hoping to continue the fight, but his friends intervene. "Cultac, you can't! Suppose the council hears of your misdeeds? You'll have to wait for another day."

"What care I for the council? I am to be the Eldest. I will not let this demon cheat me out of my victory. He left the ring, and I won the fight against the traitor who fought in his stead. The demon must pay for his treachery!" Cultac spits out with indignation.

"You accepted the fight, Brother," one of the men recounts.

Cultac turns to his friend and grabs him by the neck, trying to raise him into the air. "It does not matter. I am the Eldest and he is the demon," he breathes through gritted teeth.

The other men try breaking Cultac's grip while simultaneously trying to appease him. They tell him he was most likely tired from fighting all those others beforehand, and he'll probably have better luck the next time they fight. Cultac lets the man go and marches back toward the main camp.

As soon as Chance threw Cultac out of the ring, he stormed through the crowd toward the healer tents, gathering his belongings as he went. He races there hoping to catch Kata and find out how Broltrom is doing. When he arrives, he looks down the row of tents, wondering which one they are in. He doesn't want to get into trouble by peeping into every tent and invading people's privacy. He hopes passing by them he'll hear their voices. Walking along the path in front of the tents, he spies Kata emerging from a nearby tent. When she spots Chance making his way towards her, she tries hurrying back to take care of Broltrom.

Chance catches up and grabs her shoulder. "Kata, wait! I want to talk to you. Cho nano hulne chu.[95]"

"Whe, Chanz! No! You, Reshiara famly. No I!" Kata protests.

"What? Kata, please! Please talk to me. Losheer chu hulne cho.[96] Reshiara and I are not a family," Chance explains, hoping she stops and talks to him.

"Yez, you, Reshiara," Kata looks emphatically at Chance and joins her hands together, interlacing her fingers, holding them in front of his face, implying the pair had joined.

Chance knows what she is implying and shakes his head. Kata pauses and looks at Chance in confusion. "You, Reshiara no famly? No Reshiara Hewold?"

"No," Chance replies.

Confused how that's possible, knowing they ran by her tent after the ceremony, she looks curiously at Chance. "Broltrom zay you, Reshiara famly. Broltrom zay you, Reshiara," she explains with an inquisitive tone, interlacing her fingers again to explain her meaning.

---

95 *I want to talk to you.*
96 *Please talk to me.*

Chance sighs and runs his hand through his hair. "Kata," he pauses, feeling awkward about the conversation. "Reshiara and I didn't," he admits, hesitantly interlacing his fingers.

A twinge of excitement races through Kata's chest. She pulls Chance further away from the tent so as not to be overheard. "Chanz, po?[97]" she quietly asks why.

Chance isn't sure what to say to answer her question. He told Resha it wasn't because of Kata, but being with her now; if he had the choice, he would have chosen Kata. "It's because I didn't choose her. Cho whe lujre Reshiara.[98]"

Kata is overjoyed and can't help jumping into Chance's arms. She squeezes him tightly, not wanting to let him go, and fights the desire to kiss him again. Not wanting to be spotted either, she pushes away from him and composes herself. She looks around to make sure no one else is around and steps closer. "Chanz, you zay no famly?" she asks quietly, pointing to the surrounding area.

Chance understands she's asking if he's told anyone else about not consummating the marriage, but he finds it curious she wants to keep it a secret and insists on speaking in his language. Her sudden outburst of excitement and then quick composure has him confused as well. "No, I didn't tell anyone. Cho whe..." Kata interrupts his response by placing a finger over his mouth.

"Chanz no zay no famly. You, I ," Kata points at the spot where they are standing and then points at the sun and traces a line across the sky.

Chance guesses she wants to meet here when the sun reaches that point in the sky, but he wonders why the secrecy. He wants to continue talking, but Kata stops him and points

---

97 *Why?*
98 *I didn't choose Reshiara.*

to the tent behind them. "Cho sushu, Chanz. Cho joua Brol-trom.[99]"

Chance remembers the sorry state Broltrom is in, and is also anxious to see him. He understands the reason for meeting later on, and agrees to hold off on their conversation. He motions for Kata to lead the way.

They enter the tent, which is larger than the one Chance was kept in. There are three empty beds, apart from the one Broltrom is in, arranged around the single room. There is another healer attending Broltrom when they enter. She looks up and smiles at Kata, but her smile is swept away when she sees Chance entering. She nervously looks back down at her patient and keeps herself busy. Chance rolls his eyes, wondering how long it will be before the people are able to get over their fears of him.

He looks at Broltrom as he lays still on the bed. His leg is already in a splint and wrapped in bandages. His chest is covered in welts and bruises, and his face is swollen. Seeing one of his only friends in this state causes Chance to be filled with guilt. The reason Broltrom is in this condition is because he refused to fight. He feels worse acknowledging he was so focused on being with Kata he allowed his friend to suffer for the contempt, fear, and enmity the people held for him. If he hadn't hesitated going back, he may have saved his friend from such severe injuries.

"Katalariana!" the other healer calls out, showing her the stab wound in Broltrom's side that won't stop bleeding.

Kata rushes over with her satchel and pulls out a poultice and packs it onto the wound and re-covers it with a bandage. Seeing the stab wound enrages Chance even more. He can tell

---

99 *I'm sorry, Chance. I'm going to Broltrom.*

from the position of the wound he was stabbed from behind and the fight wasn't fair at all. He regrets letting Cultac off so easily and turns to go rectify his decision.

"Chazhewold?" a weak and raspy voice stops him.

He turns and looks at the swollen face of his friend who tries smiling in spite of the pain and swelling. Chance kneels at his bedside and grabs his hand. "Thank you, Broltrom. Cho loshome chu.[100]"

Broltrom slowly shakes his head. "Chuem gardhrallim. Chu om Ruc Aerulk, Chazhewold. Chu shere om amogar.[101]"

"We are brothers. Chuem gardhrallim. You can count on me to watch your family. Cho shere chu amogar, gardhrall,[102]" Chance reassures him.

Broltrom nods, wincing from the pain moving causes. Kata grabs a wooden vial from her satchel and pours a few drops of the liquid into Broltrom's mouth. Chance walks to the door to let his friend rest. The door flap lifts open and Imelka, Broltrom's wife, steps briskly into the tent. She looks at Chance for a second, then marches passed him to her husband's side. Chance catches a glimpse of anger in her eyes, knowing she must blame him for her husband's injuries.

Chance leaves the tent and gathers his items and heads to the woods outside of camp. He feels terrible for what happened to Broltrom and wonders how he can make it up to him and his family. Beating on Cultac might make him feel better, but Chance knows it won't help things. It might make more people angry.

Arriving at a grove of small trees deep in the woods, Chance grabs the ax tool and cuts down several trees of similar

---

100   *I thank you.*
101   *We are brothers. You are my Blue Angel. Take care of my family.*
102   *I'll take care of your family, brother.*

size. All the while, he ponders on his plight and what he can do to get people to trust him and not be so afraid of him. He doesn't mean to hurt anyone. It's the furthest intention from his mind. It doesn't take long before Chance's thoughts wander to Kata. He is filled with an eagerness to see her later in the afternoon. As excited as he is to spend time with her, things are complicated now that he's supposedly married to Resha. He contemplates what it means for him and what he plans to do about it. He hates to lead her on, but he doesn't want to destroy her either. Who knows what will happen to her if he leaves her? Judging from Resha's reactions and Kata's secretiveness, it probably isn't good.

Hours pass and Chance stops cutting. He's been so lost in his thoughts he didn't realize he's cut down a large portion of the grove; far more than he would need for a tent. He rests on a stump and looks over the pile of logs he's cut. He gets the idea to build a cabin. The advantages would certainly be greater than living in a tent, especially since it was getting colder every day.

Chance smiles at everyone stopping to watch him pass by carrying an oversized load of long, wood poles on his shoulder. It takes several trips to bring all the trees he cut down back to camp. He works cutting logs to length, building a rectangle frame as a foundation and laying logs across the top to build a floor. Using strips of hide, he lashes the logs together and uses stakes to keep them in place on the ground. He notches the logs and stacks them to build up the walls.

People stop by from time to time to watch him work, but leave shaking their heads, thinking for sure he's crazy. Some approach and try to instruct him on building a proper tent. Chance looks them in the eye and smiles, pretending not to know what they are saying. It's not hard to convince them, since most are probably unaware he knows an extensive amount of their language by now.

The sun reaches the designated position in the sky and Chance gathers his belongings and places them on the new floor of his partially constructed cabin and heads to the healer tents. He arrives at the spot outside of the tents where Kata said she would meet him but she isn't there. He considers entering Broltrom's tent, but he doesn't want to look Imelka in the face again. Not until he can find a way to make it up to her.

After waiting a few minutes, he prepares to leave until he hears someone hissing at him. He looks around and sees Kata peering around a tent at the end of the row, signaling for him to come to her. He nervously glances around and strolls over to where she is waiting. When he reaches her, she grabs his hand and runs toward the outer edge of the camp. When they reach the wall, she lets go of his hand and climbs over to the other side. Chance looks around again and hops over. On the outside, she leads him to a sparsely wooded area with a large rock formation jutting from the ground. Kata leads Chance around to one side and pulls back the overgrowth to reveal an entrance into a small cave.

Inside the cave, Chance can see an old fire pit with some logs already set up for a fire. The light cast from the entrance shines on a low stone platform protruding from the rock wall. Several blankets and furs are stacked on the ledge. There are some clay pots and baskets set on one side of the cave. Kata goes to the fire pit and produces a flat stone from her satchel and breaks a small piece off and sets it among the kindling. She pours a small amount of water from one of the nearby jugs onto the stone, causing it to fizzle and smoke. It generates enough heat to start the kindling on fire. After a moment, the fire blazes and illuminates the small cave.

Kata stands and faces Chance. She steps toward him, wringing her fingers as she approaches. Chance tries swallowing and clearing the lump in his tightening throat. There's no doubt they won't be interrupted in here. They have all the time they need.

Kata slowly reaches out and slips her hand into Chance's and stares into his eyes. Unable to contain her emotions any longer, and feeling she no longer needs to hide them, she throws her arms around his neck, pulling herself up until their lips mash passionately into each other's. Chance holds her up tight against his body as she wraps her legs around his waist. She runs her fingers through his thick hair as their lips remain locked in a fervent kiss. Kata's heart feels like it's going to burst from her chest.

The lump in Chance's throat moves down into his chest and burns with ardent fervor. The burning passion gives way to guilt, and as much as he wants to, he can't continue. Kata senses the change in Chance's demeanor and slowly parts her lips from his. She sees the concern in his eyes, so she unwraps her legs and lets herself slide down; their bodies still pressed together.

"Sorry, Kata," Chance regretfully apologizes in her native language.

Kata stops him from saying anything by pressing her fingers against his lips. "I know," she whispers, resting her head against his chest. "You and Reshiara. I understand. I need to talk to you about you and her. To be together as partners, you must..."

She pauses and interlocks her fingers again. Chance nods to show he understands her meaning.

"What happens if we don't?" Chance inquires, imitating Kata with similar hand gestures.

"Then you are not hers, and she is not yours until that happens. The partnership is not complete."

"Then we are not together and I can still leave her," Chance declares with some relief.

"No, Chanz. That is why I said not to tell others. It is your choice, but to leave your partner before being together will bring mozhad mepkav[103] to her."

"What is mozhad mepkav?" Chance asks, not familiar with the words.

Kata holds her hands out, indicating something large. Then she tries explaining mepkav. After a lot of guesswork and charades, Chance comes to the conclusion that leaving Resha will bring great shame to her. Kata explains as best as she can that making that choice implies Reshiara is not a worthy partner and to refuse someone on the night of being joined together is one of the greatest insults you can do to someone. It would essentially destroy the person if anyone found out.

Chance sits on the platform and rests against the wall. He looks up at the ceiling and sighs. It makes sense why Resha was so adamant he didn't leave. He hadn't considered the consequences of walking out on her on their wedding night, or at least, he never considered the severity of the consequences.

Kata sits down beside Chance and takes his hand, caressing it with her fingers. "I'm sorry, Chanz. I wanted to tell you. I tried to tell you." she attempts to apologize.

Chance looks from the ceiling at her. "You tried to tell me?" his voice quivers in frustration; anger pursed on his lips. "You left me, Kata! You didn't say anything about me and Reshiara."

Kata withdraws her hand from his. This wasn't the reaction she expected. She understands his anger, but how was she to

---

103 *Great shame or dishonor*

explain it when he wouldn't have understood. He clearly didn't understand their ways or all of their words. She's hurt he would turn on her when it wasn't her fault. It wasn't her fault they were kept apart, or constantly being interrupted, or that she was denied her spot in the rites. All she wanted since seeing him was to be with him. Why was he suddenly so upset with her?

She stands up, tears falling from her eyes; not so much from the hurt she feels in her heart, but more from the anger welling up inside. "You don't know, Chanz! Don't give me your anger," her lips quiver and her body shakes.

"Kata, you knew all the time. I tried to talk to you. You never told me, and now you bring me here. You tell me now? Why not before?" Chance explodes, angry he was left in the dark, not only by Kata, but by everyone.

Unable to bear his anger toward her, Kata cries uncontrollably. She looks at Chance, her heart aching once again for losing the one thing she ever wanted. She feels her happiness and the future she envisioned slipping through her fingers, and the Chance she longed for feels farther away from her than ever before. She tries retreating from the cave, but she can't force herself to surrender her feelings for him and risk losing him for good. "Chanz, you are mine," she blurts without thinking.

"What?" Chance responds, confused by her answer.

"You are mine. You, I, us. You should be with me. I should be Katalariana Hewold."

"I don't understand, Kata. I don't know what you mean. I'm with Reshiara. You left me with her. You let us be joined. I didn't know. You ran."

Katalariana kneels in front of Chance and holds his face in

her hands. "Please, Chanz. Don't leave me. Don't give me your anger, please. I'm sorry. I was afraid."

Chance pulls away from her hands and shakes his head. "Afraid? Afraid of me?" he questions, feeling a little deceived and like he'll never truly escape the moniker given to him by the people.

"No! No, Chanz. I don't fear you. I was afraid of everyone around us. I was afraid of my mother. I was afraid of the council. I was afraid of Cultac. I was afraid of Reshiara. I was afraid to lose you. I didn't want them to kill you and I was afraid they would take you from me. They did take you from me."

"Why did you let Reshiara take me?"

"I didn't. They chose. They don't want you and me to be together," Kata tries explaining.

"Why Cultac? Why does Cultac give you fear?"

Kata grows silent. She stares at Chance with her puffy, bloodshot eyes. How can she tell him without him becoming more angry and deciding to leave her? "Chanz, please hear my words. Do not give me more anger, please. Cultac chooses me to be his partner."

"You're betrothed!" Chance yells in his language.

"Chanz, please, hear my words. I do not choose Cultac. My mother wants me to partner with him. The council wants me to partner with him. I don't want him," she pauses, staring longingly at Chance. "I choose you, Chanz. I want to partner with you."

Chance sighs, letting go of some of the anger. He understands the odds are stacked against them, and he can understand her fears. He still wishes someone had let him know what was happening, or going to happen, especially when it came to being paired with someone. Anyhow, what's done is done, and there's no changing that. Both of them are being forced to partner with someone they didn't choose.

"I'm sorry, Kata, for giving you my anger," Chance apologizes as he wraps his arms around her to console her. "It's too late for us. I was given to Reshiara and you are chosen."

"No, Chanz. You can still choose. You are not together with Reshiara. Cultac says he will choose me, but he hasn't. We can go together to the council and tell them you and Reshiara have not joined and that you choose me. They will see reason when we tell them you did not know you had a choice, but now you know," Kata urges, not yet ready to surrender.

"They will not believe me. I was with Reshiara in the night and people saw me in the morning come out of the tent with her. And I do not want to bring dishonor to Reshiara."

Kata rests her head against Chance's chest feeling heartbroken; realizing Chance is right. The council won't be so willing to believe the word of someone they don't know or trust. Without Reshiara's confession about that night's events, they won't have much luck convincing them. Reshiara won't let Chance go so easily and Kata will be the one dishonored for getting between them. "You choose to join with Reshiara then?" Kata asks, feeling defeated.

"I don't feel I have a choice," Chance sighs.

Kata looks woefully at Chance, disappointed this is how the evening turned out. She hoped finally being alone together he would decide he wanted to be with her as much as she wanted to be with him.

"Chanz," she pauses, reaches up and caresses his face; her emotions welling up inside her chest. "I love you, Chanz Hewold. I don't want to lose you. I choose us. I want us to be together. Let us go together to a far place, where no one else is.

We can go to your home. No Reshiara and no Cultac. We can be together with no fear. Do you choose me? Do you choose us?"

Chance's stomach ties in knots. This is the second time someone has expressed their love for him. He doesn't know how to answer. This is the first time in his life where he's actually felt something for someone and he's not sure if it's love or if he's caught up in the thrill of the moment. He's attracted to her and he cares for her, but he cares for Resha as well. He's drawn to Kata and has been from the day he met her, but is that enough to say he loves her? He also feels responsible for Reshiara. He may not have chosen her as his life partner, but he can't ignore his sense of responsibility toward her. He doesn't want to hurt or bring shame on her. He's conflicted and it adds to the frustration he already feels.

"I can't go, Kata. These are your people and I can't take you from them. I don't want to give shame to you or Reshiara by my choices."

Kata looks into his eyes, and Chance can see the anger building up. She slams her fist against his chest and storms out of the cave. Chance chases her out and tries grabbing her hand to stop her. "Kata, wait, please."

"No, Chanz! No! I tell you I love you and you talk to me of that girl and my people. They don't care for us. They make the choices for us that keeps us apart. I choose you but you don't choose me," Kata rages, pulling her hand away from him.

"Kata, please understand."

"I cared for you when you were hurt. I taught you to speak like the Cleridrac. I was always there with you."

"I don't want to lose you," Chance interrupts.

"Sorry, Chanz. You do not have that choice now. My heart hurts too much. I cannot see you with that girl."

Kata walks back toward camp in the waning light of the evening. Chance debates whether to chase her or not. Had he made the right choice? Then again, there doesn't seem to be a right choice. Letting her go breaks his heart and he wonders if his feelings for her are stronger than he wants to admit. Unfortunately, no matter who he chooses in the end, he's going to hurt somebody, and for him, it's the worst position to be in.

Chance hops the wall and makes his way in the dark back to his tent. When he throws open the door flap, he's surprised to see Reshiara sitting on the bed. She sits quietly, staring into the flames of the fire pit, with her knees pulled up to her chest. With everything he has on his mind, he forgot he was now sharing a home; which is something he hasn't quite wrapped his mind around yet.

Reshiara jumps up from the bed and springs into Chance's arms. Her demeanor was sullen, but when she wraps her arms around him and presses herself into his body, she's content to see him.

She holds him tight, saying nothing for a long period of time. Chance figures she must either be mustering up the courage to talk about their relationship, or she is genuinely happy he returned to her and doesn't want to risk ruining the moment with words. He clears his throat, feeling awkward standing in the doorway with a young woman attached to him.

Resha squeezes tighter before pulling herself away. Chance notices her eyes glisten with tears. He hopes tonight won't be a repeat of last night, or a continuation of the day he has already had. He smiles, hoping to cheer her up and lighten the mood. She smiles halfheartedly in return after wiping her eyes.

"Hewold, I made food. Please, eat," she quietly invites, pointing to a dish beside the fire pit.

She crouches by the fire with her arms folded and stares

into the flames. Chance grabs the dish and sits on the bed. He feels bad, realizing she must have eaten without him all while wondering whether or not he was going to return. He eats in awkward silence while Resha tends the fire.

"Thank you for the food," Chance expresses in her native tongue; finally breaking the silence.

"Where were you today?" she responds curtly.

Before he has an opportunity to reply, she continues, her voice cracking with emotion while holding back the tears. "I came to the tent to change my dress, and when I returned, you were not there. I came to the tent to make food for the morning and you didn't come. I waited until midday, and you didn't come. I made food for midday and brought it to you, but you were not there. I waited for you. I hear people speak that you fought Cultac. I went to the healer tent, but you were not there. You were not here. Where were you?"

Chance runs his hands through his hair while staring at the floor. He takes a deep breath and groans as he exhales. "I was making our home and had to cut the trees."

"I saw our home. I saw the trees you cut. Where were you?" Resha asks again.

Chance shakes his head, not wanting to have another argument. He considers going out to finish the new home to escape, but he knows he'll have to answer her sooner or later. "Resha, I'm sorry," Chance sighs, saying the first words popping into his head, hoping to end the fight before it starts.

"With her? You were with her?" she asks, unable to bring herself to say Katalariana's name.

Reshiara paces beside the fire, her anger burning as brightly as the flames. She finally turns and struts out of the tent. Chance sits, still staring at the doorway, dumbfounded at his luck. In a matter of days, he managed to run off, not one, but two women who claimed they loved him but then were enraged by him. He tells himself there's nothing to be gained chasing after a mad woman except a slap in the face, or worse, a club over the head or a knife in the stomach. He doesn't want to risk either and feels it's safer to let her calm down and return when she's ready to talk again.

Reshiara marches through the camp until she arrives at the large tent in the center. "Katalariana," she hollers loudly into the doorway.

Kata's mother parts the door flap. She squints through tired eyes at the red-headed girl standing outside her home. "Sorry to wake you, Great Healer. I need to speak to Katalariana," Reshiara greets in a demanding tone.

"It is late, my child. Can this not wait until morning?" Kata's mother whispers between yawns.

"No, I must speak now."

The older woman retreats behind the door and a moment later, Kata arrives. When she sees who is calling on her, she rolls her eyes and turns to go back inside. Resha grabs Kata's arm to keep her from leaving. Kata whips her head around to face her, her eyes furrowed with intense disdain.

"I'm not leaving until you talk to me, Katalariana. You will speak to me, or I will yell it for all to hear while you hide in your bed, but you will hear what I have to say," Resha threatens.

Kata emerges from the tent and stands with her arms on her hips, waiting to hear what Reshiara has to say. "Why are you here, Reshiara?"

Reshiara takes one of Kata's hands and presses a token into it. Kata runs her fingers over it, and without having to look at it, she knows it's her token to the rites of partnership.

"I found this when I gathered my belongings. I know you were participating in the rites of partnership for him. I know you still want him, but you were not chosen, Katalariana. You think you have feelings for him, but he is not yours. He is mine. I warned you to stay away from Hewold. I told you I would go to the council if you tried to take him from me," Reshiara whispers in a stern and threatening tone.

"Then go to the council," Kata retorts defiantly. "Let us both go and tell them how you are not joined together."

Reshiara's eyes widen in shock and embarrassment. "Yes," Kata continues; "I know that you are not joined with him. He did not choose you. Let us go tell the council, then. You see, I do not fear you anymore, and I told him our ways. He knows he can still choose. He stays with you because he does not want to hurt you, not because he loves you. He is a good man, Reshiara, and he wants to do right. It was my time to be with him when he awoke. I was denied my time and you took him from me. He should be with me, and that would be right."

Kata waves the token in front of Reshiara and then tosses it at her. It bounces off her chest and onto the ground. Reshiara ignores the token and keeps her gaze fixed on the woman in front of her. "I was not responsible for the order of the rites. It was not my doing that caused you to lose your time. I will not give you what is mine. I will not let you take what is mine. If he does know our ways, then he has chosen me and not you. You can say he does not love me, but he does not love you either. Where is he now, Katalariana? He is not with you."

Kata lunges at Reshiara with a raised fist. Reshiara winces but Kata's fist stops short of hitting her. Kata's fist trembles as she holds it inches away from Reshiara's face. Reshiara can see the moonlight glinting off the tears streaming down Kata's cheeks. Kata clenches her fist even tighter and then steps back and retires to her tent, leaving Reshiara standing alone in the dark.

◄24►

Chance is almost asleep when Resha storms into the tent. She paces back and forth beside the fire, grunting in frustration. Chance sits up on the bed but she doesn't acknowledge him. After a long time of pacing in silence, and finally able to calm herself, Resha stops and stares into the fire.

"Hewold," she finally mutters.

Chance's heart beats harder. He doesn't want to argue anymore or make her more upset tonight. He hoped she went to walk off the anger, but she came back seeming more upset. He assumes she went and confronted Kata and now he's wondering if Kata told her about their romantic interactions. This was the last thing he expected to be caught up in when he received his assignment to come to the planet. He's starting to miss the days spent hunkered in the brush, defending colonists from voracious animal attacks.

"Hewold," Resha repeats, finally shifting her gaze from the fire to look up at him.

Chance can see the loneliness and sadness in her eyes and her voice quivers with emotion. It causes a lump to form in Chance's throat as a wave of guilt sweeps over him. He never intended to hurt this poor girl.

"Yes, Resha," Chance responds quietly.

"Do you love her?" Resha timidly inquires.

Chance shakes his head slowly and sighs. "I don't know."

"How can you not know? How is it reason that you do not know your own heart?" Resha presses.

"It's not so simple, Resha," Chance replies, standing up and pacing.

Chance rubs his hands through his hair and then over his face. He sighs and stares up at the ceiling with his back to Reshiara. He feels a small hand gingerly placed on his back. He lowers his head and slowly turns to face the red headed girl standing beside him. She gently holds his face in her hands and looks intently into his eyes, as if she's searching his soul for the true answer.

"Hewold," she whispers tenderly, caressing his cheek with her thumb. "I do know my heart. I know I love you. You are all the family I have. I have no one else. My family was killed when I was young. I have no friends. They have fear of me because I am different from them. People help me only because I am Cleridrac, but they do not love me. They let me live and nothing more. I have been alone for much of my life. I am a good woman. I am a strong woman, but no one chooses me because my hair is red and my skin is fair and because bad things happened to me and my family when they lived. Just as they fear you because you are different. Your skin is fair like mine, and your eyes are a color we have not seen before. They call you a demon, but I know you are a good man.

Your heart does not tell you what you feel now, but perhaps, in your mind you must decide what you want first. I will always love you because I choose you. I will only choose you and no other. If you choose me, then maybe your heart will open. It may not tell you now, but maybe someday. I hope someday soon. I will wait for that time when you can love me like I love you, but please give me that time. Don't let me be alone. With time our love will grow together and we will not be alone anymore. We can be different together, only we won't care because we will have each other."

Chance ponders the things Reshiara is telling him. He didn't realize how closely aligned their lives have been. He certainly understands the loneliness that comes from being ostracized when others fear those things that make them different. Thinking about her situation, he feels guilty for putting her through such stress and heartache and for being another one of those people who have brought her pain.

"My heart does feel for you, Resha, though I do not know what those feelings are. Perhaps, as you say, those feelings will grow into love with time. I do not want you to be alone. I know you are a good woman, and I am sorry you have suffered so much. I am more sorry that you have suffered because of me," Chance responds sympathetically.

Resha cocks her head to one side with a twinkle in her eye, staring at him inquisitively. "Do you choose me, Hewold?"

Chance can feel his cheeks burning and his chest feels tight. His hands get clammy and his throat feels dry. He's never felt like he's ever made such an important decision before which will affect his life so profoundly. He doesn't want to disappoint or hurt her again. He already feels guilty about his disrespectful behavior toward her before and he feels honor bound and obligated to her since they've been paired. He knows it will destroy her already tragic life if he backs out now, and he doesn't have the heart to destroy someone like that. He convinces himself he really has feelings for her, and having ruined his relationship with Kata, this relationship with Resha could work. Perhaps she is right about his feelings getting stronger with time.

"I," he hesitates, clearing his dry throat. "I do."

Resha's somber demeanor melts away and her bright smile returns. The energetic and cheerful girl Chance is familiar with reappears. Overjoyed to hear these words, Resha pulls Chance's face towards her and presses her lips against his. She slides her hands over his shoulders, pushing his vest off. As it hits the floor, she eagerly pulls him toward the bed.

She sits down on the bed, dragging him down with her until he's on his hands and knees over the top of her. She runs her hands over his toned chest and arms, gazing enamoredly into his eyes. She kisses him repeatedly, waiting for him to make the next move.

Chance kisses her back, but the feelings aren't there. Every time their lips meet, his mind goes back to when he kissed Kata and how it made him feel. Kissing Reshiara doesn't have the same effect and feels forced. He pushes the thoughts from his mind, not wanting to make the experience more uncomfortable by thinking about another woman; but it's hard not comparing how he feels.

He shifts his weight and slumps over onto his side. Sensing his lack of passion, but not wanting to lose this opportunity to finally be joined, Resha moves up against him and slides her hand down over his stomach. Her touch is soft and sends a sensation through his body that intensifies the farther down she goes. He sits up with a jolt, knocking her hand away. "I can't do this," he mutters.

"Hewold, what's wrong? Am I not doing it right?" she queries, sitting up and placing her hands on his shoulders.

"No, it isn't that. I don't think I can do this. I don't feel right," he admits while getting up from the bed and moving over to the fire pit. "I think I am going to leave."

"No, Hewold. You told me you would not leave me alone.

You said you choose me. Please, do not leave me," Resha begs emphatically, reaching out to him.

"I'm sorry, Reshiara. It does not feel right in my heart."

"You did not give us time. You may not feel it now, but it can still happen," she cries, crawling toward him.

"Time will only make it harder for you. It will only hurt you more. I do not want to hurt you, Reshiara," Chance explains as he makes his way to the door.

"Hurt me? You will destroy me. I will die if you leave me. My heart hurts as if it were pierced by an arrow. Why can you not give us time? I promise I will make you happy. I am a good woman. I am very young, but I will learn. I will learn how you want me to be. I can be a good woman for you. Please, give me time," she pleads between sobs.

"I'm sorry, Reshiara. I really am. You deserve someone to love you and that will love you the way you are."

"Why do you not love me?" she yells angrily.

"I do have love for you, Resha, but it is not the same kind of love that you have for me."

Chance crouches in front of Reshiara and wipes the tears with his thumb. She places her hand over his and presses her cheek into his palm. "Why can you not love me like you love her? I know your heart feels for her, but I am yours, Hewold. You say you choose me, but then you do not give us time. Why can you not love me?" she whispers through tears.

Chance shakes his head and stands. Reshiara leaps forward, throwing her arms around him, burying her face in his neck, sobbing uncontrollably. "I need you, Hewold. You are my family. I cannot stay if you leave me and I have no one else. There is no one else to love me or to protect me. Stay. Stay." she pleads.

"It would not be right. I will speak to the elders. They will understand. They will see reason. I will not let them bring shame on you," Chance promises as he pulls Reshiara's arms from around his neck.

He stands and retrieves his vest before going to the door. Reshiara remains motionless on the floor while Chance prepares to leave. When he places his hand on the door to open the flap, Reshiara stops crying and looks up at him, her eyes now full of fury. "If you go to her, she will be destroyed," she warns, her voice full of spite.

Chance stops and looks at Reshiara on the floor. Her lips still tremble with emotion, but her eyes glare at him with a hatred that burns deep. Chance is surprised to see the sudden change again in her demeanor. "If you go to her, I will go to the council," she threatens in a serious tone. "I will tell them you were together after we were joined. Did she tell you what happens when a woman joins with a partnered man that is not her own? The punishment will be severe and they will destroy her. I want you to choose me because you love me, but I will not let you go to her. She will not have you. She is already chosen by another man. I do not want to do this, but I do not want you to be hurt. Stay with me and you will be safe. Stay with me and she will be safe. We can be happy together, Hewold."

Chance is shocked to see this side of Reshiara. She always seemed so sweet and innocent and he wonders if this is an act of desperation; her last attempt at convincing him to stay. "Then the council will know that we are not joined, and great shame will be brought on you. Is that what you want?" Chance retorts.

"I told you, if you leave me, I have no one else. I will have nothing, so my life will mean nothing, and I lose nothing that I haven't already lost. If you leave me, and the council discovers these truths, we will all lose our lives. Is that what you want?"

"Reshiara, you are young. You have a long life to live. You will get another man. You can still have a family. You don't need me. You haven't lost everything," Chance tries convincing her with the hope she'll relent.

The tears stream down her cheeks again. "No, Hewold. I won't find another man. No one will take me. Every time I try to be partnered, no man will have me. When I participate in the rites of partnership, the young men pretend to be hurt when I am there. I can see they are well, but they wait for the other women. These people do not love me, just like they do not love you. We are the same here. This is why my home is here, away from the others. They do not want me with them. But I do not care about them as long as you are with me. Because you are a demon, they will not let you be with her. She is one of theirs; chosen to partner with the next leader of the Cleridrac. You will be alone. I will be alone. Stay with me and we have us. We will be a family. Please, Hewold, be my family."

Chance can see the bitterness and pain she has lived with most of her life and why she is so desperate to hold on to him. Her life was spent overcoming a stigma placed on her and she finally found someone who could relate. Beside that, it's not only her life hanging in the balance now. He can't imagine Reshiara is too concerned with Kata's welfare, but he's sure she's omitting the fact his life will also be in jeopardy. He hates being extorted, but he can see what she's saying is true. Even if he goes to the council, it will be hard to convince them of the truth. With two opposing accounts, it's doubtful he will be the one they believe. They will surely accuse him of being a devil taking advantage of multiple women. In the end, he'll probably be the one they attempt to get rid of, and he isn't going to lay down his life over the whims of two young women and a council of old men who don't know him.

"If I live alone, and I do not go with you or Katalariana, will you go to the council? If I do not choose a woman, will you let me go?" Chance questions; hoping for a resolution that doesn't involve people's lives being torn apart.

Reshiara looks at him with a perplexed stare, still disheartened he won't choose to stay with her. After a brief moment of thought, she shakes her head. "The council will see we are not together and I will still be shamed."

Irritated, he storms passed Reshiara and slumps onto the bed, throwing himself back on top of the covers. The more he thinks about the situation, the angrier he gets. All his training and experience never prepared him to deal with women and relationships. All his strengths and abilities are useless in his current predicament, unless he intends on fighting someone, which defeats the purpose of being here in the first place. The Cleridrac may have meant well when they arranged all this, but it would have been nice if someone tried explaining the plan to him instead of assuming he was going to agree to it all.

Reshiara quietly crawls over to the bed and sits beside him. She gently rubs her fingers over his arm. "I'm sorry, Hewold, and thank you for not leaving me," she whispers before kissing him on the forehead.

She slides down and cuddles up against him. She knows nothing else she says will be any consolation to him, so she rests her head on his chest and falls asleep listening to his heartbeat.

❮25❯

Chance wakes up early and leaves to work on his cabin. Reshiara forces herself to get up as well and follows close behind him, bundled up in several furs. He marches to the plot and refuses to speak to her.

He arrives at the cabin and starts working the logs, prepping them to build up the walls. Reshiara sits on the ground, cuddled in a heap of furs, and quietly watches as he works.

It's the oddest looking tent she has ever seen, but she doesn't dare ask what he's doing, or if he even knows how to build a tent. She doesn't understand how they can possibly make a fire in the middle of a floor made out of wood.

Chance is lost in thought until he spies movement out of the corner of his eye. He looks up and spots Kata on her way to the healer tents. She stops for a moment and they make eye contact. Chance smiles halfheartedly and nods to acknowledge her. She returns the smile, but her eyes reveal the hurt inside. Chance wants to approach her until he sees Kata's mother walk up beside her, also on her way to the tents.

Wondering why Chance has stopped working, Reshiara gets up to inspect what has his attention. She stands beside him as Kata and her mother continue on their way. Seeing the two women leaving, she grumbles under her breath. She looks at Chance, who watches them for a second before returning his focus to his work. She leans over and kisses him on the cheek before returning to her spot on the ground.

Kata walks away with her emotions welling up inside again. She hoped to leave early enough that she wouldn't see Chance on her way to the tents to check on Broltrom. Her mother insisted on going with her and held her up, complaining the whole way that Kata was going too fast for her.

"Look at that rock-head," her mother exclaims, motioning toward Chance. "He doesn't even know how to do something as simple as putting a tent up. At least he has not proven to be the threat that many thought he would be. He and that girl make a perfect pair. I am so happy you are not involved with him anymore. The time of mourning will soon be over and Cultac will finally make you his partner and become Eldest. Life will return to the way it always has. Then, hopefully, this dark cloud hanging over you these last days will finally break and you will be happy again."

Kata continues in silence; feeling sick at the thought of being paired with Cultac. If only her mother would listen to how she really felt. Life is not at all going to be like it used to. Cultac is nothing like her father. He only worries about his own interests. She doubts life with Cultac as a partner will do anything to lift the dark cloud. The only other thing worse than thinking about Cultac is seeing Chance with that red-headed girl.

Even after their dispute yesterday, Kata still can't get Chance off her mind. She even dreamed of him coming to her and taking her away to the secret cave. Unfortunately, she woke up before anything happened in the dream once they reached the cave. Her dream makes it harder to quit thinking about him. The worst part about it all is thinking he and Reshiara joined together last night, ensuring their partnership is official. She isn't sure how she'll be able to carry on if she has to see them together while she's stuck with Cultac. The thought causes her stomach to churn. She hopes she'll be able to focus on her work today and not have to think about Chance anymore.

When Kata and her mother arrive at the tents, they immediately go to check on Broltrom. They enter his tent and find his wife still at his side. She wakes when they enter and moves out of the way to allow the healers access to her husband. Although Kata was his primary healer the day before, she allows her mother to take the lead today. She remains close to the door while her mother begins her inspection of Broltrom's wounds.

It isn't long before Kata hears her name whispered from outside. She ignores it at first, thinking she's hearing things. After hearing her name again, she glances at the door to see it slightly parted and a single, hazel colored eye peering through. She does a double take before slowly side stepping to the doorway. When no one is watching, she slips outside.

Chance grabs her hand and rushes her around the backside of the tents and proceeds to run the same path they took the day before.

"Chanz, wait," she hollers, trying to slow him down. "Where are we going?"

Chance doesn't stop and points in the direction they previously took. Kata stops abruptly and jerks her hand away from his. "Stop, Chanz. What about Reshiara?"

"She left to go make food. I told her I wasn't hungry so she didn't need to bring me any. We don't have much time and I need to talk to you."

He grabs her hand again and races toward the wall. Kata can't help but realize the similarities to the dream she had last night. It certainly was a change to be led by him instead of being the one leading the way. In spite of her earlier thoughts and the discussion they had yesterday, her feelings for him well up inside and the warm feeling she gets with him runs through her body. She doesn't want to get her hopes up, but the fact he sought her out and is running away with her fuels the longing she has to be with him.

After they climb over the wall, Chance stops and crouches in the tall grass, pulling Kata down beside him. He points over to a group of trees and Kata can see someone walking nearby. It takes her a second to recognize Cultac making his way into the trees.

"What is he doing out here? Where is he going?" Kata wonders.

She looks over to Chance, who gazes back at her. Simply looking into his eyes causes her heart to race and she finds herself getting nervous. For a moment, she forgets where they are and why they are even there; feeling herself get lost in his gaze. Out of habit, she reaches up and brushes some strands of hair off his forehead and caresses his face.

"Kata," Chance smiles, taking her hand. "We need to hurry."

Kata takes a deep breath and sighs. She looks around and chuckles. "Sorry, Chanz. I am happy to see you."

"I am happy to see you, but we need to go," Chance responds, caressing her cheek.

"Wait, Chanz. Cultac is that way. He cannot see us or we will be in danger."

"We go carefully," he replies, urging her to follow him.

They stay crouched and scurry toward the cave. Reaching the trees, they spot Cultac speedily heading in the same direction they are going. Kata hesitates going any farther, but Chance insists they move forward. They move quietly, sticking close to the trees, making sure they don't lose sight of Cultac. They don't want to accidentally run into him. Unfortunately, he slows down when he nears the rocky outcropping concealing their secret cave.

Kata and Chance sneak around through the trees to the opposite side of the rocks and peek around to watch Cultac. He approaches another cluster of smaller boulders near a game trail leading into a thicker portion of the forest. He appears to greet someone, but Chance and Kata are unable to see anyone else. After a short wait, three warriors emerge from the woods and approach Cultac.

"Toorkrats," Kata gasps in shock.

"Who?" Chance asks quietly.

"Toorkrats are enemies. The Cleridrac fought them when they found you. Broltrom told me long ago that Cultac was friends with our enemies. Broltrom and his brother discovered his betrayal, but Cultac killed his Toorkrat friends then told my father he found them with Broltrom and his brother. My father did not listen to reason and Broltrom and his brother lost their place of honor. They were like sons to my father, and so he did not bring great shame to them, but they were not welcome in our home any longer." Kata explains.

"Can you hear what they are saying?" asks Chance, who's able to hear them, but isn't familiar with the Toorkrat dialect.

Kata shakes her head so they sneak closer, staying low to the ground and out of view. They press up against nearby boulders and eavesdrop on the conversation.

"Our numbers are small and our people go hungry. You did not keep your promise to help our people," one of the Toorkrats complains.

"You betrayed us when your people attacked us and nearly killed all our warriors while we contended with the blue demons. You told us you would convince your Eldest not to fight us until we were strong. We sought to take the demon's power for our own until our people were destroyed by you," interjects another warrior, with obvious contempt in his voice.

"The Eldest would not listen to my reason. He thought you were moving to take our lands again. I could not stop him, but he is not a problem anymore," Cultac responds with arrogance.

Chance holds Kata tightly against him to keep her from running out and strangling Cultac. He tries to calm her and motions for her to keep quiet. She nods, but Chance can see the devastation in her eyes. He still doesn't understand every word the Toorkrats say, but he understands enough to know they are talking about her father, and he suspects Cultac's treachery has something to do with his demise.

"We are not here to make war with you," continues the first Toorkrat. "We want you to honor our alliance and let us hunt your lands to feed our people. The animals are scarce and have left our hunting grounds and we have few hunters left. The great colds are coming and our people are not prepared. We will overlook your destruction of our warriors if you will let us hunt as you promised."

Cultac smirks. "My people need to eat, too. I also lost many warriors. I need all for my people."

"You said," protests the first Toorkrat before Cultac grabs the man's face, squeezing his cheeks together to keep him from talking.

"I said? I said? I said what?" taunts Cultac, pulling the man's face closer to his own. "I said I would help when I choose; how I choose. I choose that now is not the time."

Cultac pushes the warrior away, snarling as he watches him stumble backwards.

The other two warriors prop him up and assume an offensive stance. "The Toorkrats will not tolerate this. You will pay the price for breaking your oaths to us. We will get what was promised," the humiliated Toorkrat threatens.

Irritated, Cultac lunges at him, driving a dagger into his heart. He holds the warrior close to him and glares at him with wide, open eyes. "I am the Eldest of the Cleridrac. No one threatens me," he breathes through gritted teeth.

Cultac pulls the dagger from the man's chest and swings it at the warrior on his right; slitting his throat. The warrior standing on the left stumbles back in fear and turns to run away. Cultac pounces on him and stabs him repeatedly. He stands over the body and spits on it. Before he turns to walk back, he hears branches breaking in the nearby woods. He sees another Toorkrat warrior running away. Cultac starts after him but an old, raspy voice stops him. "Let him go, Cultac. You only risk being killed yourself."

An old woman draped in trinkets made from bone, feathers, and clay, emerges from beside the boulder. Kata gasps, recognizing the voice. "Shumakra?"

Afraid the old woman will find them there, Kata pushes Chance to move back to their secret cave. Staying low, they hurry back and hide in the entrance of the cave, listening for Cultac's and Shumakra's voices and waiting for them to leave the area.

"It is not wisdom to provoke our enemies, Cultac," continues the old woman. "The winds foretell of conflict."

"The Toorkrats are weak," interrupts Cultac. "The Eldest tolerated them for far too long and now it's time we destroy them. Now that I am Eldest, no one will dare threaten us. I will destroy all our enemies. The Cleridrac will be feared. We will be the strongest people and none will dare stand against us."

"Be careful, Cultac. They were your allies until now. Toorktats may be weak, but they are cunning," Shumakra warns.

"They were allies while they were useful to me. I needed their help to get rid of the Eldest, but the demons did it for me. The old man was getting weak, and he was too tolerant of our enemies. He tried making peace when he should have gone to war and destroyed them. You see how bold the Toorkrats are growing. Their warriors walk into our lands and no one stops them. I don't intend on helping them, and I never did. Once they had served their purpose and I was made Eldest, I planned on destroying every one of them. Now that I know they are weak, I will convince the council that we must attack before they can increase their strength and become a greater threat."

"That is why I came to speak with you, young warrior. The winds whisper that the Toorkrats will bring destruction. It is not wisdom to go against them to battle."

"What do the winds say, Wise One? Do the winds say we will not be victorious?" Cultac asks impatiently.

"They only speak of danger if we go to war. I do not see our death or our victory, only that the winds are not in our favor if you go. But this is what worries me the most; that the winds do not tell me more. Instead, they whisper of a blue shadow with many faces of Blue Demon; the one they call Hewold. I fear his power clouds my sight, and I cannot follow the winds," she exclaims in a beleaguered tone.

Cultac grits his teeth and furiously stomps around. "I will take his head."

"We must take care that he does not know our intentions, or he may try to destroy us. There are many among our people who are swayed by him and may attempt to stop us as well. We do not want to kill our own people."

"What care I for the weak that allowed themselves to be swayed?" Cultac barks angrily.

"Cultac, they are still your people. As Eldest, you must care for all your own, especially the weak. They will need you to guide them once they are released from his power. As much as you may not care for them now, everyone has a part to play among our people. I warn you to take care, because we do not want them playing the part against us and interfering with our plans to rid ourselves of the demon," Shumakra chides.

Cultac reluctantly nods in compliance. When she sees Cultac has calmed down and is willing to listen again, she continues. "I have been asking the winds for a way to rid us of the demon and his powers. The winds have been silent except to warn me of the dangers of fighting with the Toorkrats. Now it is becoming clear to me. I feel the demon poses a greater threat to our people; even greater than the Toorkrats. Lead your people to war, Cultac."

"But you say there is no certainty of victory. What of the warnings?"

"Our people are strong and have overcome many threats before. As you say, the Toorkrats are weak and now is the time to attack. Lead your people to war, and I will help you convince the council. Convince them to let the demon come with you." Shumakra plots.

Cultac looks confused about Shumakra's plans, but as he thinks about her request he figures what she is plotting. "In the fight," Shumakra continues. "The demon, and everyone with him, will be too distracted to watch his back. You must not fail this time. We must put an end to him before he destroys us and before he grows stronger and his shadow spreads. We cannot hesitate, for there may not be another opportunity."

"I will see that it is done, Shumakra," Cultac affirms. "Let us go to convince the council and let us be finished with the Toorkrats and Blue Demon."

"Cultac," Shumakra calls before he's able to leave. "Keep watch on Katalariana. I fear she will fall under the demon's power. I have seen the blue shadow come for her."

"That is why I will not fail."

Cultac grabs one of the bodies by the ankle and drags it back toward the camp. Shumakra grabs her walking staff and follows slowly after. Cultac drags the body to a main pathway leading to the camp and follows it the rest of the way. When he reaches the guards posted outside the wall near the entryway, the guards rush over to help him. Cultac stops dragging the body and orders the guards to gather the council.

The council and several more warriors gather around Cultac and his victim. When Cultac sees they have all arrived, he paces around the body, pointing at it, and looking every elder in the eye.

"I found our enemy in our land trying to spy on our people. Our enemy no longer fears us and they think they can wander freely in our lands. They are planning to attack our people. We cannot tolerate our enemies doing what they want. They think that with our Eldest gone that we are weak and we will cower in our tents. I call the council to answer these crimes by attacking them and showing them that we are still strong. We must be the first to strike. If we do not, they will come and wage war in our home."

"Are you certain of this, Cultac?" one of the elders asks incredulously.

"There were four of them that attacked me. I killed three of them before one of them ran away. If I was not a skilled and cunning warrior, they would have overwhelmed and killed me. The Toorkrat people can not be allowed to live after they enter our lands and attempt to kill your future Eldest." boasts Cultac.

The council members discuss between themselves the best course of action. Shumakra shuffles down the pathway, finally catching up, and approaches the group. When the elders see her, they bombard her with their queries about what the winds say regarding a war with the Toorkrats. Shumakra closes her eyes and raises her arms high into the air, pretending to call on the winds. She shakes her hands at the sky and slowly lowers them. She bows her head in silence for a brief moment before glancing into the faces of the council members. She groans and rolls back her eyes and sways her head side to side and stops. She slowly opens her eyes again and rests on her staff, acting out of breath. Everyone leans in, eager to learn what the winds have to say. "The winds have spoken to me," she groans. "A favorable wind blows over us. It speaks of our strength and our success, but on one condition."

"What is it, Shumakra? What do the winds ask of us?" one of the elders asks.

She looks side to side and then at Cultac, pointing a crooked, bony finger at him. "Cultac must lead our warriors into battle. He must also take Blue Demon; the one who calls himself Hewold; to fight with our people."

The elders all look at one another and nod their heads. "If the winds speak favorably of our people and the outcome of this fight, then it will be done. Cultac, the council agrees that you will be at the head of our warriors to lead us to victory."

A wicked smile breaks across Cultac's face. He glances at Shumakra and nods slightly. "As the council bids me, I will bring victory to our people."

26

Chance and Kata wait until they no longer hear the voices before Chance steps out of the cave entrance to check their surroundings. He returns and informs Kata that Cultac and Shumakra have finally left the area. She exits the cave; too nervous about lingering around after what she witnessed.

"It isn't safe for us to be here, Chanz. We should return before we are found by the Toorkrats, or by our own people. I do not know what Cultac's and Shumakra's plans are with the Toorkrats, but it cannot be good. He wanted my father dead, and it would be reason to think that he is planning something more. Since he will be the next Eldest, there will be no one to stop him. I fear the council will not listen to us, and I'm sure he has a plan to deal with them. I fear his actions will bring war to the Cleridrac people. Chanz, he will make me his partner soon. I do not know what will happen to me when he does."

"Kata, I need to talk to you about us," Chance interrupts.

Kata stops her panicked ranting and stares at him for a second. She shakes her head. "No, Chanz, you told me there cannot be us. You chose Reshiara. You stayed the night with her again, and I saw you with her this morning."

"We did not join," Chance interrupts again. "I could not do it. I could only think of you, even when I was with her."

Before Chance can say anything more, Kata rushes over and grabs his face, pulling him towards her, and kisses him. She stops kissing long enough to whisper, "Thank you, Chanz."

He returns the kiss and embraces her for a moment longer before pulling away. He looks deeply into her purple eyes. "You told me we should leave here and go somewhere far. Will you go with me?" he asks.

Kata's eyes tear up when she hears his proposal. She can hardly contain her emotion realizing she'll finally get what she has wanted for so long. "Is this what you want, Chanz? Do you choose me?"

"I do choose you, Katalariana."

Kata jumps into his arms with a squeal and wraps her arms and legs around him, holding him tightly. He embraces her and holds her just as tightly. He feels himself melt into her. It's like being home when he's in her arms and he finds himself eager to start a life with her. Once he was able to tell her his decision, all the doubts and fears he had about his feelings and about being in a relationship seem to disappear. It has been a long time since he's been able to decide something for himself. The entire time he was with the CC, he was always following orders, going from one mission to the next. Even among the Cleridrac, his life was being decided for him. It's liberating making his own choice and not having it determined by circumstance or decided by someone else. What's more, he remembers what it feels like to be loved, and more importantly, how it feels to love.

"Let's not wait anymore. Let us leave now, before we are discovered," Chance anxiously requests.

"Not yet. We must gather supplies before we go."

"Let us take what is here and we will obtain the rest where we go."

"No, Chanz. The great cold is coming. We will not live without supplies, especially if you take so long to build a tent," Kata mocks in a serious tone.

Chance smiles, realizing his cabin may seem odd to a people who live their entire lives in tents. "I understand, but I do not want to risk being stopped. If I am seen leaving with supplies, the council will not let me go."

"We will go back and wait for night to come. We will meet by the healer tents when Reshiara and my mother are sleeping. It is not safe to leave without supplies. We need food, beds, and medicine. I will bring what I can, and you bring what you have. Then we will go together. And Chanz, do not join with that girl before you leave," Kata smirks mischievously.

Chance shakes his head, knowing deep down she still fears that could happen. He hesitates going back, even for supplies. He doesn't want the risk of getting caught, as well as having to go back and face Reshiara. He's been gone long enough she's surely noticed his absence by now. It wouldn't take much for her to ruin their plans. Nighttime can also be dangerous with wild animals on the prowl. He voices his concerns to Kata, hoping to sway her from going back. She explains they can meet near the healer tents and come back to the cave to sleep during the night and leave before anyone at camp notices they are gone. Hopefully they will be far enough ahead to outrun any search parties. Reluctantly, Chance agrees to follow Kata's plans.

They walk back holding each other's hands with Kata leaning on his arm. She can't help but smile at the prospect of having the life she wanted with him. She scarcely believes it's really happening and finds herself looking at him from time to time to make sure it's not a dream. She's so excited, she can barely focus on what she needs to do when she gets back. It's still early in the day and it will be too suspicious to go home and gather the supplies they'll need. Her mother will be wondering where she has been all morning. She knows she should come up with a plan, but she can't stop thinking about Chance. She wonders if there is a way to get away sooner and meet at the cave. Thinking about the cave, Kata realizes they will be spending the night together. Her heart beats even faster. She fantasizes about joining with Chance and making their union official. She squeezes Chance's arm, overwhelmed with anticipation. She considers turning around and making their union official before anyone can stop them. Then he will be hers, and she will be his, and no one can dispute it. Unfortunately, they've already been gone too long and they will already have the chore of explaining their absence.

They climb over the wall back into the camp unseen. Kata steals one more passionate kiss before parting ways and races back to the healer tents. Chance gives her time to get ahead before moving along a different path. Making his way back to the cabin, he notices several armed warriors approaching him. He glances around checking his surroundings and calmly continues forward. He hopes they are just patrolling the camp, but they seem intent on stopping him.

"Hewold, we go together," one of them orders.

The warriors escort him to a large gathering of warriors. They lead him through the crowd to the front where Cultac waits. Cultac approaches him with a crooked, devious smile and presses a spear against his chest. Chance takes the spear; looking confused and bewildered. He wonders if this will be the second round of the fight they had yesterday. Cultac steps back and grabs his spear from one of the men standing nearby. Chance grips the spear and adjusts his footing, preparing for an attack, but Cultac doesn't move against him or show any sign of aggression. Chance eases up until someone walks up beside him and pats him firmly on the shoulder. Expecting to see Broltrom, he instead sees the face of one of the elders.

"Hewold," he bellows, "we go to fight the Toorkrats. You go together with us as a brother."

Cultac sneers when he hears the elder refer to Chance as a brother and turns his back to them. He's intent on leading his warriors to battle, and the sooner they arrive, the sooner he can destroy Blue Demon. He signals for the group to move.

One warrior at the front of the party steps out in front and blows several times into a horn. In unison, every warrior fills the air with their warcry. After the horn sounds, several more men run from the camp, leaving their families with one last goodbye to join the party. While the others run to join, the rest of the party marches toward the Toorkrat camp.

Chance considers slinking to the back of the group, and when the opportunity presents itself, breaking away to later join up with Kata, but the elder beside him won't let him out of his sight. It isn't until they hear a sweet, innocent voice breaking over the crowd that he is willing to let him go. Hearing the voice calling for Hewold, the elder pushes Chance to the outside of the group to where Reshiara follows beside them.

Seeing Chance emerge from the group, Reshiara pulls him aside and hugs him tightly. "I came when I heard you were selected to fight the Toorkrats. I don't like that you are leaving so soon," she says in a forlorn tone.

Chance breathes a sigh of relief. She didn't notice he was gone all morning, or at least she isn't letting on that she noticed. She throws a satchel around his neck and over his shoulder. "Food and water for you," she says, taking his free hand.

"Thank you, Resha," he replies, noticing the tears forming in her amber eyes.

She looks longingly at him, knowing her time with him grows shorter by the second. "Tell me you will come back, Hewold."

Chance swallows hard, knowing what she is really asking him. "I won't let them kill me," he responds, trying to avoid the real answer. "Be safe and take care of yourself. I will miss you."

"I love you, Hewold. Come back to me alive."

Resha gives him a tender kiss on the lips. She wraps her arms around him then rests her head against his chest, squeezing tightly. He hugs her back, holding her tightly in return. He gently kisses her forehead and bids her farewell, knowing this will be the last time he sees her if he's able to get away. She smiles warmly and watches as he runs to meet up with the elder, who stands by waiting for him, and they merge with the mass of armed warriors.

The elder keeps a hand on Chance's shoulder and leads him toward the center of the group. Chance wonders if he suspects his plans to abandon the fight and is determined to keep him from leaving. The man doesn't say a word, but is perfectly content to be marching quietly beside him.

As the massive army makes their way to the outer wall of the camp, the group slowly forms into an organized line, with the older, more experienced warriors taking their place in the rear; the younger, strongest warriors leading in the front; and the young, inexperienced, and weak warriors filling up the middle. Several cleridrac riders follow along the outside of the line, running up and down beside them. They are positioned to respond to wherever they are needed in a hurry. They also scout the way ahead, since they are fast and quiet.

Once the line has been formed, the warriors stop, and in unison raise their weapons while crying out, "Fo oma amogan! Fo oma eshiron!"[104]

They yell it out three times as loud as they can, then march

---

104 *For our families! For our home!*

again toward the outer wall. "I wonder if this is a common warcry among tribes going into battle," Chance says to himself. "That's probably how the CC soldiers got the name Eshiron."

The line moves again and the elder makes sure to keep Chance near the middle. Chance observes the large number of young men marching beside him and recognizes a few of them from the wedding celebration, though none of them bother to acknowledge him. Although they are all traveling as one group, there are several, smaller groups within. Each group is engaged in talking among themselves, and Chance suspects they must be familial groups, or groups of close friends, which is why they don't include him.

Despite being ostracized, Chance keeps a constant watch on his surroundings, as well as on the warriors around him. Being in a group heading to battle, it's hard for him not to remember his training and get into the habits he's developed over the course of his time fighting for the CC. Eyeing the groups around him, he spots a woman following frantically beside them. His heart races when he recognizes Kata. She walks beside the men, searching among the masses for Chance, but she hasn't seen him yet. Chance wants to call out to her, but he remembers who's around him. He tries standing taller in the hopes of standing out from the rest to get her attention; as if being the tallest and palest person among them wasn't enough to set him apart.

He can tell she's distressed and extremely frustrated. He tries moving toward her, but the elder, and several other warriors, stand between him and her. Chance looks at the elder to see if he has noticed Kata, but he looks back at Chance and smiles. Chance feigns a smile and tries inching his way past.

The elder pats him on the shoulder and doesn't allow him to slow down to get behind him, or to cross in front. He urges Chance to keep up and continue moving forward.

Chance watches Kata, who seems to be growing hopeless of finding him in time. He looks around for another way to get her attention.

He clears his throat loudly until one of the young men he recognizes turns and looks his way. When they make eye contact, Chance greets him as if he were familiar with him, and cuts in front of the elder to approach him. The elder finally lets him join their group and Chance pretends to be a part of their conversation. When the elder isn't looking, Chance makes his way to the edge of the line to get Kata's attention.

She sighs with relief when she sees him, but she checks her emotions and pretends to still be looking for someone to throw off suspicion. She walks close by and smiles briefly at him. She wants so badly to be in his arms, and it pains her to have to pretend he means nothing.

"Chanz, what now?" she asks quietly; her anxiety still evident in her voice.

"I cannot leave. They will look for me," Chance whispers.

"I no wan you go," she mutters in Chance's language while looking around nervously. "I, you, uz."

Chance nods his head slightly. He looks around to see if anyone is paying attention to them, and when he's sure no one is, he leans closer and whispers, "Gather the supplies and have them ready in the cave. Go there everyday when the great light is highest in the sky. I will come as soon as I can and we will go together."

Kata nods, still disheartened Chance is leaving. So many things can happen in a fight. She remembers his condition when he was first brought to them. Chance sees the worry in her eyes. "I will come back. I won't die. I will come back to you no matter what happens."

Kata nods again and smiles, swallowing back the tears. "Be safe and come back," she pauses to make sure no one is listening, "come back to me."

Chance nods resolutely. "I love you, Katalariana."

The words fly out of his mouth before he realizes what he's said. It felt natural, so he said it without being sure he should have. He swallows nervously, but the more he thinks about it, the more he realizes he does love her. At least he feels for her like he's never felt about anyone else, and she makes him feel things he never has before. He longs to be with her every waking moment and she invades his every thought. At night, she comforts him in his dreams. He would die for her, but without her, he would certainly die. Surely, then, it's love he feels.

Kata has to turn away to compose herself. Every part of her wants to break down and weep for joy, while at the same time, every part of her wants to throw caution to the wind and jump into his arms. Regaining her composure, she faces him again, but she's barely able to look him in the eye without her emotions overwhelming her. "And I, you," she whispers.

Before they can continue their conversation or say good-bye, Chance senses his elder companion walk up beside him. Nonchalantly, Chance points to the front of the line. "Cultac is there, I think."

Confused at first, Kata sees the elder approach and understands. Playing along, she looks at the front of the line and nods. "Thank you. Good journey. Return with honor."

Chance smiles, wishing they could have said their goodbyes without the facade. Kata steps away from the marching warriors as Chance returns to the center with the elder. She waits near the pathway and watches Chance. She can see the top of his head above all the rest. Somehow, still being able to see him helps her feel close to him, but it still pulls at her heartstrings the further away he gets. She waits until he is far out of sight, wishing she listened to him; that they had taken what was in the cave and left. There's nothing she can do to change it now, other than hope and pray he returns safely to her.

27

For three days, the warriors march toward the Toorkrat camp, traveling through the day and stopping only to refill their waterskins when they cross a water source. At night, they huddle together into one large body, their backs to the center, and sleep sitting on the ground. The younger, inexperienced warriors are assigned to sit on the outside of the circle with their spears propped up, pointing outward, to form a defensive barrier from animal attacks. They avoid lighting fires to conceal their position from their enemies. A few men remain awake to keep watch while the rest try to sleep.

Chance is considered an inexperienced warrior and ends up on the outside every night, though he doesn't mind. He spends the nights staring at the moons and stars, thinking about Kata. He thinks about her all the time, wishing he could be with her. Unfortunately, he's never left alone and hasn't been able to escape. The elder has been by his side even during the night. He sits close by, and whenever Chance moves, he wakes up to check that everything is alright. Chance knows he can outrun everyone if he has to, but he isn't so sure he can outrun a cleridrac. He wants to avoid conflict if possible, and he knows there are several in the group itching for an opportunity to hunt a demon and run him through with their spears.

On the morning of the fourth day, the war party stops at a watering hole, but instead of collecting water, they dig around the edge until they pull out handfuls of bright red clay.

They take turns painting designs on each other; starting on the chest and over onto their dominant shoulder and down their arm. The younger men have few, if any, designs drawn on their bodies, whereas the older veterans cover their chest, both shoulders, and down both arms. Some have them going up their neck, covering parts of their face.

Cultac stands nearby with his arms stretched out to the side while someone draws the designs on him. On the middle of his chest in thick, bold lines is the large symbol Chance saw him draw on himself when he killed the pilot. Surrounding the symbol are several others extending over both shoulders and down one arm. Chance deduces the symbols are a way of re-counting someone's kills, or participation in significant battles. The more kills and experience one has, the more designs and symbols cover their body.

Cultac spies Chance observing him and sneers. He points at the symbol on his chest to remind Chance what it stands for. Chance shrugs and shakes his head, laughing to himself. He wants to mock him again by reminding Cultac how small his kill is compared to his gruthraller, but given the serious demeanor of everyone around him, he's sure the jest will get him into trouble.

The elder following Chance around finishes getting painted and turns to him. He tells him to remove the vest and reaches down, grabbing some of the clay. Using his fingers, he draws on Chance's chest. Chance watches and recognizes a similar symbol to the one Broltrom drew on him, but the elder embellishes the drawing with other lines and shapes. When he finishes, he smiles and pats Chance's shoulder, and turns to help another.

Not knowing their symbols, Chance stands by and watches until everyone but a few younger warriors are painted. They take up their spears and move in the direction they had been traveling.

They travel until midday before Cultac holds up the line. With a few hand gestures, the group crouches and spreads out. With Cultac in the center, the rest of the group fans out behind him, taking up positions on either side of him. Staying close to the ground, they all creep slowly up a hill.

Chance guesses they finally reached the Toorkrat camp and are hoping to take them by surprise. The elder who has been with him the whole way, stays close beside him and gives him directions to stay in sync with the rest of the party. No one makes a sound, but communicates through hand gestures and signals.

As they round the top of the ridge, they see expansive plains of tall, dried grass extending to the horizon. Nested on the plains is the Toorkrat camp, or rather, what used to be the Toorkrat camp. An empty lot, riddled with dead fire pits, dilapidated tent frames, a patchwork of dirt pathways and dried up, barren garden plots are all that mark where their enemy once resided.

Cultac motions for everyone to stay alert and sends the cleridrac riders to scout the camp and surrounding areas. The grass is tall enough to hide an ambush and Cultac doesn't want to risk sending his warriors into a trap.

The riders split up, with some running straight into the camp, while others circle around the perimeter and sweep the area for any sign of the Toorkrats. It isn't long before one of the riders returns and reports the fire pits are cold and haven't been used for days.

Cultac jumps up and yells in frustration. His yell is swallowed up in the emptiness of the plains. Agitated, Cultac shoves the rider and yells at him to go find the Toorkrats.

While they wait for word from the other riders, the rest of the warriors abandon their attack formation and take up defensive positions, similar to what they do at night. Every man keeps their eyes open for possible attacks from any direction. Those with bows take up position behind those with spears and the leaders remain in the middle.

Chance watches over the plains and listens for any unusual sounds. Everything is quiet and still, even the wind. An uneasiness creeps over him and he feels something isn't right. How would an entire group of people know to abandon their camp and hide or set up an ambush at approximately the same time they left the Cleridrac camp?

The riders return and report they found no sign of anyone being there. Cultac yells again and stomps around in circles. "Where are they?" he growls.

Fear clenches Chance's chest when he realizes where they have gone. "Kata!" he exclaims under his breath.

Without thinking, Chance darts from the defensive line and rushes back the way they came. Cultac whips around and spots Chance fleeing. He whistles and signals the cleridracs after him. The riders respond promptly and stop in front of Chance, cutting off his escape. He sighs impatiently and tries pushing his way passed. One of the cleridrac snaps at him, biting the spear in his hand. Chance lets go of the spear and punches the cleridrac in the side of the head, sending the cleridrac and rider reeling around and falling to the ground. The other rider tries stopping Chance with his spear, but Chance grabs the spear and catapults the rider over his head and into the grass. The cleridrac squawks and lurches toward him. Chance slams his fist down on the top of it's head, sending the beast crashing into the dirt.

Chance tries leaving until he hears someone running up

behind him. He adjusts his footing and shifts his weight as the assailant reaches him, sending the assailant flying over his back and onto the ground in front of him. He looks down at a stunned Cultac squirming on the ground. "You! You did this," Chance accuses sharply.

Chance picks Cultac up and grips his face, pinching his cheeks together. Cultac struggles to free himself, but Chance lifts upward, putting Cultac on his tiptoes. He grabs Chance's arm and tries breaking his grip.

"This was your plan, or no, Cultac? You brought us here together, while the Toorkrats attack the Cleridrac. That was your plan."

Cultac's eyes widen. He shakes his head emphatically, denying he had anything to do with it. Chance shoves Cultac backward, releasing his grip on Cultac's face once several warriors arrive and attempt to surround them.

"I saw you with the Toorkrats. I know this was your plan," Chance repeats.

The warriors halt their attempts to stop Chance when they hear the accusations and wait for Cultac's response. Cultac looks at them indignantly and demands they attack Chance. Members of the council run over to put a stop to the fight and question Chance about his actions.

"The Toorkrats are attacking our people. I saw Cultac with Toorkrat warriors before we came."

"The Toorkrat warriors attacked Cultac," one of the elders attempts to explain.

"No. Cultac was speaking with the warriors. After they talk, he killed them. Now they attack our people and we are here."

"Whose words will you believe speak truth?" Cultac asks. "Will you believe the words of a demon? Or will you believe the words of a Cleridrac? The words of your Eldest? His ways are to deceive you. He wants to destroy our people. I am the Eldest. I do what I do to make the Cleridrac strong."

"You are not the Eldest, Cultac," one of the elders rebukes. "The winds spoke and said you would lead us to victory, but there is nothing here. Perhaps we were deceived, but not by the demon."

"Our people are in danger," Chance reminds them. "We do not have time to stay. Stop me if you need to, but I will not let you without a fight. I do not want to fight you. There is no reason in fighting you when the enemy is in our home. I will not stop until I stop the Toorkrats."

Without listening to another word, and not wanting to waste time arguing over who's telling the truth, Chance pushes through the warriors and races back toward the Cleridrac camp. He doesn't wait for any others to join him since they would slow him down and the Toorkrats already have a head start.

He speeds toward home, not even stopping to rest or sleep, only to refill his water. Reshiara packed enough dried food in his satchel to last him the journey. Fortunately, the sky is clear and the moons cast enough light for Chance to find his way at night, hoping by traveling through the night, he can make up time.

He hopes to arrive and find out he's wrong; that the Toorkrats merely left to find a better place to live for the cold season. He hopes to arrive and find everyone is carrying on as they normally would. If not, he fears the worst. He remembers men at the CC base camp told him the natives never took prisoners. Even though he's referred to as one, he hopes that only applies to demons and not other native people. He tries not to focus on it too much, but it motivates him to keep moving no matter how tired he is.

⤛28⤜

Chance races down the game trail through familiar trees. Being so close to the camp makes him forget how tired he is. It's been two, long, arduous days since he left Cultac and the rest of the Cleridrac warriors on the Toorkrat plains and it's been just as long since he's seen any sign of them.

He's been running all morning; ever since it was light enough to see several pillars of smoke rising on the horizon. Normally their fires don't make such thick, black smoke. He fears the worst and worries what he'll find when he finally reaches home.

He jumps through the brush onto the main pathway leading to the camp. He runs as fast as his legs will carry him. The smell of smoke fills his nostrils and it's getting stronger, but it isn't the smell of normal wood fires.

He clears the woods into an open field and slows down when the remnants of the Cleridrac camp come into view. Most of the tents are nothing more than smoldering, collapsed frames. The gardens also appear to be burned, and several feathered heaps litter the fields nearby. The pathway leading to the entrance he and the rest of the warriors left through nearly a week ago is lined with spears, each with the head of a warrior on top; their hair adorned with bloody cleridrac feathers. On either side of the entrance, several rectangular, wood frames have been built. Nailed to the frames are mutilated bodies whose heads have been replaced with the heads of cleridracs, crudely lashed on to keep them in place. Other headless bodies lay heaped in small piles nearby.

Walking by the piles, Chance notices all the bodies appear to be those of men. He passes the horrid scene and searches deeper into the camp. Several small animals scurry away from the bodies and debris. They appear to be scavenging on the dead. Walking along the path, Chance spots a figure through the smoke. Eager to find any survivors, he approaches and discovers the figure is not human. A bird, as large as a man, hunches over and pecks at the remains of a body on the ground. Startled, the bird extends its extremely long wings. It screeches and spines rise on the top of its head as it wards Chance away from its prize. Seeing he's not dissuaded by its aggressive posturing, it embeds its large talons into the dead body and takes flight, carrying the body to a more private location. Chance covers his face from the cloud of dirt kicked up by the beat of the bird's wings. Watching the bird fly high over the camp with the body dangling in its grip, he hopes that's the worst of the scavengers he runs into during his search for survivors.

Running toward the main part of camp, he spots the healer tents and notices they're still intact. Feeling it's as good a place to start as any, he cautiously heads to them. He peers into each one to find the few occupants inside met with a grizzly end and were left to rot. Standing outside of the tent Broltrom was staying in, he hesitates peering in.

He slowly pulls the flap aside and looks in. The bed is empty, but on closer examination, Chance spots a hand sticking out from under the furs on the ground. He rushes over and pulls the covers back. Underneath the bed frame lay Broltrom's body. Chance flips the frame out of the way and slumps down beside the body, hesitating to check for lifesigns. This will be the first time losing someone who was a friend. He leans in close and can hear Boltrom's shallow breaths.

"Broltrom!"

Broltrom groans and slowly opens his eyes. He blinks several times, waiting for his eyes to adjust. A weak grin breaks across his face and he hefts one hand and places it on Chance's shoulder. "Chazhewold."

Chance pulls out his water and helps him drink. "Broltrom, what happened?"

Broltrom finishes drinking and rests his head back down. Tears trickle from his eyes and he shakes his head. "I'm sorry, Chazhewold. I was weak. I couldn't fight them. I should have fought. I am a warrior. I need to be strong, but I wasn't," he weeps.

"Don't worry, Broltrom. I understand. Where are the others?"

Broltrom breaks into sobs. "They took her, Chazhewold. They took Imelka. She heard them come and she hid me so they wouldn't kill me. I couldn't protect her and they took her."

"Katalariana. Was she here?" asks Chance.

"No, no she was not here. I heard screaming but I could do nothing."

"Broltrom, please. I am sorry, but I need to know where they are. Do they kill everyone?"

"No," Broltrom calms down enough to answer. "They will keep the young women for their own. The children, sometimes, too. Chazhewold, you promised to care for my family. You are my brother, Blue Angel. You must get them and bring them back for me. I need you to do what I could not do."

"I will, Broltrom. I promise. Take what's left of my food and water. I will find the others and bring them back."

Chance fixes one of the beds and helps Broltrom into it. He leaves his satchel with the food and water and goes to the door after saying his farewell.

"Chazhewold," Broltrom calls out, "in my tent, find my spear and my bow. Take them and use them. They are yours now. You must hurry. The Toorkrat will join with our women to increase their numbers. Chazhewold, they know if we get them back, the children they bear will not be Cleridrac. They will carry Toorkrat blood."

Chance nods and heads to Broltrom's tent, knowing his mission is now even more urgent. Along the way, he passes his cabin. It still stands unscathed, but all his supplies are gone. The surrounding tents have been pushed over or burned.

Further along the path, he sees a body on the ground between the tents. He walks to it and sees it's an older woman with a stab wound to the heart. Looking around, Chance can see a small number of dead bodies scattered around, all older females, each with white or gray hair adorning their heads. The Toorkrats were only interested in the younger women. They murdered the older generations of women along with all the men left to protect the camp. So far, he hasn't found the bodies of any children.

Leaving the body, he carries on to Broltrom's home. The home is partially burned and what's left standing looks ransacked. Rummaging through what's left, it appears they took the food and left everything else.

Moving the family's belongings around in search of the weapons, he comes across a small doll. He picks it up from the dirt and remembers Broltrom's little girl playing with it the last time he was here.

Thinking about the young girl having to experience such a horrific ordeal enrages him. He's also mad at himself for only being concerned about himself and Kata. He completely shirked his responsibilities and the promise he would care for this family. It makes him more determined to find them and bring them back to make amends.

Searching a little more, he finds the bow and a quiver of arrows, all in good condition. The spear, however, didn't survive the fire. He grabs the bow and quiver and races to look for Kata and Resha. He has to make sure they weren't killed or managed to hide until the danger passed.

He checks both tents, but doesn't find either one of them. Then he remembers the instructions he gave Kata before he left. Perhaps she was safely waiting for him in the cave.

Heading there, he sees a dark shape limping down the path beside the remains of several burned tents. He hurries over, hoping it's a survivor who can give him more information.

As he approaches, the figure looks up at him. Chance recognizes the wrinkled, old face and the many strands of trinkets made from bone and clay draped around her neck. When Shumakra sees Chance, she tries escaping and trips over herself. She lands on the ground and tries crawling away. "No, it can't be," she cries out. "How are you here? Away from me, demon!"

"This was your doing," Chance roars. "Where did they go?"

Shumakra scrambles over the ground, her eyes wide with fear.

"Tell me," he screams.

Shumakra stops scurrying and faces him. Her lips quiver and her dark, beady eyes tremble in terror as she looks up at him towering over her. She clenches some of the trinkets hanging around her neck tightly in her bony fingers. "It was you," she mutters. "You are the cause of it all. You're a demon.

You are what destroyed us. You deceived me. You changed the winds to deceive me, to make me send our people to their doom. How can you be here? It is not possible. It is true, you have to be a demon."

Chance bends down, bringing his face close to hers, and glares into her eyes. "Tell me where they were taken."

She raises a shaky hand and points with a crooked finger toward a mountain range in the distance. "They will take them there. Why do you care, demon?"

Her demeanor changes and she cackles. "I see. You want them to create more demons. Now I understand the winds. They warned me and showed me your blue shadow spread over our land, but I saw more than one of you. There were many with your face. Now I know. You want our daughters to create more demons. Go, then. May the Toorkrats do what we could not and destroy you."

She waves him away and crawls to the side of the pathway and sits. She rocks back and forth while she chants. Chance sighs and hurries toward the cave. "Crazy, old woman," he mutters under his breath.

He races to the cave. His heart pounds and he hopes with all his energy that Kata managed to get away unharmed. He reaches the entrance and pushes aside the overgrowth. He hears gasping and sounds of panic. For a moment, he allows himself to believe his prayers are answered. He keeps the entrance clear and lets the light shine into the cave. Huddled on the far side against the wall is a group of children.

They cower in fear and many break into tears. Chance steps closer and tries to calm them. "I'm here to help. I am a brother," he says calmly.

Some of the children dare to look over to see who it is. Chance can hear them whisper, "Ruc Zherulk.[105]"

The children calm down and the crying stops. "How did you get here?" Chance asks.

"Katalariana, the Eldest's daughter," someone calls out.

"Is she still here?" Chance asks excitedly.

The children grow silent and sullen. "No, they took her when she tried to help more people."

"Did you see them take her?"

"Yes. They left me and took my mother. I saw them take her, too," one of the children responds.

"Then how did you find this place?"

"I brought her," answers another. "Katalariana brought me here. When I heard the screaming stop, I went home, but home was gone. They only took some children and left the others. I brought them here."

"Do you know where they went?" Chance asks.

They all shake their heads. Chance sighs, hoping the old woman gave him valid information, but it's all he has to go off.

Chance lights the fire for the children and tells them to keep it going for warmth at night. He sees all the supplies Kata has gathered neatly piled against the wall.

"There is food and blankets for you to use. The other warriors are coming. Help will soon arrive, so keep looking for their return. You will be well until then. You older children must lead and care for the younger ones," he instructs before departing.

He knows time is short and the Toorkrats have a head start. He hopes it will be slow going for them, since they will be transporting food and other supplies, as well as the women

---

105 *Blue Demon.*

and children from the Cleridrac tribe. He hopes he has the strength to keep going and find them before they escape into the mountains, and if possible, save them before the Toorkrats steal their virtue as well.

Strapping the quiver with the arrows to his back, he takes the bow and his knife and heads toward the mountain range. Not only is the woman he loves in jeopardy, but Reshiara and Broltrom's family are as well. The advantage he has is this is what he was trained for. He was a tool the CC used to hunt and kill, and years of experience have taught him to do it well. The Toorkrats are about to find out what Blue Demon is truly capable of.

Jesse Harper

GREYSON GREEN has been creating and writing stories since he was a young child. He graduated from the Art Institute of Seattle with a degree in Computer Animation Art and Design. He currently resides in Missouri with his beautiful wife and four fantastic, young children.